Bound
to
Murder

Also by Dorsey Fiske:
Academic Murder

Bound

to

Murder

Dorsey Fiske

St. Martin's Press
New York

Readers familiar with Cambridge may find that elements of the town in the seventies are present simultaneously with Cantabrigian characteristics of the eighties. I do not apologise for this idiosyncrasy, but claim a writer's prerogative to telescope time when it suits me.

BOUND TO MURDER. Copyright © 1987 by Dorsey Fiske. All rights reserved. Printed in the United States of America. No part of this book may be used or reproduced in any manner whatsoever without written permission except in the case of brief quotations embodied in critical articles or reviews. For information, address St. Martin's Press, 175 Fifth Avenue, New York, N.Y. 10010.

Library of Congress Cataloging-in-Publication Data

Fiske, Dorsey.
    Bound to murder.

    I. Title.
PS3556.I81463B6   1987   813'.54   87-16385
ISBN 0-312-01002-8

First Edition
10 9 8 7 6 5 4 3 2 1

To my parents, without whose generosity I might have ended like poor Chatterton (or was it Betterton?) starving in a garret.

Thanks are due to JRH for his editorial assistance with my Cambridge books; I trust he has enjoyed as much as I the pleasant hours spent in going over mss. together.

Qui lacerat, violatve, rapit, presens epitoma
Hunc laceretque voret, *Cerberus* absque mora.

JOHN SKELTON 1460?–1529

That man who tears or harms this book, or carries it away,
Him let the hellhound Cerberus devour without delay.

Contents

1 Vivien

"I am afraid there can be no doubt of the fact that he was murdered; no doubt whatever."

A profound silence filled the room as Fenchurch halted in his pacing. Thirty pairs of eyes gazed at him intently.

"And it was a peculiarly disagreeable, though possibly not inappropriate, death: to be drowned in a butt of malmsey. One might argue that Clarence's murderer possessed a sense of humour; however," he continued severely, "humour and murder do not mix. Let us hope that the passage of five hundred years has served to make us more civilised, but I am inclined to doubt it. . . . And that, gentlemen . . . and ladies," he added belatedly, "is that for today. I trust I shall see you all again next week."

A murmur and a scuffle ensued in the lecture hall, a susurration of raincoats and a clatter of umbrellas (it had been raining steadily since daybreak) as the students girded themselves against the storm. Fenchurch removed his gown, grey-green with age and an accumulation of chalk dust, and packed it in his knapsack after first extracting a pair of ancient galoshes and a dilapidated mackintosh with which to protect himself on the journey from the Sidgwick Site to Sheepshanks. As the lecture hall emptied, a soothing silence fell, so he was startled when he looked up to gather his books to find himself confronted by a girl. Or rather, not merely a girl, but a Botticelli nymph. Of middle height and sapling-slender, she had a face modelled in a perfect oval, eyes of Aegean blue, and fair hair that fell simply but artfully to her shoulders. Fenchurch did not recall having seen her before; and he was certain that if he had, he would not have forgotten the encounter. He did not notice what she was wearing, only that it was not the usual shapeless ragbag garb affected by female students, and that it became her.

"Mr. Fenchurch? I'm Vivien Murray," she said, her eyes wide and dark and fathomless as the sea which their colour mimicked. "I've been told about your architectural walks through Cambridge, and I wondered if I might come along on one of them. Would I be in the way?"

"In the way? Not in the least, my dear," he assured her warmly. "I should be delighted to have you come with us. I'm planning one next Thursday, rain or shine, at eleven o'clock. We shall meet in front of Sheepshanks Great Gate; you may like to come to the prefatory lecture in this room on the Tuesday—ten o'clock—at which I shall give some background information. . . . By the way, what is your College?" He could not let her go without learning more of her.

"Clare," she said. Clare, to the horror of many of her sister Cambridge Colleges, had recently begun to admit women. "I'm doing research on the Metaphysical Poets, but I'm very fond of history, so I've been attending some of your lectures. I hope you don't mind."

How is it, he thought in wonder, *that I have never noticed such a divine creature?* It was a large lecture room, and she must have sat well in the back, and he suffered from near-sightedness. Even so. . . . "You are most welcome," Fenchurch said with creaky gallantry, "and I shall look forward to escorting you through the beauties of Cambridge on Thursday."

"You're very kind." She threw him a glimmering smile

and tucked a strand of hair behind one shapely ear as she turned to leave.

After her departure, Fenchurch, a short bachelor of sixty-five with a lion's-mane of white hair, stood as if transfixed for some moments before he gathered up his knapsack and pulled on his galoshes. *Vivien,* he mused to himself. What a remarkably apposite name: to look at her one could not doubt that she was an enchantress.

2 A Tale of Two Libraries

"My word!" It was a remarkably mild ejaculation, considering the provocation that evoked it. Fenchurch stared down unbelievingly at the Sheepshanks copy of Loggan's *Cantabrigia Illustrata* and ruffled the pages once more in the forlorn hope of discovering that his eyes had, after all, deceived him. Perhaps, he thought optimistically, he had been woolgathering (a far from uncommon occupation in the Abbot's Library of Sheepshanks; or in any library, for that matter) and had merely dreamed the episode. Surreptitiously he took his arm between his fingers and nipped it to make certain he was awake and alert; the inadvertent start he gave at the niggling pain of the self-administered pinch was incontrovertible proof that he was. But when, thus reassured as to his state of consciousness, he resumed his perusal of the Loggan, Fenchurch's conclusion was inevitably the same: all the handsome engraved plates depicting the Cambridge Colleges had been removed from the calf-bound volume in front of him.

"Mole. Mole, come here if you please."

Obediently an elderly Under-Librarian shuffled over to the table at which Fenchurch sat and bent over it. It was in fact his natural posture, for Mole bore a close resemblance to a walking-stick with the handle at right angles to its shaft, his head and shoulders serving as the former.

"Yes, Mr. Fenchurch? What can I do for you, sir?"

Fortunately, Fenchurch reflected, the Abbot's Library was at the moment devoid of all life but himself and Mole, thus obviating the need for secrecy. "A shocking thing, Mole; the Loggan I wanted for my class. Have a look at it; all the plates are gone!"

Mole peered with myopic eyes at the volume in question, leaning over the table until it appeared that his prominent nose might over-balance him and cause him to topple forward onto the book he was examining. However, he maintained his physical, though not his mental, equilibrium, exclaiming, "Good Gawd, Mr. Fenchurch. Who would have done such a thing?"

"I haven't the least idea," Fenchurch retorted testily; Mole's reaction was, he felt, hardly helpful. "Why isn't this book kept under lock and key? I thought orders had been given to that effect after the *Principia* disappeared a couple of years ago."

"We don't bother locking up the Picture-Books, sir," returned Mole with a faint look of hauteur as if to say, we lock up our gold, but not the pinchbeck.

"Indeed," Fenchurch said grimly. "Then I had better take a look at the Ackermann."

When Ackermann's *Cambridge* was duly brought out for his inspection it too, he found, was devoid of illustrations. The field was widened, and a number of other picture-books, to employ Mr. Mole's unflattering phrase, were examined; but so far it appeared that the damage was confined to the two Cambridge books.

"My word," said Fenchurch once more, morosely leafing through the Ackermann. The phrase, though inadequate, was the strongest expletive customarily employed by him; and in any case no vocabulary of commination, however extensive, could have produced a phrase that would sufficiently have expressed his surprise, shock, and outrage at the result of his researches. "I am astonished that such wholesale vandalism could have occurred without someone on the staff noticing," he added censoriously.

Mole, upon whose stooped shoulders the day-to-day responsibilities of the Abbot's Library lay, looked so stricken that Fenchurch relented.

"Never mind," he said kindly. "You needn't look so upset. It's not your fault, Mole. But I shall have to speak to Grierson about it."

"I don't see how it could have happened, sir," quavered Mole. "I'm sure I should have noticed if one of the readers had brought in a knife or scissors, or anything of that sort."

"I feel certain that you would, but theft of this kind does not require a knife. A length of string would suffice to remove the plates from their binding. I wonder how long they have been gone," he mused.

"I couldn't say, sir. No one to my knowledge has asked to see any of those books for some time. As a rule our undergraduates do not read frivolous books."

Fenchurch let that slur to his beloved volumes pass. "I suppose it's just possible that no one, except the thief, that is, has used them since I myself borrowed them for my architectural class last year," he said, "and if it had not come time to hold the class again the disappearance of the plates might have remained undiscovered indefinitely. This is very serious," he continued. "I shall discuss the matter with Grierson. We must begin, I fear, to take even more precautions than we have done heretofore."

"Here I am, Fenchurch, at your service— Hullo, Mole." The Abbot's Librarian had arrived without their noticing him. "What's the trouble? A book gone missing? Not a valuable one, I hope." Grierson was a recently elected Fellow, replacing one of their number who had departed from Cambridge. Rotund and somewhat fussy, he was nonetheless an unexceptionable librarian and, in marked contrast to his predecessor, an accomplished scholar and administrator; in general he was a welcome addition to the Senior Common Room.

"I'm afraid it's more serious than that, Grierson. Someone has been pinching engravings from some of the illustrated books in rather a wholesale fashion."

"Dear, dear," Grierson remarked, smoothing his thinning hair back from his forehead as he examined the evidence held out to him by Fenchurch. "I'm afraid this is my fault. I told Mole to lock up the really valuable things when I took over the Library—if you remember, a first edition of Newton's *Principia* had disappeared shortly before my arrival here—but I didn't think we had to worry about these as they were too large to smuggle out, and we've been examining briefcases for scissors and implements of that sort as well as books. I don't see how the fellow managed it; unless he used a penknife. There's no practical way to check for that kind of thing, though we do have them turn out their pockets on occasion as some of them have a disgusting tendency to cut out any pages they may fancy, for alleged purposes of study. The method has the additional attraction of making the material unavailable to anyone else. Selfish little beasts!"

"He managed it with damp string," answered Fenchurch. "The technique is amazingly simple. Put a length of string in your pocket, wet it by placing it in your mouth, lay it along the inner edge of the plate to be removed, and in a few moments you need only pull it gently out and shuffle it amongst your papers. No mess, no fuss, and if necessary you could roll it up and tuck it under your jacket or down your trousers—that is, if you thought there might be a thorough examination of your briefcase." He bent over the Ackermann to inspect it. "That's how it was done, all right," he said after a moment. "The edges are slightly ragged, not clean-cut. Have a look," he invited Grierson, who obediently inspected the volume indicated, and was convinced.

"Good God, Fenchurch," he said, nonplussed. "I've never heard of that rope trick before. I daresay he thought it up to get around the inspection. I'm frankly appalled by the wholesale aspects of this theft; the fellow has got away with a whacking great haul."

"That, with a bit of luck on our side, may make it easier to identify the culprit," returned Fenchurch encouragingly. "He could not possibly have got away with all these in one or two, or even ten trips to the Library. Therefore it must be someone who is a regular visitor, and as we are still in Michaelmas Term you haven't got large numbers of students studying yet for examinations, so the library traffic is relatively light. That ought to narrow the field somewhat, provided the engravings were recently stolen. If not, we should at least be limited to a list of those who regularly use the Library, since the thefts must have been committed over a period of time. When we contact the local antiquarian printsellers we ought to be able to recognise any description they may furnish us if someone has approached them with suspicious merchandise. And from now on," he continued severely, "book illustrations should be individually stamped to discourage theft."

"It is a disfigurement, but I'm afraid we must. You think he will try to sell the plates in Cambridge, then?"

"Not if he has any sense," replied Fenchurch. "But youth has a tendency to egotism; and having got away with the thefts for several months, he may think himself immune to exposure. The wise course would be for him to take them up to London, but he might find it too difficult to locate a buyer there; and of course the market for Cambridge prints would be likely to be greater here. I think it well worth a try to notify the local dealers first." He noticed that Grierson was looking downcast. "Have no fear, my dear fellow, but that we shall apprehend the thief."

Grierson's expression did not lighten at this assurance. "I feel very badly about this, John. Those books were entrusted to my care, and for this to happen! Particularly after we were forewarned by the incident with the *Principia.*"

"You have nothing to reproach yourself with over the *Principia,*" Fenchurch very sensibly pointed out, "since it was stolen before you took Smythson's place as Librarian. As for the Loggan and the Ackermann, the loss of the plates is highly regrettable, to be sure, but there is a limit to the number of volumes you can lock up here, and there are far more precious books than these lying about the Abbot's Library. And one thing at least I feel is certain—the *Principia* thief and the man who took these prints are not the same person. They are totally separate crimes."

"You think so? The man who made off with the Newton was never apprehended. . . . I suppose he could be responsible for this," Grierson said uncertainly.

"Highly unlikely. It is a question of taste. The *Principia* has not turned up on the market; I suspect it was stolen to keep, not to sell. Though I am not in general a betting man, I should be willing to place quite a substantial wager on it. No"—returning to his original theme—"one can lock up a great many books, but one cannot lock up all of them. A library must operate to some extent on trust, or it ceases to function. We must just check the call-slips, by the way, on the off-chance that they may provide a clue, though I think it improbable in the extreme. The thief would not be so foolish as to leave such an obvious trail, and Mole would no doubt have become justifiably suspicious at such frequent perusals of a book of that kind."

"At any rate, I should certainly have remembered it, sir," said Mole.

"It would have been unnecessary for him to request them in any event since, as I recollect, the books are shelved in a readily accessible spot, a bay moreover where there is some protection from view. Yes, upon consideration I think the call-slips will prove a wild-goose chase, though there is a faint possibility that he put through a request for one of the books before he got the idea, or before he found out where they were shelved. That may give us a lead."

But the call-slips gave no indications. Neither of the books in question had been asked for since Fenchurch had made use of them for his lecture the autumn before except once, by the Master a week after Fenchurch had returned them. Fenchurch never bothered to submit a call-slip; instead he asked Mole to fetch the books for him and gave the Librarian a note against their return.

As there was nothing left for them to do now but to check with the local printsellers, they abandoned their detective work for the time being.

Sheepshanks is not only one of the oldest but one of the most eccentric Cambridge Colleges. Founded in the fifteenth century by a pious merchant as Agnus Dei College on the site of a suppressed monastery, it was re-endowed in 1514 by Henry VIII as a monastic order. Its first (and only) prior was a French *abbé* of notable depravity, who so outraged both town and University that upon his departure the monks were ejected from their cloister and a Master appointed to the now-secular foundation. Aside from a fund of scandalous stories, the only legacy left by the Abbé Dieudonné was an architectural one, consisting primarily of a superb Chapel, the present glory of Sheepshanks.

A series of politically inept Masters left the College nearly derelict and in dire financial straits in the eighteenth century, when it was lavishly refurbished by one of its own. Sir Oliver Sheepshanks, a Nabob who had amassed a Brobdingnagian fortune in India, returned to England aflame with ambition to achieve immortality. The means he selected were the rescue of his old College from decay, and the intention of astonishing the world with the magnificence of his architectural vision. Astonish he doubtless did, for he built a gigantic folly, an Indian palace-cum-temple, in which to house the revitalised foundation. In consequence Sheepshanks is architecturally the most curious of the Cambridge Colleges, with its emphasis on domes, minarets and elephants; the last, Sir Oliver's favourite quadruped, appear in all sorts of unexpected places.

If you should wish to visit Sheepshanks you will find it at the end of The Backs, just beyond St. John's College, where it is so neatly tucked away that tourists do not readily discover it. For this reason few visitors penetrate to its courts, despite the flamboyance of its architecture and the serene beauty of the Fellows' Garden. The Fellows of Sheepshanks are in strong contrast to the fabric of the College, for the Senior Common Room is generally conservative in persuasion. Few of the tenets of modern academia have taken root here. Dr. Isaac Shebbeare, Master of Sheepshanks, mans the helm of the College with a steady if somewhat retroactive hand. On the whole this attitude serves Sheepshanks very well, as it is a mistake for the academic world to embrace popular trends too swiftly. The old saw "all is not gold that glitters" still holds true despite its standing as a platitude; and, given a little time, most brightly burnished ideas acquire a layer of tarnish. Dr. Shebbeare's motto in these matters is *Festina lente,* entirely suitable in his case since he more closely resembles a large and somnolent tortoise (though not of the snapping variety) than a hare.

On this unexpectedly sunny November day the Master was pacing the paths of the Fellows' Garden, his massive head bowed in thought. The only sign of life besides himself was the kneeling figure of a gardener preparing the flowerbeds for their winter dress. The duck pond appeared nearly empty; in the little island of reeds at its centre the ducks had all congregated, huddled together for warmth, for in spite of the deceptive Northern sunlight there was a sharp East wind that blew in off the Fens, chilling the very marrow of one's bones. Dr. Shebbeare, however, was well-armed against the wintry blast. Not only his vast bulk, but a heavy overcoat and a brown woollen scarf knitted by Mrs. Shebbeare protected him from the cold. Though he enjoyed a high degree of physical comfort, he was suffering the pangs of mental dyspepsia: any disturbance in the smooth progression of life at Sheepshanks upset him, and a theft of College property was a matter of the gravest concern. It was not merely the loss of College assets that disturbed him: far deeper struck the realisation that a Sheepshankian was capable of stealing from his own College. For Dr. Shebbeare, like his College, was cast in the eighteenth-century mould and a believer in Truth, Honesty, Loyalty and Honour; a not-very-fashionable credo perhaps in the late twentieth century, but one to which he was a fervent adherent.

As he rounded a boxwood-edged corner of the path he observed a small figure clad in plus-fours and stockings, with a knapsack strapped to its back, scurrying toward him, white hair waving in the wind like a flag of truce.

"Mr. Fenchurch," the Master greeted him. "I hope your researches have succeeded in unearthing the trail of the culprit."

"Not yet, I'm afraid, Master. So far I have only uncovered several false scents, but I do not give up hope. Mr. Rouse, of Firkin & Rouse in Green Street was away when I called (I could not speak with Mr. Firkin as he is dead), and the shop assistant could give me no pertinent information, but I have hopes of his employer's return. I have hopes, that is," Fenchurch went on frankly, "because he is the last of his kind to be interviewed. If he cannot help us, we shall be at a dead end. On the other hand, there is still London; Grierson and I have not yet begun to explore London."

"The situation weighs heavy on me, Mr. Fenchurch. I must admit that the calibre of students admitted to Sheepshanks has been somewhat lowered recently, as in the other Colleges; and then," he went on with a deep sigh, "there is Grubb. Even so, an event of this kind is most upsetting, particularly in the wake of the *Principia* and the tusks, though the latter was merely a prank. You do not suppose," he continued, brightening, "that this was the result of a prank?"

"I think not, Master. It bears none of the earmarks of a prank."

"I must confess that I fear you are right," said Dr. Shebbeare. "But it distresses me greatly to think that Sheepshanks may once more be housing a criminal."

"This time, at least, it is not a murderer," Fenchurch said in an effort to console him.

But this remark failed in its desired effect. "I should almost prefer a murderer," Dr. Shebbeare said gloomily. "Theft is such a petty offence. If a Sheepshankian were to go astray, it would be better if he were to do so in the grand manner."

Fenchurch could think of nothing to reply to this, so he made his adieux and crossed the bridge to The Backs on his way to the University Library, whence he proposed to borrow undamaged copies of Loggan and Ackermann for his Tuesday class. Passing the meadows where cattle browsed on the last of the autumn grasses, he traversed Queen's Road to Burrell's Walk, in the midst of which stands the University Library, Sir Giles Gilbert Scott's 1930s monument to advanced priapism. Oblivious to the hideousness of his objective (to one attuned to the perfection of King's and Sheepshanks Chapels, a building of such self-conscious ugliness is something to be ignored) Fenchurch climbed the numerous steps of the entrance, waved a welcome to the Porters at the desk in the main hall and mounted the stairs to the first floor and the Anderson Room.

The arrangement of the Anderson Room is as undistinguished as the rest of the University Library, known to its habitués as the UL. Baldly utilitarian in design, this repository for rare books stops far short of any degree of elegance, or even of honest comfort, except for the high windows which let in light and, in clement weather, fugitive breezes to remind the occupants that there is life, of a sort, beyond books. A large room furnished with golden oak tables and chairs of a jaundiced hue, its only amenities consist of the bookshelves containing reference works which line the walls, a desk where call-slips are handed in to an Assistant Librarian, and several low tables where the departing scholar may turn in the volumes on which he has been working. To the left of the entrance a door in the wall leads to the stacks where the rare books are kept and to the office of the Rare Books Librarian, Mr. J.H.R. Manthorpe.

As Fenchurch passed through the portal and made his way to his accustomed table, he noticed several of his colleagues busy at work. Professor Enderby, once the reigning expert on Chaucer but now sadly past his prime, sat surrounded by clutter at a table to the right, near a beautiful dark young man who glowered down at his book as he took notes. While he was in the process of removing his knapsack, Fenchurch's eye was caught by an agitated knot of people at one of the tables that serve as a location for returning books. The Assistant Librarian on duty, a pale inoffensive young man named Euston, brightened appreciably upon catching sight of him and hurried over before Fenchurch was able to settle himself in his chair.

"Mr. Fenchurch, perhaps you wouldn't mind advising us, since a member of your College is involved," he said in a low voice. "I realise this is not your bailiwick, so to speak, but

Mr. Manthorpe has gone up to London for the day and I really don't quite know what to do in the circumstances."

Mentally sighing at the interruption, Fenchurch followed him to the table. Several of the Anderson Room staff were there, all of them in varying degrees of perturbation. "What is the matter?" Fenchurch enquired of Euston.

"Well—actually it's the *Anelida,* Caxton's *Anelida and Arcite,*" he explained in a hoarse whisper; the readers in the Anderson Room, inured to blotting out the world as they conducted their researches, paid no attention to the murmurs they heard only vaguely in any case. *Anelida and Arcite,* a printing on ten leaves of one of Chaucer's poems by England's first printer, is unique to the University Library; if sold on the open market, its value would probably be set at fifty to sixty thousand pounds. "The book was requested this morning—here's the call-slip—but we can't find it anywhere."

"What has Sheepshanks to do with it?" asked Fenchurch.

"It was your Mr. Maunders who used it this morning. We've contacted him and he swears he put it on this table when he had finished with it, but it's nowhere to be found. He's on his way over here now."

"I presume you have checked the stacks."

"Yes, sir, and we've gone over the shelving trolleys and checked the locations of all the books that have been re-shelved today in case a mistake was made. We've even looked in the open reference stacks, but we can't find it anywhere. Frankly, I'm at my wit's end. I can't think what Mr. Manthorpe will say." His forehead was creased with concern.

"I shouldn't worry," Fenchurch told him encouragingly. "I feel certain it will turn up soon: it isn't the sort of thing one can readily flog, after all."

"I'm sorry to drag you into this, sir. It's just that I don't quite know what to do; and Mr. Maunders is one of your people."

"You were quite right to call me over. Not to worry; we

shall get all this sorted out in no time." Fenchurch's eye was caught and distracted by a golden head in the corner, unexpected as a primrose among the balding pates of his peers. *Could it be . . . ?* His heart skipped a beat. But no; she looked up from her book, exposing to view grey eyes and a snub nose dusted with freckles, a pert little face better adapted to Hogarth than to Botticelli.

"Which of you were actually in the room while Mr. Maunders was using the book, and after he left?" Fenchurch was slightly acquainted with Maunders, a moody youth who, unlike most of the Sheepshanks undergraduates, had been recruited from the working-classes and possibly in consequence bore a very evident chip on his shoulder. Upon his arrival in College he had been taken in hand by Grubb, the only Sheepshanks Fellow with a similar background, from whom he had acquired the displeasing habit of spouting Communistic claptrap at every opportunity. However, since Deacon, the undergraduate with whom Maunders shared rooms, came of much the same background and was a cheerful lad with no visible prickles, Fenchurch concluded that it was more a matter of temperament than of social environment.

"The only staff here at the time, sir, were myself—and Welby." Euston indicated a youngish man in his early thirties who was of medium height and somewhat overweight, with the pasty complexion of one who is rarely out-of-doors and takes little exercise. "Welby is one of our binders who was in the Anderson Room checking on the reference bindings. Those books are constantly being handled, often carelessly, so they need frequent repairs. When we discovered the book was missing, I asked him to come back down in order to find out whether he had noticed anything whilst he was here."

"Did you see anything that might bear some relation to the disappearance of the *Anelida,* Mr. Welby?" enquired

Fenchurch. The binder's gooseberry eyes slid past his, then returned to fasten on them with a disconcerting intensity.

"No, sir, I saw nothing, I'm afraid. I noticed the pile of returns on the table, but as I wasn't concerned with checking them for repairs, I took no special notice of what was lying there."

"Have you any idea of what the *Anelida* looks like?"

Welby hesitated. "Is it a little skinny thing by any chance, sir? I do recall having worked recently on a book with black crabby letters, like Mr. Euston described it. But the title stamped on the spine had a name that sounded like—like coal—*Anthracite,* or some such. The hinges had cracked, I remember."

"*Anelida and Arcite,*" Fenchurch said eagerly, tossing back his mane of silvery hair. "That's right. Bound in green morocco. So you might have recognised it if you'd seen it."

Welby looked doubtful. "At least you know the size and shape. Do you remember seeing anything of the sort, either on the returns table or in someone's possession?"

Welby cogitated for a moment, clearly with an effort, then shook his head decisively. "I couldn't swear to it either way, sir. It isn't much to look at, as I recall—it could be one of those pamphlets that we have all over the place. We get hundreds of them to bind at a time."

"Thank you, Welby, for your assistance." Fenchurch dismissed him. "I don't think we shall require you further at the moment." As the binder slouched off, Fenchurch, who had unconsciously taken charge in the absence of Manthorpe, turned to Euston. "You say that Mr. Maunders is on his way over?"

"Yes, sir; fortunately he was in his rooms when I rang Sheepshanks, and I was able to send an urgent message by means of the Porter, who summoned him to the telephone. He said he would come back here at once."

As Euston spoke, the door to the Anderson Room opened, and a tall ungainly young man entered. Perhaps later on his girth would catch up to his height, but so far he had not yet filled out, and the effect was that of a carroty-headed scarecrow. His legs were long as a stork's and his elbows jutted out at his sides, as his arms were longer than the standard issue. He was dressed in a pair of well-worn jeans that accentuated his pipestem legs and a shabby brown jersey. On his face, which was incongruously round and cherubic with a scattering of freckles and seemed to belong to another body entirely, he wore a look of sullen defiance. Making his way over to the group that stood by the returns table and ignoring Fenchurch, he growled, "Well, what is it?"

Euston glanced at Fenchurch with a mute request to take over the interrogation. The elder man nodded and said, "Perhaps we might transfer ourselves to Mr. Manthorpe's room. For the time being it would be preferable that this matter go no further than ourselves. I think that we shall not require the services of anyone else at present: just you, Mr. Euston, and you, Mr. Maunders. But I think it would be as well to see that no one leaves the Anderson Room until we have decided what needs to be done."

To this effect Euston appointed one of his assistants temporary guardian of the desk with instructions to request that anyone preparing to leave the room be asked to wait until they returned, then led the way through the labyrinth of stacks to the room belonging to the Curator of Rare Books. Fenchurch sat at Manthorpe's desk and indicated that the others were to be seated in the two upright chairs which the University Library provided for visitors. "Now," he said, resting his chin on his hands and gazing intently at Maunders, "I understand that you have been informed of the disappearance of the Caxton *Anelida and Arcite,* which you were consulting this morning in the Anderson Room."

"Yes, but I don't see what it has to do with me," was the

ungracious response. "I bloody put it on the table when I left here, like I always do. In fact," he said virtuously, "now I think of it, I turned it in an hour before I left. I went down to the tea-room for a cuppa, and I didn't think I ought to leave it laying about. Then I came back up and worked on another book for a bit."

Fenchurch pounced on this remark. "As you always do. Are you in the habit of consulting this book, then?"

There was a perceptible pause. "I've had a look at it before, if that's what you mean," Maunders replied sulkily.

"Why?" Fenchurch asked in a silky voice. "Are you studying Chaucer?"

"Not exactly." There was a silence.

"'Not exactly?' What precisely does that mean?"

"I happen to be studying rare books, not just Chaucer," said Maunders at length, goaded into unwilling speech. "I've an idea of going into the book trade when I get out of this place. So I'm looking at everything I can in the UL that's got any value to it, to train my eye and to learn as much as I can." His tone was defiant.

"How very enterprising." A thought occurred to Fenchurch. "Are all the rare books you have been examining in the Anderson Room, or have you by any chance also been making use of the resources of your own College, perhaps— the Abbot's Library and the Prye?"

Another silence fell. Then, "Yes," said Maunders reluctantly. "There's no law against it, is there? I thought that was what library books were meant for, to be read."

"When a fifty-thousand-pound book disappears, it is hardly surprising that one should be curious to know who has been consulting it recently and why," Fenchurch told him sternly.

Maunders's ruddy complexion paled beneath his freckles. "Fifty thousand pounds?" He looked as if he were about to be ill. "I knew the book was valuable, but I'd no idea. . . ."

"Not only is it a Caxton, but it is a unique copy," Euston chimed in. "I suppose"—he turned to Fenchurch—"that under the circumstances we should have been more careful, but we have never before had any trouble of this kind. There is always a member of staff sitting at the desk in the Anderson Room to keep an eye on things, and even if someone were to slip past us, the Porters downstairs check the brief-cases. . . ."

"The book is so very small, you see," Fenchurch said gently. "Mr. Maunders, for instance, could quite easily slip it under his belt beneath his jersey."

"You just wait half a tick," Maunders snapped, glaring at them belligerently. "I could prosecute you for saying that. D'you think I'd be fool enough to sign a call-slip if I'd planned to pinch the thing?"

"It does seem risky," Fenchurch acknowledged. "On the other hand, the unlikeliness of it might give you the appearance of innocence: and how else would you get hold of the volume? It might be months before another scholar requested it; and even then you would almost certainly not be in the Anderson Room when he did. "I presume you would not object to a search of your rooms? Merely to assist in establishing your innocence."

Maunders's eyes swivelled from Fenchurch to Euston. There was a glint of panic in their depths, like those of a wild animal at bay. "I most certainly would," he snarled, his gaze fastening on Fenchurch. "You've always had a down on me, haven't you? Don't think I don't know it—not up to the standard of your precious College, I suppose, with all those brats of the nobility that haven't the tenth part of a brain among 'em. You wouldn't ask Lord Henry Huntingfield to turn his rooms out for a search, would you? Not bleeding likely. Then why the hell should you ask me? You've got a bloody nerve. Anyway," he continued spitefully, "you're not the Rare Books Librarian. You have no authority at the UL. What right have you to ask me to do any such thing?"

"My dear young man," Fenchurch spoke with an asperity that was rare for him and that belied his choice of address, "I am acting *in loco domini* for Mr. Manthorpe, who has gone to London—I suppose you've no idea what return train he expects to take?"—this to Euston, who shook his head in response. "I am in any event going to propose to the University Librarian that everyone in the Anderson Room—in fact everyone in the Library—be searched before leaving the building. As you had already gone out it is natural that your rooms should be searched, as will the rooms of any other person known to have left the Anderson Room during the pertinent time."

These words seemed to deflate Maunders; at any rate he made no more protest, and almost cheerfully submitted to a brief body search by Euston. Euston insisted on having the same office performed for him by Fenchurch, after which they returned to the Anderson Room to set the larger wheels of the search in motion.

The combing of the University Library for the missing Caxton caused a considerable flap among those present. It was impossible in the short term to search the entire Library with any degree of thoroughness, so except for the reference stacks in the Reading Room and the shelves containing the Royal Library—given to the University by George I and housed in bookcases that are readily accessible to UL readers—no bookshelves were checked. On the other hand the scholars, to their great discomfiture, humiliation, and sometimes openly expressed indignation, were.

Fenchurch decided that a strip search was more thorough than a patdown of the person, as the Caxton was sufficiently thin to be overlooked, particularly if the thief had had the foresight to remove and discard the binding. In general the undergraduates found this ordeal something of a lark—even the distaff side, which considered it mildly titillating to undress in the cavernous ladies' room in front of reluctant female library staff, and shouted bawdy remarks to one another as they performed an impromptu music-hall strip-tease. Research students too on the whole took the indignity in their stride, undergoing the obligatory search with minimal fuss.

The Professors and dons, however, were an altogether different story. Oddly enough, it was not the female dons who complained. The younger women disrobed in an offhand manner, as if it was infra dig. to notice they were naked, and the older ladies accepted the disagreeable necessity with Spartan fortitude. In particular Dame Hermione Playfair, Mistress of Lady Margaret Hall, as she discarded an astonishing number of nether garments layer by layer, maintained the frozen demeanour of a tragic queen making the supreme sacrifice. But the male of the species was not so stoic. Cries of outrage arose when the dons heard what was required of them and not even the intercessions of Fenchurch, one of their own, were successful in soothing their savage breasts. The more venerable the don, the more affronted he was by the projected indecency of exposing his legs even to such a relatively private viewing. To conciliate these affronted academics, Fenchurch made the concession of suggesting that they undergo a body search by a thorough patting-down, but this was rejected out-of-hand. Peascod, one of the Sheepshanks Fellows, a tall pewter-haired don with the slightly *distrait* air of Alice's White Knight, stiffly informed Fenchurch that if he had wished to be touched by anyone but his tailor, he would have taken a wife. On the other hand Minsham of King's, small and plump and mild-featured, had looked distinctly enthusiastic at the prospect until he discovered that he had drawn Fenchurch for the task rather than one of the young library staff-assistants.

Several of the searches produced startling revelations. No one, for instance, would have anticipated that Dr. Wildbore of Jesus, a forbidding black-bearded giant of a man whose specialty was medieval French, wore long red woollen underwear; or that Cresson of Clare would have sported a Union Jack on his underpants. Professor Tempeste of Sheepshanks was as irascible as his name would imply over displaying, even to so restricted an audience, the flower-strewn shorts which his lady-wife had unexpectedly given him the previous Christmas. Fenchurch averted his eyes from these evidences of frailty shown by his peers: he did not sit in judgment on them, even though his own nether-garments were chastely white and devoid of ornament. In addition to spirited underwear, this debagging of scholars *en masse* produced an unappetising collection of knobbly knees, spindly shanks, and bow-legs; a sight which made Fenchurch reflect that as a species mankind had a lot of catching-up to do physically with the rest of creation.

None of this well-intentioned labour, however, turned up any sign of the missing *Anelida*. Even the bindery trolleys were checked, in case Maunders had mistakenly dropped it on the cart Welby had loaded in the Anderson Room that morning, but they found nothing. Nor was the book located in Maunders's rooms, nor in the quarters of any of those members of the University who were known to have visited the Anderson Room or other parts of the UL that day.

All in all, it was a protracted and wearisome task; and Fenchurch, made to assist in all these proceedings at the request of the University Librarian in deference to the Sheepshankian's superior experience of crime, was dying for a drink long before it was over. By the time they finished it was nearly time to dress for dinner—to exchange his plus-fours for garb more suited to High Table—but he downed a quick sherry in his rooms before changing. It made him feel not displeasingly raffish: his father had taught him *never* to drink alone.

3 Raphael Berni

Vivien Murray drank her tea with composure, as if she had not heard the broodingly handsome young man who sat opposite her ask her to go to bed with him.

"I adore the Whim, don't you?" she remarked inconsequently, glancing about the dark cramped little room. "As far as the tea-cake is concerned it's not what it used to be, but then nothing is."

"Damn the tea-cake!" the young man across from her exploded, shoving his cup aside with a petulant gesture. "Didn't you hear what I just said?" His scowl was Byronic, matching the luxuriant curls that casually clustered on a forehead worthy, like the poet's, to be immortalised in marble. The son of the head-waiter at the Granta Hotel, Raphael Berni had received a scholarship to Trinity, where he had recently been elected a Fellow. He had a startlingly well-attended series of lectures on Baudelaire under his belt and the sultry Mediterranean good looks that are so frequently irresistible to less vivid Anglo-Saxon maidens. A premature spate of successes had somewhat spoiled him: accustomed to having his words hung upon and his propositions accepted with flattering alacrity, he was thrown out of his stride by Vivien's lack of attention.

"Of course I heard you," she replied calmly. "I should

have had to be deaf not to. It would be surprising if there were anyone in the room who hadn't."

"Oh, come now, you needn't exaggerate," he protested, nonetheless glancing uneasily over his shoulder. "I was keeping my voice down, and anyway, what does it matter?"

"My dear, you have no idea how that magnificent instrument carries; I expect it comes of all your lecturing. You ought to remember to lower it to a dull roar, at least when you converse on rather indecently personal matters. *You* may not care if all Cambridge is acquainted with the lurid details of your love life, but I prefer a modicum of privacy, thank you very much." Her tone was severe but her limpid eyes were bright with mischief.

"I'm sorry if I embarrassed you," he said sulkily. "But I'm certain no one heard. There isn't a soul looking our way. What about it?"

Vivien examined her tea-cake with obvious disapproval. "I'm not embarrassed," she retorted. "I should have thought you might be. They're skimping on the sultanas."

"What about it, then?" he repeated doggedly. She was cool and remote as a goddess, and her very aloofness and indifference served to inflame him further. Berni was used to unbridled adulation both from the undergraduate women who took his courses and the younger female Fellows in his department, to whom he seemed as exotic as an iridescent-hued butterfly and as desirable as the warmth of the tropical sun that had hatched it. In his two years as a Fellow he had fluttered about a goodly number of hearts and left them singed; not only had their owners enthusiastically consented to being bedded, but as often as not they had begged for the privilege of paying for the tea that had led to it. Now his male pride was at stake. He could not believe that this ravishing creature was immune to the attraction that had drawn so many eager moths to the flame. Her beauty combined with her lack of interest aroused him to a fever-pitch of longing, and at the same time he was hampered by not knowing how to deal with being the adorer instead of the adored.

"Don't tell me you don't want to—I can see you do, just like I do. Now you've had your fun, let's get on with it." Though Raph's style of seduction normally bordered on the brusque, this was a trifle precipitate even for him. The brouhaha at the UL, however, had made him somewhat late since he had been working in the Anderson Room that morning and had left before the discovery that the Caxton was missing, so his rooms had been checked afterwards. As a result it had been necessary to put the rendezvous with Vivien off for an hour and now there was barely time before his next tutorial to get her to his rooms in Trinity for a quick one. He was used to these split-second calculations; it was because of its proximity as well as its cheapness that the Whim was often the scene for his seductions.

The goddess raised surprisingly dark eyebrows. "A trifle over-hasty, aren't you? A quick in-and-out at Trin. It sounds like a fence at a horse show. No finesse, no empurpled words of passion to lure me off to your incense-scented lair? I expected more from a student of Baudelaire than mere caveman tactics. Thanks ever so much for the charming invitation, but somehow I think I'd rather not."

To Raph's surprise, it was not only injured pride he felt at this rejection. Searching about for some possible reason to account for her inexplicable rejection of him, he exclaimed angrily, "I know what it is. You're a snob—you'd hop into the sack with me in a flash if I were one of those public-school twits."

Vivien raked him with her splendid eyes. "Oh, you are hopeless." Taking a pound note from her handbag, she placed it on the table. "I'd rather pay for my own tea, under the circumstances."

She left him glowering down at his tea-cup and miserably wondering why, the one time it really mattered, his never-fail stratagems had unaccountably gone wrong.

4 Tracking the Prints

Fenchurch proceeded along Green Street on his now somewhat bathetic errand of tracing the stolen Sheepshanks engravings. It was distinctly less stimulating than the search for the *Anelida,* but that had reached a temporary standstill. Manthorpe, returned from London, had taken the reins into his own hands and enlisted Fenchurch as his chief consultant, but for the moment nothing more was to be done once they had notified the police to alert rare-book dealers about the theft.

The shop window of Firkin & Rouse sparkled in the watery November sun, displaying to the view of passers-by a number of prints representing familiar Cambridge scenes; none of them, however, Fenchurch noted with regret, were Loggans or Ackermanns. The inside of the shop was no less spruce than its exterior, despite the presence of thousands of prints of various periods, shapes, and sizes. The walls of the shop, painted a warm rosy tan, were visible only around the edges of mats and frames, within which velvety mezzotints hung cheek by jowl with delicate etchings in Hogarth frames. Aquatinted hunting scenes, lithographed churches, and Gilray caricatures democratically rubbed elbows around the walls or crowded each other in neatly arranged bins.

Mr. Rouse, a gentleman of indeterminate age with a pear-shaped body that matched a pear-shaped face, was fortunately in residence. He was balding, with a fringe of lank dark hair surrounding a shiny scalp, and the suit he wore was dark in colour and conservative in cut. He exhibited a welcoming manner that approached the unctuous, but his small black eyes above the round cheeks were shrewd and intent.

"May I help you, sir?" he asked, taking in each detail of his visitor's physical appearance without seeming to do so. While he had never actually met Fenchurch, he was certain of the newcomer's identity—the Sheepshankian was a well-known sight in the Cambridge streets with his flock of students, and when all is said and done, there are not many men who roam the town wearing plus-fours and sandals and carrying a knapsack. But Mr. Rouse held to the canny belief that it was far wiser to seem to know too little than too much.

"I presume that you are Mr. Rouse, the proprietor of this shop," Fenchurch said by way of response.

"I am."

"I, sir, am John Fenchurch of Sheepshanks College. I made enquiries the other day of your shop-assistant relating to some Cambridge prints which may have been offered to you recently. I was unable to speak to you as you were away at the time."

"I am pleased and proud to make your acquaintance, Mr. Fenchurch," said Mr. Rouse, taking Fenchurch's hand in his large limp grasp and shaking it enthusiastically. "Your architectural lectures are, of course, famous in the town; and I myself was fortunate enough to acquire a copy of your work, *A Comparative Study of King's and Sheepshanks Chapels.* It was most persuasive and enlightening. I was unable to set it down."

"Very kind of you to say so," Fenchurch replied modestly. He looked about him. "Your shop seems remarkably well stocked. I was here in Mr. Firkin's time, but that was some years ago."

"Would you care to join me in some sherry? We can discuss your business over a glass. Cutler—my assistant—told me about your visit to the shop." Fenchurch acquiesced and Mr. Rouse led the way into his office, a snug cubicle filled with the choicest of his wares. Several very fine Blakes hung on the walls alongside a brace of Rowlandson's rarer productions and a superb mezzotint of a liberally endowed court lady by Rupert of the Rhine. The room, though small, was comfortably appointed and distinctly cosy. A couple of leather easy chairs stood near a leather-topped desk, and a handsome silver-bound tantalus with several wineglasses graced a Hepplewhite lowboy set against one wall. Mr. Rouse filled two glasses and handed one to Fenchurch, gesturing hospitably toward the larger of the chairs as he did so.

"Now, Mr. Fenchurch, in what way may I serve you?" he asked, settling himself into the other chair. "Cutler told me that you are looking for several engravings of Cambridge, but he was not clear as to which ones they are."

"I did not tell your assistant that the engravings after which I made enquiries have disappeared from Sheepshanks," replied Fenchurch, sipping his sherry. It was surprisingly good. "They are Loggans and Ackermanns, abstracted from several books in the Abbot's Library."

Mr. Rouse composed his heavy features into a suitably shocked expression, which Fenchurch sensibly discounted as a display of good manners.

"What would seem sacrilege to me or to the Abbot's Librarian—the removal of illustrations from a volume—is no doubt merely good business sense to you," he continued. "How, after all, could a print shop exist if books were never to be broken up? But these were both particularly fine copies—a shame to deface them; and then," he added somewhat belatedly, "there is the question of theft."

"Of theft. Yes," said Mr. Rouse. "A state of affairs to be discouraged. Too often print shops are considered the natural repositories for thieves' booty, whereas we are in actuality highly scrupulous—most of us, that is to say."

"Of course," murmured Fenchurch tactfully.

Mr. Rouse waxed indignant. "You cannot imagine, Mr. Fenchurch, the difficulties printsellers face. Because we are marketing what may be described as mass-produced objects, it is difficult to assure that the provenance (if I may use so exalted a word for my wares) is free and clear. Especially now that prices have risen, one must be very careful from whom one buys in order to avoid even the appearance of improbity."

Fenchurch nodded sympathetically.

"Unfortunately one bad apple in the barrel, so to speak, can taint the rest of us by association. That is what nearly happened in Cambridge some years ago. You may not have heard of it; happily it did not get into the papers so the trade did not suffer. A dealer, whose name I need not at present mention, was charged as a receiver of stolen goods. His source was a country house not far from Swaffham Bulbeck; as it turned out the butler had been stealing illustrated books from the library there and selling them to this man. The thief had made no attempt at dissimulation—there was no need, as the dealer who purchased them was quite agreeable to handling questionable merchandise—and when the police searched the shop they discovered the books from which the plates had been removed, each volume with the bookplate of Hintlesham Hall on the flyleaf."

None of this was what Fenchurch had come to hear, but as he did not wish to disturb the flow of Rouse's conversation for fear of missing something which might prove useful, he sipped his admirable sherry and nodded politely.

"The dealer left the vicinity shortly after his conviction—he was let off with a fine, I am sorry to say, though the butler went to gaol—and has set up shop in London, where they are presumably more tolerant of such lapses. I mention the incident because a visitor to this shop brought it to mind some months ago." He paused to refill their glasses.

Aha! thought Fenchurch, now we come to the pith of the matter. He waited.

"It was," Rouse continued, daintily lifting his glass to his nostrils with a pale meaty hand to savour its bouquet, "about six months ago, I should imagine, that a very young man, not at all well-dressed—a student from the look of him— came in to enquire whether we had any Loggans in stock. Upon my replying in the negative, he said it was a great pity as he particularly wanted the one of Nevile's Court for a present—only that engraving would do, he emphasized. Could I recommend any of the other print shops in Cambridge as being likely to carry a Loggan? I answered that I doubted it, as they are difficult to obtain, though he was welcome to try. Did I know of any place in London, then? He was very anxious to find one. I said it was possible that Witwang & Crispe in Bond Street might have one, though I added, for he did not seem especially prosperous, that they tend to be pricey as they are one of the best-known printsellers in the country. To tell the truth, I did not think that he could have afforded a Loggan from my shop if I had happened to have one on hand; but of course one never knows. Witwang & Crispe, I added, are famous for the quality of their stock; they only buy from country houses and from libraries which are disposing of duplicates or selling off books which do not fit into their collections, and even then they only accept what is first class.

"He seemed dejected upon hearing this and asked whether there were not another, less expensive, shop in London where he might look for the print he wanted. It was for a girl, he said, and he was most eager to locate one. By now I was growing somewhat weary of his company. It was obvious that he was unlikely to become a customer of mine, so there was no point in my wasting so much time on him, but I could not help but feel sorry for the boy. He was young and shabby and looked so woebegone, and the fact that he wanted it to give a girl—well, to cut a long story short, I gave him the name of the dealer I mentioned earlier, who I understand has made Cantabrigiana something of a specialty of his. I did warn my visitor, however, that the man had been known to deal in shady merchandise. I felt it my duty."

"What did he say to that? Anything that you can recall?" Fenchurch asked.

"Do you know, it was really quite odd; I could have sworn he looked pleased when I told him. I was somewhat shocked as I assumed he thought it would bring down the price if the print had been stolen, so I rather sharply said that so far as I knew the dealer had reformed, otherwise I should not have considered giving out his name. The youth thanked me profusely for the information and left. I have not seen him since."

Now came the question that Fenchurch had been reserving for last, like the favourite bonbon in a box of chocolates. But in this case it might turn out, when he bit into it, to be either a champagne truffle or one of those horrid green jellies that no one ever finishes, for Mr. Rouse might offer a vague description which could fit half the Sheepshanks undergraduates. Fenchurch mentally crossed his fingers as he said, "I gather the lad did not give you his name. Can you by any chance recollect what he looked like?"

"He never mentioned his name, but his appearance was very striking. Working with prints as I do, I am of course visually oriented, but even if that were not the case I do not think I could readily forget such a figure. He was very tall, with long legs like a giraffe; and his head and body seemed singularly ill-adapted to one another. In fact, if his body had not been visible, I should have judged his face to belong to a short, possibly plump, man. Most incongruous. His hair was an orange-red, I recall; almost vermillion in hue."

"Splendid," said Fenchurch, jumping out of his chair and pumping Rouse's hand up and down in his enthusiasm. "Absolutely splendid! I cannot thank you enough, my dear sir. Would you be willing to swear to the description in a court of law, if need be?"

"Ye-es; if I must," replied the other cautiously. "But . . ."

"It may not be necessary," Fenchurch said, reseating himself. "I hope not. We shall see. By the way, what is the name of the London dealer? You must realise that we shall require it."

"I am prepared to give it to you in the circumstances. I only regret that I gave it to that wretched boy; I see now that he must have been looking for an outlet for stolen prints, not for a picture to buy. I feel quite disgracefully naïf. But at the time I should not have dreamed . . . he seemed genuinely to be looking for the engraving of Nevile's Court. And students nowadays—they all dress so oddly. One may come into the shop looking like a pauper and then pull a couple of hundred pounds from his jeans pocket, or even more surprisingly, write a cheque in the name of a Noble House! It used to be," Rouse said in a tone of regret for the vanished past, "that one could tell who someone was by looking at him. Or at least by listening. Of course the boy's voice . . . but the most unexpected people have money now."

"No blame attaches to you," Fenchurch told him soothingly. "Actually, I am delighted you gave him the information. If he had gone the rounds of London on his own, who knows whether we should have found out where he had gone? London is such a wide cover to beat. The dealer?" he enquired once more.

"The name is Biggers—J.O. Biggers, in Great Russell

Street, very near the British Museum. There used to be rather a joke among the Cambridge printsellers about his being close to his source of supply," Rouse added unexpectedly, "though so far as I know he has been quite honest since his . . . slip. A queer little man; not one I was ever able to warm up to. I believe he started life as a rag-and-bone man."

"Thank you for your help," said Fenchurch, rising from his chair. "And for your excellent sherry. You have been of great assistance. Perhaps you will permit me to repay you in Sheepshanks some day."

"Nothing could please me more; except—wait! Might I prevail upon you to—I expect it's rather a bore, you must he asked often, but . . ." To Fenchurch's astonishment Rouse flushed the shade of beetroot as he fumbled in a bookcase behind him. "If you wouldn't mind signing your book for me," he said breathlessly, taking a volume from the shelf.

"I should be delighted." This was heady stuff for Fenchurch; never before had he been approached by an autograph seeker. The only copies he had signed had been for his friends and colleagues, as it was hardly the sort of book that attracted celebrity hunters. He took the proffered fountain-pen.

"My Christian name is Justin—Justin Anthony."

With a flourish Fenchurch inscribed the flyleaf "To Justin A. Rouse, thanks to whom the lost is found. With the heart-felt thanks of John Fenchurch and of Sheepshanks," and handed the book to Rouse, who read what he had written.

"How kind of you," he said, quite pink with pleasure, "how very kind!" And he ushered Fenchurch out of his shop amid mutual expressions of gratitude and esteem.

railway carriage swayed to and fro on the track as the which it formed a component made its leisurely way London. Instead of going to Liverpool Street they had e slower and more familiar train to King's Cross, for the latter station is more convenient to Russell Square and the British Museum. Since Fenchurch and Grierson were the only occupants of the first-class compartment, they had spread their possessions over the other red-plush seats, transforming it into a miniature Combination Room on wheels. By the time the train stopped at Audley End, fifteen minutes outside Cambridge, Grierson was immersed in proofs of a book he had written on phallic symbolism in *Tristram Shandy,* shortly to be published by the Cambridge University Press; and Fenchurch was engrossed by the *Times* crossword puzzle, half of which he had completed in the short space since their departure from the Cambridge station. In his knapsack he had Michael Innes's latest thriller (he liked to keep up with the competition) and a notebook in which to jot, if all other forms of diversion were exhausted, a few chapters of his own latest projected mystery, *Slaughter Stalks Swavesey.* Fenchurch was a closet mystery-writer, who in his spare moments rested his brain by exchanging erudition for detection. He concealed this predilection from his peers in the Combination Room as though it were a moral flaw; but he took a certain quiet pride in the success of the pseudonymous Geoffrey Saltmarsh, whose latest effort, *A Fiend in Fulbourn,* the gory account of the dismemberment of an English housewife with a Maori ceremonial *toki* stolen from the Cambridge Museum of Archaeology and Ethnology, was already in its fifth paperback printing.

By the time they reached London Fenchurch had completed the *Times* puzzle and was halfway through the Innes book, a satisfactory state of affairs as it meant it was likely he would get some work done on *Slaughter Stalks Swavesey* on the way home. As they left the train Grierson, who led the way, headed in the direction of a taxi-rank.

"Surely you're not planning to take a taxi?" Fenchurch protested, trotting along at the taller man's heels. Due to the

London trip he had had to cut short his early morning walk. "It's only a matter of a half-mile or so."

"Indeed I am," returned Grierson with a shudder. "I cannot face the thought of walking in that appalling traffic. I am terrified of London streets; I would no more wander among those clanking monsters than I would a herd of rutting water buffalo. Don't ask me to do it, Fenchurch, for I won't, I tell you."

In Fenchurch's opinion the Cantabrigian herds of lemming-like bicycles, seemingly bent on mass self-destruction by wrapping themselves about a pedestrian or hurling themselves in front of a car or lorry, were far more frightening than the relatively tame London traffic, but though he was disappointed at missing the exercise, he humoured his companion and did not insist further on walking to their destination. As their taxi turned from Bloomsbury Street into Great Russell Street, a narrow shop-window became visible with the legend J.O. BIGGERS—PRINTS inscribed in shabby black-and-gilt letters on the dusty glass. When they had alighted and paid the cab-driver they found that on the door, which was locked, a card was taped with the words PLEASE RING, a directive Fenchurch obeyed.

In the distance an old-fashioned bell tinkled, muffled by the heavy door, and a moment later a rumpled jolly rotund little man with faded rufous hair like the coat of an elderly dog-fox opened the door to them. He had something of the air of a racing tout, in part because he was wearing a plaid suit with a very large and brilliant pattern, and because his nose was rubicund and the smell of stale whisky hung about him.

He seemed startled by the apparitions upon his doorstep, rubbing his eyes as if he had been taking a nap and thought he might still be dreaming. As the silence grew, Fenchurch took matters in hand by stepping over the threshold and saying, "Mr. Biggers?"

The sound of a voice appeared to dispel his uncertainty. "That's me, all right, gentlemen," he replied. "J.O. Biggers, at your service. What," he said, giving a slight hiccup, "what can I do for you?"

"We are interested in prints," said Fenchurch ambiguously.

This remark had the effect of bringing Mr. Biggers more or less to himself. He blinked and said, "Come right in, gents; be my guests. Anything special you got in mind?"

As it had been agreed upon in advance between them that Fenchurch should be the spokesman, he moved forward slightly and replied, "We are looking for a Loggan print, one from *Cantabrigia Illustrata,* and we understand that you specialise in Cambridge material. Would you by some chance have any in stock?"

Mr. Biggers placed his finger alongside his conspicuous nose in Dickensian fashion and cogitated visibly. His hesitation arose, Fenchurch suspected, not so much from a lack of knowledge of his merchandise as from an excess of spirits befogging his brain.

"Loggan, Loggan, Loggan," he repeated muzzily. "Lemme see now. Any special one you got in mind?" he asked, clearly stalling for time.

"Any one would do, but I should particularly like to buy the one depicting the North Court of St. Jude's College, if you should happen to have it," returned Fenchurch.

"I'll go take a look. It she-seems to me I recollect having somethin' like that tucked away someplace. Won't you gents take a pew?" he added, extracting a none-too-clean checked handkerchief from his pocket and hospitably swiping the dusty seats of two rickety wooden chairs with it. "Ta. Be ri' back." He disappeared unsteadily down a staircase at the rear of the premises.

Fenchurch and Grierson gingerly seated themselves and looked about the small crowded shop. It formed a strong contrast to the premises of Firkin & Rouse, which had a cluttered elegance, an air of being dusted and looked-after, that could by no means be attributed to Mr. Biggers's place of business. A certain air of homeliness was imparted by a tumbler and a half-empty pint-bottle of whisky which stood on the desk, cunningly concealed from view by a pile of books but discovered nonetheless by Fenchurch in removing several of the volumes to inspect their title pages. That part of the print shop's floor which was not covered by the scanty furnishings was filled with more stacks of books tilted at crazy angles, and grimy cardboard boxes which, when examined, proved to contain engravings and lithographs in varying stages of dilapidation. Large sepia prints of cathedral interiors, badly foxed, in massive wooden frames, along with engraved portraits of long-dead statesmen with double chins and sharp-nosed ladies surmounted by towering headdresses hung on the grubby walls, which were embellished at the corners with festoons of ancient cobwebs. A cursory inspection would have led one to conclude that the shop had not been painted for nearly as long as some of the prints had been in existence. The very light filtering in through the window-panes, crusted with ancient dirt, was dense and fuscous.

Fenchurch opened a number of the books strewn about the shop, most of which proved to be accounts of travels or botanical and zoological works, copiously illustrated. "The man's a vandal!" he exclaimed in indignation. "It appalls me to think all these books will be broken up for their plates."

At this point a bumping noise was heard on the stairs down which Mr. Biggers had descended and a moment later his foxy head poked up the staircase. "Got just the ticket for you, gents," he panted jovially, heaving a large portfolio up the steps. "Thought I remembered where I'd put it." There must have been a wash-basin in the basement or plumbing of some sort, for his ginger curls had been slicked down and his face, still not completely dry, shone with the application of water, presumably in an attempt to sober himself up for his customers. In the main he appeared to have succeeded; his speech was no longer slurred and his eyes were able to focus on their subject. He scampered briskly over to the desk, adeptly swept the glass and bottle into an open drawer which he closed with his knee, and set the stack of books on the already overflowing floor. With a showmanlike gesture he opened the portfolio to disclose a number of engravings—all, Fenchurch saw, from *Cantabrigia Illustrata*—and sifted through them until he came upon the one he sought. Pouncing on it like an overfed marmalade cat, he cried out "There!" in triumph and handed it to Fenchurch.

After a brief glance Fenchurch took a small glass from his pocket and examined the print minutely. "You do indeed have exactly what we were looking for," he said. "Do you see, Grierson?" As he gave the engraving and the glass to the Abbot's Librarian, he pointed to the left-hand corner. "It is the one; most indubitably it is the one."

"'Ere, wot's this?" protested Mr. Biggers, who seemed to have mislaid his aitches under duress. Fenchurch's behaviour alarmed him; those fumes of alcohol that remained after his hasty ablutions were being rapidly dispersed by sudden misgiving and suspicion. He tried to snatch the picture away, but Grierson was too quick for him and held it behind his back for protection.

Without answering Biggers, Fenchurch extracted a large volume from the briefcase Grierson had been carrying and handed it to his colleague, who tried the print in question in one of the gaps left by the thief. "It fits exactly!" Grierson exulted. "No doubt about it, Fenchurch. Of course, that is not definitive, as another copy of the book might be exactly the same size; but when combined with the blot . . ."

"'Ere, then; that's my propitty you're making so free with," Biggers protested vehemently.

"It is not your property. It is the property of Sheepshanks

College, as, I have no doubt, are these other engravings," Fenchurch gestured toward the portfolio on the desk, "and, I daresay, a clutch of Ackermann aquatints of Cambridge scenes as well. Where did you get these?" he continued, fixing Biggers with a stern eye.

"I don't know what you mean," the other blustered in an effort to brazen out the situation. "If you don't give me back my propitty I'm going to ring the police."

But he had not reckoned with Fenchurch. "Ring the police, by all means," he responded coolly.

"What?" Mr. Biggers gaped at him, his small grey eyes goggling uncertainly.

"You heard what I said. Do ring the police; we shall be delighted to see them. Come to think of it, it's an excellent idea."

"Now just you wait a cock," said Mr. Biggers uneasily, employing Cockney rhyming slang *cock linnet*. He had not anticipated this turn of events. "I'm willing to be reasonable. There's no need for the police among friends, is there? Just give me back what's mine, that's all I ask."

"But we should like to buy the engraving," said Fenchurch.

"Not so fast. It ain't for sale."

"Come, come. Only a moment ago you said . . ."

"That was then. Now I've decided not to sell it." His plump little mouth was set in a truculent line as he held out his hand for the Loggan print.

"In that case," Fenchurch said, "*I* shall ring for the police." He reached for the telephone that stood on the desk but it was snatched away from him by Mr. Biggers.

"Wot is all this?" His nasal voice rose in an aggrieved whine. "Are you two coppers? You don't look like the law."

"We are not policemen," Fenchurch assured him. "We are Fellows of Sheepshanks College, Cambridge, and we are looking for some stolen property belonging to the College. We have found it"—he placed his hand on the portfolio—"here."

"I'll have you both up for slander, I will," declared Mr. Biggers. "Or is it libel? Whatever it is, you'll pay through the nose. I'm an honest man. . . ."

"What about that prosecution in Cambridge some years ago for receiving stolen goods?" enquired Grierson.

Mr. Biggers opened his mouth as if to protest further, but shut it without speaking. A moment passed and then he said sullenly, "Well, what about it, then? Anybody can make a mistake, like. I've gone straight ever since."

"I am inclined to doubt it," rejoined Fenchurch, "since there is no question that this engraving came from the Sheepshanks Library. It is barely within the bounds of possibility that a print from another copy of the book would fit exactly in our volume, but this engraving of St. Jude's has a small ink-blot shaped like a fish on its lower left-hand side, probably as the result of the copperplate being over-inked. I have seen a number of copies of the work, but I have never observed another ink-blot of that description in any of them."

Biggers's jaw dropped, but his mind was working rapidly.

"That's what you would say, wouldn't you," he sneered, "once you'd seen the ink-spot on my copy." Now that he had heard and considered the evidence against him, he had recovered some of his earlier bounce. "That ain't what I'd call proof."

"It would not be accepted as proof except that I took care to attest to that fact in front of witnesses before we left Cambridge, in the hope you might not yet have sold that print and it would be here for us to identify," Fenchurch returned.

Upon hearing this the little print dealer collapsed like a pricked balloon. His plaid coat, which only a moment earlier had surrounded his ample form like the casing of a sausage, now seemed to hang from him as though he had bought it with the intention of growing into it. "I want my solicitor," he said.

"Mr. Biggers, let me assure you that we are not interested in the propriety of your business practices. We seek only to retrieve any engravings in your possession which are the property of Sheepshanks College," Grierson told him, "and to obtain some information."

There was silence. Then, "What do you want to know?" Biggers queried cautiously, swivelling a shrewd little eye in Grierson's direction.

"Who sold you these engravings?" asked Fenchurch.

"As to that, I wouldn't have the foggiest. He wouldn't hardly leave his calling-card, now would he? Not if he'd pinched them."

"We realise that. But what did he look like? I assume it was a man. Young, old? Short, tall? Fat, thin?"

"I'm not sure what he looked like. I can't remember everyone comes into the shop, can I? Anyway, 'ow do I know you'll keep your word?—about not telling the coppers, I mean."

"You have only our word," said Fenchurch gently, "but I assure you that it is trustworthy."

The print dealer was unaccustomed to trusting the word of others, having so little faith in his own, but after looking into Fenchurch's mild blue eyes he surprised himself by agreeing to the bargain. "He was young," Biggers began abruptly, "only a lad but tall, like he was walking on a pair of stilts. Towered over me, he did, though you may say that don't mean much. 'Ad a funny little round face that didn't hardly go with the rest of him. 'Air my colour," he added, pulling at a lock next to his ear.

"Splendid, splendid," said Fenchurch, rather as if Biggers were a tutorial student who had done unexpectedly well at a scholarly task that had been set him. "Just what we wanted to know. Now we have concluded our business, except for any Ackermanns you may have on the premises. And of course we shall take these with us." He began to tie up the portfolio containing the Loggan engravings, having counted them and found them all present.

"All the Ackermanns is sold," Biggers, whose command of grammar as well as of aitches had broken down under the stress of the moment, returned sulkily.

"I very much doubt that, Mr. Biggers. I think perhaps we should all descend into the cellars while you refresh your memory. My agreement not to call in the police is contingent on the return of *all* the stolen property you still hold," Fenchurch reminded him. He thought it best to keep an eye on the man to ensure that he did not have an opportunity to squirrel away any of the missing Ackermann prints.

It was clear, even to the still slightly fuddled Biggers, that they were not to be denied. Dejectedly he led them down into the depths of a cramped and musty cellar, where by the aid of a rude alphabetical filing system applied to shelves and packing crates he was able to locate the Ackermann prints. There were not so many of them left as of the Loggans. Though Mr. Biggers insisted that he had not received the full set, they were inclined to doubt his word. It was more likely that he had sold a number and was afraid they would expect him to refund the proceeds. Fenchurch was disappointed but scarcely surprised, since their colours, their soft aquatinting and comparatively cheap price made them particularly attractive to the passing tourist. All in all, he reflected in the taxi which took them from the Cambridge railway station back to the Great Gate of Sheepshanks, a tolerably successful day; not least because during the train ride home he had managed to finish not only the Innes book but the initial chapters of *Slaughter Stalks Swavesey.*

At the Master's request the Fellows of Sheepshanks had assembled in the Combination Room. From the expressions on their oddly assorted countenances it was a sombre occasion that had caused them to foregather. The day was overcast, and what light it provided had difficulty in struggling through the narrow mullioned windows so the electric lights had been turned on, illuminating walls covered in linenfold panelling of great delicacy, for the room originally had been the bedchamber of the French abbot. Since he had been partial to his creature comforts a massive fireplace stood in one wall, ornamented with entwined gargoyles into whose activities it was as well not to enquire too closely; traditionally the undergraduates tried to bribe Bottom, the College Butler, in order to get a glimpse of its rumoured lubricity, but he was incorruptible.

Bottom and several of his underlings had ranged armchairs into a semicircle with the largest and most impressive positioned for the Master in front of the fireplace. Dr. Shebbeare's bulk filled the high-backed chair and his arms rested on its carved and upholstered arms. His aspect was grave, like a judge come to try a capital offence. Nearest him sat the older and more senior Fellows: Professor Tempeste; Fenchurch; Peascod, his handsome features abstracted as he ruminated on some especially obscure form of Carolingian minuscule; Robert Austrey, the Prye Librarian, his round kind face evincing concern over the subject about to be introduced; and Grierson. On the outskirts of the circle sat little Crippen, the College Chaplain, gentle and inoffensive; Hedgecock, quite recently elected Fellow after a brilliant undergraduate and research career at Corpus; and Grubb, a member of the Senior Common Room noted chiefly for his attachment to an ineffectual brand of pseudo-Communism and for his dedicated resentment of all privilege enjoyed by anyone except himself. About the head of the seated Master curved a great pale double meniscus half-shrouded in the gloom, which set him off from the others like a Buddha in his nimbus. The trophy, made out of the tusks of Sir Oliver Sheepshanks's favourite elephant, had recently been given to the College as a memorial to Richard Mutton, a former Fellow, by a member of the Sheepshanks family—one of the d'Ewes branch. At intervals the creamy ivory of the tusks was ringed with elaborately wrought gold bands studded with gems that flashed darkly in the tenebrous light cast by the lamps.

"We are met," Dr. Shebbeare initiated the conclave, "to discuss a matter of the gravest concern. It has been discovered that a member of this College is guilty of stealing; and, what is more, of stealing from Sheepshanks." From his tone one felt that if only the culprit had confined his thievery to some other quarter the Master might have found it easier to forgive him. "I shall leave the details to Mr. Fenchurch, who uncovered the crime," he continued, "and to Mr. Grierson, in whose domain the thefts were committed and who assisted Mr. Fenchurch in his enquiries."

Grierson signalled deference to Fenchurch, who told the assembled Fellows what had happened and who was responsible. When he had finished, Dr. Shebbeare took up the thread. "We are fortunate," he said, "in having two such assiduous hunters on the trail of this—this miscreant Maunders, and to have recovered some of the stolen items. Before they went up to London I authorised Mr. Fenchurch and Mr. Grierson to avoid summoning the police provided the man Biggers could be persuaded to disgorge what remained of the Sheepshanks engravings, since I saw no point in disagreeable notoriety for the College; we have already had more than enough of *that* in recent years. I am deeply shocked, as I feel certain we all are, to learn of Maunders's disloyalty and dishonesty; and we shall of course deal with him among ourselves. I am sure I speak for all of you when I say that he must be sent down at once."

"You just hold on a minute." Every eye turned to see who had uttered a remark so foreign to the room in which they sat. It was Grubb, his voice so hoarse with anger as to be unrecognisable. He leaned forward, his sallow face red with rage and his big hands clenched on his knees. "Don't think I don't know you all have a down on Maunders. Not one of your sort, is he? Too much like me, I reckon. I'm not going to stand by and see him framed! Yes, I know you browbeat the lad into a confession"—this to the Master—"but I'm none too sure he did it . . . not all of it, at any rate."

Dr. Shebbeare acted with surprising restraint under this attack. "He has admitted entire culpability to me," he said heavily, "and he shall without question be sent down. Under the circumstances he is very fortunate to be spared going to prison."

"This is just another glaring example of the wholesale class-prejudice that's typical of this place," Grubb burst out furiously. "If one of your young lordlings had done this he'd get off scot-free, and don't think I don't know it!"

The Master pressed his lips together in an effort to avoid any undesirable utterance, first contenting himself with saying merely, "That is quite untrue, Mr. Grubb."

"Don't tell me what's true and what isn't," Grubb snarled, encouraged by the Master's reticence. "What about Lord Henry Huntingfield," he spat the name out of his mouth as if it were venom, "when he pinched *those* last year?" He indicated the tusks enclosing the murky air behind the Master's ursine head. "*He* wasn't sent down, the young twister!"

"Don't be ridiculous." Professor Tempeste spoke up indignantly. "It is not the same thing at all. Lord Henry was merely indulging in a schoolboy prank. High spirits, not hope of profit, led him astray."

"I wouldn't call stealing something that's worth ten times the value of those engravings Maunders is alleged to have taken exactly a schoolboy's prank."

"We all know," rumbled Dr. Shebbeare, "of your unorthodox political proclivities; but just because young Maunders is by your definition one of the downtrodden, he is not thereby excused from the penalties for wholesale theft. The boy had made money out of the prints and no doubt was quite prepared to do so again by purloining another batch, until Fenchurch and Grierson caught up with him. Lord Henry Huntingfield, on the other hand, removed the tusks from the Combination Room with the intention of hoisting them onto the roof of the Master's Lodge: a deplorable action, undoubtedly, but not dishonest."

"That's what he says now," Grubb sneered, "but are you sure that was what he meant to do? He may have planned to ship the things out in a trunk and sell them, for all you know. Aside from the ivory, prising the stones out of their settings would bring him thousands. And all you did," he continued bitterly, "was to gate him for a couple of months."

"But he didn't take the jewels. Don't you see, my dear fellow," said Austrey patiently, "that these are two entirely different sorts of theft, if one can describe young Huntingfield's lark by so severe a term."

But Grubb outflanked him and brought up his reserves. "What about the time the Honourable Jeremy Longworth was caught stealing pocket money from his fellow-students' rooms?" he asked, his voice a triumphant whine. "Was *that* just a boyish peccadillo? You let him off too."

"Jeremy Longworth . . ." the Master began, but Grubb would not allow him to finish.

"A perfect example of class privilege run rampant: he thought the world owed him a living, so he helped himself whenever he could lay his hands on it."

"His psychiatrist . . ."

"His psychiatrist!" the younger man echoed contemptuously. "Pay a psychiatrist enough and he'll say anything you like. I tell you this: If you persist in persecuting poor Maunders just on account of his class, I shall release all I know about the other two affairs to the newspapers. I have contacts in Fleet Street . . . and the BBC."

"The newspapers!" A cry of horror arose from the ranks of the Senior Common Room. Dr. Shebbeare did not speak but he closed his eyes and looked distinctly ill. When he opened them, he said, "I feel certain you would not do anything so ill-advised and detrimental to the College."

"Don't bet on it," responded Grubb. "I can just see my young lord in the headlines, and an Honourable won't do too badly either. The papers will have a field-day—especially with all of you. I can see it now—'Cover-Up at Cambridge,' 'Protecting the Purloining Peer,' 'The Honourable Pick-pocket at Large.' The press have it in for nobs. Don't think they won't jump at this one," he added gleefully.

"What do you think, Fenchurch?" asked the Master help-lessly, turning to the one among them who had the greatest experience of crime and of newspaper reporters. In most mat-ters Dr. Shebbeare was a tower of strength, but this unex-pected onslaught upon the fair name of Sheepshanks by one who might by virtue of his Fellowship have been expected to be among the most determined of her defenders completely unmanned him.

Fenchurch's brow creased in thought: Though he was averse to giving in to blackmail, the situation was extremely delicate. "I think, Master," he replied after time to ponder the problem, "that perhaps we ought to let Maunders off with a gating for this offence. But it must be made abso-lutely plain to him that if he were to do such a thing again he would not only be sent down, but we should have no qualms about placing him in the hands of the police."

The rest of the Fellows showed a disposition to argue this point—Maunders was not popular in College and his offence was considerable—but since Grubb stood firm on his threat to notify the papers if Maunders were sent down, Dr. Sheb-beare reluctantly took Fenchurch's advice and agreed to mete out the lesser punishment of confining him to College for his crime. As the Fellows left the Combination Room the Master beckoned to Fenchurch to remain, and when they were alone said to him, "I must confess that it goes very much against the grain to let that young scamp get away with it. Despite all the untoward publicity it would incur I've still half a mind to send him down and prosecute him into the bargain. If you had not so strongly counselled against it, I should have done so."

"I had my reasons, Master, for advising you not to press the matter now. For one thing, Grubb has us over a barrel. There is no doubt, in my opinion, that he *would* take his story to Fleet Street at once by way of revenge if we were to send his protegé down. But I have a further purpose in my plea for leniency: Maunders is one of the prime suspects in the disappearance of the *Anelida and Arcite* from the University Library, and if he should leave Cambridge it is possible that the *Anelida* would be permanently lost. It is far better for him to stay here, where we can keep an eye on him."

"You think, then, that Maunders took the *Anelida*?" the Master queried.

"I've no idea so far. I should not have considered the two crimes similar, but he may simply have worked up to something bigger. To judge by his record he has a propensity for theft, so at the moment he is the most likely of the suspects. Perhaps he stole the *Anelida* and hid it outside his rooms, or he may already have sent it off to a prospective buyer. The police have been called in by Manthorpe to investigate the disappearance of the Caxton, and I intend unofficially to inform them of the existence of Mr. Biggers. I do not think, however, that he would be in a position to dispose of so *recherché* an item as the *Anelida*; petty profits from petty theft are more in his line than a collector with the resources to make a major purchase. Nonetheless, every contingency must be checked."

"Whatever you say, my dear John. I much dislike to see

that young scoundrel escape any sort of reasonable punishment, but I rely upon your sound judgment in the matter."

"You flatter me, Master."

"I do hope not, John," Dr. Shebbeare responded drily.
"By the way, perhaps I had better suggest confidentially to
Grierson that he keep a strict eye on Maunders whenever he
sets foot in the Library, although I should hope," he went
on, "that he would have the wit to think of it himself."

"We have already discussed it, Master," answered
Fenchurch demurely. "In addition, while it is impossible to
lock up everything of value, the most tempting illustrated
books have been put away. And so far as Austrey is concerned, the Pryevian Library, though the books there are
locked in their presses, is completely out of bounds to him."

"Most satisfactory, John; most satisfactory! I knew I could
depend on you."

And Dr. Shebbeare left the Combination Room in a better
humour than he had entered it.

5 Raph in Love

"What about some grub?" Raphael Berni succeeded admirably in keeping his voice casual. It was a new experience for him to care whether or not an invitation was accepted, since he had a lengthy roster of females from which to choose and he was a proponent of the theory that all cats are grey in the dark. But Vivien with her *cinquecento* looks had bewitched him. He could not get her out of his mind.

"What a remarkably elegant invitation." He could hear the amusement ripple in her voice, and the sound brought with a rush the memory of her scent, a wafting of bluebells over the Whim's tea-table.

He flushed, thankful that she could not see him; she made him feel like a very raw undergraduate. "What about dinner, then?"

"You must have struck it rich." Everyone knew that Raph Berni rarely paid when he took girls out and then it was only for coffee or tea, never for a meal. "Has an elderly auntie unexpectedly popped off?"

"Well, actually, I've come into some money. Prospective, but there it is. I thought we might go to Shades," he said in what he hoped was an offhand manner.

"You *are* flinging the lolly about with mad abandon. And what price am I expected to pay for this delightful repast?"

How I loathe cynicism in women, Raph thought angrily; *it makes them ungrateful.* "Price?" he repeated, as though the word were unfamiliar to him.

"I suppose I shall be expected to return to your room with you and bare all, like a maiden paying the rent in a Victorian melodrama." Suppressed laughter bubbled up in her voice like an underwater spring.

Since this was exactly what he had had in mind, Raph could not think of a suitable riposte. Images of Vivien naked as Botticelli's Venus with her fair hair fanned out about her further tied his tongue. His feelings for her were not solely lustful. For the first time Raphael Berni was in love, as thoroughly in love with Vivien as it was possible for a young man of his pronounced egocentricity to be.

"I'm sorry, Raph," she said, "but that's not really my sort of thing, as it happens. So there isn't much point in my going out with you, is there? You'd be continually trying to get me into bed and it would quite put me off my feed, so that I shouldn't even enjoy the lavish meal you've so kindly offered me. It isn't your fault, I know—it's mere force of habit. You've been unconscionably spoiled, my dear, and you've taken to it like a duck to water. But I'm afraid I find you eminently resistible. Good-bye." There was a dismissive click at the other end of the line.

Raph stood holding the receiver of the pay telephone outside the bar of the Blue Boar until he was recalled to his surroundings by an impatient customer, whereupon he stalked back to Trinity in a blind fury, unmercifully jostling people as he passed by them. As soon as he reached his rooms he took a thin volume from the bottom of a desk drawer and ruffled rapidly through its pages as if it contained an anodyne to thwarted desire and injured pride, then with a scowl he threw it viciously across the room.

6 Inspector Bunce Visits the UL

"I am delighted to see you again, Inspector," said Fenchurch, "though I should have preferred it to be under circumstances that did not involve Sheepshanks. It will be quite like old times, won't it?"

"Not exactly," Inspector Bunce replied with a grin. "There's no dead bodies littering the landscape this time."

"No, thank heavens. It was a difficult period for the College, but we managed to weather it, thanks to you."

"More thanks to you, as I recall." Compliments having been duly exchanged, the two men got down to brass tacks. They were in Manthorpe's room, which had been given over to them for their conference by its owner, who had already discussed the loss of the *Anelida* with the Inspector over the telephone.

"I see you've been most thorough as to precautions. I couldn't have done a better job myself." Inspector Bunce was a short man with a tendency toward corpulence, which was, however, kept in check by the decidedly mediocre food provided him by his wife. He kept up his strength by supplementing home fare with surreptitious visits to the Copper

Kettle and Fitzbillies—Bunce had a clandestine passion for cream cakes.

"I was able to persuade the University Library Syndicate to call in the police, my dear Bunce, by vouching for your tact and discretion, of which I have ample knowledge. As you know, both the University and the Colleges have jurisdiction over crimes committed on their property, but the value and rarity of the stolen volume are sufficient to make the authorities anxious to obtain outside assistance."

"It isn't like that other book, is it?" Bunce asked suspiciously. He was referring to Shakespeare's *Cupid and Psyche,* which had disappeared from the Abbot's Library at Sheepshanks on the previous occasion of their working together: a youthfully exuberant work whose unabashed salacity had deeply shocked the Inspector's lower-middle-class propriety.

"No, no; nothing like that," Fenchurch assured him. "For one thing, this is a printed book, the Shakespeare was a manuscript; and for another, this is quite a hundred years older."

That was not what Inspector Bunce had meant, but as clarification seemed pointless he merely said, looking at the sheet of paper in his hand, "I understand from Mr. Manthorpe that this is a list of the people who were in the Anderson Room during the approximate time the book was on the returns table, and so available for the taking."

"That's right. At the top of the list of suspects is young Maunders, who actually requested the book."

"Wouldn't that more or less take him out of the running? It makes him such a glaring suspect."

"Ordinarily one might think so, but he is a bright lad and it may well have occurred to him that that is exactly how it would look—a sort of double bluff. Moreover, it would have been difficult for him to get his hands on the *Anelida* without requesting it; he could scarcely have relied on someone else asking for the book while he was in the room. There is one other significant reason which I think justifies our suspicion of him," and he told Bunce of the incident involving the engravings.

"Ah! that puts quite a different complexion on the matter," said the Inspector when he had heard Fenchurch out. "Still, I can't get over the feeling that he wouldn't have pointed the finger at himself like that."

"No; the theft may well have been an impulsive act by someone else who saw the book, recognised its value, and tucked it in his papers, later secreting it about his person in order to smuggle it out of the UL. It is a slender volume and might easily be concealed in such a fashion; that is why we took the other precautions."

"And complete to a shade they are. Now," skimming the list in front of him, "I understand that the digs of all the people with an *E* next to their names (for *left early,* before the exposure of the theft) were searched just after the discovery was made."

"Yes, we thought it advisable, though it is doubtful that the culprit would be so foolish as to hide his booty in so obvious a place."

"The ladies' rooms, too?" His finger paused on a name. "Miss Vivien Murray's, for example?"

To his horror Fenchurch blushed a deep crimson at that name, but luckily the Inspector, preoccupied with his list, did not notice.

"Yes, the ladies' quarters as well. We sent one of the female staff with an impeccable alibi to go through the ladies' things—so as not to embarrass them." Fenchurch was old-fashioned, and he blushed again at the thought of Miss Murray's "things"—an exciting and strangely disturbing image. "Of course," he went on hastily to take his mind off such intoxicating matters, "any of them—not the ladies, I mean, but any of the people who had already left the Anderson Room—could have hidden the book anywhere in Cambridge, in a place where we should not think of looking. That is the unfortunate part of it."

"I understand you've continued to check everyone leaving the University Library to make certain, in case the book has been hidden in the Library, that it will be impossible for the thief to smuggle it out."

"Yes, Inspector. Mr. Manthorpe and I felt that it would be as well to take every conceivable precaution, since it is quite possible that none of those who left the Library early are involved in the disappearance. As you can see, there are literally thousands of places in this building where the book could be hidden, particularly if the thief were to go into the stacks."

"Is that possible?"

"Quite possible, with the exception of the rare-book stacks. In the Reading Room the readers request books, which are fetched for them from locked areas by staff members, but if they should wish to go into the open stacks themselves they have only to take a lift or climb one of the stairs which give access to the various floors. Since the book has not turned up it means that we shall be required to search the whole Library after all—a mammoth task, and one it gives the staff no pleasure to contemplate."

"How long will it take? I'd offer some of my men but we're shorthanded at the moment—half the Force seem to be down with that 'flu that's been making the rounds of Cambridge lately—and I don't suppose they'd do the job nearly as well as your people anyway. You'd have to teach them what they were looking for. On the other hand"—a thought struck him—"suppose one of the Library staff took it."

"Since we have no way of knowing who may have slipped into the Anderson Room unobserved," said Fenchurch, "we are taking no chances. Only those staff members with an unshakeable alibi for the period during which the book was left unattended, according to Maunders's account, will be used for the search, along with volunteers from the College and Departmental libraries. None of the UL staff who were in the Anderson Room at the time will be asked to take part."

"'According to Maunders's account?'" Bunce pounced on this phrase. "How do you know he's telling the truth? If he's the one who pinched the book, then he's bound to be lying about the time he took it, and everything else as well."

"We have checked with the Anderson Room staff and the tea-room; he was seen in both at roughly the times he stated, and the Entrance Hall Porters say he only left the Library once. I am inclined to give credit to their testimony, as he is a distinctive sight and they would not be likely to mistake him for someone else. If Maunders stole the *Anelida,* it was not until after he returned from having his coffee; he would be a fool to stay in the building in case someone noticed it was gone and the alarm be sounded before he could hide it. I think, therefore, that we may safely accept his story."

Bunce acknowledged the wisdom of this reasoning and went on to another question. "How long do you reckon it will take to search the University Library thoroughly?"

"The Library is generally closed a week for the annual inspection in September, but of course we shall have to search more than the shelves. Moreover, as there will be a limited staff even with the volunteers, I cannot forecast how long it will take—you realise it will involve looking behind every book on every shelf. We shall just have to soldier on until we have finished."

"I don't envy you," Bunce said frankly. "And everyone who leaves the Library in the meantime will still be checked for possession of the book?"

"Yes, and that is where we should be very grateful for the services of one of your men for a few days, if you can spare him—and of a policewoman. I know you are shorthanded, but the situation is rapidly becoming desperate. The University Librarian does not plan to close the Library for the search until Saturday, and the Porters sorely need a respite. As you know, they have been making a body search, assisted by a female staff member, of all the readers when they leave; but they are greatly embarrassed by the task, and I understand are on the verge of a mutiny. Indeed, on several occasions the University Librarian himself and Mr. Manthorpe have been called down by them to investigate the persons of some of the older and more distinguished—and most indignant—scholars."

"If that's the staff attitude, it doesn't sound as though they've been doing a sufficiently thorough job to detect the book if someone has tried to carry it out of the Library," said Bunce dubiously.

"I am certaiin," Fenchurch responded, "that the Porters' loyalty to the Library outweighs even their diffidence and deference to ingrained academic dignity, but they are undeniably near the breaking-point."

"In that case," Bunce said, "despite our manpower shortage I think I could spare a man and a woman to do the job till Saturday."

"We should be most grateful."

"Frankly, Mr. Fenchurch, I shall be happy to do what I can, as I don't feel that we're being a great deal of help in this case. Oh, we're checking up on Biggers, though we'll honour your promise not to prosecute him for possession of the prints, and we've put the word out on this book of yours—not that any reputable dealer, from what you say, wouldn't recognise it at once, and report it—but apart from that and lending you a couple of coppers, I'm afraid there isn't much else we can do at present. But just keep us posted, and perhaps something else will turn up; I hope so. In the meantime I should like to go over the place so as to have an idea of what you're up against."

"Mr. Manthorpe and I will be delighted to show you

around. Possibly your sharp eye will detect something which has eluded the rest of us."

But though Fenchurch conducted Bunce through all the highways and byways of the UL, nothing new came to light. On their way to the bindery they were joined by Manthorpe on his way out, for he had been seeing to the rebinding of one of the choicer manuscripts in his care. He returned with them to the long room where several bookbinders, Welby among them, were busy at their work. It was a cluttered and confusing place, lined with shelves and with what seemed like acres of counter-space on which stood small book presses, intricate tools for decorating the bindings, sheets of marbled paper and scraps of leather in varying sizes, knives and blades in all sorts of lengths and shapes, pieces of cardboard and paste-pots and paint jars. In one corner squatted an enormous book-press, vaguely resembling a medieval instrument of torture; in another stood a guillotine with its long and wicked-looking blade for cutting paper; scattered about the floor were trolleys loaded with books of all descriptions and in all stages of decrepitude.

After his introduction to Mr. Sonning, the head binder, Bunce said, looking doubtfully at the chaos surrounding them, "I suppose the bindery will be searched too."

"Indeed it will, Inspector," Mr. Sonning assured him, "although it's most unlikely the book in question could have made its way down here. I myself have examined all the trolleys in case it had got onto one of them by mistake, but nothing doing."

Welby, who was engaged in cutting a piece of black buckram to cover the boards of an octavo volume he was rebinding, looked up as they passed him on their way out.

"This is the man who was in the Anderson Room at the time of the *Anelida*'s disappearance," Manthorpe, a man with greying hair and the beak of an eagle, told Bunce. "He knows what the volume looks like, because he carried out some recent repairs on the binding, but he did not see it that day, nor did he notice anything out of the ordinary."

"I'm afraid I didn't see the book, sir," said Welby to Bunce, setting down his binder's knife. "Sorry I can't be more help."

"Don't worry yourself about it, Welby," Fenchurch told him kindly. "It isn't your fault. What are you working on now?" he enquired, more from politeness than from a genuine wish to know.

"Just a little something of my own." Welby's sallow face flushed an unbecoming mauve, and he flipped the pages too rapidly for Fenchurch to see anything much, except that they were printed in a bold, rather ugly nineteenth-century typeface. "I sometimes bring my own books and rebind them in my lunch hour with the scraps that are left over from the library repairs; Mr. Sonning was kind enough to say that I might work a little late to finish this one, seeing as it was so close to being done."

"Convenient for you," said Fenchurch, thinking, *I wonder what the man reads to make him so coy about it:* The Golden Bough, *perhaps, or Krafft-Ebing? Indigestible stuff for him, I should have thought. Or perhaps he has hold of the other end of the stick and reads girlish novels.* In any event, it hardly seemed likely that Welby's literary tastes were in the slightest degree edifying. "I understand from Mr. Sonning that no sign of the book we're looking for has turned up here."

"No, sir. It's a real shame. I feel sorry that I wasn't more alert, Mr. Manthorpe," he told the Rare-Books Librarian, "seeing I was right on the spot, so to speak." His unprepossessing face displayed such concern that Fenchurch, ashamed of being so uncharitable, hastily revised his mental estimate of Welby's reading tastes.

"It is a severe blow to the Library, but we still have hopes of recovering the book," said Manthorpe. "Good day to you; and many thanks, Mr. Sonning, for your assistance." They made their way out past mournful stacks of ailing quartos and folios, octavos and duodecimos, some spineless or coverless, others with bindings bearing all the clinical symptoms of a virulent tropical rot.

7 *Gloria*

Lord Henry Huntingfield gazed appreciatively at the nymph, who, to his delighted surprise, was standing at the side of his bed. He had opened his eyes after an eventful night (which had included trying—unsuccessfully—to drink several companions under the table and climbing into College by way of Sheepshanks Great Gate—more difficult to scale than its attendant wall and thus considered more sporting as a means of ingress) to find a vision of unearthly beauty bending over him.

"Hail, blithe spirit!" he declaimed, rising enthusiastically up in bed. The sudden movement made his head, which required gradual acclimatization to changes of altitude, throb like the engine of a motorcycle. "This must be a houri, and I in Paradise—or is it *an* houri? I'm never quite certain."

"Ow," said the vision, who was magnificently curved like a Caryatid and crowned with a Rossettian aureole of auburn hair.

"*Ow houri* . . . is that an Arabic article? . . . Who are you, you marvellous creature?" Harry enquired. "What's your name? Not that I need to know, because I intend nevermore to leave your side."

"I'm Gloria, sir," she responded in disconcertingly nasal

accents that were ill-suited to her appearance, "and I'll thank you not to use that word in my presence, let alone calling me one. I shall tell the Master what you said."

"Don't be silly," Harry told her impatiently. "*Houri* is Persian for a beautiful spirit. You mustn't be evil-minded: it doesn't become you. And I already know you're glorious. I could hardly avoid noticing, though I must say it's a shade immodest of you to mention the fact. Let the other chap be the one to chuck the compliments about. You won't have to wait long—as soon as you walk in the door it's bound to happen."

"Gloria's me nyme," the vision explained, very sensibly taking no notice of all the gentlemanly persiflage, to which she was accustomed from having worked as a chambermaid at the Woolsack.

"I am struck with astonishment," said young Harry, suiting the action to the word by falling back on his bed, an injudicious gesture which discomposed his temporarily fragile brain. He seized the top of his head with both hands to prevent it from flying off, and continued. "I should never have expected you to have such an appropriate name. In a world where women named Helen tend to have eyes that cross, and girls christened Grace spend half their time tripping over the furniture, I should have thought your parents would have called you Gladys, or Mildred, or even—blasphemy though it would have been—Ethel. Be my divinity, and let me worship you!" He made a profound salaam on the bedclothes. "I say, you aren't married, are you?" he asked anxiously.

"No, not that it's any of your business. But that don't mean I fool around with young gentlemen who don't do the proper thing when required." Gloria spoke from bitter experience, having indulged in a brief but all-too-fruitful liaison with the son of a baronet. This slip, the occasion of her departure from the Woolsack (the manager of whom, however, had generously omitted mention of it from her reference), had left her understandably wary of too much familiarity with the upper classes.

"If by the proper thing you mean marriage, that is unfortunately out of my power," said Harry, who had risen from his prostrate position without incident. "I was engaged at the tender age of three to the uncomely daughter of a neighbouring squire. But I can offer you my entire affection. Isn't that enough? Say it is, I implore you!" She was temptingly close, and he stretched out an encircling arm.

But Gloria, too quick for him, stepped nimbly back out of his reach. "It's well past ten o'clock. If you'd please to get out of that bed, sir, as it's high time you was doing, I shall do my job and make it," she answered primly.

"So that's why you've suddenly appeared in my room, not just to enchant and tease me," said Harry, enlightened by her speech. "You're the new bedder. I don't believe it!—a beautiful bedder is a contradiction in terms. Do forgive me for obstructing you in the performance of your duties; though I can hardly be blamed for thinking you were a spirit sent to ravish my senses—all five of 'em," he added parenthetically. "Everyone knows that bedders are the oldest and ugliest females in East Anglia—the Colleges scour the countryside to find them. No one under sixty and wartless need apply. How did you slip through?"

"Couldn't say, sir," Gloria replied stolidly. She was beginning to find his compliments tedious, particularly as she could not understand half of them. While she had to admit he was a fine-looking lad—tall, fair, blue-eyed, and well set-up—from what she could see of that part of him which was not hidden under the bedclothes, there was no future in such a flirtation. Even if he were not a gentleman and thus an unpromising candidate for her hand and the guardianship of little Freddie, she was sufficiently experienced in this line of chatting-up to recognise that half of it was just talking for the pleasure of hearing himself run on. That was the trouble with living in a University city, she reflected glumly: Education made people far too fond of nattering. Gloria preferred action to words—a tendency which, as has been noted, had already got her into trouble. "If you'd be so kind as to get out of that bed. . . ." This incident must be rapidly concluded or she would fall behind in her duties and be late for lunch, she thought with annoyance; and Gloria was a healthy girl who relished her food.

"I suppose," Harry said mournfully, "if I can't persuade you to join me in it, I might as well get out of bed." He swung his long legs over the side of the bed and prepared to rise, but his head, which by this time had so nearly cleared as to make him forget its convalescent state, chose at this moment to give a valedictory and truly Gargantuan stab of pain. He uttered a piercing yell and clutched at it once more to keep it from falling off and rolling at Gloria's feet.

Her maternal experiences with young Freddie had taught Gloria to recognise the sound of honest agony, and so she knew at once that Harry was no longer play-acting. Bending over the bed so that her superb bosom was within an inch of his nose, she enquired with motherly concern, "What is it, lad? Where does it hurt?"

It was at this moment that Grubb, on his way back from visiting one of his students on the upper floor of the staircase, passed by the outer door, which Gloria had left ajar. Possessed of a considerable curiosity, Grubb would no doubt have peered within to see if there was anything worth his notice even if he had not heard the shriek: as it was, he felt it a positive duty to investigate. There was no one visible in the sitting-room so he pushed on into the bed-room, where the sight which met his horrified and disapproving eyes explained (so it seemed to him) the high-pitched scream which had so fortunately summoned him in the nick of time. The delectable Gloria, who had until that morning been assigned as bedder to his court of the College and after whom Grubb had ardently and hopelessly lusted ever since his first glimpse of her shapely bottom as she bent over to smooth his sheets, was struggling to escape the obscene embrace of that youthful reprobate and lecher, Lord Henry Huntingfield.

It was a heaven-sent opportunity—to meet approval in the eyes of his goddess by rescuing her from unwelcome advances, and at the same time to chastise a young man whom he already thoroughly (and now for an excellent reason) detested. With justifiable wrath Grubb descended upon the couple, not noticing in his excitement that Harry's hands were clutching, not Gloria's luscious contours, but his own head. "Let her go, you young satyr. Who the hell d'you think you are? May I remind you that the days of *droit de seigneur* are over." It outraged him to see this pampered puppy engaging in what he himself had longed, but not dared, to do.

Gloria, exasperated at this intrusion, which she looked upon as a further deterrent to her dinner, and irritated at the presence of the spotty-faced don who always gazed at her as if she were a joint of mutton just out of the oven, retorted tartly, "Why don't you mind your own business? If you'd bother to look, you'd see the boy hasn't so much as laid a finger on me. Haven't you enough sense to realise he's ill?" She turned to face Grubb with her arms akimbo, a magnificent virago. Let her go, indeed! She'd like to see the man who would dare to lay a hand on her, let alone keep it there, without her express permission and enthusiastic encouragement.

Grubb quailed before the anger in her beautiful eyes, and silently vowed that in the future a debt of humiliation would be repaid at the first opportunity by young Lord High and Mighty Huntingfield, who was listening to this exchange with lips that quirked suspiciously. "I only meant . . ." Grubb stammered.

"You only meant!" she repeated scornfully, her eyes flashing turquoise sparks of fury. "I'll thank you to mind your own business—are you all right now, love?" she enquired solicitously of Harry, whose normal robust colour had begun to return.

"Much better, thanks to your tender care," he answered with a glint of mischief, observing Grubb out of the corner of his eye. "Will you always be my nurse and soothe my fevered brow? I'll more than match what the College pays you to straighten sheets. I'll give you a gown made from the finest wool, which from our pretty lambs we pull. Not to mention a belt of straw and ivy buds with coral clasps and amber studs."

"You must be all right now, since you're talking nonsense again," said Gloria. A nice boy, but he did talk peculiar. "It won't take me half a tick to tidy your bed and then you can get on with dressing. The very idea, a great lad your age laying about in your pyjamas all day long. You ought to be ashamed of yourself."

"I shall stay until you've finished, to see you aren't annoyed by him," Grubb announced. He was sure there must have been some hanky-panky; the boy looked well enough to him.

"You needn't worry about me, thank you. I'm quite able to take care of myself *if* the lad was misbehaving, which he wasn't. He's been a perfect gentleman," said Gloria, with more truth than she knew, the behaviour of gentlemen so often being no better than it should be. She made up the bed with brisk efficiency, for her stomach was beginning to feel small pangs that reminded her of the approaching meal. Though both Harry and Grubb watched her deft movements with frank appreciation as she leaned over the bed, Harry was the more objective admirer. Grubb furtively licked his

lips at the sight of such deliciously abundant flesh: While
Gloria's luxuriant form was covered by the cotton overall
she wore, it was imperfectly concealed by the garment. She
gave a final pat to the pillow, said, "Well, 'bye, dear,"
and directed a radiant smile at Harry, for whom she found
she had developed rather a soft spot. He would have been
both amused and disconcerted to learn that it was maternal
rather than amorous, probably because a woman who has
once seen a man wallow in the self-pitying throes of minor
affliction ever after retains an attitude of faint superiority toward him.

Grubb gallantly held the door open for her as she left, and
Gloria rewarded him with a "Ta" but did not deign to look
at him. As he descended the staircase behind her undulant
posterior he could not refrain from murmuring diffidently, "I
wondered if sometime you might be free to . . . a cup of
coffee . . . or perhaps a drink . . . ?"

The only thing that surprised Gloria about this approach
was that it had not occurred sooner. She was an observant
girl, and it had not escaped her notice that Grubb was apt to
hang about his rooms on some pretext or other while she
performed her domestic chores. Honest admiration did not
displease her, but Grubb had a shifty eye and a sly habit of
brushing against her which Gloria correctly surmised was far
from accidental. Such sneaking tactics did not appeal to her
forthright nature. Moreover, his actions unpleasantly reminded her of an elderly neighbour's attentions during her
triumphant sally into puberty. She had sent the old ram
home with a flea in his ear, and she proposed to do the same
with this one. But a wistful note in his voice made her pause;
and she responded more gently than she had intended.
"Can't, I'm afraid," she answered. "My young man would
have something to say about that. Ta, all the same." But she

cast a smile over her shoulder that almost atoned for the rebuff.

Nevertheless, as Grubb made his way across Great Court, there arose in his breast a fierce determination to wreak condign and pleasurable vengeance on this arrogant young sprig of the nobility who had so disastrously ventured to cross his amatory path.

8 *Sir Richard Rackstraw et Ux.*

"I stand foursquare against the idea of a new College Library," Dr. Shebbeare declared roundly, "particularly one with the name Rackstraw attached to it."

"While in principle I could not agree with you more, Master, there is the long view to consider. Later on Sir Richard might be persuaded to throw the weight of his substantial financial resources behind a more desirable project; that is, provided we handle him properly." Professor Tempeste was not entirely disinterested in the matter, since he felt that there was room for major improvement in the arrangements of the University's Chemical Laboratory.

"Perhaps a renovation of the existing Library . . ." suggested Grierson.

"That's not what he's after," Austrey replied. "Surely you can tell by the tone of his letter that the man is hell-bent on erecting a monument to himself, the bigger the better. Renovations, however convenient for us, simply won't do the trick."

"Austrey's quite right," Peascod chimed in unexpectedly, running a long finely modelled hand through his beautiful silvery hair. One never knew whether Peascod was listening or not, and it was always something of a shock on those rare occasions when one found that he had been. "I've met men like that. Galloping mad, they are, to have their own way and God help anyone else. Saw at the reins as much as you like, you'll never turn his head from the bit of hedge he's got his eye on." Besides having been a rugger Blue in his youth, Peascod had also graced the hunting field and occasionally he salted and peppered his speech with half-forgotten phrases from his days as a Nimrod.

"What's wrong with the man's money?" asked Grubb disagreeably. Usually he was too much in awe of his colleagues to offer much at meetings of the Senior Common Room, but his victory over them the other day had been heady stuff; and having imbibed such an intoxicating draught of power, he was not about to relinquish it. "Is it because he made it in the marketplace that it isn't good enough for you? Do you have to wait a couple of hundred years to purify it? Fumigate it, more likely. You lot probably think any money that hasn't had a hundred years or so to lose its nasty commercial taint is full of bugs. I propose we accept Sir Richard's generous offer."

The other dons ignored this speech, as those with good manners will talk around someone who has been unpardonably rude.

"Algy has a point," said Fenchurch. "Though Sir Richard Rackstraw's preferences may not run to chemistry"—here Professor Tempeste looked moderately indignant— "it would not be a bad idea to keep him sweet, for the sake of the University as well as of Sheepshanks. One never knows when a few million pounds may come in handy; indeed, it can always be put to excellent use." Fenchurch was thinking of repairs to his beloved Chapel. "Moreover, it would be discourteous to treat such a munificent offer as if it were a penny in the gutter which we couldn't be bothered to pick up."

"You are not suggesting that we accept the Library, are

you, John?" asked the Master, looking much as Dr. Johnson (whom he closely resembled) must have looked on finding a misprint in his Dictionary. "Two Libraries," he pronounced, glaring about him testily, "are enough for any College."

"Good heavens, no, Master. I stand absolutely firm with you on that subject, as I presume we all do." Fenchurch deliberately ignored Grubb's outburst.

A murmur of assent, like wind sweeping through the boughs of an orchard, arose from the group of Fellows; Grubb, who did not have the temerity to gainsay such wholesale unanimity, had the sense to keep silent.

"There is no question that the Abbot's Library and the Pryevian Library more than adequately serve the purposes of the College. I only meant that as Rackstraw has tendered a large sum—such a very large sum—and has hinted that his book collection may someday follow it, it would be judicious of us to convey our reluctance to accept his offer of a Library gently and tactfully, so that we may still have a shot at his collection; and later we might be enabled to seek his assistance for some other, more desirable, project."

"There's no harm in trying," Austrey said, "though I'm not at all certain it will do any good. Still, it's worth an effort."

Dr. Shebbeare heaved an immense sigh, his chins trembling like a well-made blancmange. "I am inclined to agree with Austrey that nothing will satisfy this man but the Library upon which he has, for some unknown reason, set his heart. However," he went on sternly, "just because he collects the odd manuscript or incunable does not mean he has the right to go strewing College libraries all around the shop. One might wish he had been a Kingsman or a Johnian— anything but a Sheepshankian. These City men," he complained, "are like juggernauts. They are far too accustomed to having their own way, and subtlety is wasted on them. I

shall draft a firm letter filigreed with pretty phrases of gratitude and send it off to him indicating our decision."

"I'm afraid that won't go far toward keeping him sweet,"
said Austrey. "His feelings will be hurt."

"Damn it all," Dr. Shebbeare said irascibly, "am I to cos-
set the fellow? Shall I tuck it into a nosegay, or ship it off in
a box of Fitzbillies chocolates?" It was unlike him to swear,
or even to display a degree of anger, but the presumption of
this unknown tycoon in attempting to inflict an unwanted
and unnecessary Library on his College infuriated him.

"Perhaps," timidly suggested little Crippen, who had been
so quiet that the rest of the Fellows had nearly forgotten his
presence, "we could show our gratitude by inviting him to
Pullets Feast."

Pullets Feast, a dinner held by the Master and Fellows of
the College, is a red-letter day on the Sheepshanks calendar,
traditionally so Lucullan in scope that it eclipses in culinary
splendour even the most lavish repasts of other Cambridge
Colleges. An invitation to Pullets Feast is an honour avidly
sought by those who do not regularly dine at Sheepshanks
High Table, the origin of this historically disreputable feast-
day being conveniently ignored both by hosts and guests.

"Pullets Feast? Nonsense. Can't have the fellow to the
Feast. None of us has so much as clapped eyes on him. We
might ask him to lunch someday," said Tempeste.

But Austrey overrode him. "That's just the ticket," he said
to Crippen. "He was up at Sheepshanks; he must have an
inkling of what an honour it is to be invited to the Feast. If
anything will keep him on tap, that will." It had occurred to
Austrey that the Prye Library had certain deficiencies—gaps
on the shelves caused by Prye selling a few volumes when he
was hard-up—that were not likely to be remedied under the
current College budget and which, if this man proved at all
pliable, might intrigue him sufficiently to unloose the strings

of his formidable purse. He was, after all, interested in libraries. . . .

"Rackstraw, Rackstraw . . . Come to think of it, I remember him," said Peascod suddenly. "He came up during my first year as a Fellow. Got seasick once during rowing practice, and we never heard the end of it. A tiresome lad."

The Master glanced at Fenchurch, whose advice he greatly valued. "Well?" he asked.

"Peascod's anecdote notwithstanding, that is the solution," Fenchurch said. "It would be a pity to let this money slip through our fingers without attempting to interest Rackstraw in other projects; the College coffers are deep but not inexhaustible. And I agree with Austrey that in order to avoid offending him it will be necessary for us to make rather a major effort in his direction. Inviting him to attend Pullets Feast will assure him of our gratitude and considerable regard, even as we are forced to decline his ill-advised gift."

Dr. Shebbeare allowed himself to be persuaded and at length they were able to bring Tempeste, who by this time had thought of several additional projects for Sir Richard to sponsor, to agree to the invitation.

"If we must invite the creature," Peascod said querulously, "I do not wish to sit beside him."

"What luck Pullets is less than two weeks away," Fenchurch observed, ignoring this remark, "otherwise we should not have a treat with which to console him."

"Somehow," said Austrey in a low voice to Fenchurch as the Fellows took their departure, "I doubt whether we shall succeed in prying Rackstraw loose from his cash except on his own terms. But it is certainly worth the attempt. Besides, I confess to a great deal of vulgar curiosity: I have always wanted to meet a Captain of Industry, just as I have always wished to encounter—from a distance, that is—a white rhinoceros."

"I suspect, dear boy, the same holds true of Captains of

Industry as of white rhinos: that to see one of the species is more than sufficient," remarked Fenchurch as they strolled together out of the Combination Room.

"Those ivory-tower sons of bitches have turned down my Library!" fumed Sir Richard Rackstraw of Rackstraw Consolidated Industries, Ltd. He again read the letter in his hand, unbelievingly.

"Really, darling," said his wife, who was lunching with him and had stopped in his office early in order to freshen up before the Rolls took them to Le Gavroche, "what do you care if a bunch of old fossils are stupid enough to turn down a few million of the best? You can just give the money to someone else." She continued to outline her lips with deft precision, using a gold Asprey compact which she had taken out of her Hermès handbag to monitor the results.

"You simply don't understand, Julia." Sir Richard stood up and moved restlessly over the thick grey carpet to a large window overlooking half of London—the half that mattered—and gazed unseeingly at the superb view spread before him like a fillet on a plate. He was a burly man, like a prizefighter, not tall but powerful in build, and his large head with its still-dark hair and piercing eyes was a match for the rest of him. His less than patrician form was encased in a Savile Row suit and a shirt and tie of exquisite design; the overall effect was one of brute authority somewhat inadequately clad in a velvet glove. "I want my bloody name on that library. There isn't much that's class left in this world, and Sheepshanks is class. I want to see Epstein's face, and Vining's, when they hear I've had a library at Cambridge named after me. Not many people can have something at Oxford or Cambridge with their name on it."

"Too true, darling; apparently you're one of the ones that can't," Julia pointed out unkindly, putting away her lipstick and compact. Her husband's massive brow furrowed and his lower lip protruded, making him look like a small boy whose favourite toy has just been snatched from his grasp. She rose and put her arms about his waist to take the sting out of her words and added, "Cheer up, my love, you have me. Aren't I infinitely better than a mouldy old library?"

Indeed she did present a very fetching picture. Julia was in her late thirties, some twenty years younger than her husband, and a shade taller. Her heart-shaped cat-face, with translucent white skin and large green eyes fringed with dark lashes, had an unexpectedly voluptuous mouth newly emphasized with a vibrant magenta lipstick, a colour many women find difficult to wear but one which suited her perfectly. Although the prevailing style was for short curls fluffed forward, her sleek black hair was drawn back in a coil at the nape of her neck. It had been said of Julia Harlowe (she retained her professional name) that she did not follow fashion, fashion followed her. She was dressed in a deceptively simple black suit that outlined her sleek figure, her only ornament a necklace with an enormous pigeon's-blood ruby in its centre. Another, lesser, woman would have seemed overdressed, but she carried it off effortlessly.

Taking her in his arms, Rackstraw bestowed a thoroughgoing kiss upon her, necessitating a further adjustment of her lipstick. "No doubt about that," he agreed, "but there's no bloody reason why I can't have both." He moved to his vast mahogany desk and picked up the offending letter again to study it. "I'm not so sure old Shebbeare really means it; I think he may be playing hard-to-get."

"Why would he do that?" Julia sat in a deep armchair covered in pale suède and swung her elegant legs back and forth, idly admiring them.

"These elderly academics—they may pretend to be unworldly but they don't miss a trick. Either he wants even more money than I've offered him, or maybe he just wants to get the upper hand. I don't know, but I'm sure as hell going to find out."

"How will you do that?" The subject was beginning to bore Julia. She was a popular BBC personality with little affinity for books and libraries.

"I'm going to find out when I attend Pullets Feast, that's how. I ought to be able to worm something out of the old boy under the influence of all that hock and claret and vintage port and madeira the place will be floating in. It shows they want something from me, or they wouldn't have sent me an invitation. As I recall from my undergraduate days, that's one of the most coveted invitations in Cambridge—or the rest of England, for that matter. High Table is full of the Establishment, and sometimes the guest list even runs to Royalty."

"Oh?" Julia's ears pricked up. "And just what is Pullets Feast? Masses of chicken at every course? How desperately dull."

"Not a bit of it. Pullets is one of those anachronisms the Oxbridge set can't get enough of. All Colleges have Feasts, but this is one of the really slap-up kind; high-toned beyond belief. Pretty funny how it began," he said reminiscently. "As I recall the story was that a bunch of the junior Fellows during the Regency invited some local whores to dinner— that's how it got its name, not from eating a lot of hens. Of course they don't talk about that much nowadays."

Colourful history was right up Julia's street; besides the interviews she undertook so successfully on television, she produced a show called "A Peep at the Past," which specialised in racy retrospect. "It sounds fascinating," she said enthusiastically. "I might just fit it into this season. I could throw out that show on Charles the Second's mistresses— Nell Gwynn's been done to death. It's bound to be soup and fish, isn't it? I wonder what I should wear. Should I be madly demure, or shall I knock the old boys cold?"

There was an appreciable silence before Rackstraw answered. "Well, actually," he said uneasily, "you aren't invited."

Julia's opulent mouth set in a compressed line. "What do you mean, I'm not invited? I'm your wife, aren't I? Of course I'm invited."

"It's a men-only thing," he explained. "College tradition. Women are never invited."

"That's ridiculous. If women are never invited, what about those trollops who started the whole business? Anyway," she decided, "there's always a first time. It's high time those old buggers were dragged kicking and screaming into the twentieth century. Now come on, darling," she cajoled him, her voice purring in the way made famous in her interviews, "you can fix it up for me, and it would be a smashing coup. 'Peep' has been getting a trifle stale lately. Just tell the Sheepshanks bunch you won't give them a penny unless I come along."

"I was mistaken, Julia," Rackstraw said with relief, having read further down Dr. Shebbeare's letter. "I was so angry when I first read this that I skipped a line. You are invited—there's to be another dinner party at the same time, and you're asked to that. So it's all right after all."

"Another party?" she said suspiciously. "What do you mean, another party?"

"It says here that the Master's wife has asked you to dinner at the Master's Lodge along with the wives of the other guests at Pullets. You'll be asked to join us after port and cigars. I seem to recollect hearing," he added in a misguided effort to reconcile her to this substitute entertainment, "that there's a peephole from the Master's Lodge into Hall, so you should be able to see something of what goes on."

Divulging this piece of information was a gross error;

Julia's green eyes narrowed and her nostrils quivered until she looked like a panther about to pounce. "So the little women get to watch through the lattices of the seraglio, do they, and then they're graciously allowed in once all the fun is over," she said. "I call that bloody insulting. Too sickeningly Victorian for words. Of course you won't go without me, will you, darling?" Her purr deepened.

"Julia, my angel," said Rackstraw desperately, for he had his heart set on attending the Feast, "you'll only be next door."

"I might just as well be a million miles away for all the good it will do me. I don't want to dine with a lot of ghastly old frumps, I want to be in the thick of things. How can I do a programme on the Feast if I'm only allowed to peer through a keyhole? A great idiot I should look."

"It's a peephole, not a keyhole; and after all, your programme *is* called 'A Peep at the Past,'" Rackstraw reminded her. "And really, my darling, I have a strong feeling that the Fellows would not take kindly to having a television programme made on Pullets."

His feeble joke, attempted to lighten the tension, was not a success. Julia eyed him coldly. "Very funny, I don't think. Anyway, your precious Fellows needn't know about the programme until it's too late for them to do anything about it, if only I can attend. We can use stills of the Combination Room—there must be photographs of it somewhere about—and we'll take pictures of the Hall and the rest of College before they know what we're up to. Besides, my darling, it isn't just because of the programme that I want to go. We've only been married six months," she said, her lovely mouth drooping, "and I shall be miserable if you go off and leave me behind. It would be too degrading to have to sit around with a bunch of old hags knowing you were next door without me, having all the fun." In fact it was difficult to imagine her spending a gynaecian evening with any degree of patience; she was distinctly a man's woman.

"Julia, darling, it won't exactly be fun," Rackstraw protested.

"Then why are you so keen on going?" asked Julia shrewdly. "Anyway, even if it isn't fun, there's a *cachet* to it, and I mean to go. You said even Royalty scheme to get invitations." Her eyes glowed with enthusiasm. "Darling, do you know what it would do for my career if I were the first woman to be invited? Just think what a shot in the arm it would be. I'm sure you could talk them into it, especially if you offer them enough money, and goodness knows you have masses of the stuff," she said cajolingly.

"Julia, my love, you know you needn't worry about that job of yours. I can give you anything your tiny heart desires." His eyes strayed to the pigeon's-blood ruby at the base of her white throat.

"It isn't just the money," she said impatiently. "I know you'll buy me whatever I might fancy. It's all those eyes out there—envying, admiring. Heads turn and people stare when I walk down a London street; some of them come up to me just to make certain I'm real, to touch me. I see myself as I'm mirrored in their eyes, and it's unbelievably exciting." Her eyes widened and she seemed to be looking at something very far away.

"Aren't I enough?" he asked, in an unwontedly humble tone.

"Darling Dickie." She focussed her gaze on him and smiled brilliantly. "Of course you are! But it's like those musty old books you collect—having one Caxton is good, but owning twenty of them is a hell of a lot better." Realising that this explanation was scarcely likely to reassure him, she went on. "I mean, you're my vocation, darling, my viewers are just a hobby. . . . Dick, my poppet"—Julia's voice became like molten silk—"do make those beastly old men invite me to Pullets Feast. You know how to put on the screws. Give them another whole bloody College if that's what it takes. If they really don't want a library, find out what it is they do want. Say you will for Julie, my little lamb chop."

It would have astonished those who toiled in the multifarious enterprises which made up Rackstraw Consolidated Industries, Ltd if they could have witnessed the fatuous smile which spread over the stern features of its Managing Director at the sound of this nauseating endearment. "Will my kitten cat love her lamb chop then?" he asked.

"Even more than she does now—as if that were possible," crooned Julia. "But she can't wait to see how much cleverer and handsomer her lambie-pie is than all those horrid old academics. He will do it for her, won't he?"

Rackstraw nodded foolishly. "A kiss to seal it?" he ventured. "Or . . . why don't we give lunch the go-by and spend the time up here?" He glanced with meaning at the sofa.

My God, what idiots men are sometimes, Julia thought as she went over to him, arms open. "Later, darling," she said, pushing him away as soon as their pact had been duly solemnised. "I'm absolutely ravenous, and I must be back at the studio by three."

9 Welby at Home

It was raining, a light greasy rain that streaked the dust instead of washing it off and left the streets looking grimier
than they had before it began. Welby slid off his bicycle in
front of the house where he rented his bed-sitter. It was a
dreary house on Hills Road, not far from the railway station
and characterised by harsh red brick, peeling woodwork and
dusty lace curtains that hung despondently in the tall narrow
windows. He hauled his bicycle up the high flight of steps,
unlocked the outer door and wheeled the cycle into an
areaway whose floor was covered with worn linoleum. Passing
into the dingy hall, he encountered his landlady, a faded
skinny woman whose air of neglect and vague dishevelment
reflected the state of the house in which she lived.

"Good evening, Mrs. Rogers," he said.

"Good evening, Mr. Welby. A parcel come for you in the
post today. I left it with the letters on the hall table." Her
pale eyes displayed a flicker that in someone with a trace
more animation might have passed for inquisitiveness.

"A parcel?" he repeated, his heart thumping with excitement. It had arrived sooner than he had expected, but he
knew what it must be: the only packages he ever received
were the ones he had ordered himself.

"More books, I should think, from the look of it. You're

quite the reader, aren't you, Mr. Welby?" She looked up at him with a sort of halfhearted flirtatiousness.

"Hardly surprising, since I work in a Library," he returned shortly. Her prying displeased him. He thought it unlikely that she would ever take the trouble to look in his bookshelves; still. . . . He sought to dampen her nascent curiosity. "Just a few things I ordered on Byzantine History. Deep and heavy going, they are." He must remember what they were supposed to be when he rebound them, so as to mark the spines properly in case she decided to snoop.

"Fancy that," said Mrs. Rogers blankly. She herself was a great reader: she devoured every scrap that came out in the magazines about Princess Di and those precious babies. She had read clean through *The Royal Wedding* and *Princess Diana's Maternity and Nursery Fashion Book,* but history of the more solid variety—in fact any book that contained more text than pictures—defeated her. "Well, ta ta then. You have a nice read. Tea at six-thirty, don't forget. We're having quite a treat tonight—Scotch eggs."

"Thank you, Mrs. Rogers, but I shan't be taking tea today." Surreptitiously Welby licked his already moist lips as he looked at his package.

"Well, reelly. You might have told me sooner," she said in pallid indignation. "I've already set the table and made eggs enough for everyone. I'm afraid I shall have to charge you in any case. It's the rules, you know."

"That's quite all right," he said. "I'm not feeling well, you see."

Mrs. Rogers peered at his face, which wore a look of fervid anticipation.

"You do look a bit flushed," she said, mollified. "I'm sure I hope you'll feel better in the morning."

"I'm sure I shall—thank you, Mrs. Rogers." Welby picked up his parcel—his only mail; there were never any letters for him—and started up the narrow staircase with its faded linoleum treads. The dark uncarpeted hall was painted a dull brown, a colour selected by Mrs. Rogers on the economical basis that it did not show the dirt, and the woodwork of doors and door-frames was painted a deeper chocolate on the same principle. He opened his door, the second on the left, and entered. He would have preferred to keep his room locked when he was not there, but Mrs. Rogers did not permit this indulgence on the grounds that it interfered with her housekeeping. In his dreams Welby lived alone in a self-contained one-room flat—his dreams were as parsimonious as his soul—where he could display his books without the trouble of rebinding them, and where he might, if he could find the right kind and they were not too dear, hang a print or two upon the walls. . . . He sighed: It was a sort of accommodation rarely to be found in Cambridge, and would in any event be far beyond his means.

Welby's room was a meagre cell barely large enough for a single bed that made a halfhearted attempt to look like a sofa, a chest of drawers, a cushioned chair and two small deal bookcases—the cushion and the bookcases being luxuries supplied by himself. A window barely wide enough to permit the hanging of a curtain—made of the cheapest lace Nottingham has to offer—grudgingly displayed an unedifying view of a stretch of Hills Road, and the walls of the room were painted the unappetising shade of green referred to by small children as "caterpillar blood." The only cheerful note was provided by a red Indian bedspread, picked up by Welby in the Market from a stall run by emigrant Pakistanis, which inadequately disguised the sagging iron bed.

Welby shut the door and shot the bolt he had installed over the protests of Mrs. Rogers, then removed his jacket and hung it carefully on the back of the door. Next he undid his tie, took it off, and put it away in a drawer. His movements were exaggeratedly slow; this languid disrobing was part of a ritual he performed in order to prolong anticipation to its exquisite limit on the days the parcels came. Opening them was darkly thrilling, it was the climax of the choosing and the waiting—all the searching through catalogues for the right books at the right price, the ordering, the time-lag until they finally arrived. But the suspense while he was opening the package was the most exciting part of it all. It was like the slow arousal, the lingering caresses when love-making begins, with the best still to look forward to. When he unwrapped the books they were uncharted territory, like the body of a stranger. . . . He read them more than once: He read them over and over again until there were phrases, passages, whole chapters he could repeat from memory—sometimes he repeated them to himself before he went to sleep—but that was never quite as good as reading them the first time.

His hand stretched longingly out toward the brown-paper-wrapped parcel, fastened with tape and girded about with lengths of knotted string. No, he chided himself, not yet. He had not finished his preparations. With the slow sensuous movements of a courtesan he divested himself of the rest of his clothing, putting away each article piece by piece until he stood naked on the drab braided rug by his bed. Only then did he take a pair of scissors from a drawer and, his flabby but usually deft hands trembling and his muddy skin glistening with nervous perspiration, cut the cords. Reverently he removed the outer wrappings to disclose three volumes in Victorian trade bindings, and picked up the topmost book without glancing at the others. He would not so much as open them to their title pages until he had savoured the contents of the first book to the fullest. It was a lovely binding, he thought, stroking it as he sank onto the bed, shivering with a kind of ecstasy. Such a pity he would have to change it. The cover was scarlet cloth stamped with an intricate gilt cartouche made up of knotted whips and bastinados—hunting and driving whips, knouts, bull whips, cats-o'-nine-tails—intertwined with small naked figures to form a wreath. His fingers shaking, he turned to the title page, which was copiously adorned with more of this questionable ornamentation and inscribed in large flowing engraved letters *The Whipsters; or Flagellatory Frolics* by A. Ticklebum.

10 Seductio ad Absurdum

Mr. Poxwell was feeling exceedingly pleased with himself. He hummed a gay little tune as he bustled about his rooms in Queens', tidying them for his expected visitor; what had begun as "'Tis woman that seduces all mankind" from the *Beggar's Opera* slid into "Oh Polly you might have toyed and kissed" as he tenderly plumped the cushions of his Chesterfield sofa and straightened the papers on his desk. These minor housekeeping tasks accomplished, he stood back and admired the effect. It was a snug room panelled in time-worn oak, with a cosy fire glowing on the hearth that overheated the room (as he had carefully estimated) until it was just the right temperature for one in a state of undress. That should do the trick, he thought complacently; it was a well-tested and invariably successful formula. The hothouse atmosphere was cunningly contrived to ensure that any alcohol which might be consumed would rapidly ascend to the brain; and that, Poxwell had found from extensive experience, tended to loosen any few remaining inhibitions that might linger in the female students, whose behaviour, he mentally and piously thanked God, had undergone a radical alteration since his comparatively far-off undergraduate days. His wife, for example . . . but Poxwell did not care to think about his wife on these occasions. It was not that it made him feel exactly guilty to do so, but he made it a point never to mix business with pleasure—except, of course, in the use of his College rooms for explorations that were altogether unrelated to conventional scholarship.

Poxwell was an imposing, well-set-up man after a rather fleshy fashion, and his appearance coincided with his inclinations. He was fond of good food, good drink, and other assorted corporeal pleasures. His wife, a faded, vague, ascetic creature, did not fit in with these preferences, but she did not seem to mind. Her interest rested chiefly in a daughter who unfortunately took after her mother instead of her father in looks and disposition.

At the moment Poxwell was feeling even more disgruntled than usual with his choice of a wife. Her father (a retired Professor of English Literature) had recently died, and the contents of his will had just been revealed. To the unconcealed chagrin of his only son-in-law, there was considerably less substance to the Professor's estate than had been anticipated, as the old man had made it a misleading habit to live high on the hog (somewhat in the manner of Poxwell himself). Like Poxwell, he had harboured expectations which were not realised, and so had made the mistake of drawing on principal rather than income. Since his reception of this disconcerting piece of information, Poxwell had been feeling decidedly put upon by his wife and her family; though in this he was somewhat unfair, since it was almost solely due to his marital connection with Professor Brocklehurst that he had achieved his present academic eminence at Cambridge. Nonetheless, Poxwell's current resentment against his wife's father lent an increased piquancy to his proposed extracurricular diversion. Not, he reflected pleasurably, adjusting the sofa-cushions at an inviting angle, that he needed any additional spice to enjoy a dish so exquisitely composed.

There was a knock on the door and a College gyp entered, bearing a properly constituted tea-tray with a number of cups on it to maintain the fiction his master had employed to lure the dove into the net. The gyp departed and Poxwell checked his watch. Five minutes to go. . . . He wondered if she would be on time, or even possibly a minute or two early. It was always a propitious sign when they were early. He took a small pocket mirror from a desk drawer in order to smooth his still-abundant hair and straighten his Turnbull & Asser tie, suppressing meanwhile the disagreeable thought that unless his financial position underwent a rapid improvement, he was going to have to purchase his ties in future at Marks & Spencer.

When his appearance was to his satisfaction, Poxwell glanced irritably at his watch again. It seemed that she was not going to be one of the early ones; in fact, she was already several minutes late. The next moment, however, a tap on the door restored his rarely flagging high opinion of himself, and he opened the door with alacrity, taking care to sport his oak behind her.

"Do come in, my dear Miss Murray," he invited, radiating carefully calculated charm. "I hope," he added, in what he intended as a courtly manner but which to her seemed merely pedantic, "that I may be permitted to call you Vivien."

"If you like," Vivien assented politely. She surveyed the room in some surprise as he gallantly helped her take off her coat. "I'm afraid I must be early."

"Not at all, not at all," he assured her, refraining with an effort from adding that she had been just the opposite.

"But I understood that there was to be a seminar as well as tea."

"Indeed there was," he said glibly, "but at the last moment several of the others were forced to cry off. I was unable to reach you by 'phone, so I thought we might as well go ahead and lay the groundwork for another session."

"Oh." He could tell that she was not entirely convinced. Perhaps his last choice of verb had been unfortunate; there was a wary look about her, like a doe hearing a twig snap in the undergrowth. Poxwell attempted to distract his guest by changing the subject.

"I noticed that you were working in the Anderson Room the day the Caxton disappeared. I must say"—he gave a rich laugh—"it was most embarrassing for us elderly chaps to have to submit to that sort of search. Not so bad for you young ones, I expect—you're a bit more used to informality." He flattered himself that she would find *elderly* as applied to her host a vast exaggeration. And he hoped that the mention of the strip search would set up an inadvertent but irresistible train of thought in her mind. "Will you take tea? Actually, I thought perhaps sherry would be more suitable, as it's nearing dinner-time." She was thoroughly delightful, he thought greedily. Her porcelain skin had a wash of pale rose that would, he knew, become intensified by the warmth of passion, and the gentle curve of her small but perfect breasts was encased in some creamy knitted material—cashmere or lambswool—that cried out to be stroked.

Poxwell's gloating look was intercepted and correctly interpreted by Vivien (who in her brief life had already had considerable experience with this sort of situation), and she said brightly, "Thanks so much, but I'm awfully afraid I haven't time. I only stopped in to say how sorry I am that I'd forgot a supervision due in a few minutes. Just as well, really. You can easily set up the seminar later so as not to go through it all twice; though it was very kind of you to offer to put me through the paces on my own." *And you needn't think I don't know exactly what sort of paces you had in mind,* she thought with asperity as she began to put on her coat.

Automatically Poxwell assisted her, a chivalrous impulse that proved his undoing. Vivien's intoxicating proximity— the hyacinth scent of her hair and the tender bloom of her neck—was too much for him, and he bent his head to kiss her nape. "Please—please stay," he muttered hoarsely into her bright hair.

Oh, God, thought Vivien, who recognised in him an abnormally active vanity, *I shouldn't have stayed this long. Now it will be too awful the next time we meet: I shall feel hideously shy and he will hate me. Thank heavens the seminar isn't important.* She felt a disconcerting impulse to giggle, but managed to stifle it. The best course, she hastily decided, was to pretend that she had heard and felt nothing. "Good-bye," she said, turning toward him and holding out her hand, which he distractedly took. "I'm so sorry, but I must fly or I shall be horribly late. I hope you'll be able to rearrange the meeting soon; do let me know." She walked toward the door with a slow and measured step, but as soon as it had closed behind her, he could hear her running feet on the stone staircase.

Thwarted anticipation and unsatisfied lust had heated Poxwell's blood so much that he was constrained to fling open the leaded casement windows, letting in a chill east wind off the fens to cool him down; then he poured himself a large tumbler of whisky from a bottle concealed behind Volume W of the *Oxford English Dictionary* in his bookcase. But even the cold air and the first gulps of his drink failed to calm him sufficiently, and he paced the room with quick angry steps until his eye lit upon his desk. Frantically he pulled out the middle drawer, emptying its contents onto the blotter and raising a false wooden bottom. Within the space thus revealed a slender volume nestled, which he removed from its hiding place, holding it for a moment in shaking hands before he opened it.

"At least," he muttered to himself, "—at least I have this," as he avidly consumed the page before him.

11 A Chat with Chaucer

The Librarian of St. Jude's sat immersed in the sea of paper that billowed across the reaches of his desk—his notes for the catalogue of Sir Edmund Loosebarrow's Library, which Chase-Pippin hoped to have prepared for publication by the Cambridge University Press the following autumn. The Loosebarrow collection, which had become the property of St. Jude's upon that baronet's demise some two hundred years earlier, was copious but somewhat lacking in variety, consisting as it did primarily of volumes of long-winded sermons and ponderous works on divinity; but as Sir Edmund had been an eminent President of St. Jude's, the thing had to be done. The Librarian, a conscientious man, was absorbed in his work and so did not notice the departure of the Library's only other occupant, an attenuated figure of great age with a fringe of long white hair fretted about a shining scalp, who upon the conclusion of his labours had swept his papers into a large shabby briefcase and tottered unsteadily out.

It was an hour or so later that Chase-Pippin decided to call it a day, shuffled the papers on his desk into some faint semblance of order, and looked about him. Dusk was beginning to fall, making the wavering yellow lights in the room seem paler than usual and the shadows they cast paradoxically darker. As he glanced at his watch he recollected the presence of his fellow-scholar.

"Professor Enderby," Chase-Pippin exclaimed, "I am so sorry, but I am afraid I must close the Library now. I do hope it won't unduly inconvenience you—Professor Enderby?"

The crouching shadow in the corner where the Professor had been seated had briefly simulated his presence, but now Mr. Chase-Pippin saw that the table, with its row of chained books down the centre, was empty of human occupants. Relieved at being spared the necessity of sending Professor Enderby packing since his temper was uncertain when disturbed, the Librarian went over to the table to retrieve the volume on which the Professor had been working: a copy of the 1478 Caxton edition of Chaucer's *Canterbury Tales,* in remarkably good condition, which was one of the treasures of St. Jude's Library. Unconcerned at finding it was not there, Chase-Pippin returned to his desk and searched among the piles of books and notes, assuming that Enderby had dropped it off there when he left. But the book in question was neither on the desk nor in its proper place on the shelf. Enderby was becoming notoriously absent-minded, Chase-Pippin mused. Could he perhaps have shelved it erratically, shoving it in anywhere among similar volumes as he passed by on his way out, without bothering about its proper location? However, a cursory search conducted according to this theory along the most likely path from Enderby's seat to the door yielded no results.

Mr. Chase-Pippin became alarmed. Could someone have entered after Enderby's departure and taken the Caxton Chaucer without his noticing? He recalled the recent theft of the *Anelida* from the University Library and so feared the worst. Returning to his desk without more ado, he collected his keys from the bottom drawer, switched off the lights, locked the Library door, and went in search of Enderby.

"And so, my dear Fenchurch, I simply do not know what to do," Chase-Pippin concluded anxiously. He was a short youngish man with a round rosy face that, normally cheerful, was now set in unaccustomed lines of worry. "Can you help me in any way? I have not yet conducted a really thorough search of the Library, but I've looked in all the usual places, and I feel certain it is not there."

"Have you spoken to Professor Enderby about its disappearance?"

"Yes, and he says he knows nothing about it. He refuses to tell me what he did with the book when he left. You know what he is like. But I'm certain he did not leave it anywhere near his seat: I can swear to that. The President suggested that I come directly to you as the authority in such matters. If it should prove necessary to contact the police, he thought you would know how to avoid possible scandal."

For a moment Fenchurch mused on how best to go about such a delicate task. He was rapidly becoming the resident expert on disappearing volumes at Cambridge, but this pleased rather than annoyed him, as it gave him an opportunity to put into practice the detective theories he employed in his mystery novels. "I fear," he said at length, "that Professor Enderby has become a trifle unreliable of late. He has always been somewhat vague, of course, but recently this quality has developed into full-blown eccentricity. After the strip search for the *Anelida* at the UL, he forgot his trousers and would have gone home inadequately attired if the University Librarian had not encountered him on the Library steps. And the other day Vesey came across him in the Wren as he was arguing about the metre of *Piers Plowman* with the statue of Byron at the far end of the library. . . . You are certain he did not absentmindedly pocket the book and take it home with him?"

"I'm not at all certain," Chase-Pippin said frankly. "But if he has, I don't very well see what there is I can do about it. Enderby, after all, is not only Professor of Medieval and Modern Poetry, but a Fellow of St. Jude's. To accuse him of theft would be quite barbarous. Naturally, if I were sure . . . but I cannot believe he would do such a thing, even now that he is. . . ." A moment passed during which the Librarian seemed at a loss for words.

". . . In his dotage?" suggested Fenchurch. "I can, however. I had an uncle who was up at Jude's with Professor Enderby many years ago. He once told me that he had always suspected Enderby of pilfering his copy of Hammond. My uncle never forgave him; even then it was a difficult volume to replace. Old habits die hard, and book thieves are among the most depraved of criminals. They rationalise their actions, don't you know; they tell themselves that taking books isn't really stealing, that the volume they crave isn't properly appreciated by its owner and would be far better off with them. The lengths to which they will go to justify their crimes to themselves are quite shocking." Fenchurch spoke with authority; like most scholars, he had a natural tendency in that direction, which, however, he had wrestled with and conquered.

"But that would be appalling," said Chase-Pippin, in great distress. "If Enderby has taken the book, then there is no way to recover it without creating a scandal of the first magnitude." Overcome by the apparently insoluble nature of his problem, he buried his face in his hands.

"I shouldn't despair quite yet, if I were you," Fenchurch soothed him. "I have a trick or two up my sleeve that may work. Leave it to me for the moment; just leave it all to me." They parted company, the younger man bewildered but slightly comforted, and the Sheepshankian began the pilgrimage to Professor Enderby's abode.

His destination was out near Girton and so, although he disapproved in principle of any means of locomotion other than shank's pony, he borrowed an antiquated bicycle from Mr. Hobbs, the Sheepshanks Head Porter, in order to cover the distance as quickly as possible. Professor Enderby's house was substantial and Victorian, built of brick with stone ornament, its large, overgrown garden enclosed by a wrought-iron paling. It had originally belonged to Enderby's parents—in fact, the only changes made since their departure were the installation of an erratic central-heating system along with equally undependable electric wiring, and the name *Canterbury* that had been chiselled in almost illegible Gothic letters on the lintel above the massive mahogany front door—and Enderby himself had been born within its commodious precincts. It was a house that necessitated a large retinue, but nowadays even the salary of a Professor augmented by a healthy dollop of family money did not run to the luxury of servants, at least not in the numbers required by such an edifice. So it was that when Fenchurch alighted from his rickety old bike, parked it within the fence palings, and rang the bell (a process that involved pulling a large richly chased brass knob beside the front door), he was, after a wait of some moments, greeted by Mrs. Enderby. She was some years younger than her husband—that is to say, she was in the high seventies rather than the low nineties—and an imposing dame of regal bearing. She and Fenchurch were acquaintances, as they had encountered one another on various College and University occasions, and so she greeted him by name.

"Mr. Fenchurch! Do come in. Giles will be delighted to see you." She led him through a dark and lowering hall into a vast chamber whose pseudo-Gothic panelling was almost entirely obscured by books. There were bookshelves built to resemble Cathedral stalls; there were closed bookcases designed to look like rood-screens, though the effect was somewhat spoilt by the fact that most of the doors had been left gaping open. Books spilled out of these openings; books in varying stages of decay were piled on every available surface in the room. Upon entering the library one's initial impression was that here was a surrealist world that had been completely taken over by books: Indeed, in the dim light the volumes assumed a curious life of their own. Broad folios stood up straight on the shelves like soldiers, but these were in the minority. Most of the volumes in the room drooped languorously or sprawled drunkenly over the surfaces on which they had been carelessly dropped. Some were clad in morocco and gilding, as discreetly fine as gentlemen dressed according to the precepts of Beau Brummel; other bindings were badly worn, like shabby-genteel vagrants who had seen better days. Raffish volumes with brightly printed dust-covers sat cheek by jowl with soberly bound academic treatises and prim religious works bound in divinity calf tinted a horrid shade of puce (remnants of the library belonging to Professor Enderby's father).

In the midst of all this chaos and confusion, and even movement (as they walked into the room, the shaking of the floorboards jolted several piles of books, which tottered and toppled over), presumably sat Professor Enderby. A monastic dimness, however, held sway over the scene, making the proprietor of the library invisible. Mrs. Enderby flicked ineffectually at a superannuated light-switch on the wall in an attempt to supplement the green gloom filtering through the ivy that had overspread stone mullioned windows. "Tcha!" she exclaimed impatiently. "The electricity has gone off again. I expect it's the squirrels. It generally is."

"The squirrels?" Fenchurch asked, peering around in a vain effort to spot the animals to which his hostess alluded.

"Yes, the squirrels. Sweet little creatures, aren't they?

Such winsome faces, and those charming tails. I always think of Beatrix Potter," she confided. "But they do have a habit of nesting in the walls and chewing on the electric wiring—most annoying of them. Are you fond of squirrels, Mr. Fenchurch?" She turned her faded but still beautiful blue eyes enquiringly in his direction.

Fenchurch, feeling as if by entering the house he had stepped into a looking-glass world, was tempted to reply, "Do you mean roasted or fricasséed, madam?" but suppressed the urge, saying merely, "Delightful beasts."

There was still no sign of Professor Enderby among the Augean clutter in the library. But this did not daunt his wife, who marched over to a broad desk where a large calf-bound folio of Chaucer's *Works* (it was the 1532 Thynne edition, Fenchurch noted) stood open, propped up on its sturdy cover. Peering over the top of the volume, she shouted, "Giles? Giles! You have company. Mr. Fenchurch has come to see you."

Slowly a wrinkled head rose over the top of the book, like a literary turtle's from its carapace. It blinked its eyes in an effort to focus them and said in a querulous voice, "What did you say, my dear?"

Pitching her voice even louder, Mrs. Enderby cried, "Mr. Fenchurch! He has come for a visit. Isn't that nice of him?"

The head swivelled toward Fenchurch, somewhat in the manner of a human periscope, and said, "Fenchurch, is it? How very kind of you to come all this way to see me, my dear fellow."

"Not at all," responded Fenchurch. He wondered whether Professor Enderby had been studying the text or taking a nap.

"But of course it is," Enderby continued. He rose, shaking himself like a terrier and feebly brushing at his cardigan in an inadequate attempt to rid his clothes of accumulated dust.

"To make such a very long journey, and in the winter too. The snow must greatly have inconvenienced your horses."

This speech startled Fenchurch, who had not held close converse with Professor Enderby in several years.

"He's being someone else," Mrs. Enderby explained, leaning over to whisper in her guest's ear. "Sometimes he thinks he's Gower, sometimes Langland, but generally he's Chaucer. And why not?" she went on, as though Fenchurch had expressed disapproval of his host's literary metamorphoses. "If one is going to pretend to be someone else, one might as well pretend to be the best. Though it's all a trifle confusing sometimes—I'm never quite sure who *I'm* supposed to be."

This vagary of his colleague added another dimension to an already sufficiently difficult task: If Enderby were being Chaucer (or Gower, or Langland) in medieval England, how could one discuss the possibility of his having taken a book from St. Jude's Library in the twentieth century? Indeed, if it were Chaucer he was being, Enderby might with some validity argue that he had an inherent right to the Caxton copy of the *Canterbury Tales*. Fenchurch found himself in a state of considerable perplexity over what to do next. Ought he to attempt to reason with this dotty old academic, perhaps posing as Chaucer's patron, John of Gaunt, Duke of Lancaster, in order to do so? Or should he begin to search for the volume, which he was almost certain was to be found within the confines of the house, without bothering to obtain the permission of his host? Desperately he set the devious brain that had contrived the fiendish intricacies of *Murder in the Maze* to work. But nothing happened; no brilliant method of handling such a ticklish situation came to mind. In order to be effective, the tricks of which he had spoken so confidently to Chase-Pippin required that the man upon whom they were to be tried retain at least a small portion of his right mind; if

Enderby really believed he were Chaucer, or even Langland or Gower, they would be useless.

However, a seed fell on fertile ground in Fenchurch's brain, and in an instant had burgeoned, flowered, and fruited. Glorious, glorious fruit! He considered. It was utterly mad, as mad as Enderby himself, but . . . Of course, it all depended on who he thought he was. So long as he thought he was Chaucer or Gower or Langland, Fenchurch was on solid ground. But if that faulty mind should suddenly have slipped an extra cog or so and he had decided to be Herrick or Blake or Shelley, then all—for the moment at least—was lost. Fenchurch mentally crossed his fingers and wondered how best to begin.

His quandary was unexpectedly solved by Professor Enderby, who said to his wife, "Why don't you whip up a posset for our guest, Philippa, my dear? That will take the chill out of his bones."

"He means tea," Mrs. Enderby hissed to Fenchurch, "only of course it hasn't been discovered yet. Of course, Gi—— I mean Geoffrey, darling. I'll just pop along and make a pot." She went out, leaving the two men alone together.

"You must forgive my poor wife," said Enderby confidentially to Fenchurch. "Her memory has begun to fail somewhat of late—she simply cannot remember that a posset should be served in a bowl, not a pot. Sely creature," he continued compassionately. "I cannot think how she would get on without me to look after her. Still, I mustn't waste your time with tales of my troubles. Pray, what is your errand? A message, perchance, from my lord of Gaunt?"

"Nothing of such importance, I fear—that is," Fenchurch added hastily, "not precisely a message. I came to see if I might borrow a book—on behalf of the Duke, naturally."

A look of suspicion combined with low cunning overspread the mild old features. "A book, eh?—What kind of book? I would of course lay down my life for my lord and patron, but

I do not know that I can spare a book. I have few books, as you can see," here he waved a veined hand to indicate the thousands of volumes surrounding them, "and each is precious to me as my own child. I can ill afford to lend them out—and even Dukes are apt to be laggard about returning them."

Fenchurch made an effort to tune his brain to Enderby's own mad logic. "I don't think you would miss this one," he said carelessly, "as it doesn't exist yet."

"Doesn't exist—an imaginary book? Whatever can you mean? How can I own a book that doesn't exist? You're talking twaddle." The old man glared at him irately.

"Take a look at it and see if I'm not telling the truth," Fenchurch returned.

Professor Enderby threw him a dubious glance, but his curiosity proved too much for him. "Which one is it?" he asked, "—your imaginary book." His voice held a sardonic note foreign to its usual high-pitched gentle tones.

"It happens to be one of your own works, as a matter of fact," Fenchurch said casually. *"Canterbury Tales."* Fervently he hoped this would not queer the whole pitch. If only Enderby had decided to be Langland or Gower instead of Chaucer!

"You see," Enderby crowed triumphantly, "I knew you were mistaken. An imaginary book, indeed! The *Tales* most certainly do exist . . . in fact, I've just begun to write them."

"If you'll just let me see the book, I'll prove it to you," said Fenchurch. For a moment Enderby hesitated, but curiosity prevailed and he sidled over to a window-seat overlooking the neglected garden and raised the cushions to disclose a storage niche underneath, from which he took a calf-bound quarto and handed it, somewhat reluctantly, to his visitor. It was, Fenchurch noted with a rush of relief, the missing St. Jude's copy. As he fanned the pages he tried to remember which were supposed to be the later tales. Eventually he was bound to light on one of them, but it would be far more impressive if he could choose one right off the bat. Fenchurch seemed to recall that the marriage group was thought by scholars to have been written later on. Locating the beginning of the "Wife of Bath's Tale," he held out the volume to Professor Enderby, who snatched it back greedily and looked at the page indicated.

"But I haven't written this yet!" he announced with fine indignation. "I've got the idea in my head, and a few scraps of verse in a notebook somewhere to work in when I get around to writing the thing, but that's all so far." His eye travelled down the page. "I say, that's not bad!" he exclaimed delightedly. " 'Thou seyst we wyves wol our vices hide Til we be fast, and thanne we wol hem shewe—Wel may that be a proverbe of a shrewe!' Absolutely first-rate; I wish I'd thought of it."

"You will," said Fenchurch, endeavouring to pry the book from Enderby's grasp. "Probably in the next year or so."

But the old man held fast and his eyes devoured the page. "I *am* clever, aren't I? Do you know, I have an excellent idea, and it will save so much trouble. If I were to take some notes . . . or perhaps work from this book. . . ."

But Fenchurch had already thought of that argument. "No," he replied firmly. "That isn't cricket. You mustn't plagiarize from yourself. If you do, then you'll never write the rest of the *Tales*. It would make authorship far too easy."

Professor Enderby said wistfully, "You think not? In that case, I couldn't possibly deprive the world of the offspring of my genius."

"To do so would be a catastrophe," Fenchurch agreed solemnly. "Besides"—he waved the quarto in front of him—"look at that trumpery little volume. You wouldn't want to give such a shabby object houseroom in your library. It's on paper, not vellum, and it's not even a manuscript—it has been made by a process that hasn't been invented yet called 'printing,' which means every Tom, Dick, and Harry can own a book. Look at the crudity of the lettering; no self-respecting scribe would own to having copied it out."

Enderby looked, and with a sigh handed the book to Fenchurch. "Very well," he said, "and after all, since it doesn't exist yet . . . how very inconvenient it would be if it should disappear when one least expected it, perhaps before I had got it all written down."

"Quite so," said Fenchurch, clutching the precious volume to his bosom as Mrs. Enderby arrived with a tea tray.

"Here is the posset, all hot and lovely," she trilled, setting the tray somewhat precariously on top of a pile of books.

"I'm afraid I can't stay," Fenchurch apologised. He was afraid that the tea might have the unwelcome effect of recalling Professor Enderby to the present, and he was anxious to escape with his prize before such an untoward event could occur.

"Go back out into the snow with no posset to revive you? Nonsense," said the Professor robustly. "You must have a bowl."

"Ah, but it would never do to keep the Duke waiting," Fenchurch replied. "You know how he is when he wants a book to read."

This mention of his patron seemed to satisfy the soi-disant Chaucer. "The Duke—of course, the Duke. Yes, yes; on your way. Don't make him wait; you'll rue it if you do. So sorry you can't stay for posset, but there it is—needs must when the Devil drives." He mulled over this remark, then changed it to "I meant the Duke, naturally—needs must when the Duke drives. A mere slip of the tongue, ha ha; you needn't mention it to him. He might be offended—he's apt to be touchy, you know. Farewell. Do convey my deepest respects to him—and to the Duchess too." Creakily he executed a profound bow, which Fenchurch duly echoed.

"No, no, don't bother to see me to the door, my dear lady," Fenchurch said, as Mrs. Enderby rose. "I can let myself out of the house." As soon as he was out of sight he scuttered down the gloomy hall, descended the steps, and mounted his bicycle, first carefully securing the Caxton in the basket for the return journey to St. Jude's.

12 Return to Canterbury

"Damn!" said Fenchurch, to his own enormous astonishment. "Damn, damn, damn!" He braked the wobbling bicycle to a screeching halt. "Why didn't I think," he castigated himself furiously, "to enquire after the *Anelida* while I was there? If he took one book, he may well have taken the other." He turned the Porter's bicycle around with a flair which would have done credit to an undergraduate and started back toward Girton.

Mrs. Enderby was surprised but pleased to see him return so soon. "Giles is so much better now," she confided as she led him back to the library. "The tea has set him up famously—he's quite his old self again; that is, as much as he ever is."

Fenchurch's heart sank. To have Professor Enderby return with such alacrity to the twentieth century was the last thing he had wished. And indeed, he found there was no question about it: Though Enderby's hold upon the present was tenuous at best, he was at least no longer Geoffrey Chaucer— nor even Gower nor Langland, either of whom would have done at a pinch. "Fenchurch, my dear fellow," he quavered, nearly knocking over the tea-pot as he unsteadily rose to greet his colleague. "Do sit down and join me in a cup of tea.

You must tell me all the Sheepshanks gossip. Is Dr. Truebody still beating his wife?"

"Not at present," Fenchurch responded truthfully and a
bit stiffly; Dr. Truebody, who had ceased being Master of
Sheepshanks some thirty years earlier, was something of an
embarrassment to the Senior Common Room, who did not
care to be reminded of him. "No, thank you, no tea. I'm
afraid I am unable to stay long as I must return to College in
order to conduct a tutorial in half an hour." He was afraid to
linger lest some quirk in Enderby's brain make him recollect
that Fenchurch had gone off with the *Canterbury Tales.* "I just
stopped in to enquire about the *Anelida*—you know, the
book that's gone missing from the UL. You haven't by any
chance come across it here or there, have you?" he asked
carelessly.

"The *Anelida?*" Enderby replied, his old eyes round and
innocent as a baby's. "That Caxton someone stole, about
which they've been making such an unconscionable fuss? It
isn't as though it were a manuscript, after all. Why no. Why
should I have? Do you know," he continued bitterly, "I was
forced to disrobe in the men's cloakroom to prove I hadn't
got it on me. It was most humiliating."

"I only thought you might have seen it about somewhere
since then," said Fenchurch lamely. "If you should run across
it, you'd let us know at once, wouldn't you? The Syndics are
rather upset over its disappearance."

"Yes, yes, yes; of course I should," Professor Enderby retorted irritably. "But it's a great deal of furore over nothing.
Now if it had been one of the manuscripts—*UL Dd Four,
twenty-four,* for instance—I could understand it. But a trumpery printed book!"

"It *is* a Caxton," Fenchurch could not resist pointing out,
although he knew he was treading on dangerous ground.

"A Caxton, a Caxton, forsooth! Quite thrilling to you
modern men, no doubt"—Enderby seemed to have forgotten,

along with a number of other things, that Fenchurch too was a medievalist—"but printed nearly a century after Chaucer's death. Hardly what *I* should term worthwhile; trash, sir, mere trash! Oh," he went on, softening, "useful in its humble way, I grant you, but hardly worth making such a commotion over."

"Quite so," said Fenchurch, who knew when he was beaten. ". . . What a superb storage place," he remarked with Machiavellian cunning, glancing over at the window-seat from which Enderby had taken the *Canterbury Tales* on his previous visit. "I suppose it *is* a storage place? So often those seats are."

"Indeed it is," Enderby replied; "here, I'll show you. My father, who built this house, believed in making everything in it as serviceable as possible." He raised the seat and Fenchurch peered within, taking out and examining a book or two with cries of feigned interest to see what lay beneath; but there was no sign of the *Anelida*. For the time being there was nothing more he could do in this place, so he said, "Well, I must be off. No; no tea, thank you kindly," waving away Mrs. Enderby's proffered cup. "I shall be late if I don't hurry. Good-bye. So sorry to have disturbed you."

"Not at all," returned Professor Enderby graciously. "We are always delighted to see old friends. Do stop round again when you have more time, and we'll have a chat about old Truebody."

13 Fenchurch Plays Cupid

Fenchurch was thoughtful as he cycled back to town. It was entirely possible that Enderby, the old bibliomane, had the *Anelida* tucked away in his mausoleum of a house; and if he did, how on earth were they to get it back short of obtaining a police search warrant? If they had to rely on his fortuitously becoming Chaucer (or Langland, or Gower) again, the process of retrieval might take years; besides, there was no guarantee that he might not change his mind (what was left of it, that is) and indulge his madness in an entirely different direction: the Elizabethan poets, perhaps, or the Romantics. Thus preoccupied with his problem, Fenchurch did not notice an elderly but still sprightly MG sports car (what he would have characterised as a runabout) painted the flaunting yellow of a bumble-bee's stripes, which in consequence was forced to make an unexpected diversion to avoid running him down. The resultant swerve brought it in direct contact with another bicycle, one not at all the sort of ramshackle affair used as locomotion by the Sheepshanks Head Porter, but a trim ladies' job enamelled bright robin's-egg blue. Fenchurch pedalled innocently on, ignorant of the accident he had just caused.

"Damn!" said Vivien, much as Fenchurch had done half an hour before, but for a decidedly different reason. She picked herself up off Bridge Street, dusted off her skirt, and determined there were no bones broken, then began to examine her bicycle, which was brand new and the apple of her eye. Luckily only the tyre had come into contact with the car's bumper, and since that had glanced off it there was no other damage done.

Having ascertained this, she turned to see what idiot had run into her, and glared at a tall fair young man alighting from the driver's seat of the jaunty little car. "What the devil do you think you were doing?" Vivien demanded, but without the animosity that a scratch on the shining paint would have engendered.

"I say, I *am* sorry," said the young man. "Are you all right? I wouldn't have had this happen for worlds." A naturally polite youth, Harry Huntingfield would have apologised for the incident even if his victim had been old and ugly, but the sight of Vivien rendered him more than customarily solicitous. "What can I do to make amends? Is your bicycle damaged? I shall have it repaired, of course. Like new. Or would you prefer a new one? I'll be happy to replace it with anything you like." Dimly he felt that he was babbling, and tried to stop but was unsuccessful. "A dog-cart, a landau, a coach-and-four? Or possibly a sedan-chair lined in sky-blue silk, with your humble servant as chairman?"

"That wouldn't do at all," Vivien said, laughing despite herself at his flow of cheerful nonsense. "I should need two chairmen."

"Naturally I should supply the other," he replied with dignity. "A Nubian boy with teeth like pearls in a blue turban to match the sedan-chair. In his spare moments he shall be your page and carry your fan."

"Unfortunately I have small use for a fan, particularly in November, considering the state of central heating at Clare," Vivien answered gravely. "But he could carry my briefcase when I go to the UL."

"Are you on your way there now? And if so, can I tempt you away from duty by offering you a cup of tea? I'd make it a brandy, only the pubs aren't open yet. Perhaps we could do that tomorrow," he said hopefully.

Vivien eyed his gown, which was flung across the car's battered leather seat. One open sleeve hung down, making it clear that its owner was an undergraduate. "I'm afraid I'm a shade too elderly for you," she told him with a trace of regret. "I'm a research student."

"You could never be too old for me. For one thing you look younger than springtime, and for another, I don't go in for raw girls. Besides, I'm not as young as I ought to be— never have been, in fact," he responded. "The Huntingfields are notoriously slow starters, but when we catch up, we do it with a rush. Anyway, what does a year or so matter? Each year added to your age will only ripen and enhance your incomparable beauty—you mustn't mind the way I run on," he confided. "Hyperbole simply spouts out when I talk to pretty girls, but this is the first time I've really meant it. I do hope you won't let it put you off me." His tone was light, but his eyes mirrored his seriousness.

Several cars had managed to wriggle past the yellow MG, which Harry had pulled up with its near wheels on the pavement, but traffic was beginning to pile up behind them on Magdalene Bridge and there was a buzz of irritable honking. "If we don't move soon we'll have the law on us," said Harry. "Do say you'll come." At her nod of assent he picked up the bicycle, strapped it to the boot, opened the passenger's door in front, and chivalrously ushered her in. The concerted honking rose to a caterwaul as he deftly swung the car out into the street.

"Shall we try the Granta?" he suggested. "It's easy to park there, and I'm feeling flush—I had an unexpected win at Newmarket yesterday. It's found money, so we might as well blue it—that is, if you won't let me buy you a sedan-chair.

Don't think I'm a gambler," he added hastily, glancing over to admire her flawless profile, "because I'm not. It was my godmamma's horse, so I had to have a flutter on it for the sake of family loyalty; and to my great surprise the nag came in at astonishing odds. I'm normally not a gambling man—slow and steady, that's my motto. Just the sort of chap you ought to marry."

Vivien could not help laughing at his inconsequential chatter. "Hold hard," she said, "you're going rather too fast."

"As it happens, I'm quite in earnest," he replied, "but I promise not to bore you with it over tea."

They turned into Mill Lane and from the lane into a cul-de-sac by the river. Passing by the office for renting punts, which was closed now the season had ended, Harry parked in front of an artfully stuccoed apricot-tinted façade belonging to a seventeenth-century inn. Within, the lounge with its comfortable chintz-covered sofas and armchairs faced a garden along the river, a garden which even in late autumn still retained sufficient vestiges of colour to make the view a pleasing one despite the lowering metallic sky. Harry settled Vivien onto a sofa and beckoned one of the waiters, who took their order for tea and scones.

"By the way," he said to her when their waiter had departed on his errand, "my name is Harry Huntingfield, I'm in my last year at Sheepshanks, reading history at the ripe old age of twenty-four, birthday twenty-eighth May. What's yours?—your name, that is, not your age. Not that it matters," he hastened to add. "You may remain *incognita* if you like, so long as you promise to see me again."

"My name is Vivien Murray," she replied, "and actually I don't mind telling you my age, since it happens to be the same as yours—well, almost,' she amended. "My birthday is eight June. I'm doing research on Donne and Company at Clare."

Harry, who had read his Malory, thought—much as Fenchurch had upon his first sight of Vivien—that her name suited her very well. "Where did you do your undergraduate work?" he enquired, eager for every scrap of knowledge about her. "It can't have been Clare; they weren't accepting women then. Come to think of it, it can't have been anywhere in Cambridge because we couldn't possibly have spent two years in the same city without my catching sight of you."

"It was Somerville," she answered with a charming blush. "I thought I'd try the fens for a change of scene."

"You don't mean to say you were at The Other Place!" He gave a delighted laugh. "I expect you left to flee from your flock of admirers. You must have been a latter-day Zuleika."

"Let's stop talking about me," said Vivien, who though a thoroughly self-assured young lady was beginning to feel somewhat shy under his shower of compliments; all the more so because she sensed that, despite his airy banter, they were genuine. "Tell me about yourself."

So Harry, who like any other man expanded visibly under the flattering attention of a lovely young woman, held forth on the events of his short life and the mouldering attractions of Tantivy Hall, to which he proposed to introduce her as soon as possible.

Tea arrived, interrupting the amiable flow of his discourse—China tea, served with thin slices of lemon in thinner porcelain cups, and scones, still warm from the oven, accompanied by dishes of clotted cream and strawberry jam. It was some time before their healthy young appetites were assuaged, and even longer before their curiosity about each other was partially satisfied; the long autumn twilight had enveloped river and garden before they reluctantly parted in order to fulfill engagements previously made. But by the time Harry dropped Vivien off at Clare he had obtained a willing promise to meet again for dinner the next evening.

14 Brave Vibrations

Sir Richard Rackstraw sat at the desk in his resplendent library, surrounded by rare first editions, rarer incunabula, and rarest manuscripts. Despite the wisdom of the ages that kept him company in such expensive dress, he was engaged in reading, not his fifth-century manuscript of Aristotle nor the fifteenth-century edition of the elder Pliny as printed by Jenson at Venice but a letter, and a contemporary one at that. The gloom on his rough-hewn countenance made it clear that some modicum of the philosophy contained by the shapely volumes on his shelves would have been welcome as an anodyne to his evident distress. Sir Richard Rackstraw did not have an expressive face. It was a massive face, a bull-like face, the sort of face that, like the carven visage of Ozymandias, was made to display the manly passions—pride, anger, lust, covetousness—but it was not flexible enough to exhibit the more subtle emotions. As a result, the only outward mark of the feelings roused in him by the letter he was reading, overwhelming though they were, was an expression indicative of a nasty bout of dyspepsia. This appearance, however, was greatly misleading, for inside he was churning with an unaccustomed mixture of fear, trepidation, yearning and pusillanimity. Ah, woman, woman! Such is thy power—to turn a Behemoth of industry into a quivering jelly. The hand that without a tremor has signed cheques for millions of pounds and orders sacking hundreds of employees shakes as it holds a single sheet of paper before eyes once stern and clear, but now darkened by apprehension.

At the sound of high heels on the marble floor of the hall outside, Rackstraw hastily opened a drawer with the intention of concealing the document he held, but he was a fraction of a second too late. As she swept into the room (quite literally, since the hem of her swaying bottle-green silk taffeta skirt measured a good twenty yards across), the sharp eyes of his beloved caught sight of a flutter of white in the half-closed drawer and she demanded, "What's that?"

"Nothing, my angel, nothing at all . . . I must say," Rackstraw remarked, in an all-too-obvious attempt to change the subject, "you look very glamourous tonight. Is all this magnificence for me? I thought we were dining alone."

"So we are, but this just arrived from Xanadu, and I thought you might like a look at it."

"Indeed I should," he said, admiring her costume. Or perhaps it might be more accurate to say, admiring Julia. The fitted gold bodice was cut so low in front that it would have seemed in imminent peril of descending to meet the skirt had it not been so tightly moulded to her superb figure as to make this physically impossible; and as for the back of the bodice—there was none, only Julia's sinuous white back rising from the enormous skirt like a water-lily bud. "Most becoming," Rackstraw said, adding uxoriously, "But I'm not sure you ought to wear it out in public."

"Don't be absurd, darling. It's quite madly decent. See— there are yards and yards of material in it." She twirled around, the iridescent silk unfurling and billowing about her.

"That's undoubtedly true," he answered drily, "but they're in all the wrong places. However, so long as you're mine, let the rest of 'em gawk." He moved over to take her in his arms, on his part always a welcome proceeding and at this time, he obscurely felt, not only pleasurable but a successful diversionary tactic.

But in this he was mistaken. With a lithe movement Julia slipped out of his would-be embrace, saying, "What is it?"

"I don't know whether it's butterflies' wings or peacocks' feathers or woven moonbeams at midnight," answered Rackstraw, waxing uncharacteristically poetic in an attempt to head his wife off, "but I do know that what's inside is the most delicious, the most delectable . . ."

But Julia was not to be deflected. "Yes, darling, that's very sweet of you," she retorted perfunctorily. "But what's in that letter you've just put away?"

"Letter? . . . Oh, the letter," said Rackstraw, suddenly enlightened. "Just a letter, darling, from . . . a business letter. Very dull, really; nothing to bother your pretty head over."

But in the midst of this inept and deceptive explanation Julia flitted over to the desk, pulled open the drawer, took out the letter in question and began to read it. Her lovely face contorted into a mask of momentary fury; had a classical scholar been present, he would have been reminded of a beautiful Medusa. "So," she said, "they won't have me at their bloody little dinner-party at any price."

"Julia, darling, I'm most frightfully sorry about all this, but you know it's nothing to do with you personally. It's College tradition. I did warn you. I bet there's not one of the old boys who isn't panting to meet you."

But Julia was not to be mollified. "And why, may I ask, did you try to hide this from me?"

"I didn't hide . . ." But this statement was so blatantly untrue that Rackstraw quickly abandoned it. "I just wanted to avoid hurting your feelings; I knew you were counting on going and I didn't want to upset you."

Julia's green eyes narrowed and her generous mouth set in

an ominously thin line. "That isn't the real reason, and you know it. The *real* reason is that you want to go, with or without me."

Rackstraw's response to this undeniable truth was to try to refute it with bluster. "That's utter nonsense! I've never heard—"

"Oh, no, it isn't," retorted Julia; the famous purr now held a razor-sharp edge. "It happens to be the truth. But I won't have it, I tell you. I won't be humiliated by a bloody bunch of rotten old men. Of course you'll turn down the invitation, won't you, since it's such an insult to your wife."

"But, my darling, don't you see . . ." In his eagerness to bring her round to his point of view Rackstraw stumbled over his words. "Don't you see that it's nothing of the sort? All the wives are in the same basket; and it isn't as if provision weren't being made for your entertainment."

"I'm not just any wife," Julia replied coldly. "I happen to be a professional, and I don't care to be lumped together with all those others." Briefly she toyed with the idea of demanding that her husband give up Pullets Feast, but she was a shrewd woman and sensed that this might be going rather too far. In general she kept Rackstraw well under control, but her typically feminine art lay in keeping him unaware of it. With a toss of her head, she said petulantly, "Go if you must, but don't expect me to sit next door being bored to death by the bitch-pack. I won't be dragged around behind you like a monkey's tail."

"But, dearest," Rackstraw urged, "it will look so odd if you don't come, particularly since Dr. Shebbeare wrote such a kind invitation, saying how much he admires your programme and that he is especially looking forward to meeting you." He looked down at the letter in Julia's hand in order to point out the passage; it was fortunate for his peace of mind that he did not see the dangerous glint which suddenly came into her eye. There was a pause while she reread the letter.

Then, "Very well," she conceded, with the aspect of a princess who has reluctantly consented to go slumming. "I suppose I must. On condition," she continued significantly, "that you book separate rooms at the hotel."

Relieved at so readily gaining his way, Sir Richard made no objection to the harsh stipulation set by his lady wife. Two, he reflected, can comfortably fit in a single bed as readily and far more enjoyably than one. Just because a room has been paid for does not mean it must be used; and he recollected seeing a remarkable necklace of cabochon emeralds the size of quails' eggs, once the property of the Maharajah of Baroda and now reposing in a velvet nest at Cartier, which just matched Julia's eyes and might go far toward softening the harshness of her attitude long before it was time to make the journey to Cambridge.

15 At Jahangir

Exotic scents pervaded the dim, crowded room, emanating from the minute kitchen in heady waves; all the spices of India seemed to swirl about the small square tables in the restaurant, assailing the diners' nostrils with a mélange of aromatic fumes. Jahangir was the best of Cambridge's Indian eating places, which meant that the wallpaper was flocked red-and-gold in imitation of brocade, the tablecloths were changed every evening, and the paper napkins were larger than those provided by rival establishments. It was a Friday, always a busy night, and the restaurant was filled to overflowing with students bent on impressing their young women by the comparative extravagance of their outlay. Unlike most of the customers, Grubb was seated on his own: he usually sat alone at restaurants because he had few friends upon whom to call for company, and in any event it would never have occurred to him to offer to stand treat. Jahangir with its tinkling brass chandeliers and gaudy pottery elephant standing guard in the entranceway was rather above his touch, and on an ordinary night he would have made do with the curry at the less up-market Taj Mahal or Calcutta; but he was feeling bucked over his recent Combination Room triumph and consequently had decided to do himself proud.

It was a proper treat, he thought, to have supper (he used

the plebeian word defiantly to himself to exorcise the spectre
of dinner at High Table) away from all those arrogant old
bastards: for once he did not have to mind his table manners.
Grubb would dearly have loved just once to pick up his chop-
bone at High Table and gnaw it in approved working-man's
fashion for the sake of seeing old Shebbeare's face, but he did
not quite dare.

A supple sari-clad waitress brought his chicken tandoori
(the cheapest dish on the menu) and set it before him. Grubb
tucked into it with enjoyment and had half-finished when he
happened to look up in the direction of the entrance. A fair
and gracious girl was pushing her way through the strings of
beads that masked the doorway. She made Grubb, whose
mind was not normally of a poetic cast, suddenly think of
springtime and pale-yellow daffodils and bluebells growing
in deep moss. But these unaccustomed thoughts were rapidly
dispersed when, to his great disgust, this dryad was followed
almost immediately by an all-too-familiar figure, his *bête
noire*, Lord Henry Huntingfield. The sight of Harry, especially in proximity to the girl, who was obviously in his company, quite spoiled Grubb's usually voracious appetite. He
glowered at them over his now-ruined meal as the waitress
ushered them to a table directly opposite.

It wasn't fair! What did young Huntingfield have that he
hadn't got, except a title, and a nearly bankrupt one at that?
Savagely Grubb crumbled his poppadums into dust. But just
look at him—sent up to Cambridge as a matter of course,
whereas Grubb had had a job of it talking that mean old
bugger his father into letting him go up to University at all.
The old sod had thought he was getting above himself, and
Grubb had to work like a navvy to make ends meet, since he
had got no help from home. No doubt young Harry would
end up as the chief ornament of a Board of Directors for some
high-powered City firm, raking in the lolly through no effort
of his own. Grubb, on the other hand, had slaved to get as

far as he had; he still did not quite know how he had managed without connections to pull off his Sheepshanks Fellowship, and his perch there felt precarious. And as if Harry had not had quite enough undeserved spoils tossed his way, the most beautiful girls in Cambridge quite unaccountably took to him. It was the title; it must be the title. Grubb was as good a man as that overprivileged brat Harry Huntingfield any day, only he didn't have a stinking moth-eaten class-ridden title that was useless except to impress the snobstruck.

Morosely Grubb took another swig of his beer and eyed Vivien covertly. Damn all women anyway! What did she see in that young twit? It infuriated him to watch the way she was looking at her companion. He took another pull at his beer until his glass was almost empty, and his thoughts took a maudlin turn. God, she was lovely. . . . Why couldn't she look at him like that? Women were all alike. Grubb finished his glass and beckoned to the waitress to fetch him another of the same, casting a look of sour malevolence at the couple across from him. Women didn't give a damn what a man was really like. They were only impressed by externals—looks, clothes, money, titles—not by what a man was capable of thinking and feeling. Despite his recent rebuff Grubb's heart was still firmly attached to the matchless Gloria, but no one who saw Vivien could fail to be touched by her bright and gallant beauty. If he had not seen Gloria first . . . he thought drunkenly to himself. Poor Grubb! forever doomed to lust after the unattainable. He drank more deeply yet and brooded. Not only was that noble blight who smugly sat across from him unfairly overendowed with what the world values, but he had two beautiful women dancing after him as if they were puppets and he the puppet-master. It wasn't right. It wasn't fair.

Once more Grubb raised his hand to summon the waitress and a third beer was brought to him. No man, he fumed to himself, should have two women, even plain ones. Two women, no matter what they looked like, were one too many for any man. And selfishly to take two *beautiful* women out of circulation . . . No consideration for anyone else, none whatever. But then what would you expect from a swinish representative of the degenerate aristocracy? All for one, and one take all. Winner take all. Nobody left for poor Grubb. . . . By this time he was well into his fourth beer. The first three had been drunk in rapid succession and his head was starting to feel muzzy: Grubb was not accustomed to strong waters as his parents had both been teetotal, and his thoughts were becoming somewhat confused, but one thing at least was clear to him. That spoilt pup was being unfaithful to Gloria—to Gloria, who could command Grubb anything. How dared Huntingfield insult the loveliest woman in Cambridge?

Fired with alcohol and virtuous indignation, Grubb rose unsteadily to his feet, nearly upsetting the now-congealed dish of chicken tandoori, threw some money on the table, and crossed over to stand wavering in front of Vivien and Harry. They looked up from their curries in surprise. "Here, you! What about Gloria?" Grubb demanded loudly.

"Gloria?" Harry replied, understandably startled by this unexpected intrusion. "Oh," he said, enlightened. "Gloria. What about her?"

"Lovelies' woman in worl'. Where is she?" He looked as severely at Harry as his slightly crossed eyes would permit.

"I haven't the remotest idea, I'm afraid," Harry said politely. "Why, have you lost her?" He had noticed Grubb sitting glumly alone and thought that perhaps he had been stood up by the beautiful bedder.

"'T's you. You're the one. Trifling with her affections. Reckon you're trifling with this one too. Watch out for d—decadent upper classes," he said to Vivien. "R—rotten to the core, all of 'em. Poor girl"—here Grubb began to blubber—

"it'll break her heart when she finds out you been two-timing her." He glared at Harry. "For twopence I'd bash in your nose, 'n then you wouldn't look so pretty, leadin' poor girls astray, only it wouldn' be dignified, a m—member of the Senior Common Room bashin' an undergraduate. You—you be careful, miss." He wagged an uncertain finger in Vivien's direction. "Prolly got two or three wives already. Or . . . you know." He leered at her; the expression did nothing to enhance his already unprepossessing features. "Bastards strewn all over the shop. *Droit de seigneur* and all that." Apparently feeling he had said enough, Grubb staggered away, nearly colliding with a tray-bearing peri on his way out.

"Good God," Harry remarked, considerably shaken by this tirade. "The fellow must have *droit de seigneur* on the brain."

"By the way, who is Gloria?" enquired Vivien. While Grubb was busy inveighing, she had resolved she would not ask Harry about the mysterious Gloria; but under the circumstances it would have been astonishing if she had managed to restrain her natural curiosity.

"Gloria," Harry explained, "is an angel of mercy, and as fair as she is good; though nowhere near up to your standard." He described his recent encounter with Gloria and Grubb, and Vivien was laughing by the time he finished. "Clearly he's got the hots for the beautiful bedder," he concluded.

"Poor man," said Vivien compassionately. "Need you have teased him quite so much? He seems desperately unhappy. Perhaps he really loves her."

"I couldn't resist it," Harry replied. "I'm a flirt by nature. That is, I was, until I met you. I shall never, ever flirt again," he declared, taking her hand under the table. "Except with you, of course."

"I won't hold you to that. As it happens, I'm fond of flirting myself. It's great fun and quite harmless." She smiled at him. "Isn't it?"

"If you think I'm flirting with you now, you couldn't be more wrong. For once in my life I'm dead serious. And it's not bloody well harmless—nothing really worth doing ever is."

"I don't know," Vivien said pensively. "I suppose it could be more than flirtation, but it's too early to tell."

"Look," said Harry frankly, "I know I'm rushing things. I hope it's not too much of a bore for you. You must be fed up with people chasing after you all the time. I'll try to go slow," he told her, "but it will be hard as hell. Not because I always get my own way—I don't, as a matter of fact; my brother and three sisters are all born bullies—but you're so damned important to me that I can't help wanting to make sure of you."

"I think I may feel that way about you too," Vivien replied slowly, "but everything's been so sudden that I can't be sure yet. After all," she reminded him, "we've only known each other for a single day."

"For twenty-nine hours and thirteen minutes," Harry corrected her, consulting his watch. "Besides, 'Love, all alike, no season knows, nor clime, Nor hours, days, months, which are the rags of time.'"

"Now you're poaching on my preserves," Vivien told him, amused. "You didn't tell me you were studying Donne."

"I'm not. I hadn't read the old boy since sixth form until I dug out a copy of his poems in my College library last night after meeting you. He isn't half bad. In fact, for a Dean of St. Paul's he's pretty hot stuff; I stayed up most of the night reading him. Reading him and thinking of you."

Her smile dimmed a little. He noticed it and said, "Look, I don't want to push you too hard. You can be my Belle Dame Sans Merci if you like, and I'll follow you without reward my whole life through. Only I shouldn't exactly mind if you tossed an occasional bone my way."

Vivien's laughter bubbled up at the sight of Harry's

woebegone expression. "You won't have to go that far! But I need to be certain. When I fall in love, I think it will be for keeps. So let's just be silly and have fun. Let's not worry about what comes next. If we don't, it might before we know it."

"Whatever you say," returned Harry, encouraged. "Your slightest wish is my command. What can we do now that's silly and fun?—I say," he became inspired, "—I say, let's go punting."

"Punting? But all the boats are put away for the winter."

"So they are, but I happen to know where I can put my hand on one, and the moon is full tonight. The evening is quite the best time to go punting, particularly when it's chilly," Harry said practically. "No one else is on the river then, and with the lights from the Colleges gleaming on the water, one might be in Venice—or in Cambridge five centuries ago. Don't worry about the cold; a blanket or two and a hot-water bottle will fix you up all right and tight."

"I won't need them, thanks; the curry has warmed my blood quite enough already."

"Only the curry, cruel fair one?" Harry asked in a mock-mournful tone. "So be it. Come, my ice-queen—next stop the Grand Canal." As he helped Vivien on with her coat he thought, *She'll come round. She must come round. If she doesn't, I don't know what will become of me.*

16 A Conversation on Caxton

The telephone on Rackstraw's vast polished desk shrilled peremptorily and he picked up the receiver. "Yes?" he spoke irritably into the mouthpiece. "What the hell do you want?" He did not like being interrupted, and his secretary was extortionately paid to minister to his likes and dislikes.

"I'm ever so sorry, Sir Richard. I know you gave instructions not to be disturbed, but a Mr. Grimes is on the line and he insisted that you would wish to speak with him." His secretary's usually bland voice sounded apologetic and somewhat aggrieved; she had been got round by Mr. Grimes, and she was unaccustomed to being got round. She prided herself on her impenetrability, and it irked her that she had been bested, she did not quite know how.

"Very well; that's all right. I'll have a word with him." Somewhat to her surprise her employer sounded eager, much as he did when his wife telephoned him. There was a click, and the voice of Mr. Grimes came on the line, smooth, faintly oily, with the merest hint of a guttural quality underlying the suavity.

"Do I speak to Sir Richard Rackstraw?"

"You do," replied Rackstraw. "Have you got something for me, Grimes?"

"Ah, Sir Richard, how delightful to hear your voice. Yes, I may quite possibly have a little item in which you would be interested. I am telephoning in my private capacity, you realise, not as an employee of Scunthorpe's."

"Yes, yes; I quite understand," said Rackstraw impatiently. "What is it?"

"Better perhaps not to discuss the matter over the telephone, but I can tell you this: It is choice, very choice indeed. I am sure you will find it well worth examining. Our old friend De Ricci is most impressed."

De Ricci, eh? thought Rackstraw to himself, pricking up his ears. That meant it was a Caxton, as De Ricci had compiled an illustrious catalogue of Caxtons. However, it would not do to seem too eager, so he said casually, "I might just have a look at . . . whatever it is. Of course"—deprecatingly—"it may be a duplicate of something I already own."

"I think," murmured the insinuating voice, "that the condition does not duplicate anything you presently have. It is superb. Also"—here Mr. Grimes was heard to hesitate, but evidently decided to continue—"also I may soon have access to something even better; something, shall I say, unique."

"Oh?" said Sir Richard, suddenly alert. In the usual way Mr. Grimes's merchandise was undeniably superior, and if he claimed one of his offerings was out of the ordinary, that meant it was a pearl of great price in both senses of the phrase, for the cost of Grimes's wares came high, but the goods were worth it. And of course when one considered the risks he took. . . .

"I should like to have a look at them both," he said. "They sound promising."

"Most promising, I assure you," answered Mr. Grimes. "I am afraid, however, that I can show you only one at the moment. The second item of which I spoke is not yet—available."

Damn it, thought Rackstraw in annoyance. He'd made the cardinal mistake of indicating his interest too soon. Now would commence the game of cat and mouse, with the catnip mouse being withdrawn every time the cat's clutching paw nearly captured it, and each time the price would go sky-rocketing up. But greatly though he coveted these as-yet-unknown treasures for his private library, Sir Richard was a man of steel, a Damascene blade forged in the heat of Big Business. "If I can't see them both this evening," he said, his voice brusque, "then I'm afraid I'm not interested; forget it."

"I do assure you, Sir Richard, that I am not tantalising you in order to raise the price," replied the purring voice reproachfully. "The second object is still . . . in transit, as it were."

Rackstraw had a sudden flash of enlightenment, fueled by recent newspaper stories which had been printed despite the efforts of the University Library Syndics to prevent their pub-lication. If Grimes had got hold of the *Anelida,* he would pay any price to add it to his clandestine collection. "What is it?" he enquired breathlessly.

"I fear I cannot disclose that at present, but I give you my word that it is a magnificent acquisition. However, for the time being I regret it is unavailable for inspection. When the moment is ripe you shall see it. In the meantime, what about the first item? I shall be happy to bring it round whenever it suits you."

"Yes," said Rackstraw, "yes, do that. But not to my house. My office would be preferable. I shall be working late this evening. Shall we say—at seven?"

"At seven, then. And if you find it acceptable, there will be the usual transaction. Cash, of course."

"Naturally," Sir Richard responded. "Far better for both of us."

"Under the circumstances," agreed Mr. Grimes. "I could not agree more. So I look forward to seeing you, dear Sir Richard, at seven."

He rang off, leaving Rackstraw to gloat over the prospect of privy possession.

17 Pullets Feast

"Darling, don't you think you're being rather silly to insist on separate rooms? It's unhealthy to bear a grudge, you know. I shall miss you dreadfully. I do so hate sleeping by myself," Rackstraw said in a fretful voice.

"What a sentimental old idiot you are, Dick, my love," retorted Julia. She was in high spirits despite her impending banishment to the outer regions of Sheepshanks. "I shall only be next door, don't forget. I may even pop in to warm your bed if I'm in the mood."

"But I don't understand," Sir Richard complained pathetically. "I quite thought you'd have changed your mind by this time. After all, it's not as if we hadn't. . . ."

"Don't you realise, darling, it's the principle of the thing. A hell of a life I should lead if you knew how easily you can get round me." Julia patted his cheek with an emerald-encrusted hand, and her eyes sparkled as brightly as her rings. They were motoring to Cambridge in the Rolls. Rackstraw was driving; whenever possible, he made it a habit to chauffeur himself on the motorways. He enjoyed putting the powerful car through its paces as an antidote to the long hours of enforced inaction spent behind his desk.

"You're no longer angry with me, then," he said with relief.

"Darling," purred Julia, nestling against his shoulder, "how could I be, after that heavenly necklace? Did I seem angry last night? Or the night before? Or . . . ?"

He glanced down from the road at her Nefertiti profile. "No, thank God. I couldn't bear it if you were cross with me. Julie, darling, I'm really more sorry than I can say about tonight. If there were anything I could have done—anything! It's quite an honour, you know—the next best thing to having the Queen lob a peerage my way. Otherwise I would have turned it down for your sake."

"Don't worry, my little Dickie-Bird," Julia responded, delicately running a slender finger around his ear. "I'm not the least bit cross. At the moment I feel in charity with all the world. You're much more likely to be angry with me today than I with you," she added with perfect truth.

As they neared Cambridge the car began to slow down in order to thread its way through the outskirts of the town. They entered Trumpington Street and Sir Richard turned into Mill Lane, expertly manoeuvering the Rolls's sleek bulk along the narrow passageway until they arrived at the entrance to the Granta Hotel.

Rackstraw had reserved the only suite at the Granta—a charming sitting-room furnished in soft-coloured chintzes and overlooking a garden and the river, with two bedrooms and a bath that opened off the main room. Over his protests Julia ordered her suitcases put in one bedroom and her husband's in the other. "Now, my darling," she said when the porter had departed, pocketing a lavish tip, "you remember that was our agreement. Anyway, so long as we have two rooms, we may as well use them to dress in."

"But I like to watch you dress, Julia," he protested, his tone plaintive.

"I'm afraid you'll simply have to do without it this once, darling. I want to surprise you, as well as everyone else."

"I thought you had decided to wear something appropriately demure," said Sir Richard uneasily; as a rule he did not greatly care for surprises.

"There are limits, my sweet, to my ability to suppress my personality, even for a pack of seedy old dons. You needn't worry, though," Julia added consolingly over her shoulder, "it's one of your favourites."

This remark did not serve to reassure Rackstraw; nor, to tell the truth, was it calculated to do so. Nonetheless he knew from experience that it was useless to remonstrate further, so he went to his room to change for dinner. Julia too entered her bedroom, but unlike her husband she did not immediately commence her toilette; instead she spent a longish period on the telephone, murmuring instructions into the receiver in a voice designed to be heard only by its intended recipient. When she reappeared in the sitting-room a considerable while later (Rackstraw had been ready for more than half an hour) he gave a gasp of mingled admiration and horror. Her beautifully modelled figure was set off by a dress of scarlet silk that sheathed it in artful draperies and so closely moulded itself to her body as to leave very few desirable inches to the imagination. As if this display were not enough, most of her ravishing bosom was exposed by a practically nonexistent bodice—her favourite style—and a slit in the skirt revealed one long dazzling leg whenever she moved.

Julia took his gasp as a compliment. "I told you you'd like it."

"Like it—my God, Julia! Haven't you brought something else you could wear?"

"But, Dickie, you said you adored me in this dress," she returned, pouting.

"And so I do, but there's rather too much of you visible for the public to adore, if you take my meaning."

"Pooh, don't be absurd. Everyone in London is wearing this sort of thing. Anyway it will just have to do—unless you'd rather I wore my nightdress." Her eyes glinted with suppressed mischief.

Rackstraw knew when he was beaten. "Very well," he said hopelessly. "At least the male guests are bound to appreciate it, even if it does give the old boys a shock."

"Yes," she agreed. "When we're let out of our cage after dinner. Besides, there's sure to be someone else fashionable at the ladies' bash; not all the guests are academic wives, thank God."

Rackstraw looked at his watch. "Time to go," he said.

"I'm ready. At least—very nearly ready. I must just fetch my wrap and do a minor adjustment to my makeup."

As she went to collect her coat Julia closed the door to her room, picked up the telephone receiver, and dialed. "Is everything set?" she asked, her voice purposely kept low. "Good—then we're off. Don't forget what I told you. Get all the shots you can, short of committing murder. That's right. Break a leg." She rang off and caught up a sable coat from the bed, slinging the furs carelessly over her shoulders before joining her husband.

Sheepshanks Great Hall was in fine fettle that evening. High Table—the long mahogany table on the dais at the end of the Hall—had been rubbed down with lemon oil by the assiduous Bottom, the College butler, and his minions until its depths glowed in the light of the many-branched silver candelabra which it darkly mirrored. For the past week the staff had been hard at work cleaning the College silver: chargers and salvers, ewers and candlesticks, beakers and claret jugs held the mellow gleam only found on silver that has been lovingly tended for generations.

Deep shadow enveloped the richly carved ceiling of gold and crimson, shrouding the Tudor roses that formed its chief adornment. Now and then a log caught in the great stone fireplace next to High Table, fitfully illuminating the carvings so that they seemed to blossom and wither almost in the same breath. The colours of the famous (or rather, infamous) stained-glass windows, bestowed upon a less-than-grateful College by Sir Oliver Sheepshanks, were fortunately subdued because of the absence of light outside; in consequence the portraits on the panelled walls of past Masters and Benefactors, headed by a glowering rendition of Henry VIII, hands truculently placed on substantial hips, were thrust into greater prominence.

Pullets Feast was in full swing. The long table effortlessly accommodated a number of visitors in addition to its usual party of Fellows. Besides Sir Richard Rackstraw the company of distinguished guests included the Duke of Northcote, a hearty florid Rowlandsonian gentleman of the old school; Lord Payne, the Fleet Street nabob; and Henry Huntingfield, Earl of Cavesson, whose features and mien were those of a Romney portrait. Mr. Cyril Lapwing, the celebrated playwright, tall, languid and epicene, graced the assembly with his presence, as did Lord Kaplan, high in the ranks of industrial magnates. The Bishop of Barstow, whose imposing figure and full head of iron-grey hair made him look the precise picture of a prelate, was there—he was known the length and breadth of England for his BBC chats on "Is God or Isn't She?"—along with the mathematical genius Professor-Doktor Friedrich Blumenreich from the University of Munich, and Mr. Simon Poxwell, a renowned Harley Street surgeon who, it was rumoured, would appear on the next Birthday Honours List in acknowledgement of his recent deft removal of a royal appendix.

Although the Bishop was an old Sheepshankian, most of the Fellows were regretting his inclusion in the guest list for Pullets, since the excellent wine had infelicitously unleashed in him a bibulous flow of information and reminiscence which threatened to overwhelm all discourse but his own.

"Yes," he remarked pensively, his large ruddy pudding of

a face wreathed in a perpetual if slightly artificial smile, "I feel the fact that I have never held a parish has been a positive advantage to me as Bishop." He held up his glass of claret in order to admire its colour and drank. "Since God is an abstraction, God's vicars therefore should not become mired in the concrete—that is, always supposing there *is* a God, which is purely a matter of opinion. I myself prefer the theory of a Life Force . . . the Church has become confoundedly old-fashioned. We of the clergy have a duty to modernise it, both in language and in thought." He turned to Lord Payne. "You, sir, will understand that the media are the answer. Television and the Press, they are what is needed to educate our flock in the new ways."

Lord Payne, who despite the cynicism engendered by his years in the newspaper business (or perhaps because of it) was a fervent High Anglican, returned with some asperity, "Suppose your flock, as you call them, does not choose to be educated along the path you indicate?"

"Oh, but they're bound to be, you know. I must confess that I don't often take the Bible literally—myths of Heaven and angels, some of them red as a lobster, with three pairs of wings! Now really!"

"'. . . That hadde a fyr-reed cherubynnes face,'" murmured Fenchurch under his breath, eyeing the Bishop's temulent complexion.

"—All those absurd miracles; and the Virgin Birth and Resurrection, which are both absolute nonsense; but when it describes the people as sheep and the clergy as shepherds—well!" He lifted up his plump hands in an attitude of pious approbation. "Whether they like it or not, we shall herd them toward the Truth . . . as we see it. The Church, after all, is Christ; and Christ is merely what theologians choose to make Him."

"God help Him, then, and all of us as well," muttered

Tempeste, who by this time had more than had his fill of the Bishop.

"But what of Man's ability to recognise the Truth for himself and choose his own direction?" Fenchurch enquired in his gentle voice.

"Free choice?" The Bishop, who had imbibed rather more wine during the evening than is wise in a man of the cloth, gave a scornful laugh. "Most people wouldn't know what to do with free choice if it was handed to them on a platter. Don't you see," he leaned forward and spoke confidentially, "there are two kinds of people in this world—leaders and followers; and most people want to be followers. They *want* to be told what is good for them. That is where the Romans have got the better of us—they tell their people what to do, and their people do it and like it, or else. They don't wish to have the responsibility themselves of deciding what is the right thing."

"I should have thought," said Fenchurch, interpolating a remark primarily in order to break up what was rapidly threatening to become a running monologue, "that the right choice would be obvious."

"Good Lord, no!" replied the Bishop, shocked by this antiquated heresy. "That's like saying it's easy to tell the difference between Good and Evil, whereas everybody nowadays knows that there is such a thing as evil done in a good cause, and good done for the wrong reasons. When you come right down to it, there is no such thing as Absolute Good and Absolute Evil—I daresay even Hitler *meant* well."

This last statement was patently too much for Lord Kaplan and for Professor-Doktor Blumenreich, who had narrowly escaped incarceration in Auschwitz, to stomach; and for the others as well, most of whom (unlike the Bishop, who had spent the war years lecturing on Religion to rich clubwomen in America) had seen active service against the Führer's armies. There was an instant nervous resumption of the general conversation, which the Bishop had for a short time succeeded in monopolising, as an excited gabble led by the deep tones of Dr. Shebbeare broke out to cover, too late, what had already been said.

"I expect," remarked Fenchurch to Sir Richard Rackstraw, seated at his right, in an attempt to change the subject, "that you, as an Old Sheepshankian, are familiar with the origins of Pullets Feast. . . ."

"Ach, but I am not, Mr. Fenchurch," interposed Professor-Doktor Blumenreich, who had been placed on his other side. "Pray elucidate. I find these quaint English customs so whimsical, so *gemütlich*. We have them not in Germany; it is, I feel certain, due to a difference of temperament."

"I must confess," remarked Simon Poxwell, who sat opposite Fenchurch, "that I have never heard the account of how Pullets began. But then I was an undergraduate at Queens', not Sheepshanks."

"It is one of those stories that the College generally prefer to keep under wraps as it tends to diminish the undergraduates' respect for their SCR. At least it used to do so," Fenchurch said rather wistfully. "Nowadays I very much doubt it would make a shred of difference. It is, as so many naughty stories are, a product of the Regency."

By this time dessert had been cleared away and the decanters of port and madeira were in process of circulation. Bottom passed a silver box of snuff and another of cigars (cigarets were not permitted, being too new-fangled for Sheepshanks), and the men near Fenchurch leaned forward in anticipation of the sort of tale that traditionally accompanies port and cigars.

"At the turn of the last century," Fenchurch began, "the College contained a number of young Fellows who, naturally high-spirited, found themselves unduly restricted by the cloistered atmosphere in which they worked and lived. Perhaps fired by the somewhat indelicate friezes on the buildings bequeathed to us by Sir Oliver, their blood ran hot; and so one evening when the Master had gone up to London to attend to some College business, they arranged a dinner which was graced by the presence of some local young ladies who were notable for their—ah—compliance."

By this time the entire table was listening to Fenchurch, and the Bishop, whose application to the port decanter had turned his face almost as red as the cherubs' wings, chortled, "Bully for them!" Noticing the startled and censorious looks cast upon him by the rest of the company, he explained at large, "As Sh—Saint Paul said, 'Oh, Lord, make me chaste, but not yet.'"

Fenchurch hastened on with his account in an attempt to gloss over this unseemly interruption. "The fair guests made their appearance at the appointed hour suitably attired in academic gowns but otherwise completely *au naturel*; and their hosts, I regret to say, carried courtesy rather too far by rapidly following their example."

"Well done!" declared the Bishop. "'When in Rome,' and all that."

"One of the perpetrators, a wealthy man in his later years," Fenchurch continued, studiously ignoring his lordship, "left an endowment in his will (and the remains of a superb wine cellar) for the provision of an annual Feast to commemorate this scandalous event. It is said that the then Master was reluctant to accept the bequest, but the amount designated was such a generous one (and the contents of the wine cellar so commendable) that he was at length persuaded to change his mind."

The absorption of the guests at High Table in this narrative had prevented their heeding a rising commotion in the passage outside the Hall. As Fenchurch concluded his tale, the noise swelled and became recognisably a clatter of footsteps and a shouting voice, overlaid by a crescendo of giggles. The assemblage scarcely had time to wonder what this portended when the doors into Hall were unceremoniously flung open and a remarkable procession erupted into the room to the accompaniment of funereal tolling from the clock in Great Court. In front tittuped a number of comely young women clad in academic dress. Of the fact that they were women there was no possible room left for doubt, since their gowns fluttered open as they ran, revealing that underneath the scholarly attire they were indisputably, even to the imperfect vision of the older dons present, stark naked. Behind this barefaced bevy of beauties trotted a lanky young man with shoulder-length hair and blue jeans, a large video camera perched on his bony shoulder; and rounding up the rear in desperate pursuit heavily galloped Mr. Hobbs, the Sheepshanks Head Porter, like a Shire horse vainly trying to overtake a field of Thoroughbreds.

"'Ere, where do you lot think you're going? You can't enter the College dressed like that! I'll 'ave the pack of you harrested for Hindecent Hexposure, I will," he bellowed in outrage.

The group of ecdysiasts and the cameraman, far swifter than he, paid no attention to his indignant cries but approached High Table, the cameraman photographing the scene as the girls reached the dais and the astonished diners. After a moment of stunned incredulity Dr. Shebbeare prepared to take command of the situation. Before he was able to do more than push back his chair, however, one of the unbidden guests playfully landed in his capacious lap, forcing him to remain seated. "Away, madam! Away, I say!" he panted furiously, not unmindful of the peephole in the Master's Lodge.

The other occupants of the table were frozen in the horror of nightmare—all except the Bishop, who enthusiastically seized a damsel in the scarlet robe and dove-shot sleeves of a Doctor of Divinity about the waist, saying, "An angel! My very own angel! The Bible was right after all. Red as a lobster! Come to me, my lovely seraph."

Several of the other guests philosophically resigned themselves to the seeming inevitability of their fate, the Duke of Northcote and Lord Kaplan among them; while the attitude of the remainder, in their futile struggles to break loose from their temptresses, bore a powerful likeness to Laocoön's attempts to extricate himself from the sinewy toils of the sea-serpent. With commendable promptitude Cyril Lapwing barricaded himself into a corner of the room with a brace of chairs for protection, a look of revulsion on his chiselled features as he viewed the indecorous scene in front of him. Naked women were decidedly not his dish of tea.

The dons meanwhile were endeavoring to free themselves from these unexpected succubi, who had swooped down upon them with coy giggles.

"Cease and desist! Unhand me, madam!" roared the unhappy Master, whose lovely burden had twined her arms about his neck and was sportively nibbling his ear. Fenchurch found himself grappling with a magnificently endowed wench several inches taller than he. Peascod had retreated to the fireplace and was holding a persistent nymph ferociously at bay with a large poker; little Crippen, luckily for himself, had fainted from the shock. Professor Tempeste had crawled under High Table in a desperate search for sanctuary; and Austrey, who had leapt upon the table to escape his unmaidenly pursuer, was looking indecently amused. Of all the Fellows only Grubb was seen to succumb to the blandishments of the fair intruders: a redhead in an M.A. gown looked somewhat taken aback to find herself wrapped in a pythonesque and far from academic embrace.

Sir Richard Rackstraw gazed on this appalling scene with a wild surmise; and inside the Master's Lodge Julia had taken over the peephole by callously thrusting aside the horrified

Mrs. Shebbeare. "What is it?" cried the wives in frantic chorus. "What is it?" Mrs. Shebbeare responded with a groan, and Julia, her eye glued to the aperture, with a burst of unseemly laughter.

"All right, girls, time to be off. I've enough footage," called the cameraman, "and the old geezer's gone out to ring up the law. We'd best hop it."

Instantly the doxies halted their lewd advances in mid-air, gathered their gowns modestly about them, and fled the Hall, led by the man with the camera and pursued by the puffing Hobbs, who had returned as their leader was speaking. A deadly silence fell in the great coffered chamber. Those present stared wildly about them as if they had just wakened from a dream. And indeed they might have persuaded themselves that it all had been a dream, if they had not heard the distant sounds of high heels tripping on the path that crossed Great Court, and a muffled shriek as they died away.

18 The Undoing of Maunders

The night was black as pitch. No moon had yet risen over the courts of Cambridge, and the only light visible was an occasional firefly gleam piercing the stone fabric of Great Court. Fleet of foot, the girl in the scarlet robe who had so enthralled the Bishop of Barstow had outpaced her companions and was first of the pack racing toward Great Gate. It was she whose scream the unnerved group at High Table had heard when she tripped over a huddled object on the path; as she instinctively reached out a hand to keep her balance, she encountered a warm and sticky substance, "Oh, my Gawd!" she exclaimed.

"What is it, Janice?" asked the girl directly behind her.

"It's a man," answered Janice. "I think he's hurt."

"Probably one of the undergrads too pissed to make it back to barracks," said the cameraman unfeelingly. "Let's get on to the van. Make it snappy. We don't want the coppers to pinch us."

"But he was wet where I touched him. Maybe he's injured."

"He's just been sick, that's all. Drunk as a lord, that's

what he is. Or boozy as a bishop." He gave a snicker. "Come *along,* I say."

In a body they raced out of the gate and turned right into Sheepshanks Lane, where they had left the van that had carried them down from London. Everyone piled in, the cameraman taking the driver's seat after quickly stowing away his photographic apparatus. As he swung the van at a fast clip into Bridge Street and on toward the London road, they heard a raucous siren in the distance. "Just in time," the man said with satisfaction. "Not a bad night's work. And damn good pay." An eldritch cry came from Janice, who was sitting next to him in the front seat. "Watch it—you nearly made me have an accident," he said irritably. "What the hell's eating you anyway? You're nervy as a kitten."

Janice stared down at her right hand, which was visible in the light cast by the street lamps as they flashed by. "Christ. It's blood," she whispered. "I've got blood on my hand."

Maunders's body sprawled, ludicrous, pathetic and terrible, in the harsh glare of the hastily erected police lights. Graceless and gangling in life, in death he seemed even clumsier—a motley collection of shabby clothes and scarecrow limbs surmounted by a round foolish face wearing a comical expression of surprise, and incongruously daubed with blood brighter than the red hair that framed it—a discarded puppet from a petit guignol.

Fenchurch mused upon these pitiful emblems of mortality as he waited for Inspector Bunce, who had indicated that he wished to speak privately with the don. On the face of it this was an even more senseless and poignant death than the murder of Ernest Garmoyle, a member of the Sheepshanks SCR, several years earlier. The victim then had been some thirty years older than this boy, who was on the threshold of manhood with most of his life still before him. In point of fact, however, Garmoyle, though cruelly sarcastic and a drunkard, had nonetheless borne the stamp of a brilliant scholar, while this lad seemed at most to have had the makings of a thief, and not a particularly competent thief at that. During a brief interrogation by the police at which Fenchurch had been present no one had had much good to say of Maunders, not even Deacon, who had shared rooms with him; though to his credit the boy had tried—a sad enough epitaph, in all conscience.

The police photographer was finishing up his grisly task. He had been off-duty when the call went in to headquarters, so Bunce had conducted most of the necessary background work before his arrival. It was almost midnight. The Inspector had questioned the distinguished guests at the Feast first, permitting them to depart severally to their hotels or rooms in College afterwards. He had noted with the deep disapproval of a confirmed low-churchman the inebriated condition of the Bishop of Barstow, whose uninhibited consumption of wine had very thoroughly caught up with him by the time of his questioning, rendering him barely coherent and necessitating the aid of Austrey and the College chaplain to assist him, rubber-legged and shambling, to his quarters. There was no question that any of those present at Pullets Feast were involved in Maunders's murder, but their evidence helped to fix the probable time of death, since Hobbs was certain that the body could not have been on the path when he followed the interlopers into Hall.

An hour after the arrival of the police at Sheepshanks, Bunce was gladdened by the news that the van in which the trespassers had fled had been picked up on its way to London, thanks to the sharp eyes and photographic memory of one Catesby, a second-year man who had noticed the vehicle parked in Sheepshanks Lane on his way home from a concert at King's. The Inspector was quite content to leave the culprits cooling their heels while he attended to more pressing matters; serve 'em right for having scarpered, he thought, even though Maunders's body had been discovered only a moment or so later by the pursuing Head Porter.

Most of the Fellows were delighted to receive their *congés* and go home to bed after a most unsettling evening. Only Fenchurch and Professor Tempeste remained to observe the police at their work; Tempeste's wife, long accustomed to the late hours he spent in the laboratory, was driven home by the Austreys. "Nasty, isn't it?" remarked Tempeste to Fenchurch, gazing down with scientific detachment at the gaping wound that had recently been Maunders's throat. It yawned horribly wider as the body was moved to enable the police photographer and the surgeon to continue with their various occupations. "Garmoyle's death was a lot prettier. I daresay the Gate passage will have to be scrubbed down to-morrow and the path sluiced to dispose of all the traces," he went on with distaste, indicating gouts of blood that glistened wetly on the stones like oily patches in the light shed by the police lamps. "'Who would have thought the boy to have had so much blood in him?'" he aptly misquoted. "He must be nearly drained dry," Tempeste continued dispassionately. "Cruor all over the shop. The wonder is that he got as far as he did before collapsing."

"Don't," said Fenchurch with a shudder. He had rather more personal experience of violent death and murder than most men, but he had never seen (nor yet imagined, even for his thriller, *A Friend in Fulborn*) a scene remotely like this one. This was not mere murder, but sheer butchery. Now that Maunders's body had been turned over, his clothes, both jersey and jeans, were revealed as dyed a deep theatrical crimson; only at the edges of the stains was there a brownish crust of drying blood. The pea-jacket he had been wearing, which was flung back to expose the clothing beneath, was too dark to show colour, but under the lights the texture of the wet cloth had an unpleasantly viscous sheen. It was, Fenchurch supposed, partly a result of the heavy dew that so little blood had dried. The wound in Maunders's neck, he noticed with a kind of sick horror, resembled nothing so much as a second mouth, wide and lipless, displaying a rictus that bore a horrid likeness to a grin. *It used,* thought Fenchurch, *to be believed that the wounds in a body would bleed afresh at the presence of the murderer. Surely there is not enough blood left in this poor corpse thus to identify its killer; but if the author of Maunders's slaughter were now to pass by, would the mouth he has so brutally ripped open give tongue and accuse him, shrieking infamy?*

"Well, I'm off to bed," Tempeste announced prosaically. "The night air is beginning to affect my lungs. Besides, there's nothing more of interest to be seen here." The remains of what had been Maunders were in process of being neatly bundled into a large canvas bag by two constables. "Good night, Fenchurch."

"Good night," Fenchurch responded. He wondered what Tempeste would dream about that night; probably, judging by his temperament, of two soft-boiled eggs and a rasher of bacon. Fenchurch decided that he would not attempt sleep: Indeed, he would avoid it. He feared dreams filled with gushing blood—runnels, fountains, oceans of blood; streams of ichor bright and dark, flowing into each other like tributaries to form a giant river. He would hedge himself about with books until dawn—with amusing, diverting, nonsensical books, books into which no hint of death had crept. Yes, that was it; he would read until the rising of the sun and the dispersing of the shadows. But he would not write to dispel the darkness, as he usually did. At the moment Fenchurch felt he could never again write another detective story.

He stood gazing down at the pitiable wreck of a man until Bunce came over, having seen to the disposition of his forces. "If you don't think it too late, sir, I'd like to have a word with you, as I mentioned earlier," the policeman began, then looked at Fenchurch's face. The powerful lamps brought out every crease and furrow, unmercifully revealing his pallor and the bruised smudges beneath his eyes. Fenchurch had an elfin, childlike quality and until now Bunce had not thought of him as old, or even ageing, in spite of his white hair. "Perhaps it'd best wait till tomorrow," he said with sudden compassion; but Fenchurch, to whom the prospect of human companionship during the long night ahead was a life-line better even than books, his more usual comrades, replied eagerly, "I shall be happy to speak with you tonight—unless you have work to do at the police station. We shall have a fire to warm us after our exposure to the night dew, and tea with whisky to drive the chill from our bones."

It was evident that his enthusiasm was genuine, so Bunce, who was inclined to let the pullets wait a bit longer, accepted with pleasure. In any case, once his duties were ended for the night he would be returning to the cold comfort of tea brewed and drunk by himself in a chilly kitchen and, awaiting him in bed, Mrs. Bunce swathed in flannel, anointed with vanishing cream, spiky with hair curlers, and snoring; he had his own reasons for being in no hurry to wind up the evening.

Fenchurch led him up to his rooms where in the sitting-room a snug fire, requiring only the touch of a match, had been laid ready. "I'm afraid you will have to put up with my notion of tea," Fenchurch apologised, bending down to light the fire. "As it is so late all the College servants will have gone home, but I flatter myself I'm rather a hand at it. I always brew my own when I'm on a walking tour. And the whisky, at any rate, should redeem any deficiencies the tea may possess," he added, taking from a cupboard a bottle whose label bore a name hallowed in the annals of whisky-making, a distiller with whom Bunce (who fancied himself something of an authority on whisky) was familiar by repute, but of whose potions he had never had the good fortune to partake.

He gave an involuntary gasp of mingled anticipation and horror. "Surely you're not intending to put *that* in the tea?" he exclaimed before he could stop himself.

"You may take yours in a separate glass if you like," answered Fenchurch, "but I implore you to try it in tea first. It's just what we need, both of us, to set us up; and you may find," he added with a sly glance at the policeman, "that it is not so much a sacrilege as you might think."

To his surprise Bunce found that Fenchurch was right. The whisky, golden and glorious with the mingled tang of smoke and salt air and heather, was not lessened by the addition of tea but rather, like a god who deifies the mortal he lies with, raised it to heights of previously unimagined sublimity.

The two men sat companionably in capacious armchairs beside the hearth in a warmth that derived partly from the fire, partly from the whisky. For a moment neither spoke. Then Bunce enquired, "Who do you think could have done it?"

"At least we know, thank God, who could not have done it," rejoined Fenchurch. "The entire SCR are in the clear. And the guests for the Feast as well."

"The ladies too—the Master's wife vouched for the continual presence of all the guests at her dinner," Bunce said, "at least during the time Maunders could have been murdered. Not that there was much likelihood of any of *them* having done it. Still, in a case like this one we must cover all contingencies. If you don't mind, I'd like to go over the timetable for the Feast with you to make sure I've got it right—the guests, as I understand it, were invited for seven-thirty."

"That is correct. We generally dine at High Table at that time, but on Feast nights dinner is put back half an hour. Sherry was served in the Combination Room at seven-thirty, and we were seated in Hall by eight. It was a rather more leisurely meal than usual, as we had considerably more than the ordinary number of courses, and wines to accompany them."

"You had finished dinner, then, by roughly a quarter past ten?" asked the Inspector, consulting his notebook.

"It was precisely quarter past by the time dessert had been cleared away and the port and madeira decanters put into play; I know the exact time because I glanced at my watch when Bottom set them on the table."

"That's all right so far," said Bunce, scanning his notes, "but I must confess to being somewhat uncertain about the next section of the timetable. Mr. Hobbs said it was around ten-thirty when you had your unexpected invasion, but he couldn't be certain of the exact time. He was too busy chasing the intruders, he said snappishly, to bother looking at clocks."

"The contingent arrived in Hall at ten-thirty on the dot," Fenchurch told him positively.

"How can you be so sure? Did you have occasion to look at your watch again?"

"No; there was no need. As the door to Hall opened and the, er, ladies made their appearance, I heard Old Noll—the clock in Great Court, you know—strike the hour."

"Strike the hour? But you said they arrived at ten-thirty," exclaimed Bunce, perplexed by this aberration. "They couldn't have arrived at ten, seeing as you didn't start the port rolling till ten-fifteen."

"Forgive me for not explaining the situation. Old Noll is a law unto himself; he does not follow the movements laid down for ordinary clocks. But he does have a mad logic of his own: While he rarely tells the time in accordance with common usage, he alters his vagaries only on a Sunday. If one looks on a Sunday to see how early or how late he is and at what time he is striking (for the chime does not often agree with the clock-face), he invariably holds to that scheme until the Sunday following. This week he is forty minutes fast but striking half an hour slow; as tonight is Friday, you will see for yourself in the morning. On Sunday he may strike twelve minutes slow or five hours fast, but tomorrow morning, as tonight, he will infallibly strike a half hour late."

Typical of the place, calling a clock "he," thought Inspector Bunce. "Why doesn't someone fix it?" he asked.

"Repairs were attempted in eighteen twenty-four and again in nineteen-ought-two, but without success. There is a story that the clock ran perfectly until the hour of Sir Oliver's death—Oliver Sheepshanks, you know, the latest Benefactor of the College—but ever since has pursued its eccentric course. The clock was modelled after Sir Oliver's favourite elephant, which was used to carry him in its trunk," Fenchurch added, as if that explained it all.

"At any rate, it's pretty certain the filming lot arrived at ten-thirty," said Bunce, making a mental note to check the extent of the clock's departure from accuracy in the morning, "and fairly sure as well that Maunders couldn't have been on the path then, or they would have tripped over him—that is, providing they stayed on the path that time too. It's a pity Mr. Hobbs didn't return to the Porter's Lodge to ring the police instead of going to the Kitchens—then we should have it pinned down even closer."

"It was exceedingly dark, I understand; even if they all took the path on their way into Hall, mightn't Maunders have been elsewhere in Great Court without anyone noticing?"

"The Porter states definitely that he had not seen Maunders in Great Court for several hours—he would have been sure to notice him since Maunders had been gated. As all the other entrances into College except Great Gate were secured as usual at ten, Maunders must have re-entered whilst Hobbs was chasing the intruders, otherwise he would have seen the lad. The surgeon's findings make it plain that Maunders couldn't have reached Great Court before ten—with that wound he couldn't possibly have lasted more than a few minutes on his feet, let alone half an hour. Dr. Scarlett said it was surprising the poor kid made it as far as he did."

"And you believe that the attack on Maunders must have been made in All Saints Passage?" queried Fenchurch.

"No doubt about it. We've found traces of blood there that lead to Sheepshanks Great Gate."

All Saints Passage runs from St. John's and Sheepshanks Streets (the one becomes the other in the offhand way Cambridge streets have of changing nomenclature every hundred yards or so) over to Bridge Street. At the Bridge Street end it is a single alley, but toward St. John's and Sheepshanks Streets the passage branches into two paths with a wedge of ground separating them, so that the whole resembles a Y laid on its side.

"The blood begins at the Bridge Street end. He would have started spouting the stuff directly, poor bastard! so his assailant must have attacked him there. Nice quiet place at that time of night—the shops are closed, of course, and there's only occasional foot-traffic: people walking from Bridge Street and Jesus Lane over to the Colleges or the Woolsack. And the surgeon says the attack would only have taken a few seconds at most. It was a hellishly sharp blade."

Fenchurch shuddered. "Can he tell what sort of weapon was used?"

"Dr. Scarlett said only that whatever it was was sharp as a razor. He'll know more after the post mortem. And that's about it," said Bunce. "It's too late tonight to begin to hunt for a motive—we'd best go to work on that tomorrow. With your leave I'd like to have you with me when I have more of a talk with Deacon in the morning."

"I should be happy to be present," Fenchurch responded, pleased that Bunce wanted his assistance. Another murder in College was decidedly distressing, and this was a peculiarly horrible one; still, he could not repress a shiver of anticipation, like an old war-horse that scents gunpowder on the breeze. Fenchurch had the grace to be ashamed of himself but at least, he thought in partial self-extenuation, this time the SCR were not involved.

"I reckon it's time to stir my stumps and let you go off to bed," the Inspector remarked. But he showed no immediate disposition to leave the deep-cushioned chair and flickering fire, and he made only a token show of resistance when his host topped up his tea-cup with a dollop of the legendary whisky. After performing this hospitable duty Fenchurch took up a poker and stirred the dying coals into a momentary brightness, gazing intently at them like a seer searching out portents. He set down the poker and asked abruptly, "What is it like to be married?" then blushed profoundly, astounded by his own temerity. The question had unintentionally popped out. It was a question which until recently had held only a theoretical interest for him; for most of his life Fenchurch had been quite content with his comfortable bachelor existence in College, his books, his scholarship, and his writings—both scholarly and profane. But now he felt he had to know; and despite the disparity in rank and occupation, he felt an affinity with Bunce. It was easier, Fenchurch felt, to ask the policeman than to enquire of any of his fellow dons, except perhaps Austrey.

Bunce managed to conceal his surprise at this unexpected query.

"Is it cosy?" Fenchurch asked wistfully. "I do not ask for a frivolous reason. I hope I am not being unduly inquisitive, but you see . . ." His voice trailed off. "One feels lonely at times. One used to feel quite self-sufficient, but now . . ."

Bunce meditated. Obscurely he sensed that his reply held a vast significance for Fenchurch. "Cosy?" It was not a word that applied to his marriage. Kathleen Bunce did not seem greatly interested in what her husband felt or thought: There was no real closeness between them. So far as he could tell, after a marriage of nearly forty years, her mind only skimmed the surface of things. She cared chiefly about appearances and the proprieties, and was more concerned with her clothes and the condition of her house than with her husband. He replied cautiously, "It depends on the marriage." Fenchurch's face fell.

His weariness, the lateness of the hour, and the generous amount of whisky in his refilled cup, in combination with a wish to be honest with his friend, caused Bunce to elaborate on his statement, though he had never before spoken of his marriage to anyone. "Mine, for instance," he continued, "is pretty much routine—what you might call run by rote. But that's not altogether a bad thing, you understand," he added hastily, as much to himself as to Fenchurch. "It counter-balances my job, gives me a sense of stability." Even to himself Bunce sounded as if he were quoting from a psychiatrist's article on successful marriage in one of the women's maga-zines that formed his wife's principal reading-matter. The well-worn phrases rang hollow as if he were trying, not al-together successfully, to convince himself of the desirability of his situation.

"Oh," said Fenchurch doubtfully; hymeneal bliss as deline-ated by Bunce did not sound altogether appealing. But then Austrey with his radiant wife, Helen, Fenchurch thought, might have described the matrimonial state quite differently.

"Cosy? My parents' marriage was cosy, now I think on it," the Inspector continued. "I remember when my dad had closed up shop (the butcher's in Silver Street; we lived on the first floor), he'd have a romp with us kids as soon as he'd changed his clothes. And then afterwards he'd read the eve-ning paper with my mum sitting on his lap—they used to quarrel, joking-like, about when it was time to turn the page. As my sisters and me grew a bit older we were embar-rassed about that—her sitting in his lap, I mean, as if they were our age and courting—it wasn't dignified. But my mother just laughed at us and said, 'who'd have thought I'd have raised such a nest of young prigs? It's more fitting,' she told me, 'that I should sit on your dad's lap than that young vixen Nancy should sit on yours. Don't think'—wagging her finger and putting on the stern look that always meant she were teasing, like, 'don't you think I didn't see your shenanigans when you was out on the river the other day. And here you are complaining about a respectable old married couple!' They shared the same bed until the day Dad died. Yes, you could call that a cosy marriage, if you like. . . . Of course, Kathleen and I have no children," Bunce added in extenuation. "I daresay that makes a bit of a difference." He took another swallow of his tea and stared into the fire. ". . . I wonder whatever became of Nancy?"

Fenchurch could think of no suitable response to these remarks; sympathy for Bunce overwhelmed him and kept him silent. But it would not be like Bunce and his Kathleen, he told himself fiercely; it would be like Bunce's parents, warm and happy and loving. If only she would marry him he would make it so; and she—how could anything connected with her be otherwise? He knew it was all a pipe dream. He was far too old for her, he reminded himself, and yet there was Professor Heseltine, whose wife was half his age, and she seemed contented enough.

Bunce's voice broke in on his thoughts. "Sorry to have gone on so long. But I had a happy childhood, all in all, and the recollection of it is a pleasant task. It quite took my mind off murder. I must be off now and interview those young reprobates at the station. Would nine o'clock be too early for me to show up tomorrow?"

"Come to breakfast at eight, my dear fellow. We can discuss motive then, and go over afterwards to have a chat with young Deacon." Fenchurch hesitated, and then said shyly. "I suppose you don't want me to come along with you now?" Though he dreaded to face the instruments of his recent humiliation, he was anxious (for the sake of his College, he told himself) to find out all he could about Maunders's murder.

"Nothing 'ud please me more," Bunce told him heartily. "I'd have mentioned it before, only I thought it 'ud be asking too much. You're sure you don't mind?"

Fenchurch shook his head.

"Let's be off then, and have at those scamps," said the Inspector.

"I keep telling you," the cameraman, whose name was Peter Pence, reiterated peevishly. "I don't know a bleeding thing about it. Janice just happened to stumble over the poor bugger on our way out, and none of us had a glimmer there was anything more the matter with him than a skinful." He glared with manifest dislike at the unfortunate Janice. It was two in the morning, and he and the erstwhile pullets were sitting morosely in the Cambridge police station on Parker's Piece under bleak fluorescent lighting that made the exhausted faces beneath look the colour of uncooked veal.

"Why didn't you turn back when Miss Parkins told you she had blood on her hand?" demanded Bunce sternly.

"Look," Peter Pence explained in the patient voice used when speaking to a mentally deficient child, "I had a schedule to keep. Ms. Harlowe wants this programme ready to fly by next Thursday at the latest"—upon hearing this Fenchurch gave an involuntary *frisson*—"and I didn't see what earthly good we could do by coming back to Cambridge. Someone was bound to find the poor bastard any minute—probably had by the time Janice noticed her hand was bloody."

"Your business arrangements are no excuse for ignoring murder. It's your public duty to notify the police directly you find a crime has been committed." Bunce's normally good-natured features were unwontedly severe. "I ought to lock up the lot of you for obstructing a murder investigation, and for malicious trespass as well."

"Aw, come on now, Inspector," pleaded Peter Pence, seriously alarmed by this potential interruption to his schedule. "Why can't you let bygones be bygones? We're here now, and we've done everything we can to help."

"You're only here because one of the Sheepshanks undergraduates was sharp enough to spot the number on your licence plate," grumbled Bunce. He was still put out with himself for having lost a contest of wills with Julia who, in order to enable the filming crew to escape with the precious footage, had disclaimed knowledge of any but the most rudimentary aspects of her scheme.

"But we had no idea it was murder," Peter Pence protested. "We just thought the kid had been boozing and hit his head on a stone or something. Give us a break, Inspector. Who'd expect a murder in a place like Sheepshanks?"

Judging by Bunce's previous experience, Sheepshanks was one of the more likely venues for a murder, but he saw no point in mentioning this fact to Peter Pence. "I want to know exactly what all of you saw," he told them, "both on the way into Hall, and after you left." Moodily he surveyed the group before him. The girls had discarded their academic disguises and scrambled into street clothes while travelling in the van. If their previous dishabille had left any doubt in the matter, their own garments unquestionably proclaimed them tarts—tarts, moreover, of not the highest order. In addition, their necessarily hasty toilettes had left them with dishevelled hair and crumpled dresses, a condition which gave them the raffish appearance of having been recently bed-tumbled.

"If you coöperate, I shan't enquire too deeply into the regular—or should I say irregular—profession of you young ladies." Bunce's customary good humour was somewhat restored by this mild witticism, and he smiled more benignly upon the chastened group before him.

"We didn't see a thing," volunteered Janice. "Not while we were outside. We couldn't; the place was black as a coal-hole. Peter was grousing because he hadn't thought to bring a torch. There were some lighted windows, but they were no help."

"Couldn't you tell there was an obstruction on the walk?" Bunce asked.

"Not till I tripped over it—that's why I didn't go around. Even after I fell and knew something was there, I could only just see what it was."

"Did any of the rest of you actually see the body?" Bunce enquired of the rest of the vanload. But no one had; upon hearing Janice's cry they had simply avoided the path and run around the obstacle onto the sacrosanct grass that only the feet of dons are normally permitted to tread.

"How did you keep to the path before Miss Parkins stumbled, if it was so dark that you could literally see nothing?" demanded Fenchurch suddenly. "And why did you not just walk across on the grass? Though it is against our rules, one would scarcely expect that you would heed such an interdiction in the circumstances; even assuming that you were aware of it."

These questions stumped them briefly, but at length Janice was able to come up with a reasonable explanation for one of them. "The path is the shortest way across," she offered, "and I sank into the lawn because I was wearing high heels." She stuck out a foot clad in black rhinestone-sprinkled tights and a grimy red satin shoe perched on a tall, needle-like heel as confirmation of this fact. "So once I found the walk I stayed with it. That's why I took it both times."

"That's right," confirmed Pence. "If you want to get across the quad fast—"

"Court," corrected Fenchurch automatically.

"—it's the quickest route. If you take a shortcut across to the Hall from the main entrance gate, you just naturally land on that path. I could feel the stones under my feet, though I don't recall seeing it. I didn't have to, as I was following the girls."

"How could you make it out, since you say you weren't able to see anything else in the court?" Bunce repeated Fenchurch's question to Janice.

"It's paved with stones that showed a little paler in the grass," she explained. "They kind of, sort of, gleamed in the dark. Not much, but enough so I could follow them."

"Then since you could tell the difference between the walk and the grasss," the Inspector continued, "why didn't you notice the darker mass of Maunders's body on the path?"

The girl mulled this over, twisting a lock of peroxided hair around her finger. "I guess I wasn't looking at the ground just then," she replied at length. "There was a light in the street showing where we'd entered, and I was headed that way as fast as my legs'd carry me. We knew the rozzers was on the way—oops! No offence intended, I'm sure," she added cheekily.

This answer seemed to satisfy Bunce and he went on to the next point. "Which of you was in front the first time, when you were on your way into Hall?"

"Janice was first then, too; I was next behind her," offered the plump Amazonian brunette who had assaulted Fenchurch during Pullets Feast.

"I was the fastest sprinter in my school," Janice interpolated proudly.

"Is there any possibility that Maunders's body could have been on the path during the first occasion of your crossing Great Court?" Fenchurch enquired, blushing as he addressed his recent nemesis.

"No," both girls chorused together.

"One of us'd have been bound to trip over it—him—if he had been," the brunette explained.

"He was sprawled across the way. Not a chance of missing the bloke once he was there," corroborated Janice.

"You're absolutely certain you took the path the first time?" asked the Inspector. They nodded vigorously.

These answers concurred with the ones elicited during Bunce's interrogation of the Head Porter, who had been un-shakeable in his conviction that Maunders could not have been lying on the walk during his initial pursuit of the pullets.

"One final question, and then I shall let you all go . . . for the moment, at least," Bunce added dampingly as their eyes brightened. "You may be called back at any time for further questioning. Did any of you spot anyone or anything else in Great Court, no matter how small, either on your way in or out?"

The girls and Pence shook their heads. It had been too dark to see, and as for hearing—between Hobbs's shouts and the noise they themselves had produced—none of them had had ears for any other sound.

"Then off you go," said Bunce.

"What about my camera?" Peter Pence demanded. "I want it back."

"Your camera will be returned to you, but for the time being we shall keep the exposed film." Upon hearing this pronouncement Pence uttered an inarticulate cry of rage and Fenchurch a heartfelt sigh of relief. "As you began filming in the passage on the way into Hall there is just a chance that the film may have registered something useful to us. We shall have to hold it as evidence until it has been examined."

Fenchurch turned pink at the thought of the film being viewed, even by the police.

"What are you lot in training for—the Gestapo? I'd better get it back pretty quickly, film and all; and in first-class condition. Otherwise there'll be trouble," Peter Pence said angrily.

"Let's have a little less lip from you, my lad," retorted Bunce. "Considering the sort of passengers you've been hauling about lately, I could have you up for procuring if I liked."

This threat had the desired effect of silencing Pence, and he sullenly took his leave of the police, gathering his bedraggled flock of soiled lambs about him. Janice was still shaken by the discovery of Maunders's blood on her hands but the rest of the tarts, now that they had escaped a booking, clearly considered the episode something of a lark. Much to Fenchurch's embarrassment his erstwhile brunette blew him an airy kiss, and the ash-blonde who had rendered Dr. Shebbeare *hors de combat* gave Bunce a lascivious wink as the chattering band swept past on their way out of the police station.

After Inspector Bunce dropped Fenchurch off at Sheepshanks on his way home to Balmoral Cottage, the don found that it was unnecessary after all for him to resort to his library in order to obliterate his last sight of Maunders. Instead he composed himself into a peaceful and genial slumber by imagining himself improbably but blissfully married to his loving and beloved Vivien.

19 Fenchurch Amoroso

In the morning both Bunce and Fenchurch were refreshed and ready for the task ahead, despite their lack of sleep. Fenchurch had been restored by the sweetness of his dreaming in the few hours that had remained of the night; and the Inspector, with even less rest under his belt, was revivified by the hearty breakfast served them by Fenchurch's gyp. Since Mrs. Bunce rarely arose in time to prepare a cooked breakfast for her husband, his usual fare was cold cereal, laid out the night before, and tinned orange juice that tasted as metallic as its container. The tea at least was always hot, and strong enough to hold a teaspoon upright, since Bunce brewed it himself.

The breakfast provided by Fenchurch, on the other hand, was breakfast as it was meant to be, Bunce thought as he gratefully tucked into it—fresh grapefruit, fried eggs accompanied by fat sausages and hot toast, a glorious plate of kippers, four kinds of jam and three of marmalade to choose from, and the tea every bit as good as Bunce's own.

"I always find it best," Fenchurch suggested, starting on his grapefruit, "to think whilst I am eating breakfast, and talk afterwards. Otherwise the eggs grow cold."

Bunce found this a sensible plan, and the two men consumed their meal in silence. It was not until Fenchurch had poured out a second cup of tea (a matutinal version, lacking whisky, Bunce noted with a trace of regret) that discussion began.

"I have been considering motive," the don remarked, "and I suspect we shall find that the answer does not lie in College."

"Oh?" Bunce replied dubiously. He was a great admirer of Fenchurch's abilities, but he could not avoid the thought that it would be far from displeasing for Sheepshanks if the murderer were to be found outside its confines; and that Fenchurch bore an intense loyalty to his College there was no possible room for doubt.

"You are quite right to wonder if my judgment may be clouded by wishful thinking," Fenchurch returned, interpreting the Inspector's monosyllable more accurately than Bunce had intended, "but it is more a matter of common sense than of my own inclinations. Since the entire SCR are out of the affair, thanks to our joint alibi, only the undergraduates, research students and College servants are left as suspects within the bounds of Sheepshanks. So far as I can make out Maunders was cordially disliked, where he was not ignored, by most of them; but dislike, thank Heaven, is not sufficient reason for committing murder. If it were, no doubt half the members of the University would be lying lifeless, slain by the other half. Note that I have said that the *answer* does not lie in Sheepshanks. It is barely possible that the murderer himself may, though I tend to think not. My point is that I suspect the motive will prove to have no direct connection with the College. In brief, unless we find an unexpected trail leading in another direction, I think the lad may have been killed as a result of his theft of the *Anelida*."

"But if Maunders stole the *Anelida*," Bunce objected, "why would anyone bother to kill him? If someone found out he had the book, he could take it from Maunders with impunity and count on the boy keeping his mouth shut to save his own skin, for if he didn't, he'd be bound to go to gaol too."

"Perhaps they were in collusion and Maunders was killed by his partner to avoid splitting the money. Or perhaps someone took the *Anelida* from Maunders, as you say. I do not agree with your conclusion that he would rely on Maunders's fear of going to prison to keep him quiet. Revenge can be a powerful inducement to action, sometimes more powerful even than self-interest. . . . Yes, I am inclined to think that Maunders stole the *Anelida* and was killed as a result. Other motives may crop up during our investigation of his background, but none, I feel, will prove as convincing."

"I still think Maunders wouldn't have made himself so conspicuous if he had taken the *Anelida*," Bunce said stubbornly.

"That could have been a clever means of protective camouflage. I must confess that when we discovered he had stolen the Loggan and Ackermann prints I felt he was not up to more grandiose crimes, and that relatively petty larceny was his métier," responded Fenchurch. "However, as you know, I have since revised my opinion. He has displayed a previous proclivity for thievery and it is highly probable that, given the opportunity, he would begin to expand his scope. No, I have little doubt that it was he who took the *Anelida,* and an accomplice who killed him, intending to keep the prize for himself. But I have good reason to suppose that Maunders's confederate is not at Sheepshanks. Since the Senior Common Room had confined him to College for stealing the engravings, surely Maunders would not have chanced further punishment by going out-of-bounds to meet another member of College when he could easily have met him here without risk of chastisement."

"I'm afraid I disagree with your conclusions," said Bunce. Since their conversation of the previous night he felt on a footing with Fenchurch that permitted bluntness. "I think your concern for your College may be misleading you, Mr. Fenchurch. To begin with, I'm not convinced that Maunders was responsible for the disappearance of the *Anelida*. Maybe his murder had nothing to do with the UL theft. And even if it had, his killer could still be from Sheepshanks—maybe he invented some logical pretext for meeting Maunders out of College in order to divert suspicion from himself. Anyway, it's early days yet," he added pacifically. "Let's wait to see what comes of nosing about in Maunders's background."

Fenchurch pondered this speech. "You may be right," he conceded with a sigh. "I must confess that I should be very sorry if Maunders's murderer were found to be connected in any way to Sheepshanks; it is sufficiently disagreeable that a member of College has met such a violent end within our precincts. Perhaps I am allowing my natural loyalties to lead me astray. But," he went on obstinately, "until a more credible motive surfaces, I think he was killed for the *Anelida,* and I hope you will keep the possibility in mind. . . . Will you have more tea? No? Then I think it is time for us to pay a visit to Deacon."

They left Fenchurch's rooms and walked through the Screens, the passage leading from Great Court past the Hall into Paul's Court, that part of the College which lies nearest the river. The staircase which housed Deacon and Maunders was situated on the near side to Great Court; they had only to turn right as they left the Screens. Fenchurch led the Inspector up two flights of worn stone steps and knocked on a door which opened off the second landing. The short cheerful-looking youth with merry eyes who opened it to them seemed startled by the sight of Fenchurch in company with Inspector Bunce, whom he had encountered in his official capacity the night before, but he readily invited them in. The room they entered was sparsely furnished with two battered desks, a number of unmatched straight chairs and a lumpy old sofa. Deacon gestured hospitably toward the sofa,

the most luxurious accommodation available; Bunce, however, chose one of the chairs to sit on as holding fewer
surprises.

"You met Inspector Bunce last night, I believe," said
Fenchurch to the boy. "I trust you will assist him by telling
him everything you know about poor Maunders."

"Of course I'll be happy to help out in any way I can, sir,"
Deacon said to Bunce. "But I told you most of what I know
last night. I didn't know Bob at all well, as it happened. It's
a terrible thing, isn't it? I still can't quite believe it; what a
shock it will be for his people."

"Do you know much about them?" asked Bunce. "According to the College records his mother is dead. His father has
been notified and is on his way to Cambridge now, I understand."

"He's from Liverpool and has—had—a couple of younger
sisters. He was fond of his mother, I think, but he hadn't
much time for his father, judging by the little he said about
him. I'm afraid that's all I can tell you about his family; I
haven't met any of them. Bob and I didn't see much of each
other. We didn't hit it off, you see, and we hadn't many
friends in common. We didn't fight; we just weren't especially matey."

"Who were his friends?" Bunce enquired.

Deacon considered the question, his brow wrinkled with
effort. "Actually, he hadn't got any that I know of. Except
Mr. Grubb—Bob used to go see him sometimes. He kept
pretty much to himself. He went to the UL a lot—wait,
there was a girl, I think: Letty . . . Letty something. She
works in one of the local bookshops: Bowes & Bowes. Or was
it Heffers?"

"Do you recall her surname?"

"Letty . . . Letty . . . I'm afraid I can't help you there. If
I think of it I'll let you know." Deacon was patently eager to

be of assistance and clearly sorry that he had so little to offer them.

The next step was to look through Maunders's few possessions. It did not take long. They found nothing of interest except a key in a shabby tin box which he had kept locked and hidden under a pile of well-worn underclothes; the box's padlock key had been on a chain around his neck and luckily Bunce had brought it along.

"Do you know what this is for?" Bunce asked Deacon when he had extracted the key from its hiding place. It was the only object in the box, aside from a couple of pounds in small change; apparently Maunders had not been the sort to trust his roommate.

The boy shook his head. "I've never seen it before. It looks like a locker key," he said in a tentative voice.

"Good lad," the Inspector told him approvingly. "You've got eyes in your head. That's what it is, all right. See, there's a number cut into the head. Where would Maunders be likely to keep a locker?"

"I haven't the foggiest," Deacon responded. "There aren't any lockers in College, are there, Mr. Fenchurch? And the UL hasn't got them either. Parcels are left with the porters at a desk in the hall as you go in."

"What about a locker at one of the athletic grounds?" Bunce asked.

"Bob didn't take part in sports. He said he hadn't time to waste on insignificant pastimes, but I think the real reason was because he wasn't very good at them."

"I'd be willing to lay odds then that this key is from a locker in a railway station," Bunce declared, "or an airport. He probably stashed some of his loot from the Sheepshanks Library there."

Deacon's plump face took on a look of surprise; he had

known about Maunders's gating but the reason for it had been kept quiet.

"Perhaps he managed to smuggle the *Anelida* out of the UL after all, and has hid it there for safekeeping," Fenchurch offered excitedly. Here was potential proof of his theory, in which case Sheepshanks might emerge from disaster relatively unscathed.

Bunce revolved this possibility over in his mind. "It could be," he admitted. "I'd best have a look at the Cambridge railway station first, then we shall try our luck in London if we have none here. I'll see to it as soon as I leave." Carefully he placed the locker key in his wallet. "Thank you for your help, Mr. Deacon. If you should happen to recollect anything else that might be useful—the surname of Maunders's young woman, for instance—you'll be sure to let us know at once, won't you?"

"Right away, Inspector," promised Deacon. "I hope to God you catch the bastard that did it soon. I saw Bob—what was left of him—last night before the police arrived, when I was coming back from a bit of a pub crawl with friends. I don't like to think that whoever did something like that is still wandering loose in Cambridge."

The two men left Maunders's late rooms, and Fenchurch walked with Bunce as a matter of courtesy to Great Gate. As they crossed the court, the Inspector paused to check Old Noll. Fenchurch's description of the clock's vagaries proved accurate: As Bunce checked the time on the clock face against his wristwatch, which declared the correct time to be nine-thirty precisely, Old Noll struck the hour of nine with a brazen flourish.

Don and policeman parted company at the Sheepshanks entrance. Bunce was keen on exploring the possibilities of the Cambridge railway station; he had invited Fenchurch to join the search for Maunders's supposed locker, but because of a supervision the don had arranged for ten o'clock, he was forced to forego this pleasure. The disappointment Fenchurch would normally have felt at missing what might well prove to be the recovery of the *Anelida* was assuaged by the fact that Vivien Murray was to make one of his architectural walking-tour party that afternoon. He tentatively planned (greatly daring!) to invite her to take tea in his rooms afterwards, and he was filled with trepidation as to whether or not she would accept. Though fully conscious of his prowess as a scholar, Fenchurch's estimate of himself as a potential suitor was realistically humble. Even had he been younger and more prepossessing in appearance, or she older and less captivating than she was, he still would have undervalued his chances. As it was, he hardly dared to approach her even in the most innocent and avuncular fashion.

Since the research student Fenchurch was supervising that morning happened to be one of his less rewarding pupils, the older man was hard put to it to conceal his impatience to be elsewhere; yet outwardly he managed to remain his usual affable and courteous self. After the supervision he concocted a hasty sandwich from the contents of his larder rather than suffer the conversation of his peers at luncheon in Hall, and arrived ten minutes early in the courtyard in front of Great Gate where the students were to assemble, in the hope that Vivien too might be ahead of time. In this he was disappointed, for though she was several minutes early, so were a number of others, and Fenchurch was baulked in his design of extending the invitation to tea before they set off. If the lecturer was somewhat distracted during the walk, his disciples were so engrossed by what he showed them that they did not notice.

It was not until his charges had dispersed in Sheepshanks Chapel to inspect the lofty interior that, with its foliate columns carved in mimicry of tree trunks, resembled nothing so much as a petrified Druidical forest, that Fenchurch was able to speak to Vivien without being overheard by the others.

"Perhaps, Miss Murray," he ventured timidly, "you would honour me by joining me for tea at Sheepshanks after our walk?"

Briefly Vivien hesitated. She still recalled all too vividly the results of Poxwell's not dissimilar invitation; and while she did not particularly mind being disillusioned by Poxwell, she felt that she would hate to find herself deceived in Fenchurch's character. But then Mr. Fenchurch, Vivien reflected, was a very different sort of person to Poxwell; and she chided herself that she was becoming reprehensibly vain, thus to espy a seducer under every bush. "It's very kind of you. I should be delighted to come," she replied, bestowing a bewitching smile upon him.

The remembrance of such a smile, Fenchurch felt, would keep him warm on many a cold and lonely night; and to top it off, she was actually coming to tea! It had required several of his walking-lectures for him to nerve himself to invite her, and even then he had been miserably certain she would refuse; but she was coming, she was coming! During his lecture on the Chapel, which he delivered with even more than his customary flair, Fenchurch kept a covert scrutiny on Vivien to assure himself that she was still there. So it was a shock when, somewhat later upon the walk, as they left King's Chapel (a pale imitation, Fenchurch has always maintained, of the chapel at Sheepshanks) and continued toward Trumpington Street, he discovered that she had left the group without his noticing; and a relief to find, at the entrance to Peterhouse, that she had rejoined the other students. She was carrying, Fenchurch noted with the percipient eye of love, a small parcel which seemed to explain her momentary absence, for she had not had it when starting out.

At last the walking tour drew to a close, its preceptor having somewhat abbreviated his habitual route. The band of students dispersed, chattering, to seek refreshment; and Fenchurch led his guest up to his rooms, stopping at the

Porter's Lodge *en passant* to request that tea be fetched. The tea-tray made its appearance shortly after he had shown Vivien into his sitting-room and taken her coat. The gyp, having disposed his burden on a low table in front of the fireplace, laid a fire and lighted it while Vivien was seated solicitously by her host in the best chair. Upon the servant's departure Fenchurch poured tea, offering his guest a plate of cakes and sandwiches as he handed her her cup.

"It's frightfully sweet of you to invite me," said Vivien, choosing a salmon sandwich and a pink-iced cake. She was wearing a bright blue silk blouse the Aegean shade of her eyes, and the sharp November wind had coaxed a wild-rose flush into her cheeks. Fenchurch thought that never in his life had he seen anything lovelier, not even his beloved Sheepshanks Chapel. "I can't tell you how much I'm enjoying your lectures—they're absolutely riveting; and fond though I am of the old boys, it's super to have a respite and get out in the open for a change."

"The old boys?" Fenchurch asked her, startled. For one dreadful moment he had imagined she might be referring to him.

"Donne and Friends—I do adore them, but they can be fearfully intense. I find I need a breather every now and again."

"Donne has always been one of my favourite poets," confessed Fenchurch. He reddened as some of the poet's racier subject matter came unbidden to mind. "Particularly his sacred poetry," he amended mendaciously. "And Crashaw," he added, to verify his addiction to religious poetry, though Crashaw left him cold. "I have always been fond of his poem on Mary Magdalene. '. . . Stars thou sow'st, whose harvest dares/Promise the earth to counter shine/Whatever makes heaven's forehead fine.'" They were pretty ghastly, but they were the only lines he could think of offhand that Crashaw had written. "Will you have another cake?" He proffered the plate with its prettily iced cakes and thinly cut sandwiches decorated with sprigs of small cress.

"Yes, thank you," said Vivien, taking a cake with pale green icing. "They're delicious, even better than Fitzbillies. Oh! that reminds me." She handed him the parcel which had occasioned her brief absence during their walk and Fenchurch unwrapped it to disclose a box of Fitzbillies chocolates. Like a well-brought-up child, she had brought him a thank-you present.

"How very kind," he said, enchanted by her gesture. He made a ceremony of opening the box and peering inside. "They look splendid. Will you have one?" He held out the box.

"No, thank you. They're meant for you. I hope you like chocolates."

"They are one of my greatest passions." Fenchurch happened to have a craving for chocolates but even if he had detested them, he would have lied valiantly to please her. "Thank you. I shall enjoy them very much indeed. . . . And how are you liking Clare?" He refilled their cups as he spoke.

"I'm finding it quite delightful. Cambridge is a charming place and surprisingly unlike Oxford. Though I'm not denigrating Oxford, you understand. It certainly has its points: the Bodley versus the UL, for example."

"I quite agree; there is much to be said for both Universities. So you were at Oxford as an undergraduate?" He was avid for any scrap of information he could glean about her.

"Yes, I was at Somerville. I'm not sorry, though, that I chose Cambridge for my graduate work." Delicate colour rose to her face and made her more entrancing than ever as she recollected that otherwise she might not have met Harry.

"And where are your people?"

"My grandparents live in Sussex. My parents were killed in a car crash when I was small. Actually, I'm American." At his look of surprise she amended, "Only half American, though I hold a U.S. passport. My mother was English, and I came to live with her parents when my own died, since my father had no close connections."

"How terrible for you."

"My grandparents have been marvellous, and I can hardly remember my parents. I suppose," she said, politely bringing the subject around to her host, "that you must be from this part of the country, judging by your surname."

"Very observant of you, my dear; yes, my people come from near Ely, and the family have been associated with the University for quite some time. Perhaps that is why I have such an attachment to the stones of Cambridge."

"It's a fondness you impart in your lectures. I've come to feel a strong affection for this old city in a very short time. I liked Cambridge as soon as I saw it, but now I feel that I'm growing to understand it; and understanding leads to affection, don't you think?"

"To some extent," Fenchurch replied cautiously, for he hardly knew her, he had not begun to understand the workings of her mind; and yet he knew that he loved her. "I am very glad that I have been able to enlighten you on some aspects of the city and University." *What a pedantic old fool I must sound,* he thought desolately. There was so much he wanted to say to her, but he knew he must not. Not now, perhaps never.

What a kind little man he is, thought Vivien, *what a comfortable sort of person to be around.* Instinctively she trusted him. If only she knew him better, he was the kind of person she could talk to about Harry. She was longing to talk to someone about Harry, but as yet she had no close friends in Cambridge and somehow it was not the sort of thing one cared to discuss over the telephone, even with one's intimates. She set down her tea-cup and Fenchurch, who feared her action was a preliminary to her departure, cast about him for some way to keep her there with him a little longer.

"Are you by any chance fond of detective novels?" he asked rather wildly as his eye fell on a rank of his own pseudonymous works.

"I adore them. A low taste, but madly diverting. I've gone through most of the Oxford mysteries, of course—*Gaudy Night* and *A Landscape with Dead Dons* are my favourites—but I haven't come across any that are set in Cambridge. Except that one of P. D. James's, and it doesn't *feel* like Cambridge."

"Then," said Fenchurch, "you have not yet made the acquaintance of Geoffrey Saltmarsh. Most of his books take place in or about Cambridge."

"Saltmarsh? No—no, I'm sure I haven't. I should have remembered the name; it's rather like yours. Does he come from this part of the country too? How silly of me; I suppose he must, or he wouldn't set his books in this area."

Fenchurch's colour rose to his ears as he confessed, "Actually, *I* am Geoffrey Saltmarsh. That is to say, I write his books."

"How clever of you!" Vivien told him admiringly. "How do you manage it? It must be horribly difficult."

"Not in the least; if it were I am afraid that I should not be able to write them," Fenchurch replied modestly, though inwardly he was glowing under her praise. "Would you like to have one?"

"Yes, please," Vivien said with enthusiasm. "I'll read it at once and return it to you in a few days."

"No need for that. If you would like to keep it, it will be a present." Fenchurch opened the cupboard where he kept the spare copies his publisher sent him and extracted *A Killer at King's*; inscribing the flyleaf in his precise scholar's hand, he presented the volume to her. "By the way, very few people know I am Geoffrey Saltmarsh, so I should be grateful if you wouldn't mention it to anyone." It gave him great pleasure to know she was the recipient of his secret.

"I shan't breathe a word," Vivien gravely promised, flattered that he had taken her into his confidence. "Thank you—I can't wait to read it." She rose to leave.

"I hope you will come again soon," said Fenchurch, helping her into her coat. "To tea, I mean. And in the spring I take walking tours into the countryside around Cambridge; perhaps you would care to join us."

"I should love to." Vivien took his hand to say goodbye, and to his own astonishment the close proximity of her bonny face made Fenchurch say, "May I give you a farewell kiss, my dear? If I had a daughter I should like her to resemble you." His own face burned with the consciousness of falsehood, but Vivien did not appear to notice. Nor did she hesitate, as she most assuredly would have if Poxwell had asked for such a favour, even before his intentions had been made plain.

She turned her blooming cheek to him and said, "I haven't a father, as you know; I should like someone in his place. And there's no one in Cambridge I would rather choose."

Fenchurch kissed her cheek with trembling lips. It was not the rôle he wanted, but how much better it was than nothing! *And who knows,* he thought with a sudden surge of hope, *what may happen? It's a beginning, and even if it never progresses further, how much richer am I still than I was only a few hours ago.*

20 Sanctuary

Grubb blundered aimlessly about the streets and passages of Cambridge like a wounded animal whose only recourse is movement to take its mind off its agony. He did not know where he was headed, nor did he care. An unexpected and inconsolable sense of loss, frightening him with its intensity, had taken hold of him. The fact was that Maunders, recently though they had become acquainted, had been one of his few friends, and the loss to Grubb was grievous. In his sorrow he found solace by seeking to place the blame for his friend's death on one of his customary scapegoats—the class system, for instance, or Harry Huntingfield—as one with a mortal illness will manage to forget it for a while in brooding over a toothache.

But try as he would, Grubb was unable to bring Maunders's murder home to his arch-enemy, Harry—not yet, at any rate. He had so far found it impossible to concoct a plausible motive that would explain why the stripling lord might have crept up behind Maunders and with one swift stroke laid open his throat; which was not to say, however, that Grubb did not still consider Harry's guilt a distinct and desirable possibility.

As he stumbled blindly through the town some few acquaintances noticed him on his peregrinations, but no one greeted him. It was evident to the least observant that he did not wish to be noticed. He walked with his head bent as though to avoid seeing anyone he knew, and his eyes were opaque with pain. *The poor kid,* Grubb said to himself, it wasn't fair. It wasn't fair! The grim recollection of Maunders's dead, blood-smeared face floated unbidden at the back of his vision, and he could not rid himself of it. *That rotten lot in the Senior Common Room,* he thought with a warm and comforting burst of anger, *they did it, they hounded him to his death with their talk of his having stolen a few stinking prints out of a book.* But upon closer examination he found that that convenient theory would not wash. *If only it had been suicide, now,* he thought almost longingly. The most ardent adherent of a *felo de se* hypothesis, however, would hardly have supposed Maunders to have chosen such a method or such a place in which to do it; and if he had, where was the murder weapon? The police had searched all along his sanguinary path and found nothing. No, it was murder pure and simple; but by whom? And why? And who would he find to talk to now?

In his wanderings Grubb had tried and then rejected the Sheepshanks Fellows' Garden, fearing to encounter another member of the SCR, whose company in his present frame of mind he could not bear. Leaving the garden, he crossed Sheepshanks Bridge, went through The Backs to Queen's Road, walked along Silver Street and up King's Parade to the Market, thence by means of a number of turnings eventually making his way back by a circuitous route to Sheepshanks. He was not consciously headed anywhere in particular, he scarcely knew what buildings he passed or where he was, but it did not surprise him to find himself at last in the lofty sylvan echoing nave of Sheepshanks Chapel. For a moment Grubb stood gazing about him through the dim air veiled in dancing motes of dust with the aspect of an explorer unexpectedly come upon the vestiges of an extinct civilization— he was a loudly self-proclaimed atheist and made an appearance in Chapel only on those occasions when his position absolutely required it—then he fell to his knees and fervently prayed as best he knew for the repose of Maunders's soul.

21 *The Woman in the Case*

It was some time before Fenchurch, intoxicated by his recent tea with Vivien, bethought himself of the railway station locker and its possible contents. His state of exhilaration required working off with physical exertion of some sort and so, after ascertaining that Inspector Bunce had not left a telephone message for him at the Porter's Lodge, he decided to walk over to the police station on Parker's Piece to learn the news in that quarter.

If the constable seated at the entrance desk was startled by the spectacle of a diminutive white-haired gentleman attired in plus-fours and sandals, a knapsack strapped to his back and a stout walking-stick in one hand, he managed with admirable self-control not to show it.

"Is Inspector Bunce in?" Fenchurch asked him. "If so, please tell him that Mr. Fenchurch has come to see him."

"I'll enquire, sir," said the constable, who had witnessed Bunce's arrival some moments earlier, but who very properly intended to discover whether the Inspector was inclined to meet with this peculiar-looking visitor. "May I ask what it is in reference to?"

"The Sheepshanks murder," Fenchurch explained. "I am one of the Fellows of the College."

Strike me pink, the constable thought, chagrined by his lack

of perception, *I should have known he'd be from the University.*
He picked up the telephone receiver and rang Bunce, who
said he would be down at once.

"I'm very sorry not to have got in touch with you before,
Mr. Fenchurch," Inspector Bunce said a few moments later,
greeting him. "Come up to my office, and we'll have a cup of
tea. Not your sort of tea, I'm afraid; regulations don't permit
it."

"It is growing late; I hope I am not keeping you from your
dinner. I had no word from you, and I was anxious to find
out what you might have discovered at the railway station."

"You're not delaying me in the least," the Inspector assured him heartily. "I've just been going over some routine
reports; it'll be a pleasure to take a break. I shan't be going
home for a few hours yet—the 'flu is still playing Hob with
our roster, so I'm on duty a bit longer than usual. I apologise
for not sending word to you, but as it happens I've only just
now returned from the railway station. On our way there this
morning we happened to witness a motor accident—a lorry
ran into a taxi—and by the time we'd got that sorted out,
there was other pressing business here to attend to. Just as
well for you you couldn't come along then, as it turned out.
Come on upstairs and have a look at what we found in Maunders's locker."

"Then the locker to which he held the key *was* in the
Cambridge railway station. You didn't find the *Anelida?*" But
Fenchurch posed the question without much hope; he was
sure that Bunce's manner would have been very different if
the Caxton had been recovered.

"I'm afraid not, but I don't think you'll be altogether disappointed." Inspector Bunce led the way to his bare, serviceable office, which at least had the advantage of a view
onto Parker's Piece, and offered his guest a chair. Averting
his eyes from the bilious green paint on the walls, a colour
that had the property of making him feel faintly queasy,

Fenchurch accepted a thick pottery mug filled with strong black tea and waited for the Inspector to enlarge upon his statement. Bunce took a gulp from his mug before speaking further. "Ah, that does warm the cockles. . . . I walked back from the railway station for the sake of a bit of fresh air," he explained, "and it's growing mortal chilly outside. Now to business." He opened the bottom drawer of his desk, extracting a large dog-eared and grimy cardboard portfolio which he handed to his visitor.

Fenchurch opened it and scarcely glanced at its contents before exclaiming, "The missing Ackermanns! How stupid of me not to have thought of that. Grierson and I were absolutely certain that furtive fellow in London had sold the rest but would not own up to it for fear of having to give us the money." He looked over the sheaf of prints in his hand. "In fact Biggers must have sold several before we got on to him, but not nearly so many as Grierson and I had supposed. I expect Maunders kept a number back so as not to flood the market and depress the price Biggers paid him."

"Since the lad was cagey enough to conceal this batch outside of College, I'm beginning to think there may be some substance to your theory that he pinched that book out of the University Library and has it stowed away somewhere. But I haven't a clue where he might have hidden it, if indeed he did."

"You may be quite sure, Inspector, that he concealed it with the greatest of care. I am not at all surprised that Maunders has left no indications behind him of where his prize may be located. No doubt he realised that there would be an all-out hunt for the *Anelida,* with grave consequences for the thief if he were to be identified. I am inclined for several reasons to suspect that the book may still be somewhere in the Library."

"But the University Library has been gone over with a fine-tooth comb," Bunce said in bewilderment. "If it had been hidden there, surely it would have been found by now. You've told me your people have peered into every nook and cranny."

"As a matter of fact, the search is taking longer than we supposed it would. The University Librarian had hoped to be through by now, but he says it may be Thursday or Friday before it is completed. And even if, as it is now beginning to appear, the *Anelida* does not turn up in the UL, there is always the chance that it may have been overlooked. And if Maunders was indeed the thief, that thought worries me deeply."

"Why? Maunders is dead, so if he did hide the book in the UL, provided he hadn't got round to smuggling it out, it's bound to be where he stashed it," the Inspector pointed out.

"Not if he divulged the hiding place to his killer before he died. If Maunders did steal the *Anelida* and was killed for it, we can only hope that he took the secret of its whereabouts to the grave with him. On the other hand, if the murderer did not know where to find the book, it is surprising that he would silence his only source of the information. Dash it all, it's a fearful muddle!" As Fenchurch uttered this antiquated imprecation, he threw up his hands in despair. "But I still think," he continued stubbornly, "despite the fact nothing seems to fit, that the volume must be concealed somewhere in the UL. That would be by far the safest place for it during the hue and cry."

"On the *Purloined Letter* theory, you mean?" It was with evident pride that Bunce brought out this scrap of erudition; since his first case with Fenchurch he had taken to dabbling in detective stories of all periods, and had found his way back to one of the first shapers of the tradition.

"Quite so," Fenchurch replied delightedly. "You are fond of Poe, I take it."

"Yes—of his more sensible stories, that is. Some of 'em, like *Berenice,* are queer as Dick's hatband—pulling out his lady-love's teeth for a keepsake. I ask you! I reckon Mr. Poe was right off his chump when he dreamed up that one."

"I understand," Fenchurch said in extenuation, "that he was accustomed to consume an excess of spirits; that might account for his more curious productions. Of course even when sober he was the possessor of an exceedingly vivid imagination. . . . Do you know," he went on, "that there is a neat little story about stamps which is framed along the same lines as *The Purloined Letter*? It was written by Agatha Christie, I believe."

Bunce stared at his companion in open amazement. "You don't mean to tell me you read Agatha Christie! I know you're by way of being a mystery writer yourself, but I should have expected you to stick to the high-brow detective novels."

"It is always advisable to keep a weather-eye on the competition, and Dame Agatha is the Queen of the bookstalls," Fenchurch replied demurely. "But to return to our subject: Have you discovered a more probable motive for Maunders's murder than a connection with the theft of the *Anelida and Arcite*? Or, for that matter, any other reasonable motive at all so far?"

"I must admit that for the moment we haven't. But"— Inspector Bunce raised his finger monitorially—"we haven't yet finished our investigations, don't forget. For example, I've got men out interviewing everyone who so much as spoke to the lad in the hope that some hint of an enemy will emerge. So far, I must confess, all we've found out is that he was almost universally disliked, but no one seems to have cared enough about him or his actions to lift a hand against him. No one, that is, except some of the Sheepshanks Fellows, on account of his plundering of the Sheepshanks Library," he added with a sly glance at Fenchurch, "but that would hardly constitute a valid reason for a murder. So I'm not dismissing your theory about the stolen book out-of-hand, but you must admit it's as full of holes as a Swiss cheese. Anyway, I have one more card up my sleeve—the fair Letty. If that's her name, it shouldn't be too difficult to find her. Even if Deacon is mistaken about Maunders's young woman working in Bowes and Bowes or Heffers, there aren't so many bookshops in Cambridge that we can't check 'em all out, and pretty quickly too. I've reserved that plum for myself, and for you as well if you'd like to come along. It's one of the perks of being Inspector, getting to keep the juicy tit-bits now and then," he added.

"I should like to meet Miss Letty," Fenchurch agreed. "Aside from Grubb, she appears to have been the only human contact poor Maunders made in Cambridge. I fear that he suffered from a paucity of friends."

Bunce examined his wristwatch. "The shops will all be closed by this time; and tomorrow, worse luck! is Sunday. I tell you what—I'll do some preparatory digging this evening by ringing the shop managers at home, and tomorrow we can interview any likely prospects. That will save us some foot-work. With any luck there shouldn't be more than one."

But locating the mysterious Letty proved to be rather more difficult than Inspector Bunce had bargained for. First he spoke to the manager of the main Heffers bookshop in Trinity Street, only to discover that no one named Letty or any approximation thereof was employed on the premises. The manager obligingly checked with Heffers' subsidiary operations—the children's bookshop, the stationery shop, et al.—reporting back to Bunce that his labours had been unfruitful. The manager of Bowes & Bowes had an employee named Betty Martin, a long shot (particularly as she was married), who when catechised by Bunce over the telephone firmly insisted that she had never heard of Robert Maunders before perusing the shocking headlines in the Cambridge Argus at breakfast that morning. The Inspector drew a complete blank with the Mowbrays manager, who was not at home, and at that juncture Bunce gave up his researches for the evening in disgust. The next morning before continuing his enquiries, he decided to drop in on Fenchurch and brief him on the lack of progress so far; Mrs. Bunce had gone off alone to church, in a new hat and high dudgeon because her husband was too busy to accompany her.

Fortunately Bunce found Fenchurch at leisure in his rooms, at peace with himself and the world after having fulfilled his spiritual duties. He had already attended Chapel (the Sheepshanks Chapel Morning Prayer, justly famous for the beauty of its liturgy and music, is relatively short, thanks to Dr. Shebbeare's frequently stated aversion to lengthy sermons). "Ah! Good morning, Inspector," the don greeted him. "Have you noticed Old Noll today?"

"Can't say as I have, sir," replied Bunce, who had entirely forgotten he intended to establish the sabbatical variability of the clock in order to check Fenchurch's account of its eccentricities. "Is there any reason why I ought to?"

"Only to verify the fact that he changes intervals once a week on Sundays like clockwork—I beg your pardon," added Fenchurch, embarrassed by the inadvertent and somewhat feeble pun. "In general that is hardly an accurate expression to employ when referring to Old Noll. This morning when I went into Chapel I noticed that he is striking two hours fast and showing forty-seven minutes slow, the old rascal," he continued affectionately. "He keeps us on our toes. . . . Have you had any luck yet in finding the elusive Letty?"

"Not a lead so far, I'm afraid." Bunce told Fenchurch of what little he had accomplished the previous evening, adding, "There's still Mowbrays, though, and Galloway and Porter's, not to mention the second-hand bookshops. I was wondering if you mightn't like to go over with me to the station whilst I finish my enquiries, and then if I have any luck we can go have a talk with the girl—if she exists, that is. Not that I think for a moment that Deacon was lying to us, mind, but he may have got the name wrong or made a mistake about where she works. It may be necessary to use the *Argus* to reach her, though I'd rather not. For one thing, when the newspaper laddies think you need them they get to expecting tit for tat, which can be a nuisance; and for another, girls of that sort tend to be frightened by any mention of the police. She might get the wind up on seeing herself mentioned in the paper and refuse to contact us, and then we should be worse off than when we started. Besides, if she is inclined to be cooperative, you'd think she'd have been in touch with us after seeing Maunders's murder splashed all over the front page."

"D'you know," remarked Fenchurch apologetically, "I can't help thinking that Deacon may have got it a bit wrong, as you say. Judging by Maunders's proclivities and the fact that he appears to have been in training for a career as a biblioklept, I should have expected him to frequent an antiquarian bookshop rather than one of the common or garden variety. The former, after all, would have been far more use to him."

"So you think the second-hand booksellers would be the places to check first?"

"I do. Particularly those which deal in valuable books. In this way he would have familiarized himself with current prices, and by chatting up the staff, with present trends in book-collecting; it would have assisted him to gain a good deal of esoteric knowledge more thoroughly and more readily than by swotting up the big booksellers' and auction-house catalogues."

"Not to mention that he might have made a contact for fencing anything he happened to nick from the libraries at the University," Bunce added excitedly.

"Just so; though he was a cautious creature, and I should have thought he would travel farther afield for that purpose, as he did with the Loggan and Ackermann engravings. Still, someone in a shop of that kind—possibly the girl—might be a useful source of information on the subject of venal London book dealers; Mr. Biggers would not do for the higher-priced items, I suspect."

"If that's the case, it isn't surprising that we haven't heard from the girl. However, there may be other reasons for her silence. Which of the rare bookshops would you suggest we check first?"

"Let me see," Fenchurch mused. "There's Deighton Bell, and Jean Pain; but on the whole I think we should do best to start with Gore & Plaskitt in Green Street. They are an old and well-established firm, and their wares are top-quality. In addition, they specialise in incunabula, which none of the others do, so Maunders would have found them particularly interesting if he had had a hand in the disappearance of the *Anelida*. Yes, I should think that would be just the place for an aspiring young book thief in search of serviceable knowledge to haunt."

"Let me see." Inspector Bunce pulled out his list of telephone numbers and ran a large finger down it. "That 'ud be William Akers. He lives in Comberton. Why don't we pop along to my office and ring him up now? That is, unless I might use one of the College telephones."

"I'm afraid I haven't one in my rooms," Fenchurch apologised. "Sheepshanks is rather old-fashioned in that way, and even if the College were not, *I* should be. I find it a most distracting instrument. However, you may recollect that there is one in a closet off the Combination Room, which you are of course welcome to use."

"No telephone?" Bunce replied enviously. "You *are* lucky." In the Inspector's concept of Heaven, telephones, which too often brutally catapulted him from a sound sleep into an early-morning rencontre with crime, would be voiceless. He followed Fenchurch down to the Combination Room and dialled Mr. Akers's number. The manager of Gore &

Plaskitt, newly returned from church in the village, answered the phone himself.

"Mr. Akers?" queried the Inspector. "Inspector Bunce of the Cambridge Police Force speaking. Have you by any chance a girl working for you at Gore & Plaskitt with the Christian name of Letty? I'm afraid I don't know her surname. No. No, she's done nothing at all, so far as I know. I only want to question her with reference to a murder. She may have been acquainted with the Sheepshanks student who was killed Friday night, and I should like a word with her.— No,"—as an agitated quacking arose from the other end of the line—"there's no question of her involvement. I merely need to speak with the girl about the victim's other associates. . . . Ah, Lettice, is it? Lettice Knowles." He took a pencil stub from his pocket and wrote the name at the bottom of his list. "I suppose you don't happen to have her address by you? I realise you're at home, so the shop records aren't available to you at the moment. . . . Yes, if you've something you can look it up in I should be very much obliged." He covered the receiver with his hand and said to Fenchurch, "Here's a piece of luck! He's been working on the books at home over the weekend, so he's got her address there and he's gone to fetch it . . . Off the Chesterton Road, is she? Number nine Albert Street? That's champion. Thank you very much, sir." He rang off and said to Fenchurch, "Deacon got part of it right, at any rate. Name's Letty, short for Lettice. That's a quaintish name, if you like. The manager sounded quite concerned about her. Seems a nice chap. Let's see if we can catch her at home."

"Splendid," said Fenchurch eagerly. "As I only walked five miles or so before breakfast—on account of Chapel this morning—I'm quite ready to give my legs a stretch."

This was not the means of locomotion Bunce had in mind. He had made his arrival by car, parking in the cobbled courtyard in front of Sheepshanks Great Gate, and it was by car that he wished to make his way to No. 9 Albert Street. His feet, sorely taxed by his weight and years on the Force as a constable walking a beat, had never quite recovered their youthful vigour, frequently aching after even moderate exercise, and they were still tired after his injudicious walk from the railway station the previous afternoon. He looked dubiously out one of the narrow mullioned windows. The weather was decidedly uninviting: Pearl-grey clouds scudded in the grip of a stiff wind over a pewter-coloured sky, and an icy drizzle that had begun as they were walking across the court to the Combination Room was being flung in fistfuls of needle-sharp drops onto the wavering glass. "I'd rather we went in my car," he demurred, "considering the cold and the rain. It's true Albert Street isn't so very far from Sheepshanks, but in this weather I'd as soon walk barefoot to Ely."

"Oh, do you think so?" Fenchurch, who had joined him at the window, seemed disappointed. "I had thought that a brisk little jaunt in the fresh air . . . however," he continued, courteously deferring to his visitor, "whatever you think best."

As they drew up in front of No. 9 Albert Street they saw that it was a tidy little house with freshly painted woodwork and a climbing crimson rose, which not even the freezing rain had power to daunt, still blooming against the drab stone walls. A woman with streaks of grey in her dark hair and a pleasant face opened the bright blue front door to them. "Lettice Knowles?" she repeated after Bunce. "Yes, she's here. We've just finished dinner. Do come in." She stepped aside and eyed them both curiously. "May I tell her who is calling? I'm her landlady, Mrs. Jeffreys."

"I'm Inspector Bunce of the Cambridge Police, and this is Mr. Fenchurch. It's only a routine call," he assured her, observing her look of alarm. "It's possible Miss Knowles may have information which would be of use in a case I'm investigating. Nothing directly connected to her, you understand, merely checking."

Her face cleared, though her eyes still remained a trifle wary. "That's all right, then. I'll fetch her for you. Come in, do."

They stepped out of the tiny scrubbed hall into a small sitting-room which was painted buttercup yellow and cheerful with bright chintzes. "Letty's in the kitchen, washing up," she explained. "Do sit down. I'll send her in."

While they waited several small children, still dressed for church in their Sunday best, peeped shyly, whispering among themselves, their eyes wide, through the door leading to the back of the house. They had never before seen a policeman out of uniform, and it seemed infinitely sinister to them that such personages should wish to see their mother's lodger; somehow the presence of the two men was much more frightening than it would have been had they been wearing the familiar constable's dress.

In a few moments Lettice Knowles made her appearance, her hands still reddened by their recent immersion in soap and hot water. She had taken the time to remove her apron, roll down her sleeves, and tidy her hair. She was a remarkably plain girl in her early twenties—must have been at least four or five years older than Maunders, was Inspector Bunce's mental comment—if plain was not too kind a word to use in describing her. Big and raw-boned, she had the kind of figure that, while not running to excess of fat, is lumpy and shapeless. Clearly she lacked a flair for dress, since even Fenchurch, who was unversed in the subtleties of feminine apparel, could see that her neat dark skirt and unadorned white blouse made no attempt to remedy this defect. Her face reminded him of an intelligent horse, long and broad, with large, slightly protruding eyes and a pendulous lower lip. The mental comparison of this girl and Vivien, much of an age, was painful. Poor child, thought Fenchurch with a rush of compassion: Surely life is not easy for a young woman who exhibits to the world an appearance so little conducive to amelioration. Her toilette, which bore no concession to frivolity, made it obvious that she was resigned to her limitations: She wore neither jewellery nor makeup, and her hair—thick, glossy and dark brown—was simply cut with no hint of a curl. Her heavy face and figure evoked representations of bovine peasants by the Flemish painters; only her eyes were expressive. They were beautiful— eyes of a clear grey that shone like darkened silver, surrounded by thick sooty lashes; eyes that seemed to promise far more than her prosaic features and body.

She stood in the doorway, gravely surveying the two men, who rose as she entered, and seeming neither surprised nor frightened by the appearance of the police on her doorstep. In the next room Bunce could hear Mrs. Jeffreys shoo her children upstairs in a low voice; but he noticed that her heavier footsteps did not ascend the staircase in their wake. Apparently she was staying within call in order to lend her lodger moral support.

"Miss Lettice Knowles?" he asked. "I am Inspector Bunce, and this is Mr. Fenchurch." He saw no purpose in delineating Fenchurch's somewhat ambiguous position.

"I wondered when you would come." Her voice was as unexpectedly beautiful as her eyes: not shrill, but low and flexible; and her accent, surprisingly, was that of a lady. She sat upright on a chair facing them with her feet together and her hands disposed in her lap, and the two men resumed their seats.

"You expected us?" Bunce asked in surprise.

"Yes. I very nearly contacted you when I found out what had happened to Bob—Bob Maunders. That's what you've come about, isn't it? I would have got in touch with you, only I hadn't anything to tell—nothing useful, that is. And it seemed such an effort. You see, it hurt to think about him; and so I thought, if they want to speak to me they'll find me.

Why go through it all if they don't? Now you're here I suppose I was wrong to wait, but I didn't think I'd make any difference. Honestly I didn't, or I would have come."

"We are sorry to add to your grief," said Fenchurch gently.

She lowered incredible lashes to veil the argentine eyes, then raised them again to look directly at Fenchurch. "Grief?" The word held an incredulous ring. "I was glad," she said simply.

Her hearers both gaped at her; they could not believe their ears. Death has a way of obliterating frankness, particularly a violent death whose perpetrator still remains unknown. In any event it was difficult to believe that this stolid-looking young woman could muster sufficient feeling to be glad of another's death.

"Glad?" Inspector Bunce repeated after her, with a stern look.

Her eyes met and held his in a gesture of defiance. "Yes. I was glad when I heard. I'm not now, and I'm not proud of the way I felt then. Now I don't know how to feel; I haven't yet got to the point where I can be sorry for him."

"You must have been very well acquainted with Maunders," Fenchurch remarked, "to have disliked him so thoroughly."

"For a little while I thought I loved him and that he loved me." She interpreted Fenchurch's gasp of sympathy as one of astonishment. "You needn't tell me I was a fool," she continued bitterly. "I only have to look in the mirror to realise that no man is going to fall in love with me. And besides, Bob was younger than I, and I knew from the start that he wasn't a very nice person." Her hands, big and square-tipped and capable, had begun to twist in her lap as if they had a life of their own. They made her pain so explicit that Fenchurch was forced to avert his eyes from them. "But I found out that liking someone hasn't anything to do with love. I mean, I didn't like him at all, but I loved him. I knew he was greedy and small-minded and mean, and quite probably not over-honest, but I wanted him and I thought he wanted me, so I pretended not to notice. No one had ever wanted me before." Her eyes looked blindly past her hearers to confront an un-bearable truth. "And then I found out it wasn't me he wanted, it was what I knew. About books—rare books and pricing, and other dealers, and collectors. I work at Gore & Plaskitt, you see. Mr. Akers—the manager—says I have a feel for the trade. He's given me some of the correspondence to deal with, and I've learned a lot in the three years I've worked there." She said this proudly. "Bob didn't understand how I felt about Gore & Plaskitt. I almost gave him the list, but in the end I couldn't. No matter how much I wanted to, I couldn't. So then he dropped me." She sat dry-eyed, her incongruously equine face fixed in a tragic mask.

"What did Maunders ask you for, Miss Knowles?" en-quired Bunce, when her overflow of words had stopped.

"It was our list of collectors—for the catalogues, you know; annotated with specific requests and preferences so that we would know whom to notify when a particular volume comes in. It may not sound like much, but it is very valuable in the trade, and Mr. Akers would have been terribly upset if he knew that anyone outside the firm had got so much as a glimpse of it."

"Stealing to order," Fenchurch exclaimed. "That's what he must have been up to!"

"But Maunders didn't see it after all," said Bunce to Letty.

"No. By that time I knew he didn't give a damn about me. Not that *that* would have mattered if I could have given him anything else, but even if I had copied the list, I realised once he got hold of it he'd leave anyway. There wasn't any-thing else he wanted from me," she said pathetically, "and I would have given him anything—anything that was mine to give. The last time I saw him was when I refused to copy it for him. Afterwards I thought about writing him but I knew it was no use, it would only humiliate me further, so I tore the letters up. That's why I was glad when I heard he was dead. I was glad then, but now I wish I was the one who was dead."

Fenchurch thought he heard a stifled sob beyond the doorway to the kitchen, but neither Letty nor Bunce indicated that they had heard anything; she was intent on her misery and he on analysing what she had told him. The don did not know what to say to alleviate her wretchedness; nonetheless he made the attempt. "My dear, you are still very young . . ." he began clumsily.

Letty sat up very straight, and her light eyes sparkled with anger, making her look almost handsome. "Don't tell me I shall find someone else. Women who look like me don't. I've lived long enough to find that out. Mrs. Jeffreys tells me the same thing. 'Once they see what you're like on the inside they'll think you're beautiful outside as well.'" Her voice rose to a wail; even loud in grief it had a pure and mellow timbre, like a woodwind instrument. "But they never bother to look unless you have a decent figure and a face that doesn't remind them of a carthorse— Do you know why I was christened Lettice? It's really very funny. My mother had been a schoolteacher—she'd read history at University, and when I was born she named me after Lettice Knollys. Knowles and Knollys are alike, you see, and she said it might be the same family. So she named me after Lettice Knollys, who was so beautiful that she stole Queen Elizabeth's favourite out from under her nose. She married the Earl of Leicester secretly, and Elizabeth was furious when she found out. Poor Elizabeth. And poor mother—what a joke on her it was!" Briefly she put her hands over her face, and when she took them away a moment later they saw she had regained her composure.

A look of bewilderment crossed her features and she said, "I'm so sorry I went on like that. I can't imagine what came

over me. I know I ought to feel ashamed, but somehow I feel
. . . better. I really did love Bob in spite of everything, you
see, and now the hatred seems to have gone away. I can feel
sorry for him now." At last tears for Maunders glimmered in
those shadowy-silver eyes. Fenchurch was strangely moved by
the sight of them, not only on the girl's account, but because
they were perhaps the only genuine signs of sorrow that
Maunders's death would elicit. *Now at least,* Fenchurch
thought to himself, *he has someone to mourn him.*

He hastened to offer her his handkerchief, but Letty had
already taken one of her own from her skirt pocket. She
mopped at her eyes, blew her prominent nose in a business-
like manner, and achieved a shaky but creditable laugh.
"Now," she said, "I know why Roman Catholics go to confession. But you didn't come here to listen to the story of my
life. What do you want me to tell you? I didn't kill him, by
the way, though there were times when I felt like it."

"I must, as a matter of routine, just ask you where you
were on Friday evening between ten and ten-thirty," said
Bunce, experiencing a strange reluctance at questioning her.

She thought. "I went alone to a performance of *The Magic
Flute* at the Arts Theatre that night. It began at eight and
was over at about a quarter to eleven. I walked both ways. I
did ask Mrs. Jeffreys to go with me, but she had a meeting of
the Townswomen's Guild, so she couldn't. I think I still have
the theatre ticket somewhere; as a matter of fact, I was wearing this skirt on Friday." She groped in her pocket and uttered a small cry of triumph. "I thought so! Here it is." She
handed the scrap of pasteboard to the Inspector, who put it
carefully away in his wallet. He opened his mouth but before
he could speak she added, "I know what you're going to ask
next. No, I didn't see a soul I knew while I was there."

Somewhat to her surprise he appeared satisfied with this
answer. Delicately averting his eyes from her tear-stained

cheeks, he continued, "As for the other question I came to ask, it can wait. If you prefer, we can come back later."

"No, thank you, Inspector. There's no use dragging it out. I may as well get it all over with, then I can get on with other things and put Bob out of my mind—at least give it a try," she added ruefully.

"If you're certain, Miss . . . well then, it's only a matter of knowing who his friends and associates were. Who did you meet whilst you were out with him?"

"D'you know, there was hardly anyone. Looking back, I daresay he wasn't exactly proud to be seen around with me. After all, I'm not the sort of bird that would be likely to send up his stock in College." But she sounded less bitter than she had only a few moments earlier, and her face had lost some of its unhappy look. *Perhaps,* thought Fenchurch, watching her, *the letting of her tears has reduced her fever and she is on her way to a recovery of sorts. And despite what she may think now, not all men are unable to see beyond a plain exterior.* He was both ashamed and gladdened to think that he had not had to give up one aspect of his beloved for the other—loving Vivien, lovable both in mind and body, was almost too easy. In doing so he faced no trials to prove the truth of his love, for who would not love Vivien?

Letty's voice interrupted his thoughts. "There was . . . the only one I can remember was Hal Deacon. Bob shared digs with him in Sheepshanks. We usually spent time there when I saw Bob. He hadn't much money to chuck about, but I think it was mostly so he wouldn't have to be seen with me in public. I liked Hal; he was always nice to me."

"You never saw Maunders with anyone else he knew?" enquired Bunce.

Letty shook her head. "No, never," she replied. "But I didn't mind that at the time, you see. I wanted to be alone with him."

She saw them out the front door; as it closed upon her

Fenchurch caught sight of another door opening at the back of the hall and heard a voice murmur, "Oh, my dear. I didn't know."

While they were getting into the car Bunce said, "We shall have to check the Arts Theatre, of course, though even if someone saw her there she could always have left early. Well, that's that. Not that I expected much in that direction, mind. But there, one always hopes."

"You don't think she killed him, then?" Fenchurch himself thought nothing less likely, but he felt bound to ask the question.

"I very much doubt it. She's strong enough to do the job all right, but she'd not have opened up to us the way she did if she'd done him. That was quite a melodrama, wasn't it? Maybe tomorrow she'll feel like a boozer with a hangover and wish she'd never said a word to us, but I reckon she'll be all the better for it," Bunce said comfortably. "That Mrs. Jeffreys seems a nice woman, so Miss Letty won't lack for a shoulder to cry on."

"Did the autopsy discover anything helpful? You haven't mentioned Dr. Scarlett's findings."

"That's because the P.M. report hasn't come in yet. Dr. Scarlett called in yesterday morning to say he was feeling dicky and he wouldn't be able to get to it till today. Seemed to think he'd got a touch of rheumatism from the damp in Sheepshanks court Friday evening, from the river air, I expect. I only hope it doesn't turn out to be more of the 'flu we've been having lately—it hangs on for the better part of a week. Then we shall be in the soup. Where we shall find a replacement for him I can't imagine."

But as it happened there was no need for Bunce to worry on that score. When he called in at the police station on his way home he found Dr. Scarlett's report, neatly typed, waiting for him on his desk. "High time," grumbled the Inspector ungratefully, and began to read.

22 The Murder Weapon

After digesting a great deal of medico-legal language, some of which might be impolitely but accurately described as jargon, Bunce ascertained that the blade of the implement responsible for Maunders's death had been razor-sharp and an inch in length, judging by the clean edges and relative shallowness of the wound. Dr. Scarlett pointed out in his somewhat long-winded report that an old-fashioned straight razor would undoubtedly have bit deeper into some part of the neck. The same could be said of a knife; but except for the points of entry and departure, the gash left in Maunders's throat had a uniform depth of approximately one inch. For that reason Dr. Scarlett strongly inclined to the theory that the murder weapon was an instrument with which he had great familiarity: in short, that it was some form of surgical scalpel. He had, the police surgeon wrote, arrived at this conclusion with some reluctance because the hand that had wielded it (a right hand, by the by) did not appear to possess the dexterity which he would have expected of a surgeon, or even of some lesser variety of medical man. This anomaly could, however, be accounted for in one of two ways: first, by the fact that some unauthorised person had got hold of a scalpel for the purpose of using it on the unfortunate Maunders, entirely possible since no special credentials were required to purchase one; or else that the hand employing it had, through emotion or nervousness, temporarily lost some degree of its customary skill.

"A scalpel, eh? Here's something to get my teeth into!" said Bunce to himself as he read over this section of Dr. Scarlett's report for the third time. Leaning back in his chair, he tented his fingers together, a position he often assumed when he wanted to think. At last he had a clue! Whoever had used a scalpel to kill Maunders must either have bought it in a surgical supply shop with the murder in mind, or else he had access to a surgeon's instruments. In either case it provided a lead of sorts, a trail he could follow; and the thought of it gave him fresh energy. He finished reading the surgeon's report on the post mortem, but finding nothing else unexpected in it, let his thoughts revert once again to the scalpel. "Scalpels and surgeons," Bunce mused. "And with Simon Poxwell, Surgeon-Royal, right on the premises, so to speak, *and* a book-collector—a pity he has an iron-clad alibi!"

It was absurd even to speculate on a connection between a rich and respected London specialist and a poor boy from Liverpool who had managed somehow to obtain a grant to University. And yet, who knew what contacts Maunders might have made through illicit book dealing? The theft of the Loggans and Ackermanns might not have been his first essay into that subterranean trade; and Fenchurch had told Bunce that books frequently were unaccountably missing from one or another of the many libraries at the University.

Turning to another report that a subordinate had placed on his desk while he was still busy with Dr. Scarlett's literary endeavours, he noted that no trace of a weapon had been found anywhere in the vicinity of All Saints Passage. Policemen had scoured the area from the river to Jesus Lane, to no avail. It was always depressingly possible that the culprit had taken it to Garret Hostel Bridge or one of the College bridges nearby and tossed it in the river. Bunce supposed that in due course the Cam might have to be dredged, a nasty and potentially hopeless task for something so small and easily missed; and naturally that was only one of a thousand places where the murderer might have disposed of it and whatever he had used to protect him from the spirting of Maunders's blood, for presumably he had taken precautions along those lines.

If Maunders's killer were a medical man, Bunce thought gloomily, he could simply have taken the scalpel home with him, washed it and sterilised it, replacing it in its customary case, or wherever scalpels were kept. In that event, it would not matter whether he had succeeded in removing all traces of the blood, considering the instrument's intended purpose. Once again Bunce thought of *The Purloined Letter,* but this time with no pleasure in his own cleverness.

Still, despite all the problems and questions this analysis of the murder weapon posed, it was something to go on— worlds better than the sort of kitchen knife that comes from the bargain counter at Woolworths. Bunce sighed and began to read over the police surgeon's report for a fourth time.

23 *Idyll*

"'Licence my roving hands, and let them go,/Before, behind, between, above, below,'" quoted Harry, suiting the action to the word. "'O my America! my new-found-land,/My kingdom, safeliest when with one man manned.'"

"You really have been swotting up on Donne, haven't you?" Vivien said, amused, as she came up for air.

The raw November weather had softened and turned unexpectedly balmy, and Harry had driven Vivien away from Cambridge into the countryside in his yellow MG with the top down for an out-of-season picnic. They had found a navigable lane deep in the country that ended at a gate leading into a stubble-field. Providentially Harry had several elderly and disreputable horse-blankets in the boot of his car, which served to cushion the rough stalks; and they spread their feast out under a tree next to a high hedgerow. This corner of the field was sheltered both from wind and from prying eyes, and the pale wintry sun, filtering down through branches and the shrivelled brown leaves that still defiantly clung to them, warmed the place where they sat as if it were a miniature glass-house. The wine they were drinking with their pasties, suave and velvety, contributed further to the warmth, causing Vivien to shed first her coat and then her sweater. Harry had already taken off his pullover, and he made a pillow of it for her head.

"What about a lie-down before we drive back?" he suggested. "I'm fagged out from the sun and the wine, and I don't want to risk driving off the road—not with such a precious cargo."

Vivien assented, and they lay on the blankets in each other's arms as chastely as if they had been Babes in the Woods, waiting for the robins to provide them with a coverlet of leaves. For a time they slept; and then as they simultaneously half-woke, sleep became a sweet and drowsy lovemaking, a dreamy and gentle joint reconnoitre of mouths and bodies. Gradually as they became wide awake their voyage of discovery became fiercer and more ardent.

"I do," said Vivien against Harry's mouth.

"You do what?" Harry asked, pulling away with an effort and gazing at her with delight.

"I do love you."

"You're sure it isn't just the wine talking?" he enquired teasingly, though his heart gave a great bound of joy at her words.

"I'm sure. And it's not just . . . proximity, either." She placed her hand on his thigh. "I don't know when it happened, or why, but I would follow you to the ends of the earth."

Harry took her hand and pressed his lips to its palm. Looking down at her, he said, "Then you will marry me?"

"Just you try and stop me," Vivien told him, and gave him a kiss that made his heart leap again. When it ended he leaned back his head to look on her flushed and glowing face and said in awe, tracing the tender curve of her cheek with his finger, "My God, Vivien darling, you're spectacular. You're bloody overwhelming. You dazzle me, you're entirely too good to be true. You're like those French fireworks, the ones that spray pinwheels and silver rain and fountains of goldfish all over the shop. Whatever would I have done with myself if I hadn't met you?"

"I expect you'd have thought of something," Vivien replied, laughing.

"I suppose so. But to think what I'd have missed, and never have known."

"What we'd have missed," she corrected him.

"D'you think our parents felt this way about each other?" Harry asked after time out from conversation for further dalliance.

"I don't know. I never really knew mine. What about yours?"

"I think it's impossible that anyone ever felt like this before," he replied simply, cradling her head on his shoulder. Vivien took his hand and held it to her cheek. "I know all lovers say that, but in our case it must be true. My heart is so full of you that it's hard to believe there could be more to love, and yet incredibly there is."

Vivien turned her mouth to him. "Let's," she murmured. "Now."

His loins stirred even more at her words; but at the same time they aroused in him an inconveniently timed protective instinct.

"Not yet, my darling," he said decisively, though it cost him more than a slight pang to say it. "There's a boring old family tradition that the marriage will end in sorrow if a Huntingfield bride goes less than virgin to Tantivy Hall."

In one way Vivien could not help being pleased by his firmness, but in another she was profoundly piqued. "And how, pray tell," she retorted with asperity and a rebellious toss of her head, "do you know I'm a virgin?"

Harry smiled at her so lovingly that her very bones seemed to melt within her. "You will be to me, and that's all I care about," he replied, and folded her in his arms. After a moment he added practically, "We'd better get married as soon as possible, or the family custom will go down the drain."

"But, darling," Vivien pointed out, "neither of us has a job. You're still an undergraduate, and I'm at University too."

"I know," he admitted. "It's too tiresome—I haven't a bean; nor have my parents, worse luck. But there's some sort of trust I should be inheriting any day now from a black-sheep great-uncle who went out to New Zealand, or was it Australia? It won't be a lot but it ought to be enough to set up house with. Which reminds me." He pulled a small leather box from his trousers pocket and handed it to her. "I wanted to give you this today, but I was afraid you might not accept it. Now it can serve as a stopgap until I winkle the Countess's Sapphire out of Mother."

Vivien opened the box and gave a swift intake of breath. Within on a bed of midnight velvet lay a lily exquisitely formed, its surface powdered with small diamonds that caught the watery sunlight and converted it into prismatic fire. She lifted the jewel out. Its petals and leaves shivered slightly, as though a garden breeze had ruffled them, and the diamonds paving their surface threw off spangles of light.

"It's *tremblant,* the jeweller said," Harry explained. "That means the petals are mounted on wires so they move and catch the light when the wearer moves. It's a hair ornament, supposed to be eighteenth century, the dealer told me, but it can be worn as a pendant if you like. See?" He pulled a bail, through which a fine chain was threaded, from behind one of the shimmering petals.

"It's lovely," said Vivien. "It's absolutely ravishing. But, darling, how on earth can you afford it?" *How ghastly,* she thought, *wifely instincts have begun to sprout already. I do hope he won't mind.*

"Not to worry, love," Harry replied blithely, amused by this premature display of uxorial solicitude. "My day's outing at Newmarket covered it. It caught my eye in the shop window, and it was perfect for you. The cash was in my pocket, so I bought it." He unfastened the clasp of the chain and put it round her neck, kissing the soft skin behind her ear as he did so. "I hope you really do like it," he said anxiously. "Perhaps I ought to have shown it to you first. You're not just being polite, are you?"

"Darling Harry, it's distinctly super. I adore it," declared Vivien, craning around to admire herself in a compact-mirror which she had taken from her handbag. She spoke no more than the truth, but despite his reassurance she could not refrain from thinking as she kissed him that his godmother's horse must have been a very long shot indeed.

24 A Couple of Conversations

Raph Berni slipped into the telephone booth on Silver Street that stood outside the pseudo-Gothic splendours of the Pitt Press; he had chosen this location for his call as the telephones in the Blue Boar and Trinity College were too public for his purpose. Before dialling he consulted a slip of paper and produced an assortment of coins, placing the latter on the ledge provided, then dialled one-double-o and asked for a London number. A voice answered at the other end of the line and he hastily dropped several of the coins into the box in order to obtain a connection. "It's Berni," he said. "It's been some time since I've heard from you."

"That's because we've been working on the price," a voice replied.

"What do you mean, working on the price?" he asked angrily. "I thought that had all been agreed."

"Not exactly. We've had to rethink it, as it happens, and after due consideration we've decided it may be just a shade high," said the voice smoothly.

"Too high?" Raph's voice grew shrill with indignation. "You just hold on a minute. We had a deal. . . ."

"I'm afraid you're asking too much. And you may as well face it, Berni; you can't unload this little item just any old where. You know that as well as I do. It's for a very special market."

He was right. Raph knew when he was beaten. "All right," he said hopelessly. "How much are you offering, then?"

At the sound of the figure on the other end Raph gave a yelp of disappointment and outrage. "But that's not even half of your original offer." His voice shook with fury.

"Yes, well, we've decided it's a bit riskier than we had at first allowed for. Of course," the voice continued silkily, "you could always take it somewhere else. But I must warn you, it's a buyer's market out there."

Raph realised it was no use. "I suppose I shall have to take it," he said, his tone sullen.

"Very sensible of you," said the voice approvingly. "It will all be for the best. You'll see."

Raph bit back the obvious retort and savagely slammed down the receiver. Scooping up the rest of his change and stuffing it in his pocket, he strode back to Trinity with his head combatively lowered, like a bull that has made up its mind to gore the next living creature it sees.

"Hullo, Simon, old boy," said Nigel Poxwell jovially to his brother. "I hear Pullets was quite a do."

"Yes," Simon Poxwell replied, "hardly the sort of evening one had been led to expect."

"Rather jolly, though, with all those naked ladies running about, what?"

"It had its entertaining moments. Still, I expect that's not what you rang up to discuss," said Simon warily. A telephone call from his brother generally ended in a request for money.

"No . . . well, actually, I wondered if you would consider a minor loan—just a few thousand quid to tide me over for a month or so," he added hastily.

Simon's voice turned even chillier, though it had hardly been welcoming before. "Have you the remotest idea, Nigel, how many 'minor loans' I have made you recently—none of which, I might add, have yet been repaid? They add up rather rapidly to a sum larger than the National Debt."

"That's not exactly a brotherly attitude, is it? After all, you've simply been raking in the lolly, by all accounts, whereas I have to live on a don's salary, and I have a great many family expences."

"It is high time, Nigel, that you learned to live within your income. It would not be a kindness," said Simon Poxwell piously, "if I were to encourage you to exceed it by continuing to lend you money."

"Come now, Simon," Nigel Poxwell tried to sound hearty, but his voice had a querulous note. "Surely you can spare a couple of quid for your poor old elder brother."

"Sorry, Nigel. It's just not on. I have rather a large number of expences too, you know."

"You call those expences—those damned books you're always buying? You care more about them than about your own flesh and blood. And don't think I haven't noticed that every time a Caxton sold at Christie's is put down to your account some lovely young thing with a noble name has her appendix removed by Simon Poxwell, surgeon extraordinary. Appendix indeed! What do they do when they slip twice— grow a second appendix for the occasion? Or do you fit them with a diaphragm gratis at their post-op appointment?"

"There's no need to be coarse, Nigel. I'm afraid I haven't any money available to lend you at the moment. You'll have to start trimming your sails, instead of continually expecting

me to bail you out." Brusquely Simon rang off without saying good-bye.

"Damn," muttered Nigel, holding the unresponsive receiver in his hand. "Damn, damn, damn! Whatever shall I
do now?" He took the book from its hiding place in his desk
drawer. *Perhaps,* he thought, *perhaps now was the time to sell it.*

25 Calculations

Inspector Bunce stirred restively and glared at the wrack of papers that lay on his desk. *Nothing seems to be adding up,* he thought crossly. Here it was Monday, over two days since Maunders had been murdered, and they had not come up with one decent motive, let alone a killer. There was Letty Knowles, of course, but Bunce did not think that line of reasoning would lead anywhere useful. He had to admit to himself that he'd liked the girl, but he was too much a policeman to let that liking affect his judgment. No, somehow he just couldn't picture Letty slitting her faithless lover's throat with a scalpel. And even if Bunce had thought her guilty there was absolutely nothing to connect her with Maunders's death; not a scrap of proof, though he'd talked to the Arts Theatre ushers and not one of them had been able to state definitely whether Letty had been there that night. Nor did any of them recall seeing a member of the audience leave the theatre either during the performance or in the interval; but it would have been easy enough, Bunce reflected sourly, for any number of patrons to depart unobserved at the interval. People were always going outside for a breath of air in order to escape from the fog of cigaret smoke that filled the theatre's foyer between acts.

So if Letty had done the job, he could only bring it home

to her by finding some bystander who had noticed her leaving the theatre or someone who had seen her near All Saints Passage close to the time Maunders was attacked—preferably weapon in hand, he thought glumly. If Letty had killed Maunders, however, she'd have been a fool to tell them as much as she had about her relations with the murdered man; and if Bunce was certain of one thing, it was that Letty was no fool.

That left him with Fenchurch's theory. The Inspector turned it over and over in his head, examining it closely from every angle. He had to admit it was a distinct possibility—in fact, it was the only other possibility they had. And it did seem a remarkable coincidence: a book thief—well, print thief, he amended, it amounted to the same thing—a book theft, and a murder. Surely they must be connected in some way or other.

If it were true that Maunders had concealed the *Anelida* in the UL, and if the book had not yet been removed either by him or his killer (and the Inspector thought there was a good chance it had not been, considering the precautions taken), then time was growing perilously short. According to the authorities the search of the Library would be coming to an end in the next few days, and no sign of the volume had yet turned up. If the missing book was not found before the end of the check, Maunders's killer (assuming Fenchurch's theory to be true) would undoubtedly contrive to remove it as soon as the Library reopened; and their one clue to the murderer, not to mention the Caxton, would be irretrievably lost. If, on the other hand, Maunders had hidden his booty outside the UL, then his killer must already have it in his possession and the police were left utterly clueless, in both senses of the word. Any way you looked at it, it was a bloody mess.

Bunce sighed and began to draw up a list of murder suspects, for want of anything better to do. He had detailed several constables to enquire in local shops that sold surgical instruments whether any unfamiliar customers in the past few months had purchased a scalpel resembling the description supplied, but he feared that the attempt would prove fruitless. So he took out a sheet of paper and a stubby pencil (the kind he wrote with best) and began to set down every murder suspect he could think of. There was:

1. Henry Deacon. Motive—none known. Opportunity—nil, as he was out boozing with friends who vouched for him during the time Maunders was murdered. And that was that so far as Deacon was concerned.

2. Lettice Knowles. Motive—strong. Opportunity—also strong, provided she had sneaked out of the theatre, as she could have done. Proof that she had killed Maunders—none whatever. Arguments against—the fact that she had been so open with the police about her feelings for the deceased, though here one might argue that her frankness showed a brilliant cunning. Note: Why would Letty choose a scalpel for a weapon?

3. Then there was Simon Poxwell, a long shot but a possibility if he had hired Maunders to steal the *Anelida* for his book collection, and the youth had unexpectedly raised the stakes on him. Opportunity—none, unless Poxwell had hired a bully-boy to do his dirty work. Or perhaps the bully-boy had been hired merely to soften Maunders up, and had gone too far. Proof of all this farfetched nonsense—not a shred, and if anyone in the Department were to see these notes he'd be up for early retirement like a shot.

Bunce threw down his pencil in disgust. That was it, that was ruddy it. That was the complete list of suspects for Maunders's murder, unless he wanted to append the entire population of Cambridge, always excepting the guests at Pullets. There was nothing for him to get hold of, no one to sink his teeth into aside from Letty, and he was willing to bet a year's pay that she hadn't done it. But he would have to send her photograph round to the surgical supply houses if only in order to rule her out, because so far she was the only one with opportunity and a real honest-to-God motive. Bunce picked up his pencil again and made a note to Miller to that effect. If Letty was out of the reckoning Bunce was left with Fenchurch's *Anelida* theory, in which case Maunders's killer could have been anyone in the Anderson Room— and he was right back again where he had started.

Bunce groaned and held his head in his hands. So far he had been left to manage this case on his own, and he had been grateful for the confidence shown in him by the Chief Constable, but now he was beginning to feel he would not mind so very much after all if Scotland Yard were suddenly to be called in.

26 Closing In

Mrs. Bunce was feeling hugely pleased with herself. She was fond of parties, particularly when she had just had her hair permed and was wearing a dress which she was complacently certain had cost more than the outfits of most of the other ladies present. And at this party she had achieved the crowning touch of her husband's presence. It was not because she enjoyed Bunce's company that the lack of it on a social occasion displeased her. It was merely that all the other husbands were bound to be there and she felt slighted when Bunce was not. Never mind that when he was absent he had the perfectly good excuse of a police investigation to account for it; Kathleen Bunce was of the firm opinion that a husband's proper place was at his wife's elbow at social gatherings, no matter what. Otherwise (apart from being maintained in a decent style) what real point was there in being married?

Bunce, on the other hand, did not especially enjoy parties, at least not the kind his wife dragged him to. His idea of sociability was the sort of evening he had spent with Fenchurch after the discovery of Maunders's murder, or a pint at the local with a couple of cronies. He was fond of getting together with his brothers and sisters and their families, but this practice was discouraged by Kathleen, who considered her husband's relations low-bred. She herself was a cut above them all, as her father had been a solicitor, even if only in a small way.

The party was being given by Kathleen's sister, Mrs. Ratchett, whose husband claimed vague pretensions which were never quite defined and sold second-hand cars for a somewhat precarious living. It was a drinks party, Bunce noted with disapproval. He hated drinks parties: He thought they were affected. But Kathleen had talked him into coming to this one, and as she had for the moment left him to his own devices he supposed he might as well make the best of it. Taking a swallow of his drink (inferior whisky in an expensive glass), he looked about him for someone reasonably companionable to talk to and spotted a pleasant-looking man, somewhat overweight, with greying old-fashioned side-whiskers and little black eyes like currants that twinkled when he smiled. Bunce racked his memory for the name to match the face. Trotter, that was it, the jeweller on King's Parade—the shop had been there for donkey's years. They had exchanged names earlier. For an instant he hesitated. He was not in the mood to have his brains picked about security measures, or to hear someone complain how dilatory the police were in responding to alarm-calls; but then Bunce remembered that he had not been introduced as a police official, since his hostess considered his job a demeaning one. So he was safe from that potential irritation, and Mr. Trotter looked like the only agreeable guest available to talk to in a generally rum lot. Bunce moved over and reintroduced himself.

"Of course," Mr. Trotter said genially, shaking his hand. "Amelia Ratchett's brother-in-law, isn't it?"

Bunce nodded. It used to be plain Emily, he recollected sourly, looking about the room, which had recently been redecorated; because of this he had an uneasy feeling that Kathleen would shortly find a great deal in their house with which to be dissatisfied. The fact that Mr. Ratchett had been doing well in the car-flogging trade lately was reflected in the new slipcovers and several newly acquired pieces of furniture; also in Amelia's dress, which to Kathleen's chagrin quite outshone her sister's.

"I understand," said Bunce, "that you have the jewellery shop on KP—just about the best location in town, I should think. I haven't been inside, but I often pass by it."

"That's the place," Mr. Trotter responded. "You ought to drop in sometime."

"Afraid I'm not in the market much for that sort of thing."

"Ah, but we carry ranges at all prices," Mr. Trotter told him persuasively. "Some rather nice lines too, even the inexpensive ones. Pretty little knick-knacks for a couple of pounds up to some really superb antique pieces. I'm known to have quite an interest in old jewellery, you see, so when any of the local gentry sell up to pay death-duties they generally call me in to conduct the valuations. In that way I'm sometimes able to pick up a few choice items. Not that there's much of a market for them here, but I do well with the cheaper stock, and the good jewellery serves as a drawing-card in the window. I do sell a valuable piece every so often and while the money comes in handy, I find I miss them—I grow quite attached to some of them, you see. Just the other day I sold a pendant it quite broke my heart to part with—one of the loveliest jewels ever to grace my establishment. But forgive me. I must be boring you, droning on about my work."

"No, no. Do go on," replied Bunce, with more truth than might have been expected. He was not interested in jewellery except in the way of business, but it was a pleasure to encounter a man who was enthusiastic about his wares: Nowadays selling was more a matter of putting something over on the public than of offering merchandise you were proud of.

Mr. Trotter evidently loved his work, so Bunce encouraged him to discuss it. "What's this pendant like?" he enquired.

"It is a magnificent thing, late eighteenth-century, I believe, made in the shape of a flower—a lily. The petals are encrusted with small diamonds. But the really attractive thing about it is that it is *tremblant,* mounted on little wires so that it moves when the wearer does—really most unusual—and it can also be worn as an *aigrette,* an ornament for the hair," he explained.

"It sounds first-rate," said Bunce, now genuinely intrigued by the description, for the eloquence of the man made him a veritable poet of his trade. "I reckon it must have cost a packet."

"That it did," Mr. Trotter affirmed, "though actually it was cheap at the price; and I was somewhat surprised when I sold it just the other day, for the young man who purchased it is a student, and though a member of one of our oldest and noblest families, his branch are known to be pretty impoverished. However, one never can tell," he went on, "—can one? Perhaps they have recently unearthed a Duccio or a Vermeer and sold it at one of the London auction houses."

Upon hearing this Bunce pricked up his ears: With the *Anelida* still missing, any large and unaccountable sum of money that surfaced in Cambridge was automatically suspect, since there was always the chance that the thief had succeeded in smuggling his booty out of the UL before precautions went into effect. "Who was this young man?" he asked, quite forgetting that he was not in his official capacity.

The smile that had wreathed Mr. Trotter's amiable pudgy face instantly vanished and he said stiffly, his previous approval of this new acquaintance expunged by such inexcusable inquisitiveness, "I am afraid that is an entirely private matter. I could not possibly divulge the names of my clients."

Cor blimey, thought Bunce in exasperation, *first it was doctors and lawyers who claimed privileged communications, now tradesmen have taken it up.* But despite this hindrance to his work he understood and approved of Mr. Trotter's discretion. "Sorry," he said. "I ought to have explained before I asked you. I'm a member of the Cambridge Police, and I have a professional interest in finding out who your customer was."

Mr. Trotter's congenitally cheerful expression changed to one of undisguised horror. What had begun as a mildly indiscreet conversation with an unexpectedly agreeable acquaintance at a dull party was rapidly assuming the aspect of a nightmare. "I do assure you," he replied in a choked voice, setting down his sherry glass, "the pendant was not stolen property. I should not have touched it if that had been the case. It was purchased directly from the estate of Sir Hilary—"

"I've not the slightest doubt that it has an impeccable provenance," said Bunce soothingly, eliciting a mild surprise in Mr. Trotter that a provincial policeman should have the appropriate word at the ready. "What I'm interested in is the large sum of money the student who bought it has been chucking about. I need to know his name and the price he paid for the pendant."

Mr. Trotter hesitated. Bunce fished about in his pocket, saying, "I don't expect you to give me the information without my official identification just because you've met me at my brother-in-law's house. Judging by the prices he gets for his cars," he added, "you couldn't be blamed for thinking I was on the other side of the law. Let's go into the kitchen where we can be more private."

The shabby kitchen, which Mrs. Ratchett had not yet acquired time or money to tart up, was deserted and Bunce did not think they were likely to be interrupted until it was time to clean up after the party. "Now then," he said, displaying his identification. Mr. Trotter peered at it, taking out his reading-glasses in order to examine it properly, and seemed satisfied, whereupon Bunce replaced it in his pocket and took out a notebook and pencil. "What is the young man's name?"

"He is Lord Henry Huntingfield, the Earl of Cavesson's heir, you know, who is up at Sheepshanks," responded Mr. Trotter unhappily. "Such a delightful young man. He was enchanted with the pendant; said it was just what he would have been looking for if he had known one existed. I cannot think he would be involved in anything that was not completely *comme il faut.*"

The Inspector made no reply to this somewhat naïve assertion, merely asking, "What did he pay for the jewel?" When he heard the answer he could not restrain a whistle at the price. *Hardly the kind of sum you'd expect an impecunious young lordling to stump up,* was his mental comment.

"You have been most helpful, Mr. Trotter," he said formally, "and I do promise you that I shall make no use of this information unless it should prove absolutely necessary."

The jeweller appeared only partly relieved by this assurance. "I must take your word for it. I hope you will respect my confidence, as I should greatly dislike it to be known that I had revealed the name of a customer. It is a breach of trust, and moreover," he added practically, "it might have an unfortunate effect in the way of business. Shall we return to the lounge now? I feel I could do with another glass of sherry."

It seemed the most amazing stroke of luck to Inspector Bunce when he walked into his office the next morning to find a report on his desk from one of his constables describing some potential witnesses to Maunders's murder. In his absence the evening before a call had been made to headquarters by a couple who had been in All Saints Passage at a little past ten P.M. on the previous Friday and reported seeing a young

man there whose behaviour, they said, was suspicious. Bunce
sent for Miller, the constable who had taken down the par-
ticulars of the telephone call, in order to have him enlarge
upon his report.

"What did they mean by 'suspicious behaviour?'" he enquired of the constable.

"That's just what I couldn't make out, sir, though I spoke
to them both over the phone. The girl—Lana Smith, her
name is—kept saying he acted vague, like, and Gary
Trout—the bloke—said he looked sinister. Those were his
very words. If you ask me, that's hindsight now he knows a
murder was committed in the passage only a few moments
after they left it. Trout said the man kept fingering something in his trouser pocket in a funny sort of way."

"Why didn't they come forward earlier?"

"Well, sir, apparently they're the sort that doesn't normally read the papers, and they only watch the telly for 'Top
of the Pops.' They'd both heard something about the murder,
of course—they'd have to be deaf and dumb not to—but
they didn't know any of the details. It wasn't until young
Gary bought some fish and chips last night that he realised
the murder had taken place in All Saints Passage shortly after
he and Lana had been there themselves—the cod was
wrapped in Saturday's *Argus.*"

"There just might be something in it," mused the Inspector. "We know from their description that it couldn't have
been Maunders they saw, not unless they're even more unreliable at observation than the usual man-in-the-street."

"I should think it wasn't the victim they saw, sir. This one
was fair-haired, well-dressed, and very good-looking, according to Lana Smith."

"We'd better have them in," Bunce decided. "There's a
chance we might get a bit more useful detail out of them in
person."

When the two witnesses appeared in his office doorway,

Inspector Bunce, who had fondly thought himself hardened to all the vagaries of the young, blinked. The boy was a swarthy youth (part Welsh, Bunce suspected) arrayed from head to toe in scruffy black leather, and his hair—what remained of it, as the sides had been shaved off—was bright green and stood as stiffly upright as a scrubbing brush. His skinny chest was exposed nearly to the waist and decorated with a couple of bicycle chains, and a large rusty nail dangled from one earlobe. The girl had short purple hair dressed in silver spikes, and the pouting mouth on her otherwise pretty face was painted with matching silver lipstick. When she removed her shapeless cocoon of a purple coat, she revealed a dress beneath that looked as if it were made of cellophane, worn over a silver bikini. She was very young, scarcely sixteen, Bunce guessed, and with a still-unformed body, so the effect of the transparent dress was pathetic rather than lubricious.

"Do sit down," he told them courteously. "You are Miss Lana Smith, I take it; and you"—he turned to the boy—"are Gary Trout."

"That's right," Trout confirmed, nodding his head. The nail swung to and fro like a metronome. "I reckon we told about all we know over the telephone. What else d'you want?"

"For one thing, I should like the most complete description of this man that you can furnish. But first, let me just go over the details we already have. You are both at present living with your parents?" They nodded. "And both unemployed?"

"What is this anyway?" asked Lana in indignation. "A flipping inquisition? First Gary drags me over here, then I start getting the third degree. You'd think it was us that killed the bloke."

"This is merely background," the Inspector assured her smoothly, "to put in the report. Now you say you left the

Wimpy Bar in Sidney Street a little before ten P.M. on the Friday, and you were on your way to Market Hill to catch the last bus home. Why did you take All Saints Passage to get to the Market, by the way? It's in quite the opposite direction to Market Hill."

Gary shuffled his large cowboy-booted feet on the floor. "The bus don't leave till ten-thirty, see, so we had some time to kill," he volunteered at last. "And the passage is more private, like." He sent Bunce a knowing look which that officer correctly interpreted as an attempt at man-to-man communication.

"I see. But as it happened the passage was not empty, as you had anticipated. Was this man already there when you entered?"

"No, he passed us whilst we was . . . looking into one of the shop windows."

If that's all you were doing, feller me lad, I shall be very much surprised, thought Bunce to himself. "And then?" he queried aloud.

"Ask Lana, then. She were the one as noticed him first off." Gary sounded disgruntled by Lana's lack of concentration upon himself.

"I had a glimpse of somebody out of the corner of my eye, like, and so I . . . stopped looking in the shop window. So then Gary turned and he saw him too."

"You say he was tall and fair-haired?"

"And dishy. Ooh, he was dishy." As she uttered this encomium Gary shot her a look of darkling displeasure.

"Had he any identifying features?" Seeing their blank looks, Bunce elucidated. "Can you recollect anything about his appearance that would enable us to pick him out of a crowd?"

"He had grey eyes with lashes that were ever so long, and a straight nose like a film star, and a lovely chin, and he was a couple of inches taller than Gary here," offered Lana, eliciting another annoyed glance from her companion.

"How old do you reckon he was?"

"A little older than me, maybe. Could have been twenty or so, I guess," Gary said. "He acted like he was off his nut."

"He did not!" Lana answered hotly. "He was smashing. I don't know why I let you talk me into coming here and repeating half of what we said before over the phone. I know he couldn't have had nothing to do with killing that kid."

It seemed plain to Bunce that whatever hanky-panky the pair had been up to in the passage had been interrupted by the appearance of the passer-by and that Lana had taken an immediate fancy to him, thus incurring Gary's jealousy. The boy had made her come to the police in an attempt to avenge himself on the fascinating stranger, and now she was rebelling.

"Why would someone like him want to kill anybody?" she asked defiantly. "He was a real gent."

"You stupid nit," Gary told her angrily. "I suppose you think toffs don't do people? You've got the brain of a flea."

Lana flinched as though he had struck her. "My mum's right—she says you're always talking me down. Anyway, who are you to talk? You didn't finish school neither," she flung back at him.

"Can you remember what this man was wearing?" Bunce interpolated hastily, hoping to prevent the interrogation from turning into a catfight.

"He had on a lovely grey suit, and a white shirt with green stripes—narrow ones, they was," recounted Lana reminiscently, "and a smashing tie that was grey with bright green spots on it, only they was shaped funny. Oh, and there was little spots of yellow on the green. He looked ever so posh." Evidently she had fallen hook, line, and sinker for the handsome unknown.

Gary glared at her. "Looked a proper Guy he did, if you ask me—like my old granddad dressed for church."

"What about you, then? If anyone should ask me, I'd say you look like you was got up for a rat's funeral," she retorted, sticking out her tongue at him.

"Why don't you take a good look at yourself before making remarks about other people? You're a proper sight, you are, done up like a tart parading about in her own shop-window," answered Gary, stung by Lana's gratuitous insult to the garb she had so recently admired.

"How dare you call me a tart? My mum'll fix you, Gary Trout, just you wait and see." Lana was not far from tears; despite her outlandish get-up, she was still very close to being a child.

"Now then, the both of you," remonstrated Inspector Bunce, feeling disconcertingly like a referee at an infant-school row, "there's no need to quarrel. I take it you'd recognise the man if you were to see him again?"

"That I would," Gary said vindictively. Lana nodded her spiky head and sniffed morosely.

"He kept fingering something in his pocket," Gary added suddenly. "It must've been the murder weapon."

Lana emitted a wail of grief like a Wili seeking her faithless lover. "It wasn't! I know it wasn't. He didn't look that kind."

"Them's the sort as usually does it," Gary told her brutally. "Looks smooth as butter, then cuts your throat as easy as kiss my hand. You better watch out, my girl, or you'll end up in a dark alley in the same shape as the one he did."

"I shall take care to keep out of dark alleys from now on, especially with you," retorted Lana, giving her boyfriend a malevolent glance.

Bunce rose. The amorous verbal sparring of these two wayward children was beginning to wear him out, and he wished they would go. "It says here," he consulted Miller's report of the telephone call, "that the man you saw stayed in the passage after you had gone."

"Yeah," Gary said. "He were . . . kind of lurking, like. Not looking at us, just staring off into space. Pretty freaky. Well, after a couple of minutes we left, see. There wasn't no point in staying there with him hanging about when we was looking for a bit of privacy."

"Is it your opinion that the man appeared to be waiting?" Bunce asked.

"He was mooning about like he expected someone," volunteered Lana. "I bet it was a bird. I wanted to stay and see what she looked like, but Gary wouldn't. I bet it was a ring he had in his pocket. It's ever so romantic."

"A ring!" Gary replied in disgust. "A knife, more likely, the better to cut her up with."

"Thank you both very much for being so helpful," Bunce said quickly, before they could start on another spat. "That'll be all, unless we have to call you in to identify him."

Gary attempted to take Lana's arm as they departed, but she jerked it indignantly from his grasp. When they had gone, Bunce said to his subordinate, "They weren't much help, were they? Although . . . I wonder. . . ." But he did not elaborate.

It was not until the Inspector was on his way to Sheepshanks for a consultation with Fenchurch (he walked from Parker's Piece to justify stopping at the Copper Kettle for a cup of coffee and a cream-horn) that Lana's description of the mysterious stranger began to assume a less anonymous aspect. It was a clear crisp day with a cloudless blue sky, and he found to his mild astonishment that he was quite enjoying the walk; perhaps the sugary pastry he had just consumed had produced an unwonted energy. So he strode along King's Parade, glancing in the shop-windows, including Mr. Trotter's establishment, until he arrived at Ryder & Amies across from Great St. Mary's Church at the end of the Parade. In the capacious windows of the gentlemen's outfitters an array of College ties had been set out, each with its own distinctive colours and pattern. As Bunce idly gazed at the pleasing mosaic, his eye was caught by a tie in the centre of the display which reminded him of something, but for a moment he could not place what made it seem so familiar. It had a background of medium grey with a design of miniature green escutcheons, each bearing a tiny gold dot. Bunce started in surprise and examined it more closely. Beneath the grey-and-green tie the legend *Sheepshanks,* elegantly inscribed in an uncial hand on a white card, had been placed to identify it for the prospective buyer. *By God,* Bunce thought in elation, *so that's it!* The stranger in All Saints Passage must have been wearing a Sheepshanks College tie. And if that were so, then it seemed more than likely that Maunders's assailant might actually have been spotted by that ridiculous pair. He experienced a fleeting moment of compassion for Fenchurch, whom this news would hit hard. He would not, Bunce decided, disclose precisely who it was his suspicions were beginning to settle on. That revelation, no doubt, would hit the Senior Common Room even harder. But he would try out the general theory on Fenchurch to see whether the don could add anything to it.

The Inspector found Fenchurch immersed in a proposed revision of his book on Sheepshanks Chapel and delighted to find an excuse for taking a breather. Directly Bunce mentioned the matter of the tie, Fenchurch grasped its implication but took it in his stride, only observing that a licence was not required to buy a College tie—anyone could wander in off the street and purchase whichever one he might happen to fancy.

"Of course, it may not have been a Sheepshanks tie the young man was wearing," the Inspector said tactfully, though in his mind there was no doubt, "but it does sound unusual—those little gold specks in the centre of the bigger ones, you see—and the fact that the green spots were irregularly shaped."

"I fear you are correct," Fenchurch reluctantly replied. "As you describe it, it does sound uncommonly like a Sheepshanks tie: a ground of elephant grey on which are displayed the arms of d'Ewes (vert, a lamb trippant, or). Sir Oliver preferred them to his own (which are gules, a chevron or between three sheep rampant, argent) as the colour reminded him of the Burridgehatty Emerald, the proceeds from the sale of which provided funds for those monstrous bas-reliefs on the College walls; and he used them at every opportunity. If you examine one of the ties closely you will see that the small gold spot on the escutcheon is the heraldic lamb. I'm afraid I haven't one of my own to show you," he added apologetically, "as I do not go in for gaudy ties."

"I'll take your word for it," Bunce assured him.

"This is of course most distressing news. May I prepare Dr. Shebbeare for the prospect that a member of the College may be arrested for this crime? I suppose you have as yet no idea who he may be?"

"We have his description, but it could fit any number of students," Bunce replied evasively. "However, since we have eyewitnesses we should be able to narrow down the list in short order."

"I see. You still have no indication of why Maunders was in All Saints Passage at that hour?"

"No one who has admitted to seeing him later on in the evening has come forward so far. I understand that he was at the self-service meal that was set up in the Junior Common Room, as the Hall had been taken over for the Feast that night, but after that his movements are a blank. Deacon was out, so Maunders might have returned to his rooms or he might have left College illegally by the side gate that leads into Sheepshanks Lane, so the Porter wouldn't see him and report him. Indeed he must have done so at some point in order to have met his killer. While it's possible the rendezvous in All Saints Passage may have been accidental, I am inclined to think it had been prearranged, especially as Maunders was confined to quarters. He would hardly be apt to risk further punishment except for a matter of vital importance. A planned meeting would account for the murderer having a weapon to hand, and also presumably some sort of protection against bloodstains."

"You think he was sufficiently farsighted to take such a precaution?" queried Fenchurch.

"I should think it virtually certain. Dr. Scarlett says that at the very least the arm of any outer garment worn by the murderer during his attack on Maunders would be sure to have been soaked with the stuff. Speaking of Dr. Scarlett, his autopsy report has come in, and he thinks Maunders's killer used a scalpel as a weapon."

"A scalpel?" Fenchurch exclaimed. "You amaze me. The only surgeon anywhere about at the time was Simon Poxwell, and he could not possibly have done it. Why would anyone choose a scalpel instead of a knife? Couldn't it have been a knife?"

"He says not. Few knives would have such a short blade, and he claims that a knife blade, no matter how carefully whetted, would probably not be sharp enough to have done the job on Maunders. As for why, it's a most effective weapon and it would be simple to buy one—perhaps here, but more likely in London, where there's virtually no chance of the purchase being traced. And like a Sheepshanks tie, no licence is required to buy one," he went on, rather unfairly throwing Fenchurch's words back at him. "Dr. Scarlett says he doesn't think the person who wielded the scalpel was necessarily a medical man, by the by."

"I wonder?" Fenchurch said. "Perhaps Maunders's killer wanted it to seem that way. And even though the evidence appears to indicate that the murderer may be a member of Sheepshanks, if he were sufficiently cautious to arrange his meeting with the boy outside College, why would he be so indiscreet as to wear a College tie at their venue?"

"Simple enough—he had no intention of being seen by anybody but his victim. It was a fluke that he was spotted, and even more of one that the young lady was so smitten by his charms that she observed him as though she had him under a microscope."

"What about his overcoat? According to the girl's description he wasn't wearing one," Fenchurch objected, gamely fighting a rear-guard action on behalf of his beloved College. "And surely no sane man would plan to commit such a sanguinary murder in a grey suit. Indeed, you've told me that your surgeon said he would have had some covering."

"Come now, Mr. Fenchurch. How can you ask such a question when all he has to do is buy one of those polythene macs that fold up to the size of an envelope for a couple of quid or so in Woolworths or Marks? He wasn't wearing it when Gary and Lana saw him because it wasn't raining. It would have looked downright peculiar to be wearing a waterproof leaving College on a fine night, so he kept it in his pocket till the coast was clear."

"Surely," Fenchurch argued mildly, "Maunders too might have found it odd that he was dressed in a raincoat, and been somewhat wary in consequence."

"Not if the killer came up at the back of him so his victim had no chance to see him. Scarlett says Maunders's throat was cut from behind; indeed, it's the only sensible position in which to cut a throat."

"You seem to have covered all the contingencies," said Fenchurch, greatly downcast. "I very much fear that you may be right after all. I had better prepare Dr. Shebbeare for the possibility that a member of the College will be arrested for murder."

"Probability, I'm afraid, Mr. Fenchurch," Bunce told him heavily. "Believe me, *I* don't look forward to another Sheepshanks arrest."

27 *At Bay*

In order to reduce the element of error as much as possible for the sake of his friend Fenchurch and his College (and not least for the sake of the Cambridge Police), Inspector Bunce managed to procure a photograph of Lord Henry Huntingfield from the Cambridge *Argus* which, he remembered, had published a series in early October on those sprouts of noble houses who had had the great good sense to choose Cambridge over Oxford in their quest for knowledge. By making use of a contact at the newspaper, for whom he concocted an entirely fictitious tale of a kidnapping threat, Bunce was able to obtain the original of the photograph of Harry along with those of the other young Lords and Hons. in the article, all of which had been borrowed by the *Argus* from *Country Life* and not yet been returned.

With the photographs in hand and a Sheepshanks tie purchased from Ryder & Amies, Bunce called in Lana and Gary to make an informal identification. To his astonishment the pair ushered into his office by Constable Miller at the appointed hour bore slight resemblance to the flamboyant couple he had interviewed only a day or so before. Lana's pretty face was scrubbed clean of mascara and silver lipstick, and Bunce thought it much improved. The purple and silver paint had been washed out of her hair, revealing it as pale blonde and charmingly fluffy, with little tendrils at her neck and ears; and her frock, a soft blue, was decidedly becoming. Gary was wearing jeans, but at least they were denim, not leather, and his shirt was both conventional and clean; there was not much that could be done about his haircut, but the nail that had pierced his earlobe no longer hung there.

"We both got jobs," Lana offered in explanation, correctly interpreting Bunce's look of surprise.

"Yeah. What a fag," Gary said, affecting a world-weary expression worthy of a rock star.

"It isn't so bad, akcherly," Lana confided to Bunce. "It'll be super to have some lolly of my own in my pocket instead of having to ask my mum all the time. It was our mums done it—they got together and said they was sick and tired of having a pair of layabouts around the house. I'm on Boots's scent counter—I get to try them all out!—and Gary is working in a garage. He always was good with motors. He's going to save up and buy me a ring." She laid a proprietory hand on Gary's arm.

"This gear stinks," Gary growled sullenly, deeply embarrassed to be seen looking like everyone else.

"We only wear these for work," Lana explained. "He's making a great fuss over nothing." She gave Gary a maternal pat and Bunce saw that the boy was being led willy-nilly into a state of well-tamed domestication.

Gary and Lana were shown several of the photographs lent to the police by the *Argus,* all of which showed young men similar in appearance to their description of the mysterious stranger in the passage, but after viewing each one they both shook their heads. The fifth photograph was of Harry Huntingfield, and when Bunce displayed this they nodded simultaneously.

"That's the bloke," said Gary.

"Ooh, he's even dishier than I remembered," Lana cooed

with adolescent enthusiasm, gazing rapturously at the picture. "Isn't he absolutely gorgeous?—too fab for words."

Gary stared at her with cold dislike. "Shut up and stop sounding like a broken record. He won't look so pretty once he's in the nick."

"He didn't do it, did he?" Lana appealed to the Inspector. "He was just a witness, I'm sure."

"Very likely," Bunce answered evasively. "Now, you're both of you willing to swear as to this being the man you saw in the passage that night?"

They assured him that they were, and signed the documents attesting to the fact.

"Well, that's that," said the Inspector after the pair had gone. "Add together the purchase of the jewel, his presence in the passage so close to the time of the murder, his odd behaviour while there, and the fact that he hasn't come forward yet though he's had plenty of opportunity—I think it's time we had a talk with young Master Huntingfield."

Miller nodded in agreement.

"But it's going to be exceedingly delicate, seeing who he is," Bunce went on. "I must check it with the Chief Constable before going further." He picked up the telephone and dialled, and when he had reached that august personage he explained his case.

"It's bound to cause the devil of a dust-up," said the Chief Constable after hearing Bunce out, "but your reasoning seems to be spot-on. No arrest yet, mind, we shall need more evidence for that—just interrogate the lad; and go easy as you can, there's a good chap. Just one thing more, Bunce: Make damn' sure you keep any mention of it out of the papers for the time being."

After the conclusion of this conversation, however, the Inspector still sat at his desk without moving. "Well," he said finally, heaving his bulk out of the chair, "we'd best be getting on with it."

Miller accompanied him to Sheepshanks where, before confronting Harry, Bunce went into conclave, first with Fenchurch and then with Dr. Shebbeare. The Master, as may be imagined, was horrified at any intimation of criminality in his flock, most particularly in a fledgling member of the nobility, but at length he reluctantly assented to Harry's questioning provided he and Fenchurch were present to see fair play, a condition to which the Inspector willingly agreed. Unfortunately, however, Fenchurch was on his way to a lecture and an important meeting afterward with the Vice-Chancellor, so the Master was left to monitor the inquisition by himself. Dr. Shebbeare summoned Harry to his study with a message that his presence was required immediately. The porter who was sent upon this melancholy errand found Harry in his rooms, and the young man returned with him.

"Ah, there you are, my boy. Delighted you were able to come. Sit down, sit down, Lord Henry," Dr. Shebbeare greeted him. He felt he was being unduly effusive, but it was difficult to know exactly how to treat a potential murderer who was also a member of a notable County family.

Harry sat in the chair indicated with a puzzled air.

"This is Inspector Bunce, who is investigating the unfortunate matter of poor Maunders's death. He would like to have a word with you."

Harry seemed surprised but responded politely, "Of course I'll be happy to do anything I can to help, Master."

Bunce settled himself down to the unpalatable task at hand, and his constable unobtrusively took out a notebook in which to record the interview. "That's very kind of you, Lord Henry. Now, did you happen to see Bob Maunders at any time on Friday evening?" he enquired.

"See Maunders? No, not that I can recollect. I was out of College," Harry explained.

"Where did you spend the evening, if I may ask?"

Harry seemed slightly taken aback by this unexpectedly

personal approach. "I—I had dinner at the flat of a friend of mine, as a matter of fact."

"Would you mind telling me who this friend was?"

Harry's demeanour subtly indicated that he minded very much indeed, but after a pause he replied, "It was Miss Vivien Murray. She lives in Portugal Place."

"And at what time did you leave Miss Murray's flat?"

"I'm not actually sure, but I know it was fairly early. But—see here, I don't understand why you're asking me these questions." He looked at the Master as though for assistance.

"I'm afraid I can't tell you at present, but I do assure you, Lord Henry, that they are necessary." With a visible effort Dr. Shebbeare remained silent. "Did you," continued the Inspector, "return to College by way of All Saints Passage?"

"I—don't remember. Possibly."

"You seem remarkably indefinite about your movements that evening," Bunce observed.

"I had something on my mind," said Harry, "and I wasn't noticing as much as I usually might."

"I should think, however, that you would be likely to notice which route you were taking."

"I expect so," Harry said, beginning to feel badgered. "Yes, now you mention it I think I did cut through All Saints Passage on my way home."

"Did you see anyone whilst you were in the passage?"

"I haven't the remotest idea. Wait a tick—I think there was someone there . . . a couple of people, perhaps."

"Notice anything unusual about either of them?"

"Not especially. Why?"

Bunce found this reply frankly incredible. Not to notice Lana and Gary dressed in full fig out for a night at the Wimpy Bar, and no doubt climbing all over each other to boot! Why, the lad'd have to be blind as a bat to miss seeing what they looked like. Of course, if he had been contemplat-

ing an imminent murder, his abstraction would be under-
standable. Bunce decided to give it to Lord Henry with both
barrels. "You were seen in All Saints Passage only a few moments before Robert Maunders was killed. Why did you not
come forward to assist the police when you heard about his
death?"

Harry became very still as he realised the direction in
which this interrogation was leading. "I—I didn't think," he
stammered. "I told you that I had something on my mind
that night."

"Money troubles, perhaps?" asked Bunce suavely. "Something the clandestine sale of a Caxton might relieve?"

Harry seemed utterly bewildered, but then he would, reflected the Inspector, even if he knew exactly what Bunce was
talking about. It was his best defence.

"A Caxton? I don't know what you mean, Inspector. Are
you talking about the book that disappeared from the UL a
couple of weeks ago?"

"An extremely valuable book which, sold in the right
quarters, would go far toward making someone mighty
plump in the pocket," agreed the Inspector. "My infor-
mants—who have positively identified you, by the way—say
you were fumbling with something in your pocket when they
saw you. The murder weapon, perhaps?"

"Inspector Bunce, I must ask you to stop hounding the
boy," Dr. Shebbeare cried, outraged, but Bunce had the bit
in his teeth now and took no notice. He was ready to swear
this boy had killed Bob Maunders and he wasn't about to lose
his one chance at questioning him before the Huntingfield
lawyers got into the act. "Well?" he asked Harry.

"Do I understand that you think I killed Maunders for the
sake of some book or other?" Harry demanded hotly. "I never
heard of anything so silly."

"Not so silly when the book in question has a value of

thirty to forty thousand pounds to an unscrupulous collector—perhaps more, as it is the only one in existence."

"I give you my word, Inspector, it was not money I had on my mind that night," Harry said haughtily, the skin about his proud Huntingfield nose taut with anger.

"What was it then?" Bunce pressed his advantage.

"That's none of your business, if you'll forgive my saying so."

The Inspector veered off onto another tangent. "You wore," he checked his notes, "a grey suit, a white shirt with green stripes, and a College tie that evening, did you not?"

"I may have done."

"You may have done—aren't you certain?"

"As it's my best suit, I rather think I *was* wearing it."

"I should like to have a look at it, if you don't mind."

Harry could see that this was growing very serious indeed. He became white about the lips. "If you must."

Silently all four of them—Harry, Bunce, the Master and Miller—made their way to Harry's rooms. Once there Harry took the suit from his wardrobe and handed it to the Inspector, who looked it over closely. "There seems to be a spot on the right sleeve that's been sponged off," he remarked at length.

"Yes. I cut myself while I was shaving and I must have brushed the sleeve against my chin when I was putting on my jacket, as I noticed some blood had got on it. Naturally I washed it off before I went out to dinner."

A plausible story, thought Bunce, *and just the sort of thing a cornered killer would think up in order to explain away a smear of his victim's blood.* "I'm afraid I shall have to take this in for analysis," he said, handing it to his constable.

Harry opened his mouth as if to protest, but shut it again without speaking.

"I think, Lord Henry, that you had better tell us exactly

what your movements were on Friday evening," Bunce said to him with quiet authority.

Harry thought hard. "I arrived at Miss Murray's flat for dinner at seven," he said. "Her grandmother had come to spend the night and they had some family matters to discuss, so Vivien—Miss Murray—told me it would have to be an early evening."

"May I have Miss Murray's address?"

"Twenty-three-a Portugal Place. It's not a flat, really, though it's no larger than one—it's a very small house, like a mews."

"Do you remember exactly what time you left?"

"N-no, except that it must have been a little before ten, as that was the time we had agreed I should leave."

"What were you fingering in your pocket?" the Inspector suddenly asked.

Harry blushed furiously. He remembered carrying the diamond pendant in his pocket: He had taken it to dinner that night in hopes of having a moment alone with Vivien, but there had been no opportunity to give it to her. He was, however, not about to discuss his love life with the police. "I haven't the faintest idea," he replied mendaciously.

"We have been informed that you recently bought a very expensive piece of jewellery," said Inspector Bunce, almost as if he had been reading Harry's mind. "How did you come by the money to pay for it?"

Dr. Shebbeare was hard put to it to keep quiet but he wisely forebore from speech, realising that his intervention could only harm poor Harry now.

The boy had turned so pale that he might almost have been taken for the marble effigy of Sir Ranulph Huntingfield, his Crusading ancestor, in the south chapel of the church at Cavesson Parva. "I bet a couple of tenners on a horse," he answered, thinking as he did so how lame it sounded.

"A couple of tenners bet on a horse enabled you to buy that diamond pendant?" The Inspector sounded frankly incredulous. "I must warn you, Lord Henry, that I happen to know exactly how much it cost."

"The horse came in at something like eighty to one," said Harry. Inspector Bunce looked exceedingly sceptical. "It was my godmother's horse—that should be easy enough to check," he continued desperately. "Her name is Lady Skittering and the horse is Ups-a-Daisy. It ran at Newmarket in the Swynford Stakes earlier this month, and won. I don't recall the exact date but surely you can check on that."

"You may be certain we shall." Bunce spoke ominously. "Had you gone to the races with anyone?"

"No, I was alone that day."

"Did you happen to see someone you knew—your godmother, for instance?"

"No, not a soul. Celie didn't bother coming to Newmarket for the race. Nobody thought the horse had a prayer."

"What about the bookmaker who paid out your bet?"

"What about him?"

"Do you remember the name of his firm or what he looked like?"

"I haven't a clue, I'm afraid. I was so excited over my win that everything else went straight out of my head."

"Indeed." Inspector Bunce looked down his large nose. "That's very unfortunate."

"I happen to be telling you the truth." There was scarcely controlled anger in Harry's voice. He was unaccustomed to being disbelieved.

"I hope so, for your sake." He appeared to be a nice enough lad, but in Bunce's opinion far too many coincidences were beginning to pile up against him. If they couldn't locate the bookie, and if that blood test for the jacket should match

Maunders's blood type . . . "I'm afraid you'll have to come with us for a blood test, sir," he told Harry.

The police departed with Harry in tow and Harry's best suit draped over the constable's arm, leaving behind them an atmosphere of gloom and apprehension concentrated in the corpulent person of Dr. Shebbeare.

28 Proof Positive

Bunce sat in his office the next morning reading over the lab report on Harry's jacket. The spot that had recently been sponged off the right sleeve did indeed, according to the technicians, consist of human blood. Now that the report was in, the case against Harry seemed indisputable. Maunders's blood group had been AB, a comparatively rare type, while Harry's blood tested out as O. There was very little blood left on Harry's sleeve even for the modest requirements of the wizards in the police lab, but in spite of this lack they had been able to identify the presence of the two types, O and AB. It appeared evident that Harry, having a cursory knowledge of the wonders routinely performed in forensic laboratories, had essayed to muddy the already none-too-clear waters of detection by superimposing some of his own blood over any remaining traces of his victim's in case his attempt to remove the telltale spot should fail. *Too blurry clever for his own good, that boy,* thought Bunce. Obviously Harry had not thought as far as the probability that if the lab technicians could identify the presence of blood and its type when it had been washed away, they could also distinguish between two types of blood under the same conditions.

Of course there was the remote possibility that Harry had told the truth about his shaving cut, and then had got a

splash of Maunders's blood in the same place on his sleeve—
an unlikely occurrence, but such coincidences had been
known to happen. Bunce had not been able to check Harry's
account of his whereabouts on Friday evening with Vivien,
since he had not been able to reach her the day before. Now
he tried ringing her house again and this time found her at
home.

"Miss Murray?" he enquired. "This is Inspector Bunce of
the Cambridge Police. I'm checking on the movements of all
the Sheepshanks students in connection with the murder of
Robert Maunders on Friday night." He had fabricated this
fiction so as not to alarm her and perhaps get an edited version of that evening. "Lord Henry Huntingfield tells me that
he had dinner with you then."

"Yes, that's so," a soft voice said. "He isn't . . . you're
not . . . ?"

"Purely routine," Bunce replied reassuringly. "Do you
happen to remember what time he left your house?"

"I'm quite certain it was a few moments before ten; I had
told him dinner would be over by then, as my grandmother
was visiting me and we had some family affairs to discuss.
Did Harry say . . . ?"

"That matches up with the time he gave us. One more
thing . . . you didn't by any chance notice a cut or scratch on
his face, did you?"

"No," said Vivien thankfully. "There was nothing like
that."

"Might I have your grandmother's name and address—just
for our records, you understand."

Vivien gave him the information he requested and he
wrote it down. "That's all, then," he said. "Thank you for
your help." He rang off and then telephoned her grandmother, a Mrs. Faulkner, who corroborated Vivien's account.
Harry's alibi hung together so far as it went, Bunce reflected,
but since he had known in advance that he would be leaving

Miss Murray's flat before ten he could readily have set up a meeting with Maunders in All Saints Passage on his way back to Sheepshanks. His dinner engagement would afford him a reason for being about at that hour, and he could justify asking Maunders to take the risk of going out-of-bounds with the excuse that it would be unwise for them to be seen together in College since someone might wonder what business they had with each other, as they moved in very different circles. It had been confirmed that Harry was telling the truth about his relationship to Lady Skittering and Ups-a-Daisy, but then he would have been a complete fool to have done otherwise. It was also true that the horse had won with the odds at eighty to one, but Harry could easily have picked up that fact from the racing results in the papers. If no bookmaker could be located who had paid out sixteen hundred pounds or so at Newmarket on Ups-a-Daisy to a young man of Harry's description, then, said Bunce to himself, they had an open-and-shut case against him. It would be even better to face him with the dealer or collector to whom he had sold the *Anelida,* but that was asking too much. They would have to wait for Harry to tell them who the man was. Bunce fetched himself a mug of strong black coffee and sat steeped in thought. As he was finishing his coffee Miller knocked on the door to his office and entered with a closely written sheet of paper in his hand.

"Here it is, sir—the list of the bookies who showed up at Newmarket for the November meeting. All of these men were there the day the Swynford Stakes was run," he told the Inspector, his fresh young face pink with the pleasure of a job well done. "Padgett and I have just finished trying to contact them, and so far as we can tell not one of them has a record of a large amount paid out on the horse in question. As you can imagine, there weren't many bets placed on it, and they weren't for more than a quid or so."

"So far as you can tell?" queried Bunce.

"Well, sir, there's always the chance we may have missed out on one or two. Bookies are a slippery lot, and it's hard to know exactly how many of them were there at the time. But we've been double-checking with the ones we reached, asking who else they remember seeing on the course that day, so I reckon the list's as complete as we can make it."

"Then it looks as though Huntingfield must be our man," the Inspector said, reading through the list the constable handed him. "With the positive identification we have of him in the passage, the bloodstain, and now this, there doesn't seem to be much question about it." He sat for a moment, then picked up the telephone and dialled the Chief Constable's number. When he had given his superior officer all the pertinent information, there was a gusty sigh at the other end of the line, followed by an explosive, "Damn!" Then silence. Then, "It's going to be infernally unpleasant, but in the circumstances I don't see what else you can do. Take the boy in."

29 Supplication

Dr. Shebbeare had lost no time in apprising Fenchurch of the unhappy results obtained by Inspector Bunce's interrogation of Harry, and in consequence Fenchurch spent as miserable a night as the Master. The following morning, as soon as he had got several appointments out of the way, Fenchurch planned to call at the Master's Lodge to discuss what steps they could take to deal with the situation, but as he was crossing Sheepshanks Great Court on his way there he was met by a slender flying figure that almost knocked him down. To his surprise and delight he saw that it was Vivien: One look at her face, however, made him realise that all was not well. To him she still seemed as beautiful as ever, but an unbiased observer might have found the tearstains on her cheeks and the shadows that lay like charcoal smudges under her eyes less than becoming.

"Mr. Fenchurch!" she exclaimed, her voice wavering. "Thank God I've found you. I went to your rooms but you weren't there, and I didn't know where else to look." A shade passed over her face as she recalled her disappointment and she seemed on the brink of weeping afresh.

"What is it, my dear?" Fenchurch asked her with concern. He took her arm and gently led her in the direction of his rooms. "Don't try to tell me about it out here. We'll go up to my rooms and I shall make you a nice cup of tea and then you can tell me just what is bothering you."

Gratefully Vivien allowed him to lead her to his staircase. She did not speak again until he had made her comfortable in the sitting-room and put the kettle on. The water only took a moment or so to boil and Fenchurch deftly made the tea, pouring it in deference to his visitor's sex into his mother's thin rose-tinted Royal Worcester tea-cups, rather than the mugs he used when Inspector Bunce was his guest. Correctly judging her need to be great, he poured a little of the sublime whisky into her cup before taking it to her.

Upon his return to the sitting-room, he found Vivien staring at the wall opposite with a blind and tragic intentness which he felt vindicated such extreme measures. "I have put a dash of spirits into your tea," he warned her. "You look as though you could do with a bit of warming up."

As Vivien drank, Fenchurch congratulated himself on his perspicacity, for he saw that her shivering had stopped, and her colour began to return. She swallowed the tea without a pause as if it were a medicinal tonic, setting down the cup only when it was empty.

"Dear Mr. Fenchurch," said Vivien. His heart gave a flutter at her mode of address. Clasping her hands about her knees, she leaned forward in her earnestness. "You *will* help us, won't you? You're the only one who can."

"Of course I shall do whatever I can for you," Fenchurch responded, only too happy to be of service to his lady. In his pleasure at being asked he did not notice her use of the plural pronoun. "Only tell me what is the matter."

Vivien smiled then, a heartbreaking smile to one who had seen her smile in happier circumstances. "I knew you would. You're so kind. I didn't know who else to turn to and besides, you know all about these things. It's Harry," she said, looking at him with beseeching eyes whose colour had deepened to the slate blue of a stormy sky. "Harry Huntingfield. They've arrested him for murder."

"But that's impossible," declared Fenchurch, for Bunce had relayed the Chief Constable's prohibition against Harry's arrest to his friend. It was not until that moment that it occurred to him to wonder why Vivien was the one to tell him this.

"It's true," she replied, biting her underlip to keep from crying again. "I was supposed to meet him in his rooms at noon. We were to have gone out to Grantchester for lunch, to celebrate our engagement. . . ."

For the moment Fenchurch could comprehend no more. Her voice reached his ears, but like birdsong or the sound of distant music it conveyed no manner of sense to him. He sat very still, his aerial edifices crumbling about him, and concentrated on keeping his emotions locked within. It was the end of all his hoped-for happiness but, he thought dully, hardly surprising. He was a fool not to have known that there was bound to be a Harry on Vivien's horizon. Now he would have to content himself with being an uncle to her—and even at that he was luckier than most—but because he had dared to hope for so much more it would be difficult to be satisfied with the crumbs of affection for which he would have to settle. Unless, a small voice seductively murmured, Harry had after all done what the police thought he had. . . . But Fenchurch valiantly thrust the ignoble thought from him.

"Do begin again from the beginning, my dear," he said to Vivien, "so I can get everything straight in my mind."

Obediently she repeated what she had just told him, her slim hands twisting nervously in her lap. "I went to his rooms," she reiterated, "to meet Harry for lunch, but he wasn't there. He had left a note for me which said he had been arrested for that—that murder. The one of the Sheepshanks student. But he couldn't have done anything so dreadful! Besides, he was having dinner with me at my house on Friday evening when it happened." She gazed at Fenchurch pleadingly. "You will help us prove he's innocent, won't you? Harry would never kill anyone. You write detective stories. You know how to look for clues—you're probably better at it than the police. *They* can't be much," she added scornfully, "if they've arrested Harry. The merest ninny would only have to look at him to see that he could never do such a horrible thing."

"I shall do my very best to help," promised Fenchurch, giving her hand a comforting pat and fervently hoping that he would be able to justify her confidence in him. But his heart misgave him as he remembered the already formidable evidence of the witnesses; and he feared that even more must have surfaced for the Chief Constable to have rescinded his caveat against arresting the boy.

A smile compounded of gratitude and hope broke over Vivien's face, bestowing such a radiance upon it that Fenchurch was dazzled. "Thank you, dear Mr. Fenchurch," she said simply. "I know you will. I know you will save Harry." She rose from her chair, stooped to drop a butterfly of a kiss upon his cheek, and was gone.

30 *Durance Vile*

"They weren't going to let me in to see you, the brutes!" Vivien declared wrathfully. Indignation suited her, heightening her lovely colour and lending her a charming animation. "Even though I *told* them we were engaged. But I think Mr. Fenchurch managed it somehow. Are you all right, darling? You look pale." She examined him critically in the cold light of the bare room allotted them for their meeting. "But I mustn't waffle on. We haven't much time. Mr. Fenchurch says he'll help us, and I'm sure he will. He knows all about murders, he writes detective stories—so he ought to have some idea of how to go about disproving this ridiculous charge." Her eyes gave off blue flashes of anger like the flames in a Christmas Snapdragon. "Now tell me all about it."

"There doesn't seem to be much to tell," Harry answered dismally. "It all began yesterday but I hoped it would blow over quickly, so I didn't mention anything to you. I didn't want you to worry."

"Oh, Harry," she said reproachfully, "you ought to have told me about it. I want to know anything that concerns you—you shouldn't have kept it to yourself to brood over. I thought you seemed a bit off your feed at dinner last night, but I supposed it was just that essay you've been writing. What happened?"

"Apparently someone saw me in All Saints Passage after I left you on Friday," said Harry, "and it happened to be just before poor old Maunders bought it. As if that wasn't enough, I cut myself shaving while I was dressing for dinner that night and got a spot of blood on my coat sleeve, which naturally I washed off. Now the police have run tests and they claim it's the same blood type as Maunders's."

"An Inspector Bounce, or something like that, rang me this morning and said he was checking up on all the Sheepshanks students. He asked if we'd had dinner together on Friday and of course I said yes, and then he wanted to know whether I'd noticed a cut on your chin. But, darling, I had no idea what it meant, so I said I hadn't," she mourned. "I thought he was asking because they'd found out the killer had one. If only I'd known I would have said I had."

"Look, Vivien darling, you can't save me by lying; it would only make things worse in the long run." Harry spoke energetically. "Anyway, the cut was so small that it's already quite healed, so they don't believe me, and they probably wouldn't have believed you either."

"Didn't the silly asses test your blood to see if it's the same type as Maunders's?" she demanded. "It's certain to be your blood they found."

"They thought of that; but as it happens Maunders and I have totally different blood groups. To cap it all, the witnesses who saw me in the passage claim I was loitering there and ominously fingering something in my pocket—the murder weapon, presumably."

"But that's a sheer bloody lie," Vivien cried, clenching her small fists as though she would have liked to strike those deceitful witnesses. "Surely we can prove those people are unreliable, and shouldn't be believed."

"As a matter of fact, they're not far off from the truth," he said wearily. "I was taking my time on my way back to College, thinking about you and how lovely you looked, and I was fingering something too, only it was the lily pendant, not a knife. I was so excited about the prospect of giving it to you that I'd hoped to find a suitable moment during the evening to do it in, but with your grandmother there, I . . ."

"Haven't you told the police that?" she broke in.

"Yes, finally; but they don't believe me. It's just the sort of story I should invent if I were trying to cover up the murder, you see." Harry shielded his eyes briefly with his hand. "It's all like a nightmare, isn't it? One moment I'm gloriously happy, and the next a pit yawns open before my feet. I'm so desperately sorry to be putting you through all this, my darling."

"Don't you dare to talk that way," Vivien told him fiercely. "Not one speck of this is your fault. It won't last long. It *can't* last long. They're bound to catch the real murderer soon."

"Not," Harry pointed out, "if they aren't looking for him. And there's no reason why they should be, since they're convinced I'm it. Father's been notified and he's on his way here with a battery of solicitors, but I don't see that there's an earthly thing anyone can do."

"Just you wait." Vivien spoke bravely, with more confidence than she felt, in order to cheer him up. "Mr. Fenchurch will get you out of this. He's very clever and he promised me he would." She kissed him encouragingly, then walked away as the constable approached to tell them her time was up, hoping as she did so that Harry had not noticed the tears standing in her eyes.

31 Giving Chase

It was Wednesday and the search of the UL was still on-
going. Fenchurch was growing restive, for he sorely missed
his familiar haunts; the College libraries were simply not ade-
quate for his researches. Now that his dreams of Vivien had
been so rudely dispersed—now more than ever—he needed
the distraction and consolation of work; and yet with the UL
closed, work (or at least the books he required in order to
pursue it) was denied him. He had not forgotten his promise
to Vivien, but for the moment he could think of nothing that
would help Harry and he needed to take his mind temporarily off the problem, so when Grierson suggested at
lunch that they make a visit to the reading room of the British Museum (they both disdained the recently imposed title
"British Library"), he jumped at it. At first Fenchurch
plumped for the Bodley's Duke Humphrey, but as Grierson
very sensibly pointed out, they neither of them owned a car
and the cross-country bus journey to Oxford would be far
more taxing than the train trip to London. They agreed
therefore to go up to London the next day for the purpose of
consulting the BM, and it was with the emotions of a water-
starved traveller who spies a distant oasis that Fenchurch
looked forward to quenching his intellectual thirst in that
wellspring of knowledge. An ordinary man who receives a

disappointment in love will turn to the bottle; Fenchurch found his solace in books.

While the two dons were purchasing day-return tickets for the eight-twenty to King's Cross, a somewhat earlier train to Liverpool Street Station was announced, and Fenchurch spotted a familiar back among the travellers milling about on the platform.

"There's Poxwell," he said aloud. "I wonder why he should be going up to Town?"

"No doubt he's headed in the same direction as us," replied his companion.

"No doubt. Still . . ." Niggling in Fenchurch's mind was Poxwell's family connection with that eminent surgeon and collector of incunables Simon Poxwell, who was at the moment Fenchurch's front-runner for Murderer-in-Absentia, perhaps by means of a hired assassin or through his brother's agency. Moreover, Fenchurch had caught a glimpse of a large brown-paper parcel under the Queens' Fellow's arm. Though its size apparently precluded its being the missing Caxton, it was undoubtedly a volume of some sort and thus a matter of interest in the present climate of suspicion. He pointed the object out to Grierson.

"It's probably just a book Poxwell intends to compare to one of the Museum holdings," that worthy suggested.

"Yes. Ye-es, it may well be so. On the other hand, I should dearly like to make certain," returned Fenchurch stubbornly. "Furthermore, if the man is going to the BM, why should he take the eight-fourteen to Liverpool Street? King's Cross is nearer to Russell Square. It simply doesn't make sense."

"Perhaps he has an aversion to changing at Royston; and of course the Liverpool Street trains are apt to be a little faster as well."

"Perhaps. But anything out of the ordinary is worth investigating; and since Maunders's murder may be connected with the theft of the *Anelida,* any book that goes up to London from Cambridge is decidedly out of the ordinary."

"Come now, John," expostulated Grierson, "surely you don't think that thumping great parcel contains the *Anelida?*"

"Of course I don't. However, it is certainly physically possible. Besides, I happened to run into Poxwell at the Sidgwick Site yesterday afternoon and he said nothing about coming up to London, even though I told him you and I were planning a journey to the BM this morning. If he had intended to go to the same place, one would have expected him to mention it."

Grierson felt his companion was overexerting his deductive abilities. He saw, however, an opportunity therein to avoid discussion over whether or not to walk to Russell Square from the railway station, since even Fenchurch could not expect him to proceed on foot to the BM from Liverpool Street.

"Perhaps we might take the same train as him and see what the fellow's up to," he ventured cunningly.

"A capital idea," said Fenchurch, entirely taken in by his associate's Machiavellian manoeuvre. "Just what I was thinking. We must get a move on then—the train is about to leave."

They took a compartment halfway down the carriage from the one Poxwell had entered, being careful not to be seen by him. During the journey Fenchurch racked his brain in an effort to concoct a reasonable scheme whereby he might save Harry from jail and worse, for Vivien's fair sake. Harry's exoneration would sound the final knell of all his hopes where Vivien was concerned, but Fenchurch was at heart an unselfish creature and realised now that all his glorious imaginings about a life spent with Vivien had been nothing more than pipe dreams. It should have been abundantly plain to the most nearsighted that a lad like Harry Huntingfield was the natural complement to a young woman as lovely and as desirable as Vivien, thought Fenchurch. How could he ever have been so foolish. . . . But it was profitless thus to castigate himself. Heaven knew there was no shame involved in loving Vivien; and though he could not now expect the reward he had once dared to hope for, yet he could still be her "verray parfit, gentil knyght" and shield her from any possible harm. All the more honour, he told himself stoutly, thus to nourish a hopeless passion.

Upon the train's arrival in Liverpool Street the two dons held back in order to avoid being seen by their quarry, who briskly made his way to the nearest taxi-rank. Fenchurch and Grierson followed him and commandeered the next taxi in line, to the vocal indignation of several ladies who had gone up to Town for some early Christmas shopping.

"Follow that taxi!" cried Fenchurch, the lust of the chase upon him. "We must not lose it."

Grierson, who had been secretly convinced that their colleague had come up for no more sinister purpose than a book consultation at the BM, and rather ashamed of the subterfuge he had employed to avoid a lengthy walk, found to his astonishment that the taxi in front of them did not turn in the direction of Russell Square after all, but continued onward toward Oxford Circus. Passing that landmark, they drove along Regent Street, and thence into the warren of smaller thoroughfares that open off it.

"Where can the man be headed?" Fenchurch wondered aloud. "Most of the rare bookshops are near the BM, so if he's brought something up to London to flog . . . not the *Anelida*—unless he's trying to mislead any possible observer by transporting it in a much larger parcel as a blind."

"In that case I should have thought he'd be far more likely to carry it in his briefcase or an inner pocket—it's certainly small enough," objected Grierson, who was regretting his greatly anticipated and now rapidly vanishing time for study in the BM. "What earthly purpose could he have in trying to mislead us in that way? He'd have done far better to pretend he wasn't carrying a book at all. Frankly, I think we've taken on a wild-goose chase."

"Steady on. I think he's gone to ground," said Fenchurch, from whose tongue the nearly forgotten hunting phrases of his far-off youth were flowing with as much facility as if he had never exchanged the pleasures of Artemis for those of Athene. "Hold hard! We don't want him to catch sight of us," he admonished the taxi driver, who immediately drew up to the curb of St. Edward Street some distance away from Poxwell's conveyance.

Apparently the taxi had been told to wait for him, since it remained where it had pulled over after its passenger disappeared, clutching his mysterious burden, through the doorway of an elegant establishment that bore the appellation DELL & CO. LTD. spelt out in gilded letters set into the stone lintel of the entrance. It was a good ten minutes before Poxwell emerged and in the meantime Grierson fidgeted irritably in the interior of their taxi, opening his briefcase to inspect his notes and then closing it again before he took a proper look at them. He did not think Poxwell had anything whatever to do with the theft of the *Anelida,* and he was deeply regretting the impulse that had led them there: He was embarrassed at the chance that Poxwell might notice them lurking some yards behind his taxi when he came out and wonder what the hell they were up to.

However, when Poxwell regained the street *sans* parcel and reclaimed his taxi, he looked neither to left nor to right, but quickly got in and the vehicle moved off.

"I wonder," said Fenchurch, "whether we ought to follow him again. On the one hand . . . but then on the other . . . and after all, he appears to have left the parcel within, so I suppose our first duty is to go in and see what has become of it and what it contains, if at all possible. Nevertheless . . ."

Grierson put a stop to this vacillation by saying impatiently, "Oh, do come on. He's left his package here, and that's what we are interested in . . . besides getting to the BM before midnight, that is. Not that I think it has anything to do with the *Anelida*," he added tartly, getting out of the taxi, "but I suppose you won't be satisfied until we have a look at it. Wait here, driver, if you please. We shan't be long."

"It's no skin off my nose, long as I get paid in the end," returned their taximan cheerfully. "Though if you don't mind, guvnor, I will just have a pipe while I wait." He felt about in his pockets and took out a battered pipe and a well-worn leather tobacco pouch.

"Do, by all means," said Fenchurch, relinquishing further pursuit of Poxwell with a sigh. He too left the taxi, and they approached the front door of the establishment so lately quitted by the Fellow of Queens'.

The woodwork of the doorway had been painted the pale grey of a dove's breast, and the knob and curving rococo door knocker were fashioned not from brass but silver. Grierson, who was in the lead, turned the knob as a preliminary to entering but found the door was locked. He tried the door knocker, and then for good measure rang an elaborate silver bell pull that hung beside the entrance.

They waited a moment until the door was opened by a very correct-looking man dressed in a dark pin-striped suit of admirable cut. He gave them what in more vulgar surroundings would be called the once-over; then, apparently deciding that they looked sufficiently respectable, he admitted them with a flourish into a deep-carpeted room with discreet lighting over a number of niches set into the damask-covered walls. In the centre of the room a low sofa and several leather-covered armchairs placed next to a handsome inlaid library-table suggested one of the better gentlemen's clubs.

"Do sit down, gentlemen," their guide offered, hospitably

indicating this seating to his visitors. "What may I do for you?"

This was a poser, since neither Fenchurch nor Grierson had a very clear idea of the purpose of the establishment to which they had just gained admittance. Since Poxwell had left the premises empty-handed, it might be presumed to be a book shop, but it did not look like a book shop; and after all they were not absolutely certain that the package he had left there did in fact contain a book.

"But I forget my manners," purred their host. "Will you have a glass of sherry? We have a very fine Amontillado, a Dona Isabella 'forty-seven. Or perhaps you would prefer tea."

"Tea will do very nicely, thank you," Fenchurch replied firmly. Though the bracing effect of sherry would have been welcome, he felt that he needed all his wits about him in this perplexing milieu. For an instant he had thought it might be a wine-merchant's emporium, but he was quickly disabused of this supposition by the offer of tea.

"Yes, tea would be splendid," Grierson agreed.

The man bowed and disappeared through a door in the rear wall, and the two dons rapidly took this opportunity to look about them in hopes of discovering the purpose of the place. Fenchurch went over to one of the lighted niches to see what it might contain, while Grierson did the same on the other side of the room. Fenchurch could see that the small alcove contained an open book, laid as though it were a jewel on a bed of what seemed to be velvet. Surely an incunable, he thought triumphantly as he approached it; here was proof of his theory, so recently mere conjecture of the most featherweight sort, that Poxwell was somehow concerned in the theft of the *Anelida*. But as he drew nearer he saw that neither type nor illustration bore any resemblance to the productions of the fifteenth century, rather proclaiming workmanship of some three hundred years later. This in itself was something of a blow, but an even greater shock awaited him when he moved a step closer and adjusted the reading-glasses which he had perched at the end of his nose. To his overwhelming surprise and horror he found that he was looking at a richly coloured mezzotint of indubitably French origin (even in his maidenly agitation Fenchurch did not fail to note that its execution and condition were particularly fine) that portrayed a man and a woman in a state of complete undresss. Both figures had been delineated with a passion for detail that left no doubt in the mind of the most unworldly beholder as to precisely what it was they were so vigorously enacting. For the purposes of this narrative it suffices to say only that the exercise was libidinous, unconventional, and remarkably acrobatic. After his initial glimpse of the engraving Fenchurch hastily averted his eyes from the offending object. "I say, Francis," he exclaimed, "what in the world . . . ?"

"Good God!" said Grierson simultaneously, his voice tinged with a fastidious repugnance. "John, do you see . . . ?"

"We appear to have landed in a den of iniquity," Fenchurch observed, rapidly scanning the other niches from a discreet distance so as to obtain the most impressionistic view possible of their contents.

At this stage the shop's proprietor returned laden with a superbly appointed tea-tray; the silver teapot, Fenchurch noticed appreciatively, was a delightful example of playful chinoiserie that would not have been out of place in the magnificent collection of College plate owned by Sheepshanks. "Delectable, aren't they?" the man remarked, seeing that his two clients had been inspecting the merchandise. "First-class, all of them, but by no means the rarest of our stock. Might one enquire how you happened to hear of us? Generally we operate by customer recommendation."

"Mr. Poxwell . . ." began Fenchurch. Grierson was still struck speechless by what he had just seen.

"Ah, yes, Mr. Poxwell," said the proprietor with great cordiality. "One of our better customers. A most discerning gentleman, with exquisite taste. A smallish collection, but each piece perfect of its kind—but you've seen it, of course. He was here only a little while ago, as a matter of fact. What a shame you missed each other." Deftly he poured the tea into thin porcelain cups. "Do you take milk?" he asked Fenchurch. "No? Rather a pity not. So amusing, I always think, to take a final sip and then . . . Not nearly so entertaining with lemon." As he handed Fenchurch his cup the reason for this incomprehensible speech was revealed. Coyly undulating in the amber shallows of the tea was yet another all-too-explicit representation of the art immortalised by Ovid, this one painted on the bottom of his tea-cup. Fenchurch blinked and swiftly took a swallow to fortify himself, dimly feeling that although Sir Oliver Sheepshanks's *basso-rilievos* ought to have hardened him to this sort of display, they most emphatically had not. Perhaps, he thought, it was the vivid use of colour that made such a difference. . . .

Although neither of the dons had succeeded in concealing the emotions raised by the unexpected and disconcerting sight of the book illustrations, the shop's proprietor showed no surprise, perhaps attributing their reaction to appreciation rather than shock. "Might I enquire as to precisely what sort of merchandise you gentlemen prefer?" he asked them. "I feel certain we shall have no trouble in satisfying your requirements as we have a large and varied stock, all of it exceedingly select."

To Grierson's mingled alarm and admiration his companion superimposed what could only be described as a satyric leer on his mild and guileless countenance and requested a copy of *Aretino's Postures.* It was the only salacious work he could think of offhand, as he was in the midst of reading a biography of Pope Clement VII.

"You *are* in luck," cried the shopkeeper vivaciously. "It

happens that your Mr. P. (we use initials here whenever possible—best not to bandy names about too much, you know) has just brought in his *Aretino* to sell. Quite the prize of his collection; but I expect you know it well. Such a pity he had to part with it. He told me he would never have done so if it were not for some recent financial reverses he has suffered. A particularly fine set of engravings after Romano, don't you think? And the price—so eminently reasonable in the circumstances. A mere . . ." and he murmured a sum that made Fenchurch's blood run cold.

How am I to extricate myself now that we have discovered Poxwell's errand? he asked himself desperately. Grierson, who had just discovered what was painted in his tea-cup and was staring down at it with a staggered expression, obviously was going to be no help. There was only one way, Fenchurch decided, in which they might make their escape without ignominy. He assumed an aspect of pleased expectation.

"I am afraid I never had the—ah—good fortune to examine Mr. Poxwell's copy while it was in his possession. It sounds just what I had in mind. Of course it is a first edition," he remarked casually, fervently praying that it was not.

"Naturally. We do not deal in the second-rate."

That's torn it, thought Fenchurch in despair. Now they would simply have to pick up their skirts and unceremoniously flee the premises.

"It is the first English edition, and one of the finest I've seen," continued the proprietor. "The paper is in prime condition with no foxing of any kind, and all the illustrations are early impressions. Let me fetch it for you."

He turned to go through the door leading to the rear of the shop, but Fenchurch forestalled him by saying decisively, "How very disappointing—I am afraid it won't do after all. It is the first Italian edition I am seeking; I already have examples of all the English editions, as described by Foxon. Perhaps another time. Thank you so much for the tea."

And on this triumphal note he departed with alacrity, trailing clouds of improvisatorial glory and his relieved colleague, before the shopman had time to ask him to leave his name and address in the event of a copy of the first Italian edition becoming available.

32 *Tea with the Enderbys*

"How very kind of you to come, Mr. Fenchurch," gushed Mrs. Enderby. "Giles is so looking forward to a little chat with you."

She was looking very smart in a bright blue silk suit, whose cut spoke of a London shop and whose colour matched her eyes; the house had been smartened up as well. On Fenchurch's previous visits Canterbury had had something of a neglected look, but now everything had been burnished and polished and painted until it looked much as it must have when the house was first built at the end of the previous century. Equally smart was the trim maid who had opened the door to him, and the waiters whom he glimpsed passing sandwiches and little cakes on silver platters in the room beyond.

"It's lovely to give a proper party," Mrs. Enderby confided, smoothing down her skirt with appreciative hands. "*And.* new clothes. Don't you think the house looks nice?"

"Charming, absolutely charming," Fenchurch assured her heartily; he would willingly have applied the same adjective to his hostess, had he not feared she might consider it forward of him. As they moved toward the drawing-room, he noticed that the door leading to Enderby's library was closed.

"All this has happened very recently, you know. I was

surprised to be able to get workmen at such short notice, but it is amazing what money can do. Of course, Giles mustn't know where all the money came from. Fortunately, as you may have noticed, he has a slight tendency toward vagueness now and then, but there are times when I think he suspects." She gestured in the direction of the library door. "He always locks his library now and insists on keeping the key about his neck. But I never thought he'd miss them, you see." She raised her cornflower-blue eyes guilelessly to Fenchurch's face. "Really, they didn't look like anything at all, and one was only a little scrap of a thing. I was absolutely astonished when I heard what we were being offered for them. Such a nice man, who just happened to call in while Giles was out lunching in College—Oh, there he is now. Yoo-hoo, darling," she carolled, "here's Mr. Fenchurch to see you. Isn't that nice?"

The drawing-room was filled with academics and their wives, all dressed to the teeth: at least, as dressed to the teeth as Cambridge academics ever are. Through the crowd Professor Enderby stalked unregarding, with something of the air of Hamlet's father's ghost. He was dressed as usual in an elderly and rather dusty cardigan, and wore a large key on a chain about his neck.

"My dear fellow." He greeted Fenchurch with obvious gratification and Mrs. Enderby, having performed her duty, went off to attend to her other guests. "Such a long time since I've had the pleasure of seeing you," he went on. "You'll be able to tell me where they are, I collect. It was the Duke, was it not?"

"The Duke?" echoed Fenchurch, puzzled.

"I felt certain it must have been the Duke who borrowed them—those several volumes I seem to be missing. They simply aren't to be found anywhere, though I've positively scoured the place. So I said to myself, 'Aha! The Duke!' *We* know what he's like, don't we, when it comes to books?" He nudged Fenchurch in the ribs with a bony old elbow. "I daresay it was you who took them to him without asking my leave. Not that I blame you, my dear fellow. When it's a question of your head or my books—even though they *are* my very favourite books—" he interpolated reproachfully, "I realise that your head would come first—so far as *you* are concerned, at any rate. It seems a pity, but there it is. I quite understand. But you will get them back for me, won't you?" He leaned confidentially toward Fenchurch.

"Which books are they?" Fenchurch enquired, in hopes he would thus find out whether *Anelida and Arcite* was among these fabulously profitable volumes. But in this he was disappointed.

"Ah, that'd be telling, wouldn't it?" replied Enderby archly, placing a skinny finger beside his beak of a nose. "Evidence, perhaps, for the Duke to have me up on a charge of high treason. Far better, my dear chap, to leave as much as possible unsaid." He glanced apprehensively about him at his guests, engrossed in tea-drinking and academic chit-chat, and whispered, "It may *seem* that we are alone, but cannot you see that the very walls have ears?"

Between Enderby's batty behaviour and the wild conjectures it aroused, Fenchurch's brain was whirling. Suppose . . . just suppose Enderby had stolen the *Anelida* from the UL, and some less than scrupulous dealer had, with the connivance of Mrs. E., made off with it (though to be fair, Fenchurch had to admit that the dealer appeared to have given her a pretty fair price for whatever he had bought). Well then, that meant Harry had no motive for Maunders's murder after all. Fenchurch's heart grew light. But in that case, he wondered, who had killed Maunders? They were still as far as ever from a solution to that puzzle.

Enderby was waiting for Fenchurch's assurance that he would return the books, but luckily his attention was diverted just then by Manthorpe, who was newly arrived at the tea party and came up to have a word with his host.

"Good afternoon, Professor Enderby, what a delightful gathering," he observed. "Hallo, Fenchurch. You'll be pleased to hear that we've finished turning out the UL at last—that is, we shall have finished by this evening, thank God. The Library will be open at the usual time tomorrow morning. The Librarian did think of giving the poor devils a holiday till Monday, but there's been so much fuss made over the idea that he's decided it's simply not on. Still no sign of the *Anelida,* I'm afraid."

Was Fenchurch imagining things, or did a cunning light gleam in Professor Enderby's rheumy old eye as he heard this intelligence? At any rate the sight of Manthorpe had caused him to revert more or less to the present. "Who are you?" he enquired. "Don't tell me. I know. You're the fellow that's been writing a biography of poor Betterton. When may we expect to see it?"

As the work in question had been published some ten years earlier, Manthorpe tactfully dodged his query. "It's out now," he answered. "But it isn't about Betterton. I wrote about Chatterton."

"That's what I said—Betterton, the lad who poisoned himself because he was starving in a garret. Though why he bothered I'm sure I don't know," said the Professor pensively. "If only he'd waited a few days he could have saved himself the trouble. These young men—so impetuous. Ah, my dear, there you are," as Mrs. Enderby came up to them. "Charles Manthorpe has just been telling me about his new biography of Betterton—you know, the young chap from Bristol who committed those literary forgeries and killed himself when Horace Walpole was so nasty to him."

"Don't you mean Chatterton, dear? It's confusing because they were both named Thomas, but Betterton was an actor."

"That's what I said, you silly girl," he replied impatiently. "Of course I know Chatterton was an actor. Now do stop bothering your pretty head with matters you don't understand and see to it that our guests have some tea. I look forward to reading your book," he said to Manthorpe. "It sounds decidedly interesting. I trust it is available in the book shops."

"Not at the moment, I'm afraid," Manthorpe answered. It had been out-of-print for several years. "I should be happy to lend you a copy, however."

But Enderby had gone off once again into his cloud-cuckoo land. "A copy? A copy of what?" he queried distractedly.

Manthorpe was not unreasonably startled by this phenomenon. "Why, a copy of my biography of—of Betterton," he rejoined.

"Betterton? Nonsense, you mean Chatterton, don't you? You needn't lend me the book after all if your scholarship is so slipshod that you can't tell the difference between Betterton and Chatterton," Enderby scolded, unexpectedly picking up the thread of their former conversation. "Betterton, indeed! What is the University coming to? It's true he turned out a few trifling plays, but no one would trouble to write about *him*." He transferred his attention to Fenchurch and relapsed into the fourteenth century. "Pray tell your master that I have great need of those books, if he can spare them. And do convey my respects to the Duchess and all the little Gauntlets." He drank from his tea-cup. "Faugh! Rotgut!—I beg your pardon, my dear"—he inclined his head courteously to his wife—"but I don't know what the world is coming to nowadays. I cannot find my pipe, my bowl is undrinkable, and as for my fiddlers three—I haven't seen the scoundrels for days. A poor time in which to be a King, forsooth." He balanced his tea-cup and saucer precariously on his head and stood on one leg like a stork, surveying them benignly.

For the first time Mrs. Enderby displayed faint signs of

uneasiness. "Giles, darling, perhaps it's time for your nap," she suggested, rescuing the cup and setting it on a nearby table.

"My name, madam, is not Giles but Cole, as you very well know," Enderby returned with hauteur. "You're quite as bad as Manthorpe thinking Chatterton is Betterton. Or is it Betterton is Chatterton? . . . Chatterton, Betterton . . . Betterton, Chatterton," he repeated, after the fashion of the Red Queen introducing Alice to the haunch of mutton, his voice trailing away as he obediently followed his wife past the groups of guests to the staircase in the hall.

She came down in a few moments, seemingly unconcerned, and when Fenchurch enquired after Enderby she said, "Giles is perfectly all right now, thank you. It's just that he sometimes finds crowds a trifle mixing. He only needs a little nap to be quite himself again."

But which self, Fenchurch wondered, would he be after his nap—Enderby, or Chaucer, or possibly King Cole? He felt no inclination to stay and find out; for the time being he had had his fill of Professor Enderby and his *alterae personae*. Before he left, however, there was one fact which he needed to discover from Mrs. Enderby if he could.

"You don't by any chance recollect the name of the book dealer who came to call?" he asked her. "The one who bought those books from you? I may have to dispose of some of my own soon," he improvised, "and it could prove useful."

"Oh, dear, I'm afraid not. Perhaps he gave me his card. If I should find it, I'll let you know," she said brightly.

Fenchurch had to be content with this promise; and thanking his hostess, he withdrew.

33 In the Bindery

As Manthorpe had foretold, the long-awaited conclusion of the UL search and subsequent reopening of the Library took place on Friday morning, despite the fact that the whereabouts of Caxton's printing of *Anelida and Arcite* was still unknown, and much to the disgust of the toilers in the stacks. Welby, however, was pleased that the normal scheme of things had been resumed. It was just on lunch-time and all the workers in the bindery had gone off to the staff tea-room or home except Mr. Sonning, who had stayed behind to tinker with a bit of gold tooling on the first edition of Mocquet's *Voiages*. Welby glanced covertly at his boss out of the corner of his eye. He was eager to be alone so he could look at his book, the one he had rebound which was presently reposing in one of the book presses. It was always like this if he had any of his books at work with him. He knew it was dangerous, the furtive excitement that fizzed in his veins whenever he had one nearby; it was safer to wait until he took it home that night, but the constant itch to look at it was too much for him even though it was risky to draw attention to his private library.

Welby had formed the habit of taking his precious volumes into the men's lavatory where he could enjoy them in comparative privacy—a far from satisfactory procedure, but better than nothing. Recently, however, he had come into possession of a key to the tower, found when a careless Under-Librarian had left it in a keyhole and pocketed by Welby on the theory that one never knew when it might come in handy. Since then, he had begun to take his books at lunchtime to the seventeenth floor of the Library tower where it was more comfortable and he could pretty well count on being undisturbed. There was always the off-chance that a member of senior staff might find him in the tower and ask him what he was doing there, but the fear of discovery lent a certain spice, an additional thrill that heightened his enjoyment of the adventure.

Welby did not dare to remove the book from the press while someone else was in the bindery for fear of attracting unwanted attention to it; luckily his colleagues, preoccupied with their own tasks and swamped by books to repair, were sufficiently incurious to take his word for the contents of the volumes he bound with bindery scraps in his own time. It was not only the humiliation if anyone should see his books, or the threat of losing his job should their contents become known that alarmed Welby: For someone else to see them would be prying open the door that concealed his holy of holies. It would be desecration, blasphemy to expose them to other eyes. For Welby's dirty little secret had grown and grown until it had become his religion, his all-in-all. Unattractive to look at and too shy to make even the most innocuous advances to a real woman, in his lurid imaginings he was hotly pursued by the most irresistibly pneumatic females. In any event, few women in existence could have lived up to his exaggerated ideas of concupiscence gleaned from Victorian erotica: the knowing courtesans expertly trained in lascivious exercises, the pert schoolgirls with long black stockings and an inexplicable aptitude for debauchery, the demure nuns whose prim habits hid willing bodies lavishly overendowed. Poor Welby—his reading had forever ruined him for real life.

"Not going down to the canteen, lad?" asked Mr. Sonning. Welby was relieved to see that he had finished fiddling with the binding he was working on. "Shall I bring you up something then?"

"No, thanks," Welby responded. "I brought a sandwich with me today." To his consternation his voice sounded hoarse with suppressed desire, but fortunately the older man did not notice.

"I'll be off then. Don't work too hard," he admonished. "Give yourself a rest. You know what they say about all work and no play, and now that the Library has reopened and we can accept books for repair again, I daresay we shall have more than our share of work."

Welby waited for a cautious but impatient moment after Mr. Sonning had left to make certain the head binder was not coming back, before making his way over to the book press. It was lucky for him that the search for the *Anelida* had halted the flow of repairs to the bindery and that most of the bindery staff had assisted in the quest, since as a result the book presses had been idle, enabling him to keep his book in one of them, where it was hidden from prying eyes.

There it was, safe in the massive jaws of the press. Welby permitted himself a few seconds of gloating, and the exhilaration in his blood rose to his brain, making him drunk with anticipation. Which chapter should he reread first, he wondered, unscrewing and loosening the press; perhaps the one where the young monk discovers his cellmate is really a woman—that, he thought, licking his lips greedily, was an especially good one. . . . But as soon as Welby picked up the book he realised it was not his. It was approximately the same size and bound in the same black buckram, but it was not his! His eyes darted, glaring like a madman's, about the long room. He tried to calm himself down, to think rationally about where the book might have got to. His body was shaking uncontrollably as though he were suffering from a fit of ague; he sat down on the nearest stool to keep from falling and forced himself to think sensibly. Someone who had needed to use the press that morning must have taken his book out when he was not looking; so much was clear. Then, he reasoned, it ought to be on one of the shelves in the bindery. Methodically Welby examined each shelf and trolley, fiercely concentrating on finding a black cloth-bound octavo. But it was useless. A constriction clasped his chest and his breath came in short gasps as he arrived at the end of his search and the inescapable conclusion that his book was not there.

It was not there! In rage and desperation Welby flung open drawers, scattered books on the counters, overturned trolleys till their contents were strewn about the wooden floor. When all was chaos he sat down again and held his throbbing head in his hands. Though his head felt hot and heavy his face had become numb and icy, and where he touched it he could feel nothing at all—it was like touching a block of marble. The blasted book must be here, Welby said to himself—but it was not. *What,* he thought despairingly, *could have happened to it?* He would not think about the possibility that one of his co-workers had noticed the subject matter and hidden it as a joke. Besides, they were all a sobersided lot. No, it was far more likely, he decided hopefully, that some idiot had put it on a trolley and shelved it, thinking it belonged to the Library. What, after all, could be more natural? While the volume had no shelf mark on the spine, its lack of one might not have been noticed, and it would not be the first time a careless shelver had lazily and incorrectly shelved a book without checking its class mark or contents. *That,* thought Welby excitedly, *must be what had happened. It must be!* But where in the miles and miles of Library shelving was he to begin his search? Feverishly he tried to recollect the title he had lettered on the spine to mislead his landlady in case she decided to snoop. *Battles of Byzantium?* No, that wasn't right. Something about the Emperor Constantine—*Constantine and His Court.* No, no! Welby clutched his pulsing temples and willed himself to concentrate. *Chronicles of Constantinople,* that was it. Then it would make sense for him to begin by looking in the history stacks.

He gazed at the wreck of the work-room with wild, unseeing eyes that gradually came to focus upon their surroundings. He must have been mad to generate such a muddle; he would have to straighten it up before he went into the stacks, before any of the other staff returned from their lunch. As is always the case, it took longer to tidy the room than it had to overturn it, but now that Welby had a plan of action he worked rapidly and efficiently to set the place to rights. When he had finished his task, he looked at his watch and saw that only a few moments remained until the other binders were due to return from their lunch-hour so, wheeling an empty book trolley to establish his *bona fides,* he set off at a frantic gallop for the history stacks.

34 Fenchurch Remembers a Lady

It was good to get back to the Anderson Room at long last. Fenchurch gazed with approval and affection at the unprepossessing golden oak furniture and his (for the most part) equally unprepossessing colleagues, who were hunched possessively over untidy piles of books and papers. The place, he thought appreciatively, looked just as it always had. One would never guess either from the condition of the room or of its scholarly occupants, some of whom looked as though they had not left it for a week, that the Library had been closed to enable a thorough search of the premises to be made. An unavailing search, Fenchurch reflected ruefully. He sighed. He was still convinced that the *Anelida*'s disappearance was in some way connected to Maunders's murder, and his promise to Vivien weighed heavily upon him, but he was as far away from a solution as ever. For the time being he dismissed all thought of crime and filled out a request slip for the *Chronicles of England*—the edition printed by Wynkyn de Worde in 1497–8—handing it to a new young woman, a member of staff he had not seen before. Apparently she was still learning her way about the rare-book stacks as it was some moments before she returned with his book, and he whiled away the interval in going over the notes he had brought with him. By the time the girl delivered the volume he had asked for Fenchurch had so thoroughly immersed himself in his work that he did not notice her presence. So it was not until nearly a quarter of an hour later that he glanced down at the book she had fetched for him and uttered a "Tcha!" of annoyance. It was manifestly the wrong one. Nonetheless he could not resist picking it up, for there was a tantalisingly familiar look about it that he could not place, like a person once encountered whose name has been forgotten; and Fenchurch, whose life was lived out among books, had the same reaction of mild curiosity to this strange volume that most people have to a half-remembered acquaintance. It was a medium-sized octavo, recently rebound in stout black buckram boards, with the title *Chronicles of Constantinople* stamped in gilt along the spine. Fenchurch turned the book over in his hands and idly opened the cover for a glance at the title page. To his great astonishment that title was not the one imprinted on the spine; instead, he read in slightly cramped and very black late nineteenth-century type the words *Two Little Maids in a Monastery; Or, From Priggery to Friggery* by the Reverend H.A.V. Atem.

"Good gracious!" exclaimed Fenchurch aloud. A scholar at a nearby table glared at him ferociously, infuriated by the untoward interruption, before resuming his labours. Fenchurch inadvertently covered the offending title with his hand, then shut the book with a snap. He was in a quandary as to what he ought to do. The sensible course, he felt, was to return the book to the desk, explaining that he had been given the wrong one and that, considering its contents, it ought to be replaced in the Deputy Librarian's room, where the Arc (short for *arcana*) class books were kept, at once. But despite his instinctive distaste for the volume's subject, Fenchurch could not help being intrigued by the mystery that surrounded it. Why had the binding been given the wrong title? He looked for a class mark, but there was none. Suddenly he recalled seeing a stamp of some sort during his horrified perusal of the title page, and gingerly opened the book again. Sure enough, near the lower right-hand corner of the title, stamped in purple ink and enclosed within a lozenge, was the inscription COX & SON, LTD., CURIOSA, 15 BELFRY STREET, LONDON.

As he shut the enigmatic book once more, Fenchurch noticed that its covers were unusually thick and clumsy for the size of the volume. He inspected them more closely and found somewhat to his surprise that the workmanship itself was excellent: The only fault he had to find was in the proportions of the boards, an odd mistake for an experienced binder to make. At this discovery something clicked in his mind and a nascent glimmer flickered at the back of his brain. *Binding . . . book covers . . . bawdy books*—the juxtaposition set up an unexpected train of thought—*book covers . . . bawdy books . . . fanny.* For one dreadful moment Fenchurch feared that the proximity of *Two Little Maids* was infecting him with improper ideas. To think anatomical thoughts at all was deeply shocking to his innocent and gentle soul; but to think them in the Anderson Room! *Hill.* Why Hill? He was acquainted with no one named Hill. Market Hill? No, Fenchurch realised with a great flash of revelation, *Fanny Hill,* that was it; that was what his brain had been searching for. Delighted to find that his unconscious had not reverted to infantile body references, Fenchurch pondered this result of free association and found it small improvement. *The Memoirs of Fanny Hill,* though somewhat sanctified by the passage of two hundred years, was a bawdy book if ever there was one. Or so Fenchurch had been given to understand, for he had never read it.

But why had John Cleland's boudoir masterpiece come to mind, triggered by the sight of the Rev. H.A.V. Atem's *oeuvre*? Why not *Aretino's Postures,* in light of his recent exposure to it at Dell & Co.? No, Fenchurch decided, there must be some reason aside from its dubious subject matter that had made him think of *Fanny Hill*. He worried the name like a terrier playing a rat. Perhaps it wasn't Cleland's book that was attempting to surface after all; perhaps the word he was really after was Hill. Hill . . . Gogmagog Hill . . . Peas Hill . . . Castle Hill . . . hills in the fen country were a comparatively scarce commodity. After much cogitation the only association Fenchurch could make with the word was the name of an American visiting scholar who had dined at Sheepshanks High Table some years earlier. As he made this connection the glimmer flared into a bonfire, and Fenchurch viewed the conundrum with sudden comprehension, as though the last pieces of a jigsaw puzzle had unexpectedly fallen into place. *Of course,* he told himself, *how stupid of me, how incredibly thick-headed*—the first known American edition of *Fanny Hill*, of which only a few leaves are extant, discovered by a wide-awake binder inside the covers of an eighteenth-century botanical work that he was rebinding. The paper-, cloth-, or leather-covered pasteboard protecting the leaves of a book is often formed by glueing together waste paper; and in the case of the American *Fanny Hill*, an enterprising printer had used up his unsold stock of Cleland's novel by turning it into book covers for his newer and less controversial publications.

It was a very long shot, thought Fenchurch, but just suppose that one of the UL binders had stolen Caxton's *Anelida and Arcite*. It would be a piece of cake for someone with a bindery trolley to pick up the book from the returns table in the Anderson Room without being noticed as he passed by on his task of collecting and returning volumes. And then suppose that he had glued together the ten leaves to make a cover for a book he was binding, or better yet—Fenchurch amended—hollowed out a space for them in a piece of cardboard. Less messy all round and no chance of damage to the precious leaves. It might be necessary to make the covers thicker than usual, so the hollowed-out cardboard would be strong enough. A mental image of Welby in the bindery and his embarrassment when Fenchurch had remarked on the book he was binding for himself came to Fenchurch, illuminating his newly hatched theory even more vividly. So much the better for the thief if it happened to be his own book into which he was binding the *Anelida*; once the search of the UL was discontinued, as it would have to be eventually, he could walk out with his book under his arm and no questions asked. And to cap it all, Welby had been in the Anderson Room when the book vanished.

The noise of a volume being clapped shut at a neighbouring table woke Fenchurch from his musings. All pure conjecture, he thought ruefully, and just as likely to come crashing down as the dreams he had once erected about Vivien.

Vivien! If his theory was correct, Harry Huntingfield would be safe. For if Welby or someone else from the bindery *had* stolen the unique Caxton, then Harry was left without the ghost of a motive for Robert Maunders's murder. Harry would be safe, and Vivien would be happy again. But, on the other hand, if Harry were convicted of killing Maunders . . . A pleasing vision arose of Vivien, lovely in her sorrow, being comforted by him. The imaginary scene became even more seductive as sorrow turned to gratitude, and then perhaps . . . Who knew? It was an entrancing picture, and he smiled as it passed through his mind.

I should drop that harebrained theory about the book-covers if I were you, whispered a small voice that sounded disagreeably familiar. *It's a pretty notion for one of those detective stories of yours, but in real life it's just not on; you'll look a prize fool if you so much as suggest it. If Inspector Bunce were ever to get wind of it, he'd think you were mad as a hatter. That's it,* said the voice triumphantly, *you see you've a perfectly good reason to forget all about the idea. No point in going off half-cocked. It's certain to be wrong, and you don't want people to think you've gone batty, now do you? You're getting on a bit, you know.*

What the voice said seemed eminently logical; and in Fenchurch's vision Vivien went over to sit affectionately in his lap, as Bunce had said his mother had sat in his father's. But without warning that picture faded and another showed itself to him unbidden: Harry, no longer young and good-looking and cheerful but grey-jowled and haggard, hopelessly pacing out his life in a prison cell. *Damn you,* said Fenchurch in answer to the voice, *I never knew you were there. I did not think I could be so wicked.*

The voice laughed, a strangely enticing sound. *You needn't get on your high horse with me,* it replied. *Don't forget I know you through and through. Besides, the idea's absurd. But go ahead if you want to,* it went on airily. *Make an ass of yourself. See if I care.*

I can open up the binding myself, and if there's nothing in it, no harm will have been done.

No harm? the voice jeered. *What if someone finds you at it? Oh, they'll all be very kind, but they'll think you've gone crackers. They might lock you up; you'll certainly be asked to resign your Fellowship.*

Not if the Anelida's *leaves are there,* Fenchurch insisted stubbornly.

But you know they aren't, the voice wheedled. *It's a schoolboy's trick that no one in his senses would entrust fifty thousand pounds worth of book to. It shows you're achieving your dotage, my boy, even to think of it. Just turn in the bally book and forget all about it,* it murmured alluringly, *there's a good chap.*

What it suggested was very tempting. It would be easy to persuade himself that such a long shot was not worth the effort, and then Vivien would be free to love someone else. For a while Fenchurch sat staring at the rows of reference books in front of him with unseeing eyes. Then he picked up the volume and carried it over to the desk where Euston was sitting. "Is Mr. Manthorpe in?" he enquired.

"I believe so, Mr. Fenchurch. Let me just check," replied Euston, picking up the telephone and dialling an extension. "Mr. Manthorpe?" he said into the receiver. "Mr. Fenchurch would like a word with you." He handed the instrument to the Sheepshanks Fellow.

"Manthorpe, Fenchurch here. Sorry to disturb you, but I've found something you might like to take a look at. . . . You're free? Splendid. I shall be right in."

Book in hand, he was escorted by Euston through the progression of bookcases beyond the Anderson Room until he came to Manthorpe's room.

"What do you make of this?" Fenchurch demanded without preamble, placing the volume he carried on the Rare Books Librarian's desk.

Manthorpe glanced curiously at the title on the spine, then opened the book to its title page. His eyebrows rose in surprise and disapproval. "What in the devil . . . ?"

"On the face of it one would say it was simply a refugee from class Arc," Fenchurch said. "But it seems exceedingly odd that the title on the spine should be so much at variance with the subject matter of the book; moreover, there is no class mark nor, for that matter, the Library's stamp. I have an idea. It may be foolish, but will you bear with me for a moment?"

"Gladly," Manthorpe responded, mystified by his colleague's behaviour.

"Have you such a thing as a penknife or a razor blade handy?"

"Why, yes. I keep a penknife in my desk for sharpening pencils. Will this suffice?" He opened a desk drawer and handed Fenchurch a blade folded in a silver case.

"Capital." Fenchurch retrieved *Chronicles of Constantinople* from Manthorpe's desk and painstakingly slit the cloth on each of the exposed edges of the front cover, peeling it back after he had done so to reveal several layers of cardboard glued together rather than a single thick piece. *So far, so good,* he thought; that was what he would expect to see if his theory were to be proved correct. He set himself to prising with exquisite care at the topmost layer as Manthorpe watched, bewildered and intrigued. At length the glue attaching the upper sheet to the rest of the cardboard gave way and the top layer sprang up, disclosing a recess carved into the cover. Within the compartment thus formed lay a number of sheets of rough creamy paper, the uppermost page with lines of verse printed in a rounded black-letter typeface and headed by a title written in an early sixteenth-century hand: *Annilida and false Arcyte.*

Fenchurch gave a deep sigh of satisfaction as Manthorpe clapped him on the back and grinned. The search for the *Anelida* was over.

35 Pursuit

"Once I happened on that method of hiding the *Anelida,* it was obvious," Fenchurch said modestly to Bunce. The Inspector had brought several subordinates with him to the UL, and the presence of four large policemen made Manthorpe's room seem even smaller and more crowded than usual. "The members of the bindery staff," Fenchurch continued, "like the proverbial postman, are virtually invisible in the Library—one so frequently sees them going in and out with books to be repaired that one takes no particular notice of their presence. Oh, we checked up on Welby, of course, along with the rest of the UL staff, but we never seriously considered him as the thief."

"And so you reckon he made up the book covers with the leaves of the Caxton inside them during his lunch-hour that day?" asked Bunce.

"Yes; he had already established the habit of staying on in the bindery at lunch-time to work on his own books, so it was easy enough to do so. It was imperative that he hide the leaves as quickly as possible since a great hue and cry was bound to be set up once it was discovered that the *Anelida* had disappeared. I daresay we actually saw him working on the book the day you were shown over the Library."

The Inspector seemed dissatisfied with this solution. "Jolly enough for you to get your ruddy Caxton back, but now we're left with a murder that has no apparent motive," he grumbled. "Lord Henry must have killed Maunders, but why?"

"Of course he didn't." Fenchurch spoke sharply, perhaps all the more so because he remembered his small inner voice's attempts at persuasion. "You cannot convict a man just because he was in the wrong place at the wrong time."

But Bunce remained unconvinced. "Maybe he was blackmailing Maunders on account of another theft—one we haven't uncovered yet. Anyway"—he brightened at the prospect of a hole in Fenchurch's inconvenient theory, even though incontrovertible proof of its accuracy lay in front of him—"how did Welby dispose of the Caxton binding? You didn't come across that while you were scouring the Library," he pointed out. "Maybe he and Maunders were in it together, and Maunders smuggled the binding out when he said he was down in the tea-room. Then as he was dumping it in the Cam or somewhere," he rather ineptly improvised, "Huntingfield caught him at it and demanded part of the loot."

But Fenchurch punctured that hopeful balloon. "Nothing simpler than for Welby to rid himself of that binding, my dear fellow. He probably shredded it with one of the implements they use in the bindery and flushed what was left of it down the w.c. . . . ." His voice trailed off. "I say, Inspector," he ventured, "you did tell me it was a scalpel Maunders was killed with, didn't you?"

"That's right, sir. That's what the police surgeon says anyway, and he ought to know."

"I have been inexcusably stupid," Fenchurch said quietly. "Directly that fact came to light I ought to have spotted the murderer."

Manthorpe was suddenly enlightened. "By God, Fenchurch, you don't mean—?"

Fenchurch addressed Bunce, interrupting the librarian as

though he had not heard him, which indeed he had not, so intent was he on his revelation. "I was endeavouring to think of some way to connect Simon Poxwell with Maunders's death because he is a surgeon as well as a book collector, and thus would have ready access to a scalpel; but I was criminally remiss in forgetting the fact that scalpels are also sometimes employed by bookbinders in their work. Since a scalpel is an incomparable cutting instrument, binders sometimes use them for trimming cardboard, cloth, or leather. They are, as it happens, occasional tools of the binding craft. Maunders probably saw Welby take the book from the Anderson Room and blackmailed him, just as you thought young Huntingfield had done; then Welby silenced him by killing him, using what came naturally."

Bunce was silent as this vital and hitherto undreamed-of piece of information sank in. Then his usually genial face settled into lines of grim determination and, picking up his hat from Manthorpe's desk, he said, "Let's go, then. We have no time to waste, I fancy. If Welby should find out the book has gone from wherever he kept it he may get the wind up and take off, and he's too dangerous to leave running about, perhaps with a scalpel in his coat pocket."

However, when the police (accompanied by Fenchurch, who felt that it was his prerogative to be in at the kill) arrived at the bindery, Mr. Sonning told them that Welby had not been there when he returned from his lunch. "He appears to have taken one of the book trolleys, so I expect he's somewhere in the stacks. I should think he'll be along any moment now," he added. "The lad must be getting hungry, he's left his sandwich behind." The head binder indicated a packet wrapped in oiled paper lying on the counter.

"I suppose you've no idea what floor of the stacks he's gone to?" Fenchurch spoke up.

"I'm afraid not, sir." The binder tried to look incurious at the presence of so many policemen, but failed signally.

"We shall have to see to it that he doesn't leave the building. Would it be possible to lock all the entrances to the Library except the front door?" Bunce asked Fenchurch.

"Under the circumstances I feel certain it can be arranged." With a word of apology to Mr. Sonning, Fenchurch picked up the bindery telephone, spoke briefly to the University Librarian, and then said to the Inspector, "He assures me that all entrances except the main door will be secured at once."

"That's champion. Now if I may, Mr. Sonning, I too shall borrow your telephone to ring for reinforcements." When he had done this, Bunce said, "There's no point in going out looking for him until we have some help. In the meantime you lads go on down to keep an eye on the main entrance. I'd best go with you, I suppose, as I'm the only one among us who's clapped eyes on the bloke and I can't very well go after him on my own. Coming, Mr. Fenchurch?"

"In a few moments," replied Fenchurch innocently. "You don't need my services now: I can see you have everything splendidly in hand, and there are one or two little matters I want to attend to."

He trailed them out of the bindery, but as soon as they had gone down to the ground floor he made his way to the history stacks, like a hound hunting his own line. It did not occur to Fenchurch that by going off alone to look for Welby he might be running any particular danger, and now that the main outlines of the puzzle had been filled in, he was eager to clear up the tag-ends—such as, for example, how Welby's mind worked. Had he entered the history stacks (the obvious choice when searching for a work titled *Chronicles of Constantinople*) or did he possess the extra-clever sort of mind which leapfrogs over itself and comes to unexpected, illogical, yet sometimes surprisingly accurate, conclusions? In that event he might even now be rummaging through the rare-book section, having somehow guessed that the volume he sought had been misshelved according to the first word in the title rather than with reference to its subject or period. But for him to do that would indicate a general familiarity with the titles of early English printed books, a desirable though not absolutely necessary prerequisite to stealing one that was not likely to be possessed by Welby.

Fenchurch moved cautiously along the narrow bays between tall metal bookcases that stretched from floor to ceiling. In the dim and dust-ridden light one might almost fancy oneself wandering in a queer kind of catacomb where countless volumes entombing the thoughts of men long dead took the place of more conventional remains. Fenchurch was small and light-footed and accustomed, on his walks in the Cambridgeshire countryside, to move silently through the marsh-reeds in order to view the microcosmic worlds they sheltered; and he made remarkably little noise in his progression along the paths of the bibliotaphic maze. Even so, several corridors away, a figure stiffened and froze in the middle of its frantic scanning of the shelves.

The book spines and their titles had begun to jerk and dance meaninglessly before Welby's eyes like colours in an abstract tapestry. No longer was he able to think objectively; the one idea that kept pounding in his mad and swollen brain was that all was lost, all was lost, unless he could find that damned book. Common sense would have told him that no one could possibly guess what it contained and that it was bound to turn up sooner or later, but common sense had long since departed, leaving sheer unreason in its stead. So much depended upon those ten slight leaves of paper—a flat of his own, where for the first time in his life he could live as he liked, free of prying Mrs. Rogers and the eternal cabbage smell, a place where he could display his treasures and look at them openly whenever he chose, where he could take a girl— a soft and plump and pliable girl, bashful yet eager like the girls in his books. All those riches so long counted upon, so long waited for, fled in the flicker of an eyelash. Black rage possessed him. All that he had thought, had contrived, had done—all of it wasted. The cleverness and the calculation, the risks taken, the blood and the whistle Maunders's windpipe had made after he sliced it open, like the piping of a wounded bird; sometimes Welby thought he heard it at night when the wind was blowing among the chimneys of Hills Road—all endured for nothing.

He stood motionless with one hand resting on a blackbound volume which he had been about to pull off the shelf—the letters stamped on the backs of the books had become a senseless jumble and now he had to open a book at its title page, holding it close to his eyes, to make any sense of the words. The irrationality that possessed Welby gave him the instincts of a hunted beast. If he had paused to think he must have realised it was virtually impossible that anyone could have guessed where the *Anelida* was concealed, or supposed that he had anything to do with its disappearance. No one holding the volume that purported to be the *Chronicles of Constantinople* would think there was anything out of the ordinary about it, aside from the difference between its spine title and its subject matter. But logic had flown out the window; and uncontrolled panic reigned within the small misshapen soul of the bookbinder.

The sound of a light footstep in the next bay made Welby realise he was unprotected, for in his haste it had not occurred to him to bring anything that might serve as a weapon. Eyes fixed and wide with the frenzy of fear that gripped him, lips drawn back from foam-flecked teeth, he snatched the heaviest object that came to hand and waited for what he knew, from its stealth, must be his pursuer.

Though Fenchurch was patently enjoying the rôle of bloodhound (it was sometimes pleasant to abandon the theoretical for the practical) he had decided not to be foolhardy. Recollecting all too vividly a perilous hour or so spent with a murderer in the loft of Sheepshanks Chapel some years ago, he inwardly vowed to indulge himself in no more than a brief reconnoitre of the stacks despite his certainty that Welby could not suspect they were on to him. Nonetheless, Fenchurch surmised, it would be far more prudent to let the police deal with the man once he had been located.

But the don had reckoned without two circumstances: the state of Welby's nerves and the fact that as Fenchurch rounded a corner of a bookcase he came unexpectedly upon his quarry who stood silent as a statue only a foot or so from him, his face an unrecognisable mask of terror and his arm upraised, a weighty volume in his work-hardened hand. There was barely time for the thought that he must run to cross Fenchurch's mind before the heavy book came crashing down with unerring accuracy on the top of his head. For an instant his ears sounded with the clangour of barbaric instruments, and his vision misted over as though he were wearing spectacles out in a Cambridge mizzle. Shifting crimson shapes wavered and surged like amoebae at the back of his closed eyelids. And then all his senses fled.

36 *Taking Flight*

Welby did not stay to see what damage he had done. He fled—out the door leading from the stacks, down the echoing corridor, totally abandoning the previously all-important search for his book. The volumes which lined the high shelves loomed overhead, menacing him, threatening to topple and crush him beneath their combined weight as he had just smashed Fenchurch's skull. He was stifling in this mote-filled, mould-scented air. The nidor of books permeated the building and assailed his unwilling nostrils—an effluvium of ageing hides and crumbling animal glues; decaying skins of lambs, scraped and beaten; oils and unguents, long gone rancid, that had been massaged into the leather to keep it supple—a gamut of odours eddied in the draughts and blanketed the place, nauseating him. First-century Greek philosophers, clapped between worm-eaten wooden covers; fifth-century Coptic Bibles wrapped in stiff hairy goatskin; medieval books of hours, their thin vellum leaves, brittle as crackling, protected by jewelled boards; musty volumes of sermons with pages still uncut, bound in flaccid divinity calf—the mephitis pouring out of these untold thousands of volumes permeated Welby's brain, obscuring all his other senses. Perplexed, he halted in midflight, uncertain where to go or what to do: His mind, clouded by the deluge of odours, was hopelessly muddled.

He started down the stairs leading to the front entrance, only to look down and see Bunce and his constables stationed in the hall below. His fear of pursuit had not been foolish after all. He stood uncertainly at bay, quivering like a stag with the hounds at his heels, that has no place to run. He was convinced that somehow they had found his book and discovered that he was responsible for Maunders's death; he knew beyond a doubt that he would be charged with the murder of Fenchurch. He would be sent to prison for life and never see his books again. All his dreams shattered: Instead of a cosy flat of his own, a prison cell and day following dismal day—each grey-tinged, lacklustre, indistinguishable from all the others—until he died. He did not notice that the only real difference between the life he had been leading and the prison life he pictured to himself would be the total absence of hope.

Welby took several uncertain steps in the direction of one of the rear entrances to the Library, only to come to an abrupt halt. If they were guarding the front of the building, he reasoned, then surely the other exits would be barred to him as well. There was only one place left where he might successfully escape detection. He made his stumbling way toward Scott's uncouth tower that rears itself above the Library's bulk, hugging the walls for support like an old man. He remembered the key in his pocket that would open a path to the tower. They would never think to look for him there! The staircase key did not provide access to the tower lift, but Welby preferred to walk: He would have been afraid to summon the lift, for if he did the door might suddenly slide back to reveal some of his stalkers; and in any case it only rose as far as the fifteenth floor.

Welby's impulse to bolt made him want to put as much

distance between himself and his enemies as he possibly could, to seek sanctuary high up on the topmost floor where he had spent so many happy hours undisturbed with his books. With this goal in mind he staggered, hot and panting, up the curvated stone staircase that spiralled upwards, receding into the gloom, twisting in upon itself like a giant corkscrew in motion. As he reached the eleventh floor Welby clung to the metal rail like a frightened monkey, his head spinning vertiginously. He wondered uneasily whether he would slip and fall, caroming against the rough stone walls that encased the narrow pie-shaped steps, until his broken and battered body came to rest at the foot of the stairs nearly a hundred feet below. He paused then to rest, his heart thudding in his ears, before continuing the ascent.

At length the steps ended beside a door and he could go no higher. Opening it, he apprehensively peered in. The room that comprised the seventeenth floor of the tower was quite empty. *Thank God,* Welby thought and scuttled in like a terrified rabbit making for its burrow with a stoat hot on its trail. Here in his eyrie he was safe, for the moment at least. No one knew he had a key to the tower, so they would not look for him up here. Metal bookcases filled the room and the atmosphere, like that of the stacks he had recently left, was dusty and close, impeding his breathing and making him inhale in short rapid gulps, his chest heaving like the sides of a fish out of water. It seemed to him that the turbid air was clogging his lungs and that soon he would be unable to take another breath. Panic-stricken, he clawed, wheezing, at his throat. Air, he was frantic for air—pure fresh air, the biting wind off the fens that would sweep away the unbearable book stench smothering him. But he must not, must not, leave this haven. He must stay up here in the tower; it was only in the tower that he was safe.

Retching and choking, his sight dimmed as though he were viewing the room and its contents through smoked glass, Welby reeled over to the metal door in the centre of the room that guarded the highest floor of the tower, and futilely wrenched at the doorknob. In his agitation he had not noticed that the door was padlocked. He lacked the presence of mind to try his key, but it would not have fitted. Another key was required for access to the platform at the top of the tower. I'm dying, Welby thought wildly, I must get air. His breath rattled in his throat, and in the depth of his terror he summoned preternatural strength to aim a volley of blows with his fists on the heavy frosted glass set into the upper part of the metal frame. Soon his hands were bruised and bleeding, to no effect; and he desperately snatched off a shoe with which to pummel the recalcitrant glass. His footwear was of the sturdy old-fashioned variety: With it he succeeded in producing a crack in the pane, which further wild hammering extended into a jagged hole.

With a gasp of relief Welby put his face to the aperture he had made, but it was not enough. In a frenzy he forced the rest of the shattered glass out of the door-frame, scratching and tearing his hands on the shards until he had made a space wide enough to heave himself through onto the metal staircase that led up to a hinged trap door. The air on the stairs was damp and chill with the must of an unventilated area, and Welby painfully clambered up the remaining steps. His respiration had eased slightly, but he still felt as if he were suffocating. His tortured lungs demanded air. He kept his eyes fixed on the entrance overhead, and when he gained the final step and pushed against the trap-door with the last of his strength, he discovered to his joy that it was unfastened. As he crawled through onto the tower roof, the sharp November air blew about his face and eased his congested lungs. He found himself on a platform surrounded by a wooden fence with palings four feet high, part of which was in process of repair: Workmen had removed a small rotted section, leaving a gap a couple of feet wide in the protective railing.

The lack of air had left Welby lightheaded, and he moved to the edge of the roof like a man in a trance. As he looked down, a familiar hiccoughing wail rose on the gusts of wind that streamed about the stubby obelisk, buffeting him. A hundred and fifty feet below him the Library entrance was spread out like a model on a table-top—foreshortened stone steps led to the main doorway, toy cars were parked in rows, neat strips of grass and paving were laid out on the ground like green and brown velvet ribbons. Directly in front of the broad steps a miniature ambulance was drawn up with its escort of Lilliputian police cars, sirens ululating. *So,* Welby thought numbly, *it was all up with him—they had found the nosy old bastard.* He raised tear-filled eyes and saw two ravens revelling in the currents of air that flowed around the tower. Mesmerised by their gambols, Welby could not tear his gaze away from them. Slowly he drew nearer to the edge until he had passed through the opening in the fence; then he stepped off the roof-top as if to join them in their play. For an instant the wind capriciously supported him in midair, and for the first time in his sad, dreary life Welby felt free—clean and free, with the cold breeze surging about him, carrying him along like an autumn leaf navigating the aerial streams; then the wind dropped and he began to fall.

37 *The End of the Case*

"There's no need to fuss," said Fenchurch somewhat testily. "I'm perfectly all right. It was only a knock on the head."

Despite his vociferous protests he had been taken in the ambulance to Addenbrooke's Hospital, where a doctor had diagnosed mild concussion and bandaged the cut he had received by falling into a sharp corner of one of the metal bookshelves. After seeing to the disposition of Welby's remains, Inspector Bunce had gone to visit his friend who had insisted, disregarding the vigorous recommendations of his physician, on returning to his rooms at Sheepshanks.

"That was a plaguy heavy book," Bunce declared. "You're lucky to have a harder head than most; it'd have cracked some skulls like an eggshell."

"Not Caldicott's *Discourses on Socmanry*. His theories are far too lightweight to do any real damage," scoffed Fenchurch who, though dazed and bloodied by Welby's attack, had nevertheless retained enough scholarly curiosity to inspect the volume that had felled him before he was carried out of the history stacks on a stretcher.

"You hadn't ought to have gone into the stacks after Welby," Bunce told him severely. "You knew damned well it was dangerous. You might have been killed." Indeed, he shuddered to think how close his friend had come to death.

"If it hadn't been for one of the staff who saw Welby run out of the history stacks into the corridor, we shouldn't have had a clue where to look for you."

"Well, well, perhaps I ought not to have followed him," Fenchurch conceded, ruefully rubbing his bandaged head. "Another time I shall be more careful."

"Let us hope there will not be another time," pronounced Dr. Shebbeare, who had hastened over to render sympathy to his afflicted colleague. "Sheepshanks has already suffered from far too much undesirable publicity of late. And speaking of distasteful publicity," he continued, for notwithstanding Maunders's murder his chief concern since that ill-fated night of Pullets Feast had been for his own dignity and that of the other Sheepshanks Fellows, "what is to be done with that abominable film which I understand the police have in their possession? I have consulted the College's solicitors, and they have notified the BBC that we intend to sue if it should be shown over the air, but I am sorry to say that so far they are proving refractory. That woman perpetrated an appalling abuse of hospitality. I shall see her in the dock if she dares to attempt to expose the College to ridicule." His massive eyebrows met in a magisterial frown. Even if the culprit were sent to prison, he reflected, her incarceration would provide no balm for the shame and humiliation that the showing of the film would produce among its involuntary actors.

"You can set your mind at rest about Ms. Harlowe's little peepshow," replied Bunce. "We shall shortly be informing her that the film was accidentally destroyed along with some pornographic films we had confiscated from one of the local shops."

"How perfectly splendid!" said the Master, wringing Inspector Bunce's big hand gratefully.

"How very convenient for us," Fenchurch remarked. He was as relieved as Dr. Shebbeare that the matter was so agreeably settled, but he could not resist briefly looking the gift horse in its capacious mouth. "Is that what really happened?"

"It will have done by the time Ms. Harlowe gets the news," the Inspector informed them placidly. "We can't have Cambridge represented by that sort of filth, now can we?" Dr. Shebbeare cast Bunce a look in which gratitude and approval vied for the ascendency. It was altogether appropriate, the Master felt, that the Cambridge Police Force should feel the same kind of loyalty to the University and regard for the dignity of its Members as they did themselves—that the Police should in effect serve in the capacity of supernumerary Bulldogs—and it did not occur to him to be surprised by the fact.

"We've let young Huntingfield go, by the way," Bunce continued. "It was a mistake to have arrested him in the first place, as it turned out, but I'm not sure I wouldn't do the same again, everything else being equal. The evidence against the lad seemed overwhelming at the time; and for all we knew he had made up that story about the wager—not about the horse winning, of course, but about placing that much money on it."

"What about the blood you found on his sleeve?" Fenchurch enquired curiously. "You said that some of it was Maunders's blood type. That is surely still an enigma."

"Not any longer. Lord Henry's lady-friend, Miss Murray, gave us an explanation for that circumstance just before you rang me from the Library, but at the time I wasn't inclined to credit her account. I thought she'd made it up to try to save him. She says they went punting the other night—punting at this time of year! I ask you. What will undergraduates be up to next?" he added in a scandalised aside. "—And while she was in the boat, she scratched her hand on an exposed nail. She says she must have left a smear of blood on the sleeve of Huntingfield's jacket as he was helping her ashore. Well, you can understand why I thought she must have invented the story. It seemed much too good to be true as far as Lord Henry was concerned, and too much of a coincidence that both bloodstains should have landed in the same spot. But she insisted on having us carry out a blood test, and when I went back to the station to deal with Welby's suicide the results were in and they show that her blood is AB—the same type as Maunders's. I've also had Welby's binding tools checked over. There are several scalpels among them, one with a one-inch blade that Dr. Scarlett says is just the article we've been looking for. We ran a test on that which shows traces of AB blood in the join of the handle. Welby's blood group, by the way, was A."

Bunce fell silent at the memory of the welter of Welby's blood that had temporarily painted the UL front steps a brilliant crimson. "So your general theory was correct," he went on a moment later, speaking to Fenchurch. "It was just some of the characters we got wrong, as you realised once you found the *Anelida*. Maunders wasn't a thief in this instance, but a blackmailer who saw Welby take the Caxton from the returns table after he had put it there. When the hue and cry went out he realised the binder had stolen it and he demanded a share of the proceeds."

"It is quite possible that Welby had been planning the theft for some time," said Fenchurch. "The *Anelida* had recently been brought to his attention, since he made repairs to it only a month or so ago. On the other hand, he may have stolen it on impulse when he saw it lying unattended in the Anderson Room. Or it may have been a combination of the two—he intended to steal the *Anelida* all along, and when he saw a chance of having the theft attributed to any one of a large number of potential suspects, he seized it."

"Why do you think Maunders was willing to meet Welby out of College when he had been gated, thus risking further punishment," asked Dr. Shebbeare, "since presumably he was the one with the upper hand?"

"I suspect he was being exceedingly cautious," Fenchurch explained. "The financial stakes were high, and he did not want to take any chances of queering the pitch. Don't forget he had already been branded a thief by the SCR: If any of the Fellows heard that he was suddenly being chummy with one of the UL staff, it might have caused comment. No doubt he expected to make his way back into College undetected either while the Porter's attention was distracted or by climbing in. And of course meeting away from Sheepshanks suited Welby's purpose very well."

He was interrupted by the sound of footsteps running up the worn stone stairs that led to his rooms, and a moment later Vivien's glowing face appeared in the gap left by the half-open door. "May we come in?" she asked.

"Yes indeed, my dear," Fenchurch replied, visibly cheered by the sight of her charming countenance. "You are always welcome."

She danced through the doorway, followed by a beaming Harry. The combined glory that shone about the reunited lovers fairly dazzled the occupants of the room. "Darling Mr. Fenchurch, we've come to thank you for saving Harry," she announced, bestowing a kiss on the uninjured side of his head. "Oh! Your poor head! Are you all right? What happened? No one told us you had been hurt."

"A mere bagatelle, I assure you," Fenchurch told her, pleased by her solicitude. "I am too tough an old nut to be so easily cracked." There was a poignancy in seeing them together, so obviously right for each other: a golden lad and girl, bright with promise.

"I can't thank you enough, sir," Harry said awkwardly. He cast a fleeting glance at the Inspector and nodded a greeting to Dr. Shebbeare. "If it hadn't been for you I'd have been done for—Father's solicitors just stood around looking glum when they saw the evidence the police had against me. But Vivien wouldn't let me give up hope even when it seemed as if I didn't stand a chance. She said you'd be sure to turn up trumps, and she was right." He gave Fenchurch's hand a heartfelt shake.

"After all," said Fenchurch, embarrassed by so much gratitude, "we can't have a member of College kicking his heels in the lock-up. That wouldn't do at all." Their happiness was incandescent, but oddly enough he did not feel shut out by it. Such joyous warmth kindled an answering glow in him, and he smiled back at them. Perhaps, Fenchurch thought only a little sadly as he gazed at their radiant faces, perhaps I *am* too old for her. Perhaps it would not have done. But at least she is fond of me—I am fortunate to have that much—and I shall dance at her wedding.

The success of Raph Berni's slender volume of French poetry, written in imitation of Baudelaire but considerably more explicit, was astonishing, not least to Raph himself. What had been conceived as versified pornography tailored to a sophisticated underground smut-trade unexpectedly burgeoned into a best-seller of the *literati* when the reviewer for the *Guardian* happened across it and sent readers and booksellers scrambling for copies with his description of the poems' "exquisitely steamy depravity" and "captivating vice." "A worthy scion of Baudelaire," trumpeted the *Times Literary Supplement,* rapidly following suit; "verse to seduce a saint."

The popular papers soon jumped on the bandwagon, proclaiming Berni's verse "deliciously evil and lusciously vile" and hinting of film-rights discussions. As usual, television was not slow to take over the titillating topic, particularly when it was discovered that the author, far from being the typical pallid, balding, and distinctly unphotogenic academic, was blessed with the sultry good looks which are more commonly the possession of a Romantic poet or a rock star. He became an instant celebrity: the airwaves were full of him. Julia Harlowe interviewed Raph on her new BBC programme, *Piquant Personalities,* the New York publishers Matthew & Meldrum bought the American rights for a fabulous sum, Raph was signed to make a lecture tour across the States the following spring, and the poems went into their fifteenth printing. One of the surest signs of his success was the fact that all over the country adolescents were vainly searching their French dictionaries for words whose English versions were condemned in polite conversation.

This was heady stuff for a struggling young academic, and Raph was basking in his new-found fame. His already well-developed ego had been further inflated until it was close to bursting, and it occurred to him that his newly acquired eminence might induce Vivien, after whom he still yearned with a calf-love as unsettling as it was unfamiliar to him, to view him in a more favourable light.

"Hullo," he said, ringing her with some trepidation. "It's Raph."

"Raph?" The word hung questioningly in the air like a bell that has been tapped and whose ghostly resonance continues to reverberate.

He replied rather crossly, for he had begun to regard his name as a household word, "Raph Berni, *Les Pousses Pervers.*"

"Oh, Raph *Berni,*" answered Vivien, enlightened. "Why didn't you say so? And what on earth is Papoose whatever-it-is? Don't tell me you've taken up studying American Indians; I thought Frog Lit. was your line."

"*Les Pousses Pervers.* That means 'The Evil Seedlings'; it's a pastiche of Baudelaire," Raph explained kindly. "Don't tell me you haven't heard of it." He sounded incredulous. "It's had the most marvellous reviews: 'Delectable debauchery,' 'Out-Baudelaires Baudelaire and out-Sades Sade,' 'A young archangel of evil'—that's me. I've been on the box quite a lot lately, explaining it," he went on casually.

"Smashing for you. Actually, I'm afraid I haven't heard a

word about it—I've been far too busy with matters of life
and death and all that sort of thing to bother watching television." She did not elaborate.

"Oh," said Raph, somewhat crestfallen. "Well, I had
thought that you might . . . we might. . . ."

"Oh, Raph, I *am* sorry." In her newfound happiness Vivien could not find it in her heart to be unkind. "But I'm
afraid I can't. I'm engaged."

"But I haven't even told you which night I'm inviting you
out yet," declared Raph, outraged. "You can't be permanently engaged."

"That's exactly what I am, my dear—I'm engaged to be
married. Affianced, if you prefer. Banns and bridesmaids and
lashings of rice and all the trimmings. Otherwise," said Vivien, who was really a very nice girl, "I should have adored
to."

There were distinct advantages to the month of November,
Fenchurch thought contentedly, peering over the balustrade
of Sheepshanks Bridge to watch the ducks on his way to the
UL. The plague of tourists was growing worse each year: in
the summer it was often impossible to push past an impedi-
ment of Japanese sightseers strung across the bridge like
pearls on a necklace, too busy taking snapshots of the river
and The Backs to make way for the indigenous inhabitants of
the town.

He sensed a presence near him and glanced sideways at a
muffled back and a pair of hands that were occupied in tearing pieces from a scrap of bread to throw to a congregation of
greedy ducks. The hands, large, square and capable, seemed
oddly familiar. Fenchurch had a mental image of those same
hands twisting nervously in a grey-clad lap. Could it
be . . . ? He looked up into the unforgettable face of Lettice
Knowles. He was uncertain whether to speak—perhaps she
would not wish to be reminded of their previous meeting.

But Letty solved his quandary by smiling and extending her hand to him, having tossed the last of the bread to the quacking multitude below.

"Mr. Fenchurch!" she exclaimed warmly. "How pleasant to see you again." She hesitated and then added, "I must apologise for my behaviour the other day. I'm not usually so—so silly."

"Not at all," replied Fenchurch. "I thought you were a very courageous young woman. You handled yourself remarkably well in an extraordinarily difficult situation. I hope you will forgive my intrusion in a painful matter which did not directly concern me."

"It helped, somehow, having you there," she said simply. "I've read your book, you see—the one about the chapels— and so I felt you were a sort of friend. What a fool I was about Bob!" She spoke without rancour.

"Love makes fools of us all," Fenchurch said gently.

"Yes—yes, I suppose so."

He wanted desperately to give her something that might serve as an anodyne to her deep hurt, and shyly offered the only gift that lay in his power. "Perhaps you might like a tour of Sheepshanks Chapel someday," he said diffidently, "since you have been sufficiently interested to wade through my work on the subject."

Her beautiful eyes lit up. "I should love to. Thank you so much."

"Are you free now?" he asked. His research suddenly seemed trivial compared to the possibility of distracting her from her trouble.

"Yes, as a matter of fact. Kind Mr. Akers gave me the day off, and I'm rather at a loose end."

"Then I should be delighted if you would honour me with your company. . . . Of course you know that the Abbé Dieudonné brought a number of workers in stone with his entourage from France, to assist with the carving. . . ."

Fenchurch took her arm, and they moved companionably off together toward the lawn which was crowned with the graceful bulk of Sheepshanks Chapel.

"Those too utterly foul old sons of bitches!" Julia stormed, stalking back and forth in her sitting-room like a caged tigress. "They must have bribed that bloody Inspector to get rid of the Pullets film. I never heard of anything so incredibly false as claiming the police accidentally burnt it. It would have been absolutely superb on my programme," she mourned. "The Fellows' behaviour was hysterically funny. The Master was simply priceless—one could see it was a case of 'I would if I could but I daren't,' with his dumpy old wife staring pop-eyed at the antics through that peephole. Then there was the bawdy old Bishop! I wondered how many men it was going to take to pull him off that girl—he had as many arms as an octopus! And poor Cyril, who was surveying the scene with a look of the most utter revulsion. Well, it certainly wasn't *his* scene at all." She gave a reminiscent chortle.

"I failed to see anything even remotely amusing about the incident," Rackstraw said coldly, mentally thanking God that he had managed to retain some few tattered shreds of dignity during the débacle. Despite this fact he was profoundly grateful that the film had disappeared, though he had the good sense to realise that it would be a fatal blow to connubial peace if he were to say so.

"That's because you weren't in on the joke. However, you needn't worry, pet, you behaved impeccably, more or less." Like a good general, Julia did not waste time regretting her failures, but concentrated her formidable energies on future campaigns. "Oh, well, it can't be helped; but of course you'll withdraw your offer of a Library from that dreadful College of theirs. They've been hideously ungrateful about it anyway . . . I've been thinking that it wouldn't be a bad idea to found a College of our own; it would have far more *éclat* than a mere library. Rackstraw College."

She drawled out the syllables in her most mellifluous BBC tones, and Rackstraw had to concede that it sounded very well indeed. Certainly a College would create considerably more splash than a library, and would be one in the eye for the Sheepshanks SCR besides. Anyway, he had gone rather off book collecting ever since the deal with Grimes for the *Anelida* had fallen through. A pragmatic man, Sir Richard was beginning to feel it was a bit pointless to spend so much money on books. It was true rare books were a high-class hobby and there was a thrill to owning one of Grimes's illicit treasures, but it wasn't, after all, as though he ever read any of his holdings.

"Having a College named after you would really be giving you your money's worth," Julia went on. "You can make it a College with an emphasis on video communication," she continued, inspired. "Television is a lot trendier than books nowadays. It's high time Cambridge stopped living in the eighteenth century. Print is out and electronics are in. And I," she decided, patting her husband's beefy shoulder with a slender predatory hand, "shall be a Fellow in your new foundation. It would be rather a kick to be Mistress, but it would take up too much of my time. There must be a portrait of me in Hall—and one of you too, of course," she added as an afterthought. "Just think how amusing it will be to choose an architect for the project. Something different, I think, to set Cambridge on its antiquated ear. What about a mirrored skyscraper, with a helicopter landing-pad on top? Convenient for my commuting. Or we could build it out in the river, on stilts, with a prow like a Chinese junk. . . ."

"Whatever you say, my darling," replied Rackstraw meekly. He had had a taste of what happened when his

Julia's wishes were flouted, and was now thoroughly broken in.

"Then that's settled . . . do you know, Dick, darling, I've just had the most marvellous idea." Julia sat up and her eye lit with the gleam of creative fire. "Norman has been after me lately to try my hand at investigative reporting. I think I shall take him up on it, and do a really riveting exposé of corruption in the Cambridge Police."

The atmosphere in the Sheepshanks Combination Room after dinner was considerably lighter than heretofore. Although none of the dons had been a suspect in Maunders's killing, the sensation of possible cohabitation with a murderer had nevertheless been decidedly uncomfortable. During the past week more than one Fellow had found himself, on his way to his rooms or to his car after dinner, uneasily peering into the shadows to see if he was being followed. And all the Fellows (except Grubb) rejoiced that Harry had been cleared of suspicion. The Huntingfield name had long held an illustrious place in the annals of the College, and they would have been sorry to see it disgraced; moreover in their different ways they were all (except Grubb) fond of the boy.

When they were settled with their postprandial coffee, the Master announced, "I have received a communication today whose contents will be of interest to you all. It is in reply to the letter that you authorised me to send to Sir Richard Rackstraw, definitively refusing his offer of a Library and making it clear that the College will accept no gifts of any kind from him until the Senior Common Room receive an apology from Lady Rackstraw for her irregular and outrageous behaviour on the night of Pullets Feast. Sir Richard writes that Lady Rackstraw declines to apologise and that he is therefore withdrawing his offer. He plans instead to endow a new College."

At this news a silence born of surprise and deep disapproval briefly reigned in the Combination Room. It was broken by Professor Tempeste. "A College, forsooth!" he remarked with strong distaste. "Rackstraw College? A paltry name to attach to a Cambridge College. Upon what meat doth this our Rackstraw feed, that he is grown so great?"

"I trust the Vice-Chancellor will put his foot down. Certainly we cannot have a College named after someone in Trade," Peascod put in, conveniently forgetting the methods their founder Sir Oliver had employed in amassing his fortune.

"I must say, it seems a bit puffed up for the man to expect to set his name next to Sheepshanks and Sidney and Pembroke and Caius," said Grierson.

"Not to mention Jesus and Christ's," Hedgecock added drily, mildly scandalising the Chaplain with his levity.

"I fear Sir Richard will find himself disappointed in his ambition. There are already," the Master pronounced with finality, "far too many Cambridge Colleges." Dr. Shebbeare was a purist whose opinion of any College founded later than the sixteenth century was that it was an upstart that wanted weeding out.

"I, for one," Fenchurch confessed, "am delighted that Sir Richard is no longer attempting to foist his Library upon us. While it is a pity to lose all prospect of a gift from him, in the circumstances it would not be seemly to accept one. Moreover, in his own milieu he is a formidable force and I suspect that he would demand his own way in anything he chose to finance at Sheepshanks, to our detriment. There is also the reprehensible influence of his wife to consider."

"Beware the monstrous regiment," quavered Professor Enderby, who had been invited to dinner by Fenchurch as reparation for his unjustified suspicions concerning the *Anelida*. "It puts me in mind of the Duke once he had made an honest wench of Kate Swynford—the poor fellow couldn't call his soul his own."

No one could think of a suitable response to this remark. After a moment Grierson said wistfully, "Of course now his book collection is bound to go elsewhere."

"The books in themselves are no doubt eminently desirable," answered Fenchurch in an attempt to cheer up the Abbot's Librarian, "but I fear the collection *qua* collection would prove meretricious, and therefore unworthy of enshrinement in a Sheepshanks Library. So often nowadays collecting is not inspired by a seeking after knowledge, but is rather the endeavour to achieve immortality by means of propinquity. Why, I should not be at all surprised to find that Rackstraw has not read half the works in his library! I suspect," he went on disapprovingly, "that there is an increasing tendency for modern book collectors (when they are not scholars) to be more interested in the provenance and binding of an acquisition than in its text."

"That would be less to be wondered at if some of their bindings hid treasures comparable to the *Anelida*," said Austrey in facetious compliment to Fenchurch's discovery.

"It's all very well to be rid of Rackstraw's importunities, but having an unwanted library forced upon us pales beside the humiliation we would all have undergone at his wife's hands had not the police inadvertently destroyed the film recording the . . . the infestation under which we suffered during Pullets," announced Professor Tempeste. "Once that film was shown our lives would not have been worth living. Thank God for constabular bungling!"

"That," replied the Master, "is the official account of the fate that befell Lady Rackstraw's ill-conceived project, and the one I promulgated in deference to Inspector Bunce's wishes. He has, however, at last acceded to my request that I be permitted to reveal the truth to the members of the SCR."

And he told them what had really happened to the film.

A murmur of approbation reverberated about the room like

a hiveful of contented bees. "Stout fellow," said Tempeste approvingly. "We must have him to dinner soon."

"And to next year's Pullets," Austrey added.

There was another loud hum, this one of agreement, and the conversation once again became general.

"Whatever became of that Caxton you made such a fuss over losing?" Professor Enderby suddenly enquired of Fenchurch. "The *Anelida and Arcite,* was it not? I can't imagine why you thought *I* might know anything about it."

"We discovered that one of the bindery staff had stolen it, but happily it has since been recovered," Fenchurch replied. He did not explain more fully, suspecting that Enderby's hold on lucidity might not be sufficiently robust to sustain a detailed account of the incident.

"Shocking behaviour; simply inexcusable. Hope they hang the feller. Book stealing is the one unforgivable crime, what?" said Enderby, his wrinkled face bland as a baby's. He appeared sublimely unconscious of his own record in that respect.

"No need for such drastic measures. As a matter of fact, the thief killed himself," Fenchurch told him.

"Driven to it, I expect." Enderby was unsurprised. "The curse got him. Just like Carter and that Tutankhamen business. Nasty things, curses. Better to steer clear of 'em."

"The curse?" Fenchurch had thought he was growing accustomed to Enderby's dottiness, but this remark took him aback.

"Skelton's curse. You know—*Qui lacerat, violatve, rapit, presens epitoma, Hunc laceretque voret,* CERBERUS *absque mora.* Serve the blackguard right!" Having made this pronouncement, Professor Enderby gazed nearsightedly about the room. "What's happened to old Truebody? Appalling want of manners, not turning up after inviting a chap to dine," he said severely. "Ah, well, I daresay he forgot the time—far too busy beating his wife."